The Hidden Cottage

ALSO BY ERICA JAMES
FROM CLIPPER LARGE PRINT

The Real Katie Lavender

The Hidden Cottage

Erica James

W F HOWES LTD

This large print edition published in 2013 by
W F Howes Ltd
Unit 4, Rearsby Business Park, Gaddesby Lane,
Rearsby, Leicester LE7 4YH

1 3 5 7 9 10 8 6 4 2

First published in the United Kingdom in 2013
by Orion Books

A CIP catalogue record for this book is available
from the British Library

ISBN 978 1 47122 884 1

Typeset by Palimpsest Book Production Limited,
Falkirk, Stirlingshire
Printed and bound in Great Britain
by MPG Books Ltd, Bodmin, Cornwall

To Edward and Samuel for always saying the right thing.

CHAPTER 1

'Expect the unexpected' was Owen Fletcher's new personal mantra.

And the unexpected was exactly what he got when he turned off the main road and dropped his speed to enter the village of Little Pelham and saw a floral sofa hurtling by at considerable speed.

Now that's something you don't see every day, he thought with an amused smile.

With two lads riding the sofa down the narrow street and a motley gang of children chasing after it, their happy laughter and boisterous cries of encouragement rang out in the peaceful still of the afternoon.

Keeping his distance, Owen carefully followed behind. Passing the stone-built cottages, their tiny front gardens vibrant with spring flowers, he recalled a time when he had used this very street to ride his bike at breakneck speed. He had to admit, though, sofa racing was a lot more inspired, much more of an extreme sport.

Ahead of him the sofa and children had come to an abrupt stop near the water trough, where the slope levelled and the village green with its semi-circle of thatched cottages began. Seeing that the sofa had tipped over – its wheels had dug into the grass, and its two riders had tumbled out to great cheers – he pulled alongside and with the top back on his car, he leant over. 'Everything OK?' he asked. 'Anyone hurt?'

Judging from the laughter, he was fairly sure no one was injured, but there was no harm in checking. Without answering his question, two boys came over; they looked to be about eleven years old. The smaller of the pair said, 'Cool car.'

With a roll of his eyes, the other boy said, 'Of course it's cool; it's a Jaguar E-Type.'

'You're very knowledgeable for one so young,' Owen said with a smile.

'My dad's into classic cars,' the boy replied with a shrug of his shoulders, casting what appeared to be an expert eye over the Henley green bodywork of Owen's pride and joy. 'He takes me to the car shows.'

'Well, I've got to say your turbo-charged sofa is pretty cool,' Owen said with a laugh. 'I wouldn't mind a go on it myself.'

'You can, if you help push it back up the hill.'

Owen laughed again. 'Another time, boys. You take care now.'

He drove slowly on, passing the Fox and Goose on his left; it bore all the hallmarks of having been thoroughly updated to suit the needs of a discerning gastro-pub clientele. He doubted there would be a dartboard inside any more. Nor a bunch of old boys playing dominoes in a quiet dusty corner. In the late-afternoon sunshine, the pub's pale walls, built of local Northamptonshire limestone and partially covered with wisteria, were mellow with age and added to the quintessential English village vibe. Stretching the full width of the building was a raised decking area with tables and chairs and umbrellas. A number of tables were occupied; Owen noticed a few curious glances being cast in his direction. The likelihood of anyone recognizing him was zero.

Next to the pub was a general store; it wasn't dissimilar from the shop he remembered from his childhood. On the pavement, a man was tying a sign to a telegraph pole. On closer inspection Owen saw that it was a poster advertising Little Pelham's forthcoming May fete.

His speed still low, he drove on. To his left was Cloverdale Lane, where he had once lived. He'd been nine years old when his father had been taken on as a farm labourer at Cloverdale Farm. He could remember so clearly the day they had moved into the terraced cottage. The sun had been shining, just like today, and the next-door neighbour had called round with a fruitcake she had baked. 'Welcome to the village,' she had said. 'Anything you need, just knock on my door.' A jolly elderly woman who lived alone with her two cats, she had been quickly labelled as an interfering busy-body by Owen's father, the sort of woman he didn't want nosing around in his business. And with good reason: Ronald Fletcher got up to plenty of stuff he didn't want people to know about. Despite his father's predictable disapproval, Mum had been the happiest Owen had seen her. 'Everything's going to be all right here,' she had said when she had kissed him goodnight that first evening. 'From now on, things are going to be different.'

But things hadn't been different. Within the year his father's vicious temper had once again got the better of him. Just as it always did.

Owen made no effort to turn left for Cloverdale Lane, not even for old times' sake, but kept to the main street through the village, towards the church on his right with its squat Norman tower, where he had once been allowed to have a go at ringing the bells.

Running adjacent to the churchyard was a foot-path and on this side of it was the vicarage where, for a short time, before his father put a stop to it, Owen's mother had worked as a cleaner for the vicar and his family. The house had backed on to gently sloping green fields with woodland beyond. He wondered if it still did. Perhaps now a development of houses had been built on the land. It was then that Owen spotted something that was definitely different – the sign on the gatepost no longer said The Vicarage.

He stopped the car and blatantly stared at the handsome five-bay-fronted Georgian house with its elegant sash windows and front door painted dark blue and the sign that read: Medlar House. What was that all about? Another example of the Church of England hitting hard times and selling off more of the family silver? Very possibly.

Idly wondering where the present incumbent of St George's lived, Owen pressed on, and the nearer he got to his destination the more his excitement and anticipation grew exponentially.

Expect the unexpected.

Some would say that his expectations for coming here were too high, that the reality couldn't ever live up to the dream. But it was a risk he was prepared to take. After all, what was life without taking a risk, or more importantly, chasing a dream?

Ever since the day, thirty-four years ago, when he was ten years old and had left Little Pelham he had dreamt of returning. It had not been a case of casual or wistful daydreaming, but an actual and very persistent dream. And it was always the same. It was a hot summer's day and, alone and lost, he would be drawn in to the cool and leafy shade of a dense copse of trees. Wandering amongst the trees, he would find a path that led to a house. But the only way to reach the house was to cross a small lake in a wooden dinghy. Untying the rope that was looped around the stump of a dead birch tree on the bank, he would row across the lake, somehow not destroying the perfect reflection of the house in the glassy-smooth water. The front door would always be open and music – faint and beguiling – would reach out to him, inviting him in like a beckoning finger. Exploring the house, searching for the source of the music, he would discover that behind every door was a room with yet another door that led to yet another room and another door, and he would be endlessly surprised and fascinated.

Always when he woke from the dream, he felt a sense of pleasurable contentment. And a pull, as if a tiny thread was attached to him and was being tweaked.

The house he dreamt of so regularly was not entirely the product of his imagination; it was based on something very real right here in Little Pelham. It was where he was going now.

To The Hidden Cottage.

CHAPTER 2

The woman turned around from the mirror. 'What do you think? And be honest.'

Mia picked up a medium-sized brimmed hat that was softened with a pretty layer of gauze and trimmed with a silk bow. 'I still think this one suited you best,' she said with well-practised diplomacy.

Wrinkling her nose, the woman scrunched up her face, giving herself the unfortunate appearance of a bulldog. 'But it's so boring,' she said. 'Every other woman will be wearing a hat like that at my son's wedding. Whereas this little beauty will make me stand out from the crowd.' Sighing like a love-sick teenager, she patted the red and black miniature top hat that was perched at a jaunty angle on her head. 'Yes,' she said decisively, 'this is the one I want.'

Mia knew when she was beaten and with a smile firmly in place and agreeing that the woman would indeed stand out from the crowd at her son's wedding, she thought of her own son, Jensen. It was his thirtieth birthday today and they were having a family get-together.

It was a while since she'd managed to get everyone in the same place and she was looking forward to seeing Jensen and Eliza and Daisy. She was also looking forward to meeting the girlfriend Jensen was bringing with him. A girlfriend they knew nothing about, as Jeff had been only too quick to point out when Jensen had phoned last week to ask if he could bring Tattie.

'Tattie,' Jeff had said in response to Mia relaying the news, 'what sort of name is that? What is she, some kind of potato?'

'It's short for Tatiana,' Mia had replied. 'I think it's nice.'

'More like short for something very affected.'

Her husband had no time for affectation or anything of an ostentatious nature. Nor did he believe in 'pussy-footing about', as he called Mia's reluctance to speak her mind. He wouldn't have held back with this woman; he would have come right out with the truth and informed her that she was choosing the wrong hat. Moreover, he probably would have said that a dustbin lid would flatter her more. 'The trouble with you, Mia,' he regularly said, 'is that you're much too middle-class and polite for your own good.'

An hour later Mia had shut up shop and was letting herself in at the back door of Medlar House: her commute took all of forty seconds.

Four years ago when Daisy, the youngest of their children, had left for university Mia had had the idea of converting the unused barn to the side of the house into a light and airy space from which she could run her own business. Jeff had been sceptical. 'You really think the demand is out there?' he'd asked. Mia knew, from listening to friends bemoaning the difficulty of tracking down the perfect hat to complete an outfit for a special occasion and how wasteful it was to buy something that would only be worn once or twice, that the demand was most definitely there. She was proved right. From day one, after Jensen had helped her to create a website to promote the business, Mia's Hats was a success. Women came from miles around to her showroom in the village of Little Pelham, where, in a relaxed and welcoming environment, she gave them the opportunity to try on as many hats and fascinators as it took to find what they were looking for. With changing rooms on offer, she encouraged her customers to bring their outfits with them so that nothing was left to chance. She had recently extended the service and started selling handbags and costume jewellery as well.

She opened the fridge and focused on dinner that evening, not that it was going to tax her too much. At Jensen's request she was making his favourite meal – corned beef hash followed by apple crumble. It was hardly the last word in haute cuisine, but when she'd asked him what he wanted for his birthday dinner, he'd said, 'The usual, of course, Mum.' It was what he always wanted her to make; it had been his meal of choice as a young child.

There had been many times in his life when Jensen had been averse to choice and to change, to the extent of making him seem awkward and obstructive. As his mother, Mia knew all too well his faults and failings, but she also knew that at heart he was fiercely loyal to those he cared about. He might have an odd way of showing it, but that was just his way.

As she peeled the potatoes, Mia thought of this day thirty years ago when she had given birth to Jensen. She had been nineteen years old, alone and terrified. Well, not entirely alone – the delivery room in the hospital had been buzzing with activity: there had been the midwife, a doctor and two junior doctors, one of whom had been Chinese. Even now she could remember that the doctor had been wearing absurdly large-framed spectacles and a blue and yellow bow-tie. He'd been the epitome of a pompous ass as he'd questioned the junior doctors on the procedures currently being performed on Mia. The midwife had rudely shoved him out of the way just as Jensen had made his appearance into the world. When she had been allowed to, Mia had hugged her newborn son close and tearfully promised him the world. A tall order given that she had no husband, few friends and no support from her parents.

But look at me now, she thought wryly as she put the saucepan of potatoes on the hotplate of the Aga. A husband, three grownup children, a successful business and a beautiful home that when she was nineteen she could never have dreamt of living in.

They had moved into Medlar House ten years ago; the previous owners having bought it from the Church of England and renamed it. With Jeff's new job basing him in Milton Keynes, the picturesque village of Little Pelham on the Northamptonshire and Buckinghamshire border had been the perfect location for the family. It had a good school close by for Daisy – Eliza was then away at boarding school and Jensen was at university – and offered the family a chance to put down some roots in an idyllic country setting. They had moved house three times in the preceding decade, each time because Jeff had tired of his current job and had traded up to something bigger and more challenging, and more financially rewarding. The ten years they'd been at Medlar House was the longest Mia had lived anywhere.

But last year Jeff had sprung another move on her and announced that he'd been offered the job of divisional managing director of a large Swiss engineering company and that his office would be in Brussels.

'A job offer like that doesn't materialize overnight,' she'd said with a sinking heart. 'How long has this been going on for?' She'd sounded like a wife asking how long her husband had been seeing another woman.

'For the last four weeks,' he'd answered.

'Hmm . . . and you didn't think to tell me when the proposal first came up?'

He'd had the grace to look guiltily shamefaced. 'I was waiting until the final details had been thrashed out. You know how these things can drag on; I didn't want to worry you unnecessarily.'

'Have you accepted the job?' she'd asked.

Silly question. Of course he had. 'I'm fifty-five, Mia,' he'd said. 'This could be my last big hurrah. And wait till I tell you about the financial package. We'll be set for the rest of our lives.'

'I thought we already were.'

'Don't be like that. I'm doing this for *us*. So that we won't have to worry about the future.'

More concerned about the present, about losing the life she had created for herself within the village, she had said, 'I'm sorry, Jeff, but I can't do it. I want to stay here. What would I do in Brussels?'

'You could do what you do here. Or better still, take it easy and have some fun. Just think; we could bob over to Paris for dinner whenever we liked. We could go to Antwerp, Amsterdam, Bruges. You've always wanted to go there, haven't you?'

'What about the children?'

'Oh, Mia, they have their own lives now. Which means we can have *our* lives back. We can start to enjoy ourselves.'

As much as he tried to sell the idea to her, Mia wouldn't budge. It was one of the few times in

12

their marriage that she said no to Jeff. In the end he reluctantly accepted her decision but still went ahead and took the job, saying that since the flight was such a short one it would be a manageable Monday to Friday commute and he would divide his time between Brussels and Little Pelham quite easily. He found himself a furnished one-bedroom apartment in the centre of Brussels, just off Avenue Louise and a short walk from his office. Mia stayed there a couple of times with him when he moved in, but she hadn't returned.

She would never openly admit this, least of all to Jeff, but she liked the new routine they had settled into. She enjoyed having some time to herself. She particularly enjoyed the peace and sense of calm being alone gave her.

She glanced at her watch. Under normal circumstances she would take with a pinch of salt Jeff's promise that he would catch an earlier flight home to be here for Jensen's birthday. However, in this instance he was picking Daisy up in Luton where she now lived, and if there was one thing he would never do, it was go back on his word to Daisy.

CHAPTER 3

Eliza was not a daydreamer, for the simple fact she didn't have the time to daydream. As a technology consultant for Merchant Swift – recently named Global Technology Leader of the Year – her every waking moment was as good as accounted for and duly charged to the client.

But recently occasional bouts of daydreaming had started to slip into her busy schedule. Usually she spared these diversionary thoughts no more than a nanosecond of her precious time, but this evening, sitting on the packed rush-hour train out of Euston, bone-weary and unable to keep her eyes open, she granted herself the luxury of dwelling on the most persistent of her daydreams, that of Greg being a permanent and long-term fixture in her life.

The first time this thought had popped into her head she had been shocked. She wasn't that kind of girl. Marriage. Kids. Lunch boxes and school runs. That wasn't for her. But meeting Greg had changed something in her. Her long-term perspective had been altered. Having him in her life made her consider things she had never considered before. And that terrified her.

She had lived the greater part of her childhood inside her head, which in turn meant her natural inclination was to be a loner, so sharing her space, her feelings, her hopes and dreams with another person was uncharted territory. But she had begun to do that with Greg. In some ways it had felt liberating and exciting, and in other ways it scared her rigid, flew in the face of all she'd understood about herself.

She had met Greg four months ago on a flight from Frankfurt where she had been visiting a client. They had got chatting after she had dropped one of the reports she'd been reading and he'd picked it up for her. By the time their plane had landed at Heathrow, they had exchanged mobile phone numbers and arranged to meet for a drink two days later. The drink had turned into dinner and the following evening they met again. Within ten days of meeting, they were officially 'seeing each other' and reeling with happy disbelief, Eliza confided in her closest friend, Serene, that she was in a relationship. A special relationship.

Strictly speaking she was in a long-distance relationship as Greg worked in the legal department for a group of venture capitalists based in New York with an office in London. He spent about a third of his time in the London office and the arrangement suited Eliza perfectly. She didn't cope well with a twenty-four-seven boyfriend. Her last boyfriend had never understood the demands of her job or appreciated that at times she needed to be alone.

But Greg understood this need in her because, as he said of himself, he was wired the same way. At thirty-three, he was older than her by seven years and she liked that his age and experience gave him a depth of maturity that most men her age didn't possess. He had been briefly married – 'We were much too young, didn't have a clue what we were doing' – and the marriage, by mutual agreement, ended within a year. 'We were very grown up about it,' he said. 'No recriminations on either side.'

She might not see Greg as often as a conventional relationship would allow, but when they were together, they were truly together. Instead of staying in a serviced apartment as he used to before they met, he now stayed with her in her rented ground-floor flat in Victoria Park. It was really only big enough for one person, but since Greg didn't live there full time, they just about coped with the lack of space. She loved waking in the morning with him in her bed and had reached the stage when she felt his absence when he wasn't there.

As brief as their time together was, it had what she called the ring of authenticity to it. Better still, they never argued or bickered over the trivia, as most couples did, but then that was probably because they saw one another so infrequently they didn't have time to get bogged down in the tedious minutiae of everyday life. There was no silly talk about whose turn it was to put the bin out or empty the dishwasher: it was her flat, so those were her jobs as far as she was concerned.

Lately Greg's trips to London had become increasingly more erratic and often arranged or postponed at the last minute. Which meant it was difficult to make plans. She had wanted him to come with her this evening to meet her family – a terrifyingly big step for her – but he hadn't been able to make it. 'Another time,' he'd said on the phone when she'd explained about her brother's birthday.

She had been surprised at the extent of her disappointment and had heard herself saying, 'But there won't be another time like this, Jensen will only be thirty once.'

He'd laughed. 'While that's undoubtedly true, it's the most illogical thing I've ever heard you say. Your brother's age has no bearing on my meeting your parents.'

'It's just that it's a special occasion and I'd like you to be there with me,' she'd said defensively, knowing that she was sounding needy, something that was pitifully out of character for her.

'I promise you I'll meet your family the next time I'm over.' He'd laughed again. 'You can't imagine how much I'm looking forward to them vetting me.'

She had relaxed then herself, grateful that he

had diffused the moment for her. 'They'll love you,' she said.

'I wouldn't bet on it. After all, I'm a man who couldn't hack his marriage after only a few months. That's not exactly going to impress them, is it?'

'Everyone's allowed to make a mistake. And my father is in no position to judge anyone else when it comes to commitment.'

Eliza snapped open her eyes. The man sitting next to her had jolted her arm hard. He was either oblivious to disturbing her or he simply didn't care, but having put his laptop away into a large bag, he stood up and without a word reached for his jacket from the rack above. Through the window she could see they were approaching Watford Station. Hopefully no one would get on and take his place.

Her wish was granted and she once more relaxed and closed her eyes as the train picked up speed. But this time her thoughts weren't of Greg, they were of her family and what lay in store for the evening. And the weekend.

The last time they were all together was for Christmas, although Jensen had managed no more than twenty-four hours and had left early on Boxing Day after he and Dad had argued over the stupidest of things. But that was par for the course. She hoped there would be no arguments tonight, that their father would behave and not goad Jensen as he often did. She couldn't bear that for her brother. Not in front of his girlfriend.

As soon as Eliza had heard from Mum that Jensen was bringing someone called Tattie to his birthday dinner, she had rung her brother. But typically he hadn't answered. She had then texted him, but again he hadn't responded. Communication wasn't his strongest suit. But then he would have known all too well that she was only getting in touch to interrogate him. Mum had said that she had no idea as to how long Jensen had been in the relationship – like Eliza, Jensen played his cards close to his chest – but for him to want to introduce this girl to the family, there had to be something special going on between them.

Just as there was between Eliza and Greg. Funny that their lives should have taken the same turning at exactly the same time. She couldn't speak for her brother, but for her own part – and she wasn't proud of this – she had wanted to bring Greg with her this evening to prove to their father that despite not being as pretty as Daisy, she could still attract someone as amazing as Greg.

Of course, given their father's track record, it was no surprise that she and Jensen should be so secretive about their relationships. The only surprise for Eliza was that her brother hadn't already confided in Mum. On several occasions in the last month Eliza had come close to telling Mum about Greg, but each time she'd held back, irrationally anxious that by uttering the words out loud she would be tempting fate and she would lose Greg. Maybe Jensen had had the same irrational fear. Until now.

At Milton Keynes, her head down in the scrum of commuters, she hurried along the platform wheeling her overnight case behind her, her heavy workbag slung over her shoulder and banging against her hip. Mum had offered to come and meet her, but she had said she'd be fine with a taxi.

Outside she found one, gave the driver the address for Medlar House and took a deep breath as she felt the familiar knot of apprehension in her stomach tighten. Twenty-six years old and she still felt like she was thirteen and returning home after a term away at school.

She had been the only one of the family to go to boarding school; it had been entirely her choice. When she was twelve years old, without her parents' knowledge she had sent off for a selection of brochures and when she had read them all and made her choice she had presented the school's prospectus to Mum and Dad and asked if it would be possible for her to go. Mum had been shocked and upset, but Dad, once he'd checked out the fees, had been all for it. 'Let's face it,' he'd said to Mum, 'she's running rings round those ruddy useless teachers of hers. Has been for some time. Do you remember that new teacher who accused her of cheating in a maths test because she did it in double-quick time and got every answer correct?

Smaller class sizes, more attention – that's exactly what our very own little Einstein needs.'

Einstein had been Dad's nickname for her. It had started when she was three and a half years old after Mum had found her in bed one morning reading Roald Dahl's *James and the Giant Peach* to herself. And not just reading from memory, mimicking her mother's telling of the story, but actually reading the words. By the time she had started school, she already knew her times tables, could name all the planets and play chess with Jensen and beat him. Her favourite book was an encyclopaedia that was so big and heavy she could hardly carry it.

It was Mum who took Eliza to visit the school, to see whether it was as good as the prospectus portrayed, and it was Mum who drove her there two months later for her to begin her first term. 'If it's not what you thought it would be,' Mum had said, trying to hide the tears that were filling her eyes, 'you can come straight back home.'

But they both knew that wasn't going to happen. Even at that young age, Eliza was resolutely independent. She had no concept of relying upon anyone else for help. Any problems she encountered, she resolved them herself. She put this down to being the middle child of the family, the in-between child who had to fend for herself.

School life away from home was exactly as she'd imagined it would be. She loved the structure, the order and the discipline. Never having really felt the need of friends before – other than friendship with Jensen – she discovered the joy of a best friend, a girl who was also new to the school. With her sleek black hair that fell to her waist and her unfeasibly slight body that didn't look strong enough to withstand the worst of the British weather, let alone survive the rigours of cross-country running, netball or lacrosse, Serene Tay, who barely spoke a word of English, was the prettiest girl Eliza had ever laid eyes on. They were in the same class and shared the same dormitory with two other girls, and within no time they were firm friends, and had been ever since.

After graduating from Cambridge, Serene, whose razor-sharp intellect made Eliza look like a half-wit, returned to Singapore to help run the family printing business. The expectation was that when her father retired as chairman, she would step into his considerable shoes.

Fathers, thought Eliza as she stared out of the taxi window at the familiar passing scenery, they want and expect so much of us. Her father's words to her when she'd gone away to school had been: 'Make me proud of you.' And hadn't she always tried to do exactly that? Because at the end of the day, it was the only way she could really gain his attention.

Jensen had been furious with her when Eliza had told him that she was going to boarding school. He didn't speak to her for three days and when finally he did, he came into her bedroom and threw himself on her bed. 'I suppose now it'll be down to me to babysit the Special One,' he'd said sullenly. That had been his nickname for Daisy.

The morning Eliza was due to leave, when Dad was away on a business trip and Jensen was helping to load her things into the boot of Mum's car, with Daisy getting in the way as usual, he'd hugged her fiercely, then abruptly, without saying anything, let go of her and walked back inside the house. When it was time to leave, she had looked up at his bedroom window and spotted him there. She had waved goodbye to him, but he hadn't waved back. Even now that memory saddened her, knowing that she'd hurt him so much. She had written to him every week while she was at school and she still had the few letters he'd written to her.

The taxi driver slowed the car and then stopped. 'This it, then?'

She looked up at Medlar House. 'Yes,' she said. 'This is it.'

CHAPTER 4

While her father filled the car with petrol, Daisy went inside the shop for a copy of this week's *Grazia*. Minutes later she was back out on the forecourt and Dad was replacing the petrol cap on the car. 'Found what you wanted?' he asked as he passed her to go and pay.

'Got the last copy,' she said, waving the magazine at him.

She'd just got herself settled in the car when her mobile rang. It was Scott. 'Hey,' she said, 'what's up?'

'Have you missed anything yet?'

'You mean, other than you?'

He laughed. 'No, not me. You've left your brother's present on the kitchen table.'

'Oh hell! I didn't leave my head there as well, did I?'

'Give it time and you will one day. How's it going?'

'OK. We've just stopped for petrol. Should be home in about ten minutes.'

'Have you told him?'

24

'Not yet.'

'I thought the idea was to tell him in the car when it was just the two of you.'

'It was. Now I've decided to wait until the evening's under way. Then when the bickering starts, I'll slip it in while no one's looking.'

'Are you sure that's such a smart move?'

'Probably not, but—' She saw her father approaching the car. 'He's coming back,' she said hurriedly. 'I'll speak to you later.'

'Just remember, Daisy, you're all grown up.'

'Yeah, try telling my father that. Bye.'

She stuffed her mobile back into her bag and guiltily opened her magazine. No reason to feel guilty, she told herself as her father got in beside her. He leant over, peered at the open pages on her lap and pointed at a photograph of Janice Dickenson in a dress that couldn't have suited her less. 'Bloody hell,' he said, 'she's got a tan on her like an Oompa Loompa! What is she, our latest deterrent against global warfare? Because I'll tell you for nothing, she's scaring the hell out of me. One look at her and I'd run in the opposite direction.'

'She's an American model from a squillion years ago.'

'Oh, well, that explains everything.'

He switched on the engine and pulled out of the forecourt onto the road. They'd been driving for a few minutes when he said, 'You OK? You seem a bit quiet.'

'Busy week, that's all.'

'Been overdoing it?'

She shrugged and turned the page of her magazine.

'So how's the job going?'

Oh God, she thought. Where to start? How to answer his question without blurting the whole thing out? How to avoid telling him that the job he'd wangled for her through a friend of a friend was doing her head in? That every morning she woke up, she felt like calling in sick and hiding under the duvet for the rest of the day. And yes, she knew all too well that, as Dad would be quick to remind her, in these difficult times, she was lucky to have a job.

Graduating last year while the recession was still in full swing meant she hadn't had a hope of landing her dream job, but then Dad had stepped in and pulled some strings and before she knew it she was a bored-out-of-her-mind graduate trainee designer for a manufacturer based in Luton that supplied hotels with the dullest furniture imaginable.

When she'd been studying for her degree in furniture design her work placement had been with a small, award-winning design team in London that had produced gorgeously one-off funky and cutting-edge pieces of furniture. All her hopes had been pinned on working there when she graduated. But the recession put paid to that. Every job she applied for, she got the same response – if she was lucky to hear back at all – that they were not taking on anyone new currently. It was then, when she had so badly wanted to prove to her father that she could stand on her own two feet, that there was no need for him to keep holding her hand, that he waded in with a wave of his magic wand and found her a job. It was what he did, stepped in and put things right for her.

Or so he believed. The truth was, he didn't make anything right for her. Repeatedly he said all he wanted to do was protect her and keep her safe, just as any parent did. But what he didn't understand was that his protective care totally suffocated her.

It hadn't always been that way, not when she was a small child, when she had idolized him, had thought there wasn't anything he couldn't or wouldn't do for her. In those days she had revelled in knowing that she was his favourite child, that she could do no wrong. She had happily gone along with it because who doesn't want to be more loved than anyone else?

She would be the first to admit now that she must have been a difficult child, a bloody nightmare more like it. But once she was old enough to understand what was really going on, she realized that she could only ever disappoint her father by ultimately wanting to wriggle out from his protective hold, to have the same freedom and control over her life that her brother and sister had.

She had tried to take control some years ago and had got herself into a hell of a mess. She hated to think of that time and what she'd put Mum through. As for Dad, he'd been at a complete loss how to treat her.

This time, though, it would be different. This time she was older and wiser and stronger. And she had Scott. Wonderful Scott.

'In your own time, Daisy.'

She turned to look at her father and realized that he was waiting for her to say something. 'What?' she said.

He smiled. 'I asked how the job was going.'

'Oh, that. Yeah. It's fine.'

How the lie tripped off her tongue.

CHAPTER 5

Since Jensen had yet to make an appearance, Jeff did what he always did when he arrived home from Brussels: he took an ice-cold bottle of beer from the fridge and went upstairs for a shower.

Now dressed, he got himself comfortable on the bed, placed the bottle of Budweiser to his lips and filled his mouth with the welcome cool beer. He swallowed it appreciatively, enjoying its light freshness. In Brussels they were always banging on about the beer there, the enormous choice, the superior quality, the complex this, the aromatic that, but for him there was nothing like the straightforward, crisp, dry taste of a Bud. He drank some more, wiped his mouth with the back of his hand and sighed the sigh of a tired but relatively contented man.

With the low evening sun shining through the window on him, he reminded himself of the promise he'd made Mia, that he'd be on his best behaviour tonight for Jensen's birthday. As if he wasn't always on his best behaviour! Any chance she'd asked Jensen to do likewise? He doubted it.

He put the beer to his mouth again and drank some more and wondered as he so often did why he and Jensen couldn't get on better. Life would be so much easier if they did. One of the things that really irked him was Jensen's inclination to drift through life without a clear idea of where he was going. A website designer – was that really a job? Wasn't that just another name for lolling around at home watching daytime telly?

Jeff, on the other hand, had known from an early age where he was going in life and that you had to take life by the scruff of the neck and wring out of it exactly what you wanted. And that took guts. You see an opportunity, you take it; that was his motto. You didn't dick around on the sidelines waiting for an opportunity; you got stuck in and made it happen. Which was why he had taken the position in Brussels. He was looking at another three years in the job and then he'd call it a day and cash in on the package he'd negotiated for himself. And who knew what he'd do then? Retirement was an option. But then so was consultancy work. Or sitting on the board of a company or two.

For now, though, he was enjoying the continuing challenges in his role of divisional MD of the Rieke Hirzel Group. Since his appointment last year, his sector of the business was bucking the trend and exceeding all expectations. The first thing he'd done was to increase the budget on technical research and instil a far more aggressive approach when it came to targeting new customers; for obvious reasons it was the latter that was showing immediate results. The research investment was the slow-burner part of his strategy. But let no one be under any misapprehension: there'd be no resting on any laurels on his watch.

Whenever he was foolish enough to question Jensen's lack of ambition, Mia always rushed to his defence, claiming that his work as a website designer was going well. She would also point out that Jensen's early years had not been the same as those of Eliza and Daisy and therefore Jeff had to accept there would be differences and inevitable consequences.

In contrast Eliza had drive and ambition in spades. Truth to tell, she probably had too much. He'd never told anyone this before but as proud as he was of Eliza, he'd always been a bit unnerved by her. She'd been an extraordinarily bright child, but not an easy one to be around – too distant and self-contained. She still was.

Daisy was, and always had been, a different kettle of fish altogether and was easily his favourite child. With her ivory skin, her dark hair and her startlingly violet-blue eyes – so like Mia's – she had been such a spirited and beautiful little girl and so very affectionate with him. People had regularly said that they ought to approach a children's model agency with Daisy and he had been all in favour of it, happy and proud to show her off, but Mia had put her foot down. Seven years old, Daisy had been furious with her mother, having devoted herself to hours of prancing about in front of the mirror practising her poses. To make up for her disappointment, he'd bought her a Swiss chalet-style playhouse for the garden, which immediately led to ructions from Jensen and Eliza about him always spoiling Daisy.

He knew that this partiality bothered Mia, but he reckoned he wasn't the first parent who had a special bond with a favourite child. It was hardly a crime, was it?

His beer finished, he reluctantly raised himself off the bed. Time to go downstairs and join the party.

CHAPTER 6

So far so good, Jensen thought as he snatched a look at Tattie. But then this was the easy part of the evening – his father had yet to make his appearance.

He had agreed to this dinner, knowing that Mum wanted to arrange it for all the right reasons. One of them being that she was concerned that he and his sisters didn't see enough of each other, despite he and Eliza both living in London. By no means was she a meddling or a possessive mother, quite the contrary; she was a great mother, the best in his eyes. She never made demands of anyone and rarely did she lose her temper or behave irrationally. Sometimes he wished that she would, that she would let rip and lose control and go a bit crazy. But when it came down to it, they had all, with the exception of their father, become adept at hiding their feelings. It was a defence mechanism, a way to keep Dad at a manageable distance.

Jensen had regularly spoken to Tattie of his mother and his sisters, but as to his father, he'd kept a lid on that one. She wasn't stupid, though, the omission inevitably alerted her to something being amiss. 'You never speak of your dad,' she'd said. 'It's as if he doesn't exist.'

'Oh, he exists all right,' he'd replied. 'He's what you call a larger-than-life character.'

He's certainly that, Jensen thought now as he watched his father throwing the spotlight on himself as he made his entrance into the sitting room where they'd congregated and where Phase I of Operation Scrutinize Tattie was under way by his mother and sisters.

'Ah, I see everyone's arrived,' he said.

Tattie along with Daisy and Eliza and Mum turned round from where they had been standing at the French windows. Tattie had earlier let out a whoop of delight at the sight of a peacock on the lawn. 'Oh my God, is that thing for real?' she'd cried, rushing to the window. Her American accent was always more pronounced when she was excited. Or angry. Thankfully the latter didn't happen too much. Mum had then explained to her that the peacock was called Putin and had free rein of the village, where he roamed at will. When he wasn't wandering the neighbourhood gardens he was holding court on the village green and waking the inhabitants of Little Pelham obscenely early with his screeching. 'You're winding me up,' Tattie had said. When they'd all confirmed that it was true, she'd shaken her head and puffed out her cheeks. 'Well, fancy that.'

'This is Tattie,' Jensen said now and registered with satisfaction his father's expression – never would he have expected his loser of a son to attract a girl as spectacular as Tattie. 'Tattie, this is my dad.'

Tattie offered her hand. 'Hi, Mr Channing. We were just admiring Putin in the garden. He's quite something, isn't he? I thought it was a set-up, you know, put on a show of Englishness to educate the dumb-ass Yank.' She beamed him one of her dazzling killer smiles. 'But take it from me, sir, I'm all educated up now.' Jensen suppressed a smile of his own. When it came to making first impressions, Tattie was in a class of her own.

'Err . . . yes, well, it's a pleasure to meet you. And please, call me Jeff. Now then, what can I get you to drink? You look like a glass of champagne kind of girl.'

Tattie laughed. She had the best laugh Jensen had ever heard. Sparky and irrepressible, it was one of the things that had first caught his attention. That and her curly white-blonde hair and her trademark bright red lipstick. 'Goodness no,' she said, her voice suddenly serious. 'I'm a strict teetotaller. It's against my religion.' She crossed herself exaggeratedly.

In the stunned silence, knowing the punch line, Jensen watched with yet more satisfaction as his father's face took on a look of startled awkwardness. Gone was Mr Bonhomie and in his place stood Mr Seriously Stuck For Words.

'Hey, Jeff, I'm just kiddin' with you. Gets people every time that one. I'll have whatever everyone

35

else is having.' She laughed and Jensen laughed too. God, he loved this girl. She was a much-needed breath of fresh air in his life.

'Mrs Channing, you just have to give me the recipe for this corned beef hash. JC's been telling me all the way here that no one makes it like you do. Not that I'd ever be able to cook it properly – I'm pretty much hopeless in the kitchen, aren't I, JC?'

'Hardly that bad. And anyway, you have plenty of other talents.'

'Please, Tattie, it's Mia. You make me sound so ancient calling me Mrs Channing.'

'You, ancient, with that flawless complexion? No way! You could easily pass for another of JC's sisters. You must have had him when you were a child.'

Clearing his throat and topping up his glass of wine, Jeff said, 'So what are your other talents, Tattie? I should imagine a bright girl like you would be good at many things.'

Tattie put down her knife and fork. 'Well,' she said, carefully dabbing the corners of her mouth with her napkin, 'I like to think I'm a good mother. Apart from not being able to cook for my daughter as well as maybe I should. But then she's gotten real good in the kitchen herself these days. Flips pancakes like a total pro. JC's taught her how to do that.'

'*Mother*,' repeated Daisy and Eliza in unison.

'You have a daughter?' asked Mia with a slight

lifting of her chin. 'How old is she?' Jensen had to hand it to his mother; there wasn't a hint of shock or surprise in her voice or expression.

Tattie smiled back at her. 'I have an awesome nine-year-old daughter. Her name's Madison and she's just beautiful. And real smart. I couldn't be prouder of her.'

'Nine years old,' echoed Daisy. 'But you don't look old enough.'

'Don't be fooled, I'm plenty old enough. I had Madison when I was twenty.'

'And her father?'

'Mia, let's just say that he wasn't cut out for fatherhood and therefore chose not to be involved.'

Jeff gave Jensen a sidelong look, so quick it was barely noticeable, but Jensen saw it and turned away.

'So what brought you to Britain?' asked Eliza.

'Oh, you know,' Tattie said, 'the usual thing for us foreigners, your beautiful weather.'

Everyone laughed.

'Actually, my great-grandmother was British,' Tattie went on, 'and she moved with her family to the States when she was a little girl. I'd always wanted to visit and then when a friend of mine moved to London, I visited her with Madison and we loved it so much we decided to make our home here in England. That was more than two years ago.'

'Wow,' said Daisy. 'And your mum and dad back in America didn't mind you doing that?'

'Oh, they put up a token show of resistance, but deep down they accept that I have to find my own way.'

Daisy turned to her father. 'You'd be the same, wouldn't you, Dad? You wouldn't ever stop us from doing something we felt we had to do, would you?'

'I suppose that rather depends on what it was,' he said.

Something in the way Daisy had put the question to their father made Jensen look at his sister closely. Watching her now chewing on her lower lip and examining one of her fingernails, instinct told him she was up to something, that she had a very real reason for asking Dad what she just had. He wondered if she had a shocker hiding up her sleeve.

In the silence, Mia stood up. 'If you're all finished, I'll get the dessert.'

'I'll help you,' Jensen said, eager to have a few moments alone with his mother.

Out in the kitchen, the door closed to the dining room, Jensen began stacking the dishwasher. 'Come on, then, Mum, what do you think? Do you like her?'

'Yes I do. She's great.'

He smiled. 'She is. She really is. I think she's the one I want to be with for the rest of my life.'

'Even with a nine-year-old daughter?'

He stopped what he was doing. 'Does that bother you, that she has a child?'

'No, not at all. I just don't want . . .' her voice trailed away.

'What, Mum? What don't you want for me? To be happy?'

'Don't be silly. Of course I want you to be happy. It's what I've always wanted for you. And if Tattie makes you happy, then that makes me happy. But taking on the responsibility of someone else's child isn't something you should do lightly. It's a big step.'

'I know that. I've given it a lot of thought.' He went to his mother and hugged her. 'Thanks for tonight, for my birthday dinner. I still can't quite believe I'm thirty now; it feels like a properly grown-up age.'

She hugged him back and laughed. 'How do you think it makes me feel? There should be a law against such things happening. I'm officially banning you from having any more birthdays!'

He laughed too and, letting go of her, he said, 'Then I'd better make the most of this one. But seriously, your approval of Tattie is the best birthday present you could give me. I meant it when I said I want to be with her for ever. I've never known anyone like her.'

'And her daughter, you get on with her?'

'I haven't pushed it, but yes, Madison's a great kid. You'll love her too.'

'I'm sure I will.'

He watched his mother open the oven and take out his favourite dessert of apple crumble. He only had to smell it and he was transported back to being a very young child. He associated it with rainy Sunday afternoons, the two of them on the sofa, Mum reading to him, the light fading outside. Strange that he could still feel nostalgic for those days.

'How long have you known each other?' she asked.

'We met five months ago at a party given by a client of mine.'

She set the hot dish on a mat on a tray, then slapped him playfully with the oven gloves. 'Five months and we're only *now* having this conversation?'

He smiled. 'I wanted to wait until I was sure how Tattie felt about me. I mean, as Dad would be the first to say, I'm not much of a catch, am I?'

She tutted. 'Stop putting yourself down, you're a fine catch.'

'Yeah, but you're biased.'

'And that, darling, is a mother's prerogative. Now take the jug of cream for me and before you're gripped with any more self-doubt, listen very carefully. From what I've seen so far, I think you and Tattie make a great couple and, what's more, I think she'll be good for you. I certainly like her sense of humour. She's refreshingly open.'

So unlike our family, he thought as he followed his mother out of the kitchen.

Back in the dining room, Eliza was asking Tattie

if it was difficult for her to balance work with having a child.

'I manage pretty well,' she answered as his mother began spooning the crumble into bowls and Jensen helped by passing the bowls around the table. 'I actually have two jobs, one of which I run from home. I run my own online business supplying eco-friendly party bags for children's parties.'

'Eco-friendly party bags,' repeated Jeff. 'That's a new one on me. Is there much call for such a thing?'

'Oh yes, and it's going from strength to strength. I'm twenty per cent up on this time last year.'

'And your other job?' asked Daisy.

'I work as a celebrity lookalike.'

'No! Really? Who do you do?' asked Daisy.

'Guess. And I'm not giving you any clues.'

Everyone stared at her.

'I think I know,' Eliza said. 'Is it Marilyn Monroe?'

Tattie laughed. 'Clever you, Eliza, you've got it right.'

'Do you remember that schlocky advert on the telly last Christmas,' Jensen said, sitting down and putting his arm round Tattie, 'the one with Marilyn Monroe and Elvis opening the door to Father Christmas? That was Tattie.' He couldn't keep the pride out of his voice.

'*No!*' Daisy said. 'That advert was so cool. Does that mean you're an actress as well?'

'Sort of. But not really.'

41

Daisy sighed. 'You have such an amazing life. We all sound very boring compared to you.'

'Not true. JC's told me all about Mia's hat business, which I'd just love to see. I also know about Eliza being such a whizz, and you, Daisy, I hear you're the queen of furniture design.'

Daisy slumped in her chair and shook her head. 'I wish. It's all very dull and mundane what I do. Naff hotel furniture. Not at all what I thought I'd be doing.'

'And what do you do, Jeff? What's your thing?'

'*JC* not told you?' he responded.

Without missing a beat, Tattie said, 'I expect he did, but I've had a ditzy Marilyn moment and forgotten.' She leant towards him encouragingly. 'A captain of industry, that's what I've got you down as. Am I right?'

'Dad's in sealing and vibration control,' Jensen said, not liking his father imitating the way Tattie called him JC. 'And let's face it, it doesn't get any more interesting than that, does it?'

The atmosphere crackled and as spoons scraped against dessert bowls in the sudden silence, and knowing that a family gathering could so easily turn on a moment such as this, a moment for which he was responsible, Jensen tried to salvage things by quickly changing the subject. Turning to his sister, he said, 'So, Daisy, what's up with you then?'

Daisy raised her eyes, clearly taken aback. 'What do you mean?'

'You said that work was dull and mundane a few minutes ago – why's that?'

'Yes,' their father joined in, 'I thought you liked that job. I went to a lot of trouble to get it for you.'

'I know you did, Dad, and I am grateful. It's just that—'

'It's just what?'

'I don't like it very much. If you really want to know, I hate it.'

Jeff looked shocked. 'Mia, did you know about this?'

She shook her head. 'It's the first I've heard. Why didn't you say something before now, Daisy?'

'Because I knew Dad would tell me there's a recession on and I should be grateful for having a job, blah, blah.'

'But not if it's making you unhappy, darling.'

'Mum's right, Daisy,' said Eliza. 'No job's worth that. Have you got anything else in mind?'

Daisy chewed on her lip. 'We-*ll* . . .'

Uh-oh, thought Jensen, here it comes. Here comes the shocker, just as he'd suspected. And perhaps this was the moment when the evening would turn on its axis.

'The thing is,' Daisy said, 'and you promise you won't get angry with me, Dad?'

'Of course I won't. Just so long as I'm sure you've really thought it through.'

'I have. Trust me I have.' She paused. 'It's Scott,' she went on, 'my flatmate. He's going back to

43

Australia and has said I should go with him, that I'd easily find work there. The job market is heaps better there than it is here.'

'*Australia?* Daisy, you can't be serious.'

'It's a great opportunity, Dad. There's nothing here for people my age. Nearly everyone I know who graduated when I did can't get work. They're all stuck at home on benefits getting more and more depressed.'

'But you've got work.'

'I know. But it's not what I want to do. I hate it. I absolutely hate it and it's making me miserable. Is that what you want for me?'

'Of course it isn't. It's just the first step, the first rung on the ladder. Everyone has to start somewhere.'

'Where in Australia are you thinking of going?' asked Mia.

Daisy swallowed, her eyes dark against her pale, anxious face. She looked so worried Jensen felt genuinely sorry for her; she must have been dreading making this announcement. 'Sydney,' she murmured. 'That's where Scott's from originally.'

Jensen watched their father carefully rearrange his facial expression, replacing shock with his standard look of indulgence when it came to Daisy. Shaking his head, he said, 'Daisy, I can absolutely see the attraction. I really can. You think the grass will be greener, but take it from me, it won't be. Now come on, admit it, you haven't thought this through at all, have you? It's nothing but a sun-filled dream that your irresponsible housemate has put into your head.' Smiling, he reached across the table to pat her hand, but Daisy snatched her hand away.

'No, Dad, you're wrong. And I knew you wouldn't take me seriously. It's what you always do. You patronize me and rubbish anything I come up with.'

'Sweetheart, that's simply not true.'

'It is true! It's what you do all the time. It's why I need to get so far away from you!' She let out a small cry and pushing back her chair, she rushed from the room.

In the awkward silence Daisy left behind her, Jensen glanced at Tattie and thought, welcome to my world.

CHAPTER 7

*E*xpect the unexpected.

Twice now in one day Owen had experienced something out of the ordinary. First the racing sofa, and then, as if waiting for him, a peacock had been standing guard at The Hidden Cottage when he'd arrived.

As welcoming committees went, it hadn't been the friendliest; the peacock, on seeing Owen step out of his car, had let rip with an ugly screech and put on a dramatic show of male supremacy with its magnificent plumage.

'Hey, why don't you put your feathers away and give me a hand?' Owen had told the bird as he'd carried what little luggage he'd brought with him up to the house. The peacock had given him a long hard stare with its beady eyes and then shaken its tail feathers some more and screeched some more. To which Owen had responded with, 'Pardon my bad grammar, but in the words of Shania Twain, that don't impress me much.'

The peacock had made its feelings vocally very clear for the next five minutes, plainly regarding Owen as a no-good interloper. 'Right, fella,' he'd said when he'd had enough of the awful din and addressed the bird in his sternest voice, 'if you and I are going to get along, we have to get things straight from the outset. You may have treated this as your patch in the past, but this is my home now, which means my rules apply. You either accept that, or you ship out. Got it?'

The bird must have decided these were terms it couldn't accept and had sloped off into the bushes with its tail feathers lowered, leaving Owen to get on with letting himself into the house and savouring the moment of his long-awaited arrival.

Now, several hours later, having explored and unpacked the few things he'd brought with him and cooked himself a supper of bacon and eggs, he topped up his glass of red wine, put on a fleece and went outside. In the fading light, as he stood on the veranda, the wooden floor creaking beneath his feet, he breathed in the soft honeyed night air. I'm here, he thought. I'm *really* here. It might not seem much to anyone else, this significant moment, but for him it was beyond special. He couldn't really put it into words. It was an emotion. And when all was said and done, could you really put an emotion into mere words?

He could just imagine some of his friends rolling their eyes at such talk, but he'd always been a soppy old devil; he couldn't be trusted to watch *Bambi* without making a fool of himself. Bea, his ex-wife, used to say it was one of his most endearing qualities. When he'd told Bea about his plans to come here, she'd wished him well. 'I hope it turns out to be everything you want it to be,' she'd said. 'I expect an invitation to come and visit.'

While he regretted their marriage had come to an end, he treasured the good relationship he and Bea had managed to maintain in the three years since the divorce. She had remarried eighteen months ago and was now the mother she had always wanted to be. Her new husband, Steve, was a thoroughly decent guy and Owen was happy for Bea.

Children had been one of those things both he and Bea had been keen to have, but after extensive attempts to get pregnant – let no one call him a slouch in that department! – they had sought professional help only to discover he was at fault. 'Not at *fault*,' the doctor had corrected Owen when he had used the word, 'just deficient in sperm.' Whichever way the diagnosis was served up, the net result was that Owen knew he couldn't do the one thing that had become so important to Bea, and with her body clock ticking loud and fast, the pressure between them grew. They discussed endlessly the options available, such as adoption and donor sperm, but never quite reached the point of committing to either.

He would never know for sure, but Owen couldn't help but wonder whether, had they been able to have a child together, they would have heeded the warning signs and realized sooner that their marriage was suffering because they were working too hard?

Well, they hadn't, and it was into their jointly owned business that the two of them poured both heart and soul. From his own point of view, it felt as if it was the only thing he could get right.

Four years after graduating from university, where he and Bea had met, they had given up their jobs – he had been a trader in the City and Bea had been a solicitor – and together they started running a mail order business for ski wear. They called it ObeSkiWear and being keen skiers themselves, they knew what worked and what didn't. When the internet took off, they began selling online and that was when things went stratospheric and they were working crazy hours. And failing to conceive a child.

The combination of working too hard and not being able to do what all their friends were doing so effortlessly was not a good mix. But ultimately it was the pressure they were under to sustain the success of what they'd created that was their undoing. What had once been their 'baby', conceived in their spare room, had grown into a monster that demanded all their time and energy. From their warehouse and office in Crawley, they were constantly travelling, attending trade shows, meeting new suppliers and designers, carrying out stringent quality control, devising new marketing strategies and most importantly ensuring their customers were always happy and would come back for more.

When they took the step to open some stores in carefully selected towns, friends who had known them for many years began to voice their concern, namely that he and Bea looked to be on the verge of burnout and that they couldn't continue living at the frantic pace they were. The most vociferous voice of concern had come from Owen's oldest friend. It was an opinion that Owen had dismissed as a severe case of the pot calling the kettle black because Rich, who still worked as a trader in the city, regularly put in a fourteen-hour day and often looked like hell whenever they could spare the time to see each other.

But being the man he was then, Owen refused to admit anything was wrong and even when he and Bea decided to call it a day on their marriage, he was convinced they could continue working together. Bea humoured him for about a year, but around the time that Owen's mother died, when she met and fell in love with Steve, she announced that she wanted out, saying she wanted to create a new life for herself, a life that included a family.

It was then, when Owen was trying to summon up the strength to continue without Bea, that one of France's largest ski clothing and equipment retailers made an approach to buy them out. There had been a time when he and Bea would have told them where to stick their money, but not now – now they gave the proposition all their consideration. It took months and months of legal wrangling to form an agreement, with Owen and

Bea wanting cast-iron assurances that their current employees, some of whom had been with them since the early days, would not lose their jobs. Finally an agreement was reached to the satisfaction of all parties, but being the pathologically sentimental idiot he was, Owen had had a lump in his throat when he'd signed the forms last November. He and Bea might have suddenly become absurdly wealthy overnight, but he had felt bereft.

While Bea got on with her new life with a new husband and child, Owen had felt as if he had a resounding nothing to get on with. No job. No wife. No family. Thank God for his friends! Because it was while spending most of the winter on the ski slopes, having rented a chalet in Chamonix for three months, and inviting friends to join him whenever they wanted, that he realized one very important thing: he now had to get on with his life and chase his own dream.

He had no idea what the outcome would be of returning to Little Pelham, but as he sat down cautiously in one of the seen-better-days garden chairs the previous owners had left behind and tuned into the quietness of the evening, it felt good. It felt like home.

On his return from Chamonix, back in March, going through some of the boxes of his mother's things – a task he'd deliberately put off – he'd found one of his old school books from his time at Little Pelham Junior School. He'd had no idea that his

51

mother had kept it, but flicking through the pages and coming across a picture he'd drawn of The Hidden Cottage he'd realized that it matched perfectly the exterior of the house he'd dreamt of for all these years, and it set him thinking. Which in turn had him turning to the internet and browsing the various property sites.

His search was restricted to one small area: Little Pelham. There was nothing that interested him – just a couple of small cottages for sale. He signed up to receive regular updates and to his amazement, less than a fortnight later, he received notification that a new property had come on to the market in the village; it was The Hidden Cottage.

Not surprisingly the photographs showed an interior that he didn't recognize – after thirty-four years it was only natural that the place had been changed and extensively modernized – but there was no doubt in his mind what his next step had to be. Without even going to see the house, he made an offer, instructed a solicitor and a surveyor and the deal was done.

Rich declared him as having more money than sense and finally going off his rocker, but Bea had reasoned that even if it proved to be a mistake, what did it matter when it was a mistake he could easily afford to make? Admittedly it was the most wildly impulsive thing he'd ever done, yet it felt entirely right.

Just as it had felt right to put off coming to see the house until today when he moved in. He had planned it that way to ensure maximum effect; he had wanted to capture all of his emotions into one sharply focused moment.

With that thought uppermost in his mind, he stared out from the wooden veranda that covered the full width of the back of the house and absorbed the cloistered tranquillity. The light had gone now and low in the inky-black sky, the moon shone down, skimming the tops of the trees, its reflection caught in the stillness of the lake.

He'd first come across The Hidden Cottage a few weeks after he and his parents had moved to the village. It was a Saturday afternoon, his father was working and his mother was ironing, and with nothing to do, he'd gone for a walk. He'd nosed around the allotments watching the old men at work, then followed the path up through the fields, and then slipped through the barbed-wire fence and entered the woods. He'd followed the slope down and kept on going, thinking about what he'd heard some of the other children in his class saying, that no one ever came out of the woods alive because there were witches who lived on the other side of it. He knew what they were saying was rubbish, but as he emerged into a sunlit clearing and found himself in front of a small lake perfectly reflecting the trees around it, he almost believed he'd stepped out of the real world and into some kind of magical place. Maybe a witch did live there, he'd thought as he walked cautiously towards the water.

When he turned and spotted the house, complete with a twist of smoke coming out of one of the chimneys, a sense of wonder and mystery crept over him. Staring up at the windows, their frames painted green to match the door, he imagined for a moment that he could hear the house's heartbeat, that it was a living and breathing thing and was beckoning him towards it.

As if led by the hand, he moved forward and the heartbeat grew louder and more insistent. He held his breath and suddenly realized that the heartbeat he could hear was his own. He almost laughed aloud at his stupidity. It was then that he heard music coming from the house through the open French windows. It was piano music and unlike anything he'd ever heard before.

He had no idea what he would say if someone came out of the house and asked what he thought he was doing there, but he was prepared to risk that. But for some reason, he didn't think that was going to happen. He was meant to be here. He was meant to see this place for himself. And whoever lived here would understand that. What's more it would be their secret. To his nine-year-old self, his reasoning made perfect sense, but to any parent it would have had every alarm bell ringing.

Nobody did appear that day, nor the next time he went, nor the next. It wasn't until he'd been there five times – and always just to sit by the water to watch the moorhens fossicking about in the bank and the dragonflies skimming the water's surface, but mostly to hear the extraordinary music that poured out from the house – that he saw a flicker of movement at a downstairs window, and plucking up the courage, he went and knocked on the door. He did it because, if he had been seen, he thought it a matter of politeness to explain why he was there; he didn't want the owner of the house to think badly of him.

Also he was curious now. Who really did live here?

He knocked on the door in what he hoped was a polite manner. Not too loudly, but loud enough.

The first knock went unanswered.

As did the second.

Then determined to get an answer, if only to satisfy his curiosity, he tried again. This time the music came to an abrupt end and in the sudden and complete silence he heard the sound of a lock being turned. All at once, he began to doubt the wisdom of what he was doing, and what he'd done in coming here. What if the person who opened the door was the sort of man his mother had warned him never to speak to? The sort who kidnapped children. The sort who hid them away never to be found again. The sort who—

The door slowly opened and with his legs trembling and his brain telling him to run, he took a wobbly step back . . .

A rustling sound in the bushes had Owen glancing sharply to his right. A fox appeared on the lawn and bathed in the moon's soft radiance; it looked directly at Owen as if querying his right to be there. It then trotted off towards the lake and melted away into the darkness.

Time for me to melt away as well, thought Owen. He drank what was left in his wineglass, and went back inside the house. He wondered if it was too late to ring Nicole. He really should have called her earlier, but to be honest, he wasn't that sure how well his call would be received. He wasn't exactly his girlfriend's favourite person right now.

They'd met in Chamonix in January. He'd been skiing alone and had shared a chairlift with her. When she said that she'd got separated from her group of friends and was on her way back to the hotel where they were staying, but didn't know the way, he'd offered to ski her to the door. To thank him, she invited him to join her for a drink. The next day he met up with her and her friends for lunch and then spent the afternoon skiing with her.

From there things just snowballed, as he'd joked when reporting back to Rich. A fortnight after the end of her holiday, she returned to Chamonix to stay with him for a long weekend, and did so again twice more before he returned to the UK and to the apartment he was renting in Marylebone, only a stone's throw from where Rich lived. Since Nicole also lived and worked in London they were able to spend a lot more time together and all was going well until he told her about The Hidden Cottage.

56

'You've done what?' she'd said, her face incredulous.

'I've bought a house in the country,' he'd explained, 'a very special house.' He'd tried to explain why but all she'd cared about was why he hadn't told her about it before.

'I haven't told anyone,' he'd said. 'You're the first to know.'

Her expression still incredulous, she said, 'But I'm your girlfriend; didn't you think I'd be interested?'

It was a fair comment – she was his girlfriend and it was something he should have discussed with her, but he hadn't. He was guilty of precisely the kind of autonomous behaviour he had always strongly disapproved of and he had no defence other than to say he'd acted instinctively and, yes, selfishly.

'Apparently I'm not important to you,' she'd gone on, 'not important enough at any rate for you to share something like this with me.'

Disbelief had now been replaced on her face with what he recognized as the beginnings of a sulky pout. At thirty-six she was perhaps too old to play that card, but he knew he'd upset her and putting his arms around her, he'd said, 'Of course you're important to me.'

She'd looked into his eyes. 'Really?'

'Absolutely.'

One of the things that had surprised him about Nicole was her constant need for reassurance. In all other respects, she was outgoing and hugely confident, but when it came to their relationship she seemed to want his perpetual reassurance that he cared about her. With hindsight, his buying The Hidden Cottage without telling her didn't really help matters.

Trouble was, just as he'd smoothed things over and she said that she was looking forward to seeing the house, she then realized she'd misunderstood him. She had assumed The Hidden Cottage was a weekend retreat, somewhere they could slip away to, just the two of them. 'You mean you're moving there?' she'd said. 'You're actually going to *live* there? But what about us?'

It was a good question and one they had yet to resolve.

Inside the house, despite how late it was, he rang Nicole on his mobile. But all he got was her voicemail telling him to leave a message. Which he did.

Trying not to read too much into Nicole's continued silence – she hadn't returned any of his calls for the last two days – he went in search of the sleeping bag he'd brought with him. Such was the extent of his good mood at being here that nothing – not even a sulking girlfriend or a night of sleeping on the floor – could dampen his spirits.

CHAPTER 8

By the time Mia had finished in the bathroom, Jeff was already fast asleep, his breathing heavy, his body restless. He'd never been a peaceful sleeper. But then he wasn't a peaceful sort of man.

Standing by the side of the bed, Mia felt a pang of pity for him. He'd been so very upset at Daisy's outburst earlier that evening; nothing could have hurt him more. Bad enough that Daisy had announced she wanted to move to the other side of the world, but to say she had to do it to get away from him must have been unbearable.

Too wound up to sleep or to read, Mia went quietly back downstairs, anxious not to disturb Daisy and Eliza, who were sleeping in their old rooms. Jensen and Tattie hadn't stayed the night; they'd driven home to London.

In the kitchen she filled the kettle, put it on the Aga and wrapped her arms around herself to keep warm. It was the end of May, but the nights were still quite chilly. The kettle soon boiled and after dunking a teabag in a mug and adding milk, she drew up a chair and inevitably thought again of

Daisy. After she had rushed from the room, Jensen had gone to look for her. She didn't know what he'd said to his sister to bring her round, but minutes later, they reappeared and nothing more was said on the subject. Everyone, even Jeff, tactfully concentrated on Jensen's birthday cake and him blowing out the candles, all thirty of them.

Jensen, Mia thought fondly, thirty years old. How was that possible and where had the time gone?

She and Jeff had met when she was in her first year at Bristol University. A shy and somewhat naive girl, she had been drawn to him by his charm and maturity and his extraordinary belief in his own worth and capabilities. He also made her laugh. He was the first person who made her feel that she took life just a little too seriously, that actually there was a world of fun out there. Six years his junior, she was in awe of his confidence and being with him made her believe she could be like him, that she could do anything she wanted, that the skies really were the limit.

Having left school at sixteen Jeff Channing was a world away from the man her parents had in mind for her and, of course, that only increased the attraction. The more they disapproved, the more independent and liberated she felt, elevating herself above their appalling narrow-mindedness. With hindsight, she was behaving as a perfectly ordinary rebellious nineteen-year-old girl, hell-bent on flouting convention and all the rules her parents had laid down.

Jeff came into her life in the middle of her first term and such was the effect he had on her, the newly made friendships with her fellow students were all but forgotten in her eagerness to be with him. Their paths crossed in an off-licence; she was there to buy a bottle of cheap wine to take to a party, but when she tried to pay for it, the man behind the till refused to believe she was old enough to be served. She had produced her student union card but he'd waved it away without even bothering to look at it, dismissing it as a fake. She'd explained that it most certainly wasn't, that she wasn't a liar or a cheat, and that if he'd just take the time to look at the card he'd see that it was genuine. Reluctantly he had. 'Doesn't look anything like you,' he said of the photo.

'That's because I've got my hair done differently; I'm going to a party. That's why I need the wine.'

'You can go empty-handed for all I care. I'm not selling you any alcohol. And that's that. So on your way and let me serve the rest of my customers.'

She'd had no choice but to swallow back her humiliation and leave. She was a few yards down the road when she heard her name being called. She turned to see a smartly dressed man in a suit coming towards her. 'Do I know you?' she asked.

'Not yet you don't,' he said.

She frowned. 'Then how do you know my name?'

'I was standing behind you in the off-licence just now and saw it on your student union card. Here, this is for you.'

She continued to frown, not sure what was going on. Who was this man?

He smiled. 'Take it, it's the bottle of wine you wanted.'

'But . . . but why would you do that?'

'Because I felt sorry for you, for the way that idiot treated you. Anyone can see that you're a bona fide student, and not a liar or a cheat.'

'Are you teasing me?'

His smile widened. 'Just a little. What time is the party?'

'It's started already. I'm late. I was trying to finish an essay and lost track of the time.'

'What are you studying?'

'French.'

'I'm impressed.'

She dug around in her bag for her purse. 'I must pay you.'

'Must you? Why not pay me in kind by having a drink with me?'

'But the party . . . I'm already late.'

'Then why not give it a miss altogether and have dinner with me instead?'

'Dinner?'

'I know a particularly good French restaurant in Clifton. You could help me with the menu.'

'I don't think you need help with anything.'

'Now *you're* teasing *me*. Come on, have dinner with me. You look like you could do with feeding up. No wonder the man in the off-licence thought you were underage – there's not a spare ounce on you.'

'But I don't know you. I can't have dinner with a total stranger.'

'I promise you, I'm not a danger to you. I'll be the perfect gentleman at all times, and what's more I'll drive you back to wherever you live afterwards. Come on, live a little. Have some fun.'

How could she refuse such a gauntlet? Especially as she hadn't really been looking forward to the party. Dinner at a French restaurant in Clifton sounded a much better evening.

His car – a burgundy-coloured sports car – was parked a few yards up the road and after he'd helped her in and he was behind the steering wheel, she thought of her father's Volvo Estate and said, 'I've never been in a car like this before. What is it?'

'It's a Jensen Interceptor. A classic.'

'Are you rich?'

He laughed. 'No. But I fully intend to be.'

He kept his promise that evening; he behaved impeccably and asked if he could take her out for dinner again when he was back from a business trip up north. She agreed and found herself counting the days until she saw him next. From then on she saw him as often as she could.

He was a man of grand romantic gestures, but lacked what she would later discern as any romantic sensibility. He took her to London, to expensive restaurants. He bought her clothes. Grown-up clothes, he called them. She started wearing make-up, something she had never done before. Her studies suffered. But she didn't care. She was happy. Happier than she'd ever been. She felt so alive. And in love. In love with a man who in all truth wasn't exactly handsome, but his attraction lay in his ceaseless energy and absolute certainty that he knew exactly where he was going. When he agreed to meet her parents – their prejudice against him was subsequently confirmed on sight and he was dismissed as brash and too full of himself – she knew that he was as committed to her as she was to him.

Six months after meeting she was pregnant, and that's when she realized he wasn't as committed as she'd believed. 'You can't keep the baby,' he'd said matter-of-factly. 'You have to get rid of it. You're much too young to have a child. And what about your degree?'

'I don't care about my degree. I want to have your baby. I love you, Jeff. I want us to be together.'

'I love you too, Mia, but this is all wrong. I can't be a father yet. I'm not ready.'

And to prove it, he left her. He gave her money, promised to send her money regularly in the post, but she couldn't expect any more than that from him.

By rights she should have hated him. But she didn't. She didn't have that kind of energy to waste on him – she was too mired in shock and shame. Even then, 1982, girls of her class and background didn't end up pregnant: they were meant to be smarter than that. There was a moment when she really did think that the only answer was to do as Jeff had said: get rid of the baby. But an abortion? How did one go about it? She knew nothing of such things. So, as absurd as it now sounds, she tried the cliché of sitting in a hot bath while drinking lots and lots of gin. All that happened was that she was violently sick and nearly passed out.

Still very much pregnant, she went home to Basingstoke and broke the news to her parents. It was her mother who led the charge in their combined anger and disappointment with her and declared she never wanted to set eyes on Mia again. Unless she had an abortion. In an instant Mia felt fiercely protective of the child she was carrying. No one was going to make her kill it. This was her baby. It was hers and she was going to give it the right to live.

Refusing her mother's demand point-blank, and believing her parents would come round, that they would eventually calm down and do all they could to help, she stood firm. But they didn't come round and the shock of their adamant rejection hit her more than Jeff's abandonment. Parents, weren't they supposed to be there for you, no matter what? Wasn't their love supposed to be unconditional?

Not in this case. And so she returned to Bristol in a state of shocked denial. This really wasn't happening to her, was it? Somehow she managed to continue fooling herself, along with everyone else, until finally one of her tutors took her aside and asked outright if she was pregnant. Things happened very quickly after that. She was given the opportunity to defer her place, to return after the baby was born and initially Mia was tempted to say yes, but then she thought how trivial it all seemed. She was about to become a mother; the luxury of study was no longer an option for her. She had to find a way to support herself and the baby.

She moved out of her halls of residence and, using the local paper, she looked for somewhere to live in Bristol. She ended up renting a room from a woman called Mrs Frost, whose manner was as cold as her name might suggest. She was a gorgon of a landlady, but Mia was determined to make it work, if only because the rent was so reasonable. Her parents had cut her off without a penny but at least Jeff remained true to his word and regularly sent her money. Other than that, she didn't hear from him. She had an address for him, but she had promised herself the only time she would contact him would be to let him know she'd had the baby.

When the time came she wrote telling him that he had a son and she'd called him Jensen, after his car. His response was to send her more money, and as regular as clockwork, every month, a payment was made into her bank account.

She didn't see him again until Jensen was nearly four years old and had been admitted to hospital.

CHAPTER 9

Back from her sleepover at Lauren's, Madison unpacked her overnight bag.

When she had put everything away, she smoothed the duvet on her bed and placed a large round cake tin on it. She then sat at the desk JC had bought for her. Squeezed in between the chest of drawers and the door, it was her favourite thing in her bedroom, that and her electronic piano keyboard and the pretty shell Lauren had brought back from her holiday in the Caribbean. It was a conch shell and when Lauren had given it to her she had explained that she'd bought it from a man selling them on the beach in front of the hotel where she and her family had been staying. Originally Madison had kept the shell on her bedside table, but now she had it on her desk.

JC had surprised her with the desk on her ninth birthday three weeks ago. Even Mum had been amazed and had thought it might be too big for her tiny bedroom. JC had said he wasn't stupid and that he'd checked the measurements before he'd bought it at Ikea.

So now she had her very own desk with a drawer

where she kept her diary. The diary now open in front of her, she selected the pen she wanted to use – it was Saturday, which meant it had to be the pen with the sparkly gold ink; she had a different colour for each day of the week. She placed the cap on the top of the pen and tapped it against her teeth wondering how to start and thinking that maybe if she didn't actually write what Lauren had told her, it might not be true, or might not happen. But that was silly thinking. It *was* true. And it *was* going to happen. Lauren and her family were moving away and Madison was going to lose her best friend. Her *only* friend.

Last night Lauren had told her that her parents had decided to move out of London to a place Madison had never heard of. She had said it had been a big secret, but now the new house was theirs and even though Lauren hadn't even seen it, she was dead excited about it. It had a big garden and they were going to keep chickens and Lauren was going to look after them and her brother was going to be allowed to have a dog. 'We'll still be best friends,' Lauren had said. 'We'll send emails to each other all the time. And I'll learn how to use Skype.' Madison already used Skype on Mum's computer; she used it to chat with her grandparents in America, but doing it with Lauren wouldn't be the same. Nothing was going to be the same once Lauren left. School would be horrible again. There'd be no one to eat lunch with. No one to sit next to in class. No one to play with during break-time. It would be like it was before Lauren came to the school.

And who was going to give her piano lessons? Lauren's mum had been teaching her and even she said Madison was way better than Lauren now, that she was a natural and had perfect pitch and could play by ear, something Lauren couldn't do. But then Lauren was brilliant at other things. She could do ballet and make her arms look as light as feathers. Madison would never be able to do that. She wasn't built the same way. Lauren was like a fairy, whereas Madison was tall with what Grandma Barb called big bones. Grandma Barb said they were Family Bones and that Mum had them too. But Madison didn't think that was true. Mum was beautiful. No one would ever say that about Madison. She was big and ugly and stuck with wearing glasses. Mum said that she would be able to wear contact lenses when she was older, but that didn't help her now when she was called Specky Eyes at school. She was also called Freak because she was so tall. They had all sorts of names for her. Some were cruel, but mostly they were dumb. If she wanted to, she could come up with names for them that were a lot cleverer than the ones they used. She didn't see the point, though. Why waste her thoughts on something so stupid? She would much rather read a book or play the piano.

She thought of her lessons at Lauren's and felt sad. Heather – Lauren's mum – gave her the lessons for free. Mum had offered to pay, but Heather had said that since Madison was always round at their house, it was no trouble giving her lessons or letting her practice on the upright piano they had in their dining room. Sometimes Madison and Lauren played little duets together, and that was fun. Other times, Madison would try and play something that Lauren could dance to. But that was quite hard to do.

With not a word written, she replaced the cap on the pen and put it down on the desk. Why did Lauren's parents want to move? And why did things have to keep changing? Grown-ups did that all the time. Just as you got used to something, they went and changed it. Mum was the same. It was why they were living here in London. She had said she wanted Madison to experience something more than small-town America. 'There's a whole world out there for us to discover,' Mum was always saying.

Madison worried when Mum said that; it made her anxious that they might move again. Although right now, that didn't seem such a bad idea. Especially if she could convince Mum they should live wherever it was Lauren was going to be.

But would that mean they would have to leave JC behind? That would be a shame. She liked JC. He was easily the nicest boyfriend Mum had ever had, not that she'd had that many. JC knew every-thing about computers and liked to play chess with Madison, and he didn't let her beat him; he played to win, just as she did. Before JC, she had played chess on the computer; she much preferred having a real person to play with.

Recently, on days when Mum was working or when Lauren had her ballet or speech and drama lessons, JC had started picking her up from school. The first time he'd come for her, after Mum had told her teacher to look out for him, everyone had stared at him. With his golden-brown hair, his sunglasses and his black jeans and hoodie top, and his odd shoes – he had a thing about wearing different coloured Converse trainers on each foot – he looked way cooler than any of the other dads who came to the gate. Lauren had met him a few times and said he looked like he could be famous, like he played in a cool rock band.

As a proper dad, JC would be totally cool. One of the things she liked about him was that he didn't do that boring thing grown-ups usually did – talk to her as if she was an idiot and then lose interest when she was in the middle of telling him something. He always listened properly. She liked it when he stayed for what Mum called a JC sleepover, because he made them nice breakfasts in the morning. Porridge was her favourite, with golden syrup. She'd never had it before; no way could Mum, who was the worst cook in the world, be trusted to make it.

That was why Madison had offered to make a birthday cake for JC, because Mum couldn't make one to save her life. She had made it early this morning at Lauren's, with only a bit of help from Heather. It was the piping that had been the difficult bit, that and writing Happy Birthday JC on the cake. She hoped he liked it. Mum had said that they would give him his presents this afternoon and then surprise him with the cake. It would have been nicer to celebrate his birthday yesterday, on the actual day, but he had taken Mum to meet his family last night. Madison had asked if she could go as well and JC had said, 'Yeah, why not?' but Mum had said there was plenty of time for all that.

'All what?' Madison had asked.

'Never you mind, missy.'

In the car coming back from Lauren's earlier, Madison had asked if they'd enjoyed themselves last night. Mum had looked at Jensen and said, 'It was a blast. Hey, you'll never guess what I saw in Mr and Mrs Channing's garden: a peacock. A real peacock. Imagine that. And you know what, it just wanders round the village wherever it wants to go, doing whatever it wants to do.'

'Can I come with you the next time you go?' Madison had asked. 'Can I see the peacock?'

'We'll see, hon. We'll see. So what did you and Lauren get up to?'

She hadn't said anything about Lauren moving away; she had wanted to put it in her diary first. Her diary was sort of like a friend to her – it was where she shared anything important. Good things. Bad things. Losing Lauren would be a very, *very* bad thing.

The blank page of her diary stared back at her. This was the first time she hadn't been able to put into words how she felt about something. And that made her feel so upset she suddenly wanted to cry. She took off her glasses and squeezed her eyes shut to try and stop the tears coming, but it didn't work and the first tear rolled down her cheek, followed quickly by another. She slumped over the desk and cried and cried.

A knock at the door made her jump. 'Yes,' she said, sitting bolt upright and wiping her eyes with the backs of her hands.

JC came in. 'Your mum's just gone to the shop for some milk and I wondered if you wanted to have a game of . . . Are you OK?'

She nodded, sniffed and fumbled to get her glasses back on.

He stared at her and came right into the room. 'Are you sure?'

She swallowed and nodded again, wishing he'd go away, but at the same time wanting him to stay. She didn't want to be alone. She saw his gaze flicker towards her diary still open on the desk. She quickly shut it, even though there was nothing to see.

He crouched down beside her. 'Madison, you know I'd never *ever* read your diary.'

When she didn't respond, he said, 'You're not bothered about last night, are you, about not coming with us?'

She pressed her lips tightly shut and shook her head.

'What then?' He put a hand on her arm. 'Did you and Lauren have a bust-up?'

He was being so nice to her and his voice was so soft and gentle she should have felt better, but hearing Lauren's name was too much and she couldn't stop herself from flinging her arms around him and blurting it all out.

CHAPTER 10

Originally Eliza was going to go up to Cloverdale Farm on her own to fetch the eggs Mum needed for lunch, but then her sister had said she'd come as she fancied a walk.

Given Daisy's childhood history of seismic tantrums and door slamming, nobody would have been surprised if she'd left with Jensen and Tattie in a tearful strop last night, but no, she'd stayed, and Eliza could only presume she'd done so in the hope of bringing Dad round.

Just before she'd gone up to bed last night, Eliza had overheard Daisy asking their father if she could talk to him, seeing as they'd both calmed down. 'I really don't know what to say to you right now,' he'd said. 'I think it would be better if we talked in the morning.' Eliza couldn't recall him ever sounding so cold with Daisy as she did then; it must have upset her enormously.

At breakfast this morning, with Dad not around – he'd been up early to go and play golf – Daisy had spoken in more detail to Mum and Eliza about why she wanted to go to Australia, how Scott was absolutely convinced she could make a good life for herself there. 'I feel like I'm stuck in the rut of doom here,' she'd complained, 'and I'm only twenty-three. There's got to be more to life than the brain-numbing nine-to-five boredom I currently have to cope with. I want more than that. Is that so wrong?'

Her sister's words had resonated with Eliza in a way she would never have expected. There was nothing boring or nine-to-five about her job with Merchant Swift, far from it, but since she'd met Greg, she had begun to think that a fulfilling life outside of work was something she would like to have.

Having collected the eggs from Sue at Cloverdale Farm and heard the latest on her twin daughters whom Daisy used to babysit and who were now doing their GCSEs, they retraced their steps towards the centre of the village. The green, with its semi-circle of attractively thatched cottages that led up to Medlar House and the church, was generally considered to be the jewel in Little Pelham's crown, but Eliza thought Cloverdale Lane was the real gem. She loved the eclectic mix of stone-built cottages, the way they were squeezed in so closely they seemed almost ready to break free and tumble down the steep and narrow twisting road. She liked the tiny front gardens too, the way the owners all took such pride in them, filling the spaces with as much colour as they could. She was no flower expert, but as she and Daisy made their way down the hill, Eliza could recognize London pride, catmint, aubrietia, clematis, alliums and the frothy yellow flowers of lady's mantle.

When they reached the junction with the main road, they waited for a chestnut mare ridden by a girl they didn't know to clip-clop slowly by.

'So what do you really think about Jensen's girl-friend?' Daisy asked as they turned right to go on to Parr's, which was Little Pelham's one and only shop – a post office and food store combined. 'She wasn't at all what I imagined. Not that I have any idea what kind of girls he's ever been out with in the past. I mean, he's always so secretive.'

With all the drama Daisy had caused last night they hadn't had a real chance to discuss Jensen and Tattie in any detail. 'I liked her,' Eliza said simply. 'And as for his secrecy, we're all as bad as one another. Look what you were hiding from us.'

Daisy slowed her step. 'You're right, but come on, who'd have thought he'd get involved with someone who's got a child? He's not exactly the fatherly type, is he? I'd have had money on him running in the opposite direction the second he knew she came with that kind of baggage.'

'People change,' Eliza said. 'Besides, we all have baggage.'

Daisy let out a short, bitter laugh. 'You're not wrong there and, as we both know, I have enough baggage to warrant my own baggage handler. So what's your big secret, then? What are *you* hiding from us?'

Wrong-footed by the swerve of her question, Eliza said, 'What makes you think I have a secret?'

'You just said we're all as bad as one another for hiding things, I assumed you were including yourself in that.'

Eliza hesitated. Could she tell Daisy? Why not? Hadn't she wanted to bring Greg here this weekend to show him off to the family? She steeled herself. 'Actually,' she said nervously, 'I've met someone. His name's Greg and—' She broke off and laughed, suddenly bashful at her own daring. 'Oh God, I sound like someone from Alcoholics Anonymous!'

Daisy looked serious. 'How long have you been keeping Greg under your hat, so to speak?'

'Um . . . it's been about four months now.'

Daisy's expression intensified. 'And don't tell me, you've kept quiet about him because of Dad?'

'No, not just because of Dad. More a matter of not wanting to jinx things before they'd had a chance to become really established.'

'And things are established now?'

'I . . . I think so.'

'Well, good luck to you, Eliza. You got yourself fast-tracked to boring old adulthood at far too young an age; I reckon you deserve some fun. And if Greg is fun, you make the most of him. But what a family we are for keeping quiet about anything that's important! What the hell's wrong with us? And you know what, my going to Australia is only half the story.'

'There's something else?'

'Oh yeah, there's a lot of something else to come out yet. Hey, I haven't seen this car round here before.'

They were now outside Parr's where a green sports car was parked. Eliza looked at the number plate: OWEI. 'Probably someone just passing through or maybe visiting,' she said, pushing open the shop door and setting off the tinkling bell.

There was only one other customer inside the shop – almost certainly the owner of the car – and with a big grin on his face, Bob Parr was merrily cashing up a sizeable order. His wife, Wendy – aka, Windoline Wendy, owing to her fondness for lurid pink lipstick – was packing everything into a large cardboard box and she also was grinning like the proverbial Cheshire cat, albeit with very pink lips.

While searching the chilled cabinet for the packet of pancetta that Mum had asked them to get for the carbonara she was making for lunch, Eliza covertly scrutinized the stranger. Tall. Slim. Dark-haired – short and well cut. Sunglasses artfully placed on the top of his head. Shirt: fitted and pale blue and tucked into jeans. Next to her, Daisy whispered, 'Not bad-looking, wouldn't you say?'

'Ssh,' Eliza whispered back.

'He can't hear us, not with Bob and Wendy gushing all over him.'

'Hello, girls,' Bob said, after he'd helpfully opened the door for the good-looking man and told him not to hesitate to get in touch if there was anything he needed. 'You two home for the weekend, then?'

Before either of them had a chance to answer, Wendy said, 'I bet you're wondering who that man was, aren't you?'

'What man?' asked Daisy, all wide-eyed and looking about the shop.

Bob laughed. '*That* man,' he said, as from outside came the throaty rumble of a very powerful engine, which had them all turning to stare unsubtly out of the window.

When the car had gone, Eliza put their purchase on the counter to be rung up. 'Go on then,' Daisy said, 'give us the lowdown so we can report back to Mum and Dad.'

'His name's Owen Fletcher,' Wendy said excitedly, 'and he's bought The Hidden Cottage, just moved in.'

'Really?' Daisy said. 'I didn't know it had been on the market.'

'Apparently he got in fast, before a for-sale board went up.'

'That's the internet for you,' added Bob, struggling to get round his substantial wife behind the counter. 'He saw it online and snapped it up PDQ.'

'Is he going to live in it?' asked Eliza, unable to contain her own curiosity now.

'He certainly is,' Wendy said. 'Unlike that stuck-up couple from London who only used it at weekends and brought all their own food with them. They came in here once, just *once* mark you, and that was to buy a measly carton of milk. They had the brass-neck cheek to complain about the price of it as well.'

'And they criticized our choice of pasta. "What no organic trofie pasta?"' Bob said, imitating a woman's haughty overbearing voice. 'Good riddance to them, that's what I say.'

For the last two years, nearly everyone in the village had had an opinion or a story to tell about The Couple From London; their mean-spiritedness and unsociable manner having gained them a less than flattering reputation very soon after becoming the new owners. Despite the minimal time they'd actually spent in Little Pelham, they had fallen out with an extraordinary number of people. They had accused Joe Coffin of deliberately over-charging them for some joinery work he'd done on the house; they had told Ricky Jones who had cut the grass for them that he didn't know a thing about gardening; they'd reduced Karen Jackson to tears, claiming that while cleaning the house in their absence she had stolen a tea towel, and even the vicar, the Reverend Jane Beaumont, had come in for a tongue-lashing when she hadn't taken seriously their complaint that the church bells were rung too loudly during bell-ringing practice. Working on the basis that The Hidden Cottage was on the edge of the village and almost a mile distant from St George's, she had assumed they were joking.

Would the new owner of The Hidden Cottage

make as many enemies? Eliza wondered as Daisy surprised her by saying, 'It's such a lovely day, let's have an ice-cream.'

Bob pointed over to the freezer. 'Plenty of choice, girls; take your pick.'

At Daisy's suggestion, they didn't go straight home but sat on the bench on the green with their Magnums and watched a group of children kicking a ball about. Her sister was right; it *was* a lovely day. Eliza supposed the reason Daisy wanted to sit here was that she was in no hurry to get home, where Dad would be due back shortly.

But as cross or disappointed as he was, Eliza knew he wouldn't shout or rant at Daisy; he saw her as being too fragile for that. Which, of course, was another reason he was so protective of her.

Eliza wasn't proud of it, but as a child she had harboured an unhealthy amount of ill-feeling towards Daisy. As an adult, however, she came to realize that Daisy's horrendous behaviour when she'd been little had not been entirely her fault; she had merely reacted to the way their father treated her. Placed high upon a pedestal, she had learnt to wield the power she'd been given and had done so with tyrannical zeal and spite. One word from her perfect little rosebud mouth and their father would be in uproar with Eliza and Jensen, his ears closed to any claims that Daisy was lying or manipulating everyone. Even when Mum stepped in, as she so often had to, and defended Eliza and Jensen, he refused to listen or believe that Daisy could be anything other than perfect. In the end, it was easier to give in to their little sister, to let her have her way in whatever it was she wanted. But it was to do her no good in the long run; it could only ever lead her towards a crisis of some sort.

And that crisis happened, as these things frequently do, without any of them seeing the signs or realizing that poor Daisy was in serious trouble.

Eliza had been away at university and had arrived home at the end of term for Christmas, along with Jensen who hadn't been home in ages, and they had both taken one look at Daisy and been openly shocked. It was Jensen who had asked their sister straight out how long she'd been anorexic. Not surprisingly, she had vehemently denied it, but once the awful word had been uttered aloud, it was suddenly blindingly obvious that Daisy was ill. No more could her loss of appetite, the baggy layered clothes, the sallow skin, the hours spent alone in her bedroom, be dismissed as a teenage phase or simply the pressure of exams, which was what Mum and Dad had assumed was the case.

Initially Daisy refused to see a doctor, promising that she would now start eating properly, that there was nothing to worry about, but Mum wouldn't take no for an answer. She must have been frantic with guilt that she hadn't spotted what Eliza and Jensen had seen, but as they soon discovered, seeing a person on a daily basis often blinded you to the gradual change in them; it took a fresh pair of eyes to see the situation for what it was.

Eventually Daisy gave in to Mum's pleading and saw a doctor. Months of counselling followed, as did an excruciatingly slow gain in weight. At the same time, it all came out, that by starving herself Daisy had been taking control of her life as a way to free herself from the pressure of Dad's over-powering love and his unrealistic expectations of her.

In the process of getting herself together, Daisy dropped out of school for a year and by the time she retook that year and went on to university she was out of sync with her old friends. It was a massive understatement to say that it had been a difficult time for Daisy and, four years on, they were still sensitive around her when it came to food. Seeing her eat an ice-cream and clearly enjoy it, as she was now while they sat in the warm sunshine on the green, would have been unthink-able back then.

It was equally unthinkable that Dad would give her his blessing with regard to her wish to go to Australia. Or that he would accept that this was obviously another attempt by Daisy to loosen the intense hold of his love for her.

CHAPTER 11

Monday morning and Mia was alone.

Jeff had left for the airport not long after Putin had started up with his screeching out on the green and with no customers booked in, Mia had the day to herself. But feeling tired and edgy, she wasn't sure it was a good thing not to be busy. Left to her own devices there was a danger she would brood on what had proved to be an exhausting weekend – a weekend of vigilant damage limitation and of constantly pacifying Jeff.

Right now her husband would be 35,000 feet up in the air, while she was down here crackling with guilt and self-reproach. Why hadn't she known Daisy was so unhappy with her job? Why hadn't she known that her daughter was planning to move to the other side of the world? Oh, it was all too reminiscent of when Daisy had made herself so ill.

The shame of Daisy's anorexia still weighed heavily on Mia, that she had failed so absolutely as a mother, when all the time it had been the one thing she had tried so hard to get right. Another weight of regret and sadness for her was knowing that her relationship with her youngest daughter had always been overshadowed by Jeff's love for Daisy.

While it would be fair to say that Jeff had had no interest in fatherhood when his son came into this world, things changed dramatically when Jensen was seriously ill in hospital. From then on Jeff accepted his role as father and threw himself into it wholeheartedly. Mia could still remember the look on his face when he set eyes on Jensen for the first time; there was a softening in his expression, a tenderness combined with a look of real alarm, but then lying in bed hooked up to an intravenous drip, Jensen had looked so very weak and vulnerable.

Prior to that day, Jensen had been poorly with a bad throat infection and the GP had prescribed a course of penicillin. But then one afternoon when Mia was sitting on the sofa reading to him, Jensen just didn't look right to her; he seemed even more tired and lethargic and he had a strange puffiness around the eyes. Afraid he might be having a reaction to the antibiotics, she phoned the surgery and took him to see the doctor again. By the time Jensen was being examined, Mia could see that his hands had swollen, as had his ankles. When the doctor lifted his T-shirt, Mia winced at the sight of Jensen's distended stomach: something was very wrong. Within the hour they were at the hospital and Jensen was being examined by yet another doctor.

Numerous tests were done – blood, urine and blood pressure – and then the doctor said that he wouldn't be absolutely sure until they'd carried out a biopsy on Jensen's kidneys, but it was looking very likely that he was suffering from something called nephrotic syndrome. 'I've only ever seen one case of this before,' the doctor explained. 'What happens is that when there's loss of large amounts of protein in the urine the protein content of the blood is lowered, causing oedema – that's the swelling you can see. For now the priority is to completely flush out Jensen's system and to get his blood pressure down. We'll need to have him on an intravenous drip with fluids and hydrocortisone.'

'But how has this happened?' Mia asked, trying to hide her fear and her shaking hands as she looked down at Jensen, who was lying on the bed staring at her with glazed eyes. 'He's so rarely ill.'

'It's probable that as a result of the streptococcal throat infection he's had, his immune system has gone on the blink and attacked the kidneys. Like I said, this is very rare. But you mustn't worry, we'll soon have everything under control. It's going to take time, though.'

But she did worry; of course she did. Jensen meant the world to her – he *was* her world – and to see him so ill was utterly heartbreaking.

At about seven o'clock that evening, while Jensen was fast asleep, she was advised to go home and fetch some things for him – pyjamas, toothbrush, a few books and toys, anything that would make him feel more at home. She also needed a bag of essential items for herself as she would be staying with him in the side room he'd been put in to.

She took a taxi from outside the hospital and when the driver dropped her off she asked him to wait for her so he could drive her back. She was on her way up the stairs to their first-floor flat when Mrs Frost's door opened. 'You have a visitor,' she said. Oddly her voice didn't have its customary glacial tone; there was a cheery lightness to it that Mia had never before heard. But she didn't care who the visitor was; all that mattered to her was getting what she needed and rushing back to be with Jensen. She didn't want him to wake and find her not there. But then she registered the present tense Mrs Frost had used. Whoever the visitor was, he or she was still here. But where?

She turned and looked down the stairs at Mrs Frost and was about to explain that Jensen wasn't well and that she was in a hurry when Jeff appeared in the gloomy hallway. 'Hello, Mia,' he said, 'your delightful landlady and I have just been enjoying a cup of tea and a slice of cake together.'

She was struck by so many thoughts in that moment, but chief amongst them was disbelief that Jeff could do the impossible – that he could charm Mrs Frost. But then all the fear and worry of the afternoon, all the emotions she had kept hidden from Jensen, combined with the extraordinary coincidence of Jeff turning up just when she needed help most, overwhelmed her and she burst into tears.

Once she'd calmed down sufficiently to get the words out, Jeff was marvellous. He paid the taxi driver, helped her find what she needed for the hospital, insisted she ate something – a slice of toast and a flapjack he found in the cake tin – and then drove them to the hospital. And as he drove, he kept a firm hand on hers and told her every-thing would be all right.

Amazingly, everything did prove to be all right. Five days after he was admitted to hospital, Jensen was allowed home, but it was another month before he was back to his normal healthy self. By which time Jeff had not only supported her through the weeks of worry and anxiety but had proved himself to be a changed man, a man who wanted to play an active role in his son's life. Three months later and he said that he wanted them to be a family, a proper family. But Mia needed to be convinced that he was serious, that this wasn't just some passing whim on his part. She also needed to work out just what it was she felt for Jeff; she needed to be sure it wasn't just gratitude for helping her through Jensen's illness.

His response was to go to great lengths to prove himself worthy and he agreed to her wishes that he didn't rush things, that he especially didn't rush Jensen into calling him Daddy, even though Mia had explained just who he was. Given the close relationship he and Mia had shared since his birth, Jensen was understandably wary of Jeff at first but gradually he became less jealous and possessive and more open to having Jeff in their lives. And as time went by Mia realized she enjoyed having Jeff around; he brought a brightness into her life and regularly made her laugh with his impressions of Mrs Frost, whom he had eating out of the palm of his hand by bringing her flowers or chocolates when he visited. He had winkled out of her all sorts of stuff that Mia had never been able to, such as her having been widowed for more than twenty years and that before that she and her husband had run a B&B together in Cornwall. 'I'm beginning to feel jealous of you and Mrs Frost,' Mia said one day. 'I think you only come here to see her.'

'Good,' he said, 'I'm glad you're jealous; that means you feel something for me.'

And she did. Just as when she'd first met him, she enjoyed his positive outlook and his rock-solid belief that there wasn't anything he couldn't make happen. But only when she was convinced that Jensen was happy with having Jeff in their lives did she agree to marry him.

Ten months after their marriage, Eliza was born, and then along came Daisy. Born three weeks earlier than her due date, Daisy's birth took them unawares, so much so Mia knew they wouldn't make it to the hospital in time and Jeff ended up having to deliver Daisy. It was, he claimed for many years, his proudest achievement.

Whereas Jensen and Eliza had been very easy-going babies, Daisy was furiously demanding with only two volume settings to her cries – loud or deafening. Throughout the Terrible Twos life was virtually intolerable; Daisy could scream and hold her breath for a terrifying length of time, and afraid she could actually damage herself, that something might burst inside her, Mia would give in. Anything to stop her from crying and screaming. Life went on like that until Daisy was three and a half, when suddenly, as if a switch had been flicked, she changed. 'See,' Jeff said, 'didn't I tell you it was just a phase?'

It was as helpful as his comments when Daisy had been just a few weeks old, when he'd as good as said that Mia was to blame for Daisy being such a fractious baby. 'You're too tense,' he'd say, as if he was now the world's expert on childrearing. 'She's picking up on your anxiety; you need to relax more.'

'Relax?' Mia had snapped. 'Just how do you expect me to do that?'

'There you go,' he'd said, 'flying off the handle at the slightest thing. It's not good.'

Regrettably Daisy was the catalyst for changing the dynamics within the family. But in no way was it her fault. Jeff was to blame; it was his singling her out as his favourite that did the harm. Blind to what he was doing, divisions took hold and resentment amongst the children bubbled beneath the surface. As the years went by, Jeff changed, he became hardened; the fun seemed to go out of him and he grew increasingly dictatorial, his ears closed to any viewpoint but his own. Mia put it down to him simply replicating his behaviour in the office at home – so used to being the boss at work, he expected to be treated accordingly at home. All too frequently Mia felt guilty that despite her attempts to do so she had failed to rein Jeff in, to make him see the damage he was doing to the family and himself.

Guilt. Oh, she could gather it effortlessly, layer upon layer of the stuff. Like ornaments on a shelf gathering dust.

She felt guilty right now that she had argued with Jeff last night, having promised herself she wouldn't rise to his bait. During the day they had both been occupied – he with another round of golf and she with driving the girls to the station and then tidying the house, stripping beds, washing the sheets and towels, setting up the ironing board in the kitchen and making sure that Jeff had the shirts he wanted to pack for the week he was in Brussels.

In the evening, they had a dinner party to go to given by friends of Jeff's from the golf club. As he could so often do, he had put on an impressive act of appearing as if he didn't have a care in the world. He had charmed and joked his way smoothly through the evening with consummate skill. Only when they had said goodbye to their hosts and Mia was driving them home did he drop the act and pick up where he'd left off, that of sitting in crushing silence. She knew and understood that he was hurting, that Daisy could have given him no greater shock, but he had to come to terms with it. He had to realize that his treasured daughter was allowed to make her own decisions now, most of which wouldn't include or relate to him.

But facing up to life's great dilemmas was not something Jeff was good at. Yes, he acknowledged them, but he didn't deal with them. Anything he couldn't easily resolve, he swept aside as if it had nothing to do with him. He'd never, for instance, spoken openly about Daisy's illness; it was as if he had blocked it from his thinking. Again, that was him all over. He was acutely disdainful of any kind of introspection. He refused any sort of self-analysis; blame was so much more convenient, particularly so if he could lay it squarely at someone else's door. When Daisy was receiving treatment for her anorexia, his way of dealing with it was to bury himself in work.

Over the weekend, Daisy had calmly furthered her case for wanting to leave her job and move to the other side of the world. 'But you can get another job, here in this country,' Jeff had argued. 'It doesn't have to be so far away for pity's sake. Or why don't you come to Brussels with me? I could get you a job there. That would give you a change of scene and some excitement, if that's what you're looking for.'

'But I don't want to go to Brussels,' she'd said. 'I want to go to Sydney. Come on, Dad, there's no comparison between the two places, or the lifestyles the two offer.'

'You've never been to Sydney – how do you know what the life would be like?'

She wasn't to be deterred, though. 'Life is hardly ever what we think it's going to be,' she'd said with such solemnity and such wisdom in one so young Mia had wanted to hug her. 'All we can ever do is hope for the best.'

'Sounds like your mind's made up,' he'd said flatly.

'It is, Dad. But I want to go with your blessing; I don't want you to stay cross with me.'

Of course, Daisy was the last person he would stay cross with. That would be saved for the rest of them. As last night in bed proved all too well, when Jeff had taken out his frustration and whatever else he was feeling.

'You don't seem to care that she's doing this,' he'd said to Mia.

'I care deeply, but I just want her to be happy.'

'What if she makes herself ill again?'

'She's more likely to do that if she continues doing a job she hates. Jeff, you have to let her go; she's all grown up now – she has been for some time. You have to accept that. Why can't you be proud of her that she has the courage to do something like this, to change the status quo?'

Those words echoed now in Mia's head as she

looked out at the garden and thought of when she had wanted to do exactly that, to change the direction of her life.

She had very nearly done it. She had made up her mind she was going to leave Jeff and was on the verge of doing so when they realized Daisy was ill. In an instant, any thought of starting a new life for herself was out of the question and she focused all her energy into trying to make her daughter better, vowing never again to put her own needs before those of her children. For that was what she had done. So wrapped up in her own unhappiness she had entirely missed Daisy's far worse misery.

Still looking out at the garden and the unblemished milky-blue sky above, she decided to go for a walk, to see if it would lift her spirits.

She locked the back door and walked round to the front of the house. Over on the green Putin was circling the bench, stopping every other step to peck viciously at the grass. She recalled Tattie's enchantment at seeing the peacock in the garden the other night and thought how refreshing it was to see someone act so spontaneously and with such obvious and unfettered delight.

She turned right and paused at the noticeboard next to the gate to St George's where a poster for the village fete had been placed. As she had for the last three years, she would be running the bookstall with the vicar's husband, Richard, who was the head teacher at Little Pelham's primary school.

Between Medlar House and St George's was a footpath and taking this she headed up the hill towards the allotments. Feeling the warm sunshine on the top of her head and shoulders, she thought of Eliza shyly confiding in her about a new boyfriend. One way or another, it had been a weekend of surprises. Mia was happy for Eliza; it was about time she had something in her life other than work. 'When do I get to meet him?' Mia had asked, resisting the urge to enquire why Eliza hadn't said anything before now. She knew her middle child well enough to know that Eliza wasn't one of life's great sharers, that she found it difficult to open up to people.

'Soon,' Eliza had said. 'I'm sure you'll like him.'

'I'm sure I will. So long as he makes you happy.'

'He does. And Mum . . . I would have told you sooner, but I didn't want to jinx things.'

'It's OK, darling, you don't have to explain or apologize to me. I know you always have to do things your way and I respect that.'

Up at the allotments where it was a leafy oasis of peace and quiet, the morning air was soft with the appley scent of May blossom. Mia loved this place. She loved the sense of steady purpose it generated, the neatly dug trenches for potatoes, the canes for runner and French beans, the rows of onion sets, the walkways made out of old wooden pallets, the fencing, the ramshackle sheds, the happy camaraderie of those who were lucky enough to have a plot, the sense of time standing still. For some it was a place of refuge. Perhaps that's why she liked it so much; it was somewhere she could escape to.

She spotted Georgina unlocking her shed at the same time as talking to Muriel.

Georgina Preston and Muriel Fulshaw were Mia's closest friends in the village. Georgina was forty-eight – a year younger than Mia – but being the mother of twin five-year-old boys, Edmund and Luke, her life was very different from Mia's. Her husband had tragically died three years ago of a brain aneurism and, now that the boys were at school full time and she was cushioned by a life insurance policy payout, Georgina was able to enjoy some well-earned free time to indulge her passion of growing vegetables. By her own admission, having an allotment kept her sane.

Mia approached the two women. Muriel saw her first and let rip with a barrage of questions. 'Hello, you, how was your weekend? What was Jensen's girlfriend like? Will she do? Did you approve of her?'

A retired civil servant – something 'big' in the Treasury, of which she never spoke – Muriel Fulshaw was, as she described herself, the village battleaxe and self-appointed general pain in the backside. She was also a governor of the school and a formidable opponent of political correctness. She stood on nobody's ceremony, preferring instead to tread on their toes or get up their nose. She was the principal village activist and relished any sort of skirmish, whether it was a fight to keep the allotments and not let the Church sell the land, as they had with the vicarage, or to fight the council over their latest madcap scheme to save money.

Yet as fond as Mia was of both Georgina and Muriel, she had never shared with either of them anything of a personal nature regarding her marriage. There was a commonly held belief in the village that Jeff Channing was an all-round good egg. He was sufficiently charming with the women to make them like him and equally matey with their husbands so as not to make them jealous or suspicious of him around their wives. It seemed needlessly cruel to prick the bubble of his worth in Little Pelham.

On top of that, Mia had her own self-worth to consider. Her pride forbade her from admitting to anyone that she was unhappy. Why tell anyone that her life was nothing but a brazen deceit? As her mother had said to her often enough, 'You've made your bed, and now you must lie in it.' Her mother had written the book when it came to unhelpful clichés.

'Now then you two,' Muriel said, after Mia had given a highly edited version of her weekend, 'what have you heard about Owen Fletcher, the new man who's moved into The Hidden Cottage? Do you have a source of knowledge other than the Parrs? Because frankly I'm fully up to speed with everything they know.'

Georgina offered up what she knew by saying that for some unaccountable reason the children at Sunday school had decided he must be a rich footballer.

Muriel dismissed this with a shake of her head. 'And what would a wealthy footballer be doing living in The Hidden Cottage? It's not half grand enough. Mia, what have you got for me?'

'Only that Eliza and Daisy actually got a look at him in the shop on Saturday and they said he was "hot". That was the word Daisy used at any rate.'

Georgina smiled. 'I like the sound of him, and I could like him even more if I knew he was single.'

Muriel laughed. 'In that case, we need to be proactive. We need to welcome Mr Owen Fletcher to the village, let him know that we're a friendly bunch and not one of those villages where you're an outsider until you've lived there for fifteen years.'

'What do you suggest?' asked Mia with a smile, winking at Georgina, 'as if we can't guess.'

'I advocate we knock on his door and interrogate him thoroughly,' Muriel replied.

CHAPTER 12

With the crummy state of the offices, it was a miracle anyone could be creative here. Or was the idea that the small team of designers, so starved of beauty, would keep sane by escaping the ugliness of their surroundings and immerse themselves in imaginary idylls of splendour from which they dreamt up fabulous furniture, anything but face the reality of this ghastly hellhole?

The place was a mess. Carpet tiles held down with brown packing tape, paint falling off damp crumbling walls, windows too high to look out of, cobwebs strung between light fittings like forgotten Christmas decorations, the temperature either stifling or freezing cold. It was as depressing as depressing got. It was a hideous prison.

But Daisy was about to break free. Another five days and she would be out of here. Gone. No one would miss her. No one would wonder how she was or what she was doing. She would be as forgotten as the cobwebs above her head.

She had handed in her notice last week, something she hadn't told her parents. But that wasn't the only omission, or rather the only lie she had told. She'd had to do it; of course she had. Dad wasn't ready for the whole truth yet. One shock at a time was best. Once she was in Australia, the rest would follow – when she was safely thousands of miles away.

Scott disagreed. He subscribed to the school of thought that dumping all the news in one big truck-load was the way to go. Easy for him to say, when it wasn't him dealing with Dad. He had offered to be there with her, but she had said no, she would do it alone.

When Scott had met her at the station he hadn't rushed to ask how it had gone – he knew her too well. He knew to take his time. Crowd her and she shrank; that was how he described the way she behaved when she felt under pressure. And so he had distracted her by telling her how he'd helped their elderly neighbour – Mrs Balfour – find her cat that had been missing for several days. Scott had found it shut in a garden shed, three doors down. 'My hero,' Daisy had said with a smile. And meaning it.

Back at the flat, putting the kettle on, she'd given him a rundown on how her father had taken the news. 'And before you ask, no I didn't tell him the really important bit.'

'Ah,' was all Scott said as he leant back against the worktop while watching her dither over opening a new box of peppermint tea or settling for green tea.

'I just couldn't do it all in one go,' she said. 'I know you think I'm a coward, but I really couldn't—'

He'd hushed her with a kiss. 'You're not a coward. I've never once thought that.'

From the other side of the partition, a phone rang. It rang and rang. Just as it always did. She knew that Julienne, the very worst receptionist in the world, was there at her desk; Daisy could hear the girl's long acrylic nails clawing at her keyboard. And never would Daisy be convinced that it was important work that kept the annoying girl from answering the phone. Julienne was as lazy as she was stupid and came to work only to finance her hectic social life and then post comments about it on Facebook.

Ring, ring. Ring, ring. It was like Chinese water torture. If it went on for much longer, Daisy would answer the wretched phone herself!

Finally the phone stopped ringing and in the ensuing hush, Daisy felt herself relax. She was wound too tight, just as Scott had said. 'You should have got it all over and done with,' he'd said when she'd kept him awake during the night with her tossing and turning.

She could, of course, have played her trump card. The old Daisy would have done it in a flash; she would have threatened Dad that he would make her ill again if he couldn't be reasonable. But she was trying to be a new Daisy. She wanted to be taken seriously as a young independent

102

woman who was strong and able to make her own decisions, and mistakes. She didn't want to be the old Daisy who'd been a daddy's girl – that wasn't her any more. She wanted to be like Eliza. Eliza had always been able to do exactly what she wanted without Dad ever interfering in her life.

Well, that wasn't entirely true. The last time Eliza had brought home a boyfriend, Dad had been spectacularly awful to her and the boyfriend. It had been back when Eliza was still at university and Dad had taken one look at Eliza's boyfriend and said, 'Well, Dave, you're an improvement on the last one, I'll give you that much. But between you and me, he wasn't difficult to beat. Poor devil, he'd been thoroughly whacked with the ugly stick.' In the awful silence that followed, Dad had looked around at them all and said, 'I'm joking.' He'd shaken Dave's hand hard and said, 'You knew I was joking, didn't you, Dave? Course you did. Only someone very stupid would think I wasn't joking and you're not stupid, are you, Dave?'

In one easy and outrageous step he'd as good as called the poor guy stupid and ugly. Mum had been furious with Dad later – Daisy had heard them arguing when she'd been upstairs in her bedroom. They had been arguing a lot then. In fairness to Dad, Dave hadn't been much of a looker, but that was beside the point. Not surprisingly they never heard of him again from Eliza. But now Eliza was prepared to risk going through the same humiliation again. She had told Daisy

103

that just as soon as Greg's busy diary had a free slot, she was going to take him home. Whoever this Greg was, Eliza must have enormous confidence in him and believe he was made of stronger stuff than Dave.

Just as Scott was.

Daisy had told herself a million times that Scott was more than equal to the challenge of meeting Dad, and he'd repeatedly assured her that there wasn't anything anyone could say that would alter his feelings for her.

She had met Scott when she'd answered his advert online – *Easy-going-in-touch-with-his-feminine-side-Aussie seeks flat-mate.* He'd worded the advert like that because he didn't really want to share with a bloke. Blokes, he said, were unreliable and as messy as hell; he was the exception, he'd added. As it turned out, her only opposition had been about a thousand gay men. She'd liked him instantly, but not in a fancying kind of way – he was ten years older than her, so was well out of her sights. He was also seeing someone at the time, a girl he worked with in the company where he was a project engineer. Mum and Dad met him when they helped her move in and even Dad gave his grudging consent, viewing Scott as someone who was rock steady and would look out for his daughter and not make a move on her.

Things changed, though, when out of the blue Scott's girlfriend broke up with him. For the first time in her life, Daisy found herself in the position of comforting someone else, of being useful to someone. From there, things just sort of developed between them until eventually they both realized they were in love with each other. Being with Scott had made her happier than she'd ever been in her whole life.

None of which she'd so much as hinted at over the weekend. OK, again that wasn't wholly true – she'd hinted to Eliza that her going to Australia was only half the story, that there was more to come yet. So typical of Eliza, always so reserved and circumspect, she hadn't pressed Daisy for any further details.

Being with her sister at the weekend had made Daisy realize just how much she would miss her when she left. She would miss Jensen too. Time was when the pair of them would have been only too happy to see her move to the other side of the world, but things changed between them when she'd been ill. Jensen had been unexpectedly kind and caring towards her during that period; he'd talked to her in a way no one else did, openly and candidly. He'd even joked with her that he hadn't gone to the trouble of saving her life only for her to blow it now.

He was referring to when they'd been on a family skiing holiday in Austria. Jensen and Eliza had wanted to ski on their own and when Daisy had pestered to go with them and not with Mum and Dad, Dad had agreed so long as Jensen looked after her. 'Watch out for your sister,' he commanded. 'Don't let her out of your sight.'

'Babysitting again,' Jensen had muttered bad-temperedly.

'I don't need babysitting,' Daisy retorted. 'I can ski as well as you and Eliza. If not better.' It was a boast that was blatantly untrue, but Daisy, being thirteen years old, wanted to prove she wasn't the irritating little sister they made her out to be.

They'd been skiing for about thirty minutes when they got off a chair lift and Jensen said he needed the loo. Eliza said she'd go as well. 'How about you, Daisy?' Daisy shook her head and popped another piece of chewing gum into her mouth, despite being under strict instructions not to chew gum while skiing. She watched them remove their skis and rest them against the rack, along with their poles. They'd just taken off their gloves when she said, 'I'll see you at the bottom then!' And off she went, knowing they wouldn't be able to catch her up. That would show them! She skied as fast as she could, determined to prove that she was easily as good as them, that she didn't need babysitting. Her recall of what happened next was like a dodgy pirated DVD – there were breaks in the film and what she could actually remember was fuzzy. But apparently, so intent on looking over her shoulder to make sure her brother and sister weren't catching her up, she nearly collided with a snowboarder who'd shot out of the trees to her right. She managed to avoid hitting him, but lost control and skied into a tree. When Jensen and Eliza reached her, she wasn't breathing and her lips had turned blue.

Somehow Jensen knew what to do. He turned her over and thumped her as hard as he could, again and again, until finally the gum she'd been chewing flew out of her mouth. Meanwhile someone else had summoned help and within no time she was being taken down the rest of the slope on a stretcher and Eliza had called Mum and Dad on her mobile. At the hospital she was told her helmet had saved her head from being cracked open, but what had saved her life was the quick thinking of her brother. Dad had been full of gratitude at the hospital, but later back at their hotel Daisy overheard him saying to Mum, 'But I expressly told Jensen not to let her out of his sight. What the hell did he think he was doing?'

'For God's sake, Jeff, can't you just once acknowledge your son did something good? Something which, frankly, had he not done, Daisy would have died.'

'All right, all right. Don't go on about it. I still think that if he'd done as I asked—'

'*Jeff!*'

If Dad could be as grudging as that with someone who had saved her life, how would he treat a man who not only wanted to take her away to the other side of the world, but wanted to marry her? Because that was her big secret she was keeping from her family: Scott had asked her to marry him and she'd said yes.

The phone began to ring the other side of the partition. *Ring, ring. Ring, ring.*

Realizing she was being as lazy as Julienne, Daisy put Scott and her father out of her mind and got on with some work. But not before asking herself the big question: why did any of this matter to her? Why did she still feel, after all these years, after all the counselling she'd had, that her father's opinion in any way mattered?

CHAPTER 13

'Good afternoon, Mr Fletcher. You've heard of the Witches of Eastwick; now meet the Witches of Little Pelham.'

From his doorway, Owen worked at keeping the surprise off his face. 'I'm very pleased to meet you,' he said, addressing the woman who had spoken.

'Muriel Fulshaw,' she said, holding out her hand and giving his own a good pumping. She turned to her right, 'And this is Georgina Preston.'

On the receiving end of a warm and engaging smile, the handshake this time was a lot less vigorous.

'And last, but by no means least, this is Mia Channing.'

And absolutely by no means least, thought Owen as he shook the hand of a woman dressed in straight-legged jeans and a pale pink shirt with the cuffs turned back. She was easily the most attractive of the three envoys, doubtless here to check him out and to report back to the rest of the village.

'We've brought this for you,' the smiling woman

called Georgina said. She held out a small booklet. 'It's the village magazine.'

'We thought it might be useful to you,' the older woman said. 'I'm the editor and I can assure you it's full of helpful contacts. Plumbers, builders, joiners, cleaners, babysitters, even secretarial help, you name it, it's there in Little Pelham's *Parish News*.'

'Every eventuality covered,' Owen remarked, flicking through and seeing the name of an undertaker's in nearby Olney. He closed the magazine and tapped it against the palm of his hand. 'Thank you. Thank you very much.' Then deciding it might be fun to play along with the three women, he said, 'I was just about to take a break from the unpacking and have a drink. Would you like to join me?'

He found himself directing the question at the woman called Mia, who from beneath her long lashes was looking at him with the most extraordinary violet eyes. She was different from the other two women – friendly enough, but she didn't have their overtly cheerful, forthright manner. She was The Reserved One he decided, alongside The Smiley One and The Bossy One.

'That would be very kind of you,' she said, 'but we really don't want to put you to any trouble or give you the impression that we're being . . .' Her soft voice trailed off.

'Being what?' he asked.

The Bossy One roared with laughter. 'What my wonderfully polite friend is trying to say is that she'd be horrified if you thought we were being nosy. Which we are, of course. Can't have a new chap move in and not welcome him with a sound interrogation, can we? That really would be letting the side down.'

'You're sure we're not disturbing you?' asked The Smiley One.

'Ladies,' he said, in an approximation of Jack Nicholson welcoming the Witches of Eastwick into his life, 'I'm at your disposal. Come through to the garden and you can begin your interrogation.'

He ushered them in, shut the front door and led the way, apologizing for the mess as they picked their way through the packing boxes. The removal van had arrived on Saturday lunchtime and while he had the bulk of the important and essential unpacking done, he still had all the fiddly stuff to deal with, along with ten boxes of books to find a home for. He knew without a shred of doubt that his guests would be avidly taking in what they saw in the way of his belongings, eagerly swapping notes when they left and putting together a profile of him.

'Oh, a piano,' observed The Smiley One, as he took them into the sitting room, 'a grand piano at that. Do you play? Or is Mrs Fletcher the musician?'

A clever opening question, he thought with

111

amusement. 'There's no Mrs Fletcher,' he replied.

'And do you actually play, or is it purely ornamentation?' asked The Bossy One.

'You mean for effect, to make me look more interesting? No, I do play. Not as well as I'd like, but who knows, maybe now I have more free time I might practise enough to improve.' He knew the 'free time' comment would have them wondering, and before they had a chance to seize the opportunity to probe further, he opened the French doors and took them outside to the veranda where he'd replaced the old chairs the previous owners had left with his own table and chair set. 'Now then, what can I get you to drink? Tea, coffee or perhaps a glass of wine? Or is it too early? What are the rules on drinking here in Little Pelham?'

The Bossy One laughed. 'The rules are quite clear, as long as both feet are kept firmly on the ground at all times, any time is a good time.'

It was when he was in the kitchen, delving into one of the packing boxes he had yet to fully empty, that he had a sudden thought. The Bossy One – Muriel Fulshaw – was it possible that she was the woman he vaguely remembered moving into the village not long before he left, and into the larger of the only two detached cottages in Cloverdale Lane? His mother had described her as a 'career woman', saying the words with such hushed awe in her voice, the woman might have been the first female astronaut. 'In other words a bloody know-it-all,' his father had muttered, taking off his shoes and shoving them at Mum to polish. 'Either that or a lesbian.'

'What's a lesbian?' Owen had asked, looking up from his bowl of tomato soup, which he was stirring with his spoon, waiting for it to cool down.

'Never you mind,' his father had snapped. 'And haven't you got better things to do than sit around listening to other people's private conversations?'

'He's having his tea, Ron, leave him alone.'

His father hadn't liked women. He saw them as the enemy, something to be kept under control. But then he saw everyone as the enemy – the man he worked for at Cloverdale Farm was a thieving dictator who was robbing him of his rightful wages; the other farm labourers had it in for him; and the neighbours looked down their noses at them because they were outsiders. His paranoia was unstoppable and as a consequence he did everything he could to keep Owen and his mother firmly under his thumb. And isolated. He did it in small ways, such as deliberately not having a car so that they couldn't drive anywhere, and he never gave his wife any more money than it would take to shop locally, and every item purchased had to be ticked off against the bill, which he insisted on being given, together with any change, thereby ensuring that Mum and Owen couldn't hold back any money and sneak off somewhere on the bus. Initially he allowed Mum her cleaning job, so long as she handed over her wages, but then he banned it altogether. He claimed it was to keep them safe, that no one, absolutely *no one* was to be trusted.

The glasses unwrapped and hurriedly cleaned, a tray located and a bottle taken from the fridge, along with a dish of olives and feta, Owen went back outside.

'Ooh, champagne!' exclaimed The Smiley One. 'How decadent for two o'clock on a Monday afternoon.'

Owen smiled. 'I thought that since you're my first guests, we should do things properly.'

'I can see you're going to fit in perfectly here,' said The Bossy One. 'Very well indeed.'

The glasses filled, he handed them round. 'A toast,' he said, sitting down, 'to new friends.'

'To new friends,' they echoed, 'and welcome to Little Pelham.'

He helped the women to olives and observed that The Reserved One had moved her chair ever so slightly so that she could look down the garden without straining her neck. A neck, which, he had to admit, was attractively long and slender and on full show due to her dark hair being tied up into a pony-tail. She was sitting so still, so straight-backed and perfectly composed she was like a Madonna painting. 'I have a confession to make,' he said in the growing silence.

They instantly stilled their glasses and looked at him expectantly.

'Please don't tell us you really are a footballer,

as the children in Sunday school think,' The Bossy One said.

He laughed. 'I'm much too old to be that.'

'You could be an *ex*-footballer,' suggested The Smiley One. 'But only recently retired, of course, because you can't really be that old.'

The Bossy One snorted. 'An ex-footballer who plays the piano? What tommyrot!'

'Any other rumours about me?' he asked, amused and curious. His friends had warned him that he would be the subject of much speculation and had dared him to lie, to invent a persona with a back-story so colourful it would have jaws dropping and eyes popping. But in truth his real identity would arouse sufficient curiosity without recourse to any embellishment.

They shook their heads.

'Then I shall settle the matter for everyone,' he said. 'The thing is, it's more a case of welcoming me back to Little Pelham. I used to live here, a long time ago. I came to live in Cloverdale Lane when I was nine years old and left when I was ten. I promised myself I'd come back one day.' Looking at The Bossy One, he went on, 'This would have been thirty-four years ago. Did you live here then?'

'No. I moved into the village, ooh, getting on for twenty-two years ago. Why?'

He shook his head. 'Just wondered if our paths might have crossed back then.'

The Smiley One laughed. 'You'd have had no need to wonder; you'd have remembered Muriel all right. Once met, never forgotten. And in case you're wondering, I've only lived here for five years and Mia . . .' She turned to her friend, 'Mia, how long have you been here?'

'Ten years,' she said. She raised her chin and looked at Owen and once more he was struck by the unusual violet colour of her eyes. He noticed the faint lines at the corners of her eyes as well as her full and perfectly defined lips. She was a beautiful woman, no question. 'What made you make that promise to yourself when you were only ten years old?' she asked.

'A very good question,' he said and while he paused to consider his answer, the other two women looked on keenly. 'I was happy here,' he said at length. 'Happier than anywhere else I lived as a child. That seems reason enough for me.' He was being a little evasive, but he didn't care. The details would come out later, either when he was good and ready or when someone in the village remembered him and his family.

For the next twenty minutes he allowed himself to be put under the spotlight and answered their questions politely and as superficially as he could, telling them no more really than that he'd recently sold his business and was looking for a new direction in his life.

Eventually The Bossy One brought matters to a close. 'Come on, girls, time we left this good man to his unpacking. And you, Georgina, have the Holy Terrors to collect.'

'Holy Terrors?' he asked, everyone now on their feet.

'My sons, Luke and Edmund.'

'How old are they?'

'Five. They're twins.'

'They must keep you busy.'

'Just a bit. My husband died three years ago and it's been what could be described as a challenging time.'

'I'm sorry to hear that.'

'She's a marvel, she really is,' The Bossy One said. 'She's coped splendidly. We're all very proud of her. You said earlier, Owen, that there was no Mrs Fletcher; have you never been married?'

Feeling generous, he offered up another nugget of information about himself for them to pick over. 'Yes. And now my ex-wife has a baby with her new husband, so I've seen how much hard work just one small child can create.'

Seemingly satisfied with his answer, The Bossy One turned to The Smiley One. 'Here,' she said, 'have a mint to freshen your breath; we don't want you turning up in the playground reeking of Moet, do we?'

The Smiley One grinned. 'I can think of worse things to smell of.'

He took them through the house again and when he opened the front door, he saw he had another visitor coming up the tree-lined drive: the peacock. He was plodding along like a weary postman making the last call of his round.

'Have you made the acquaintance of Putin?' asked The Smiley One.

'I didn't know that was his name, but yes, he and I have met. Who christened him?'

'Muriel, of course,' answered The Reserved One. 'She's named them all over the years. We used to have Gorbachev and Brezhnev, but they died a couple of years ago.'

'Don't forget Yeltsin.'

'Oh, yes, alas poor Yeltsin, he got run over.'

'No peahens?'

'We had Maggie,' The Bossy One said, 'a real firecracker of a bird, named after Mrs T of course.'

'When I lived here as a boy there were five peacocks. But they didn't have names.'

'I soon changed that,' The Bossy One said.

Owen imagined she'd changed a lot of things in the village since her arrival in Little Pelham.

'Will we see you at the fete next Saturday?' she asked. 'Help is always appreciated and in my experience it's the best way to get stuck in when one is new to a place. Or perhaps you have some unwanted items you can donate to the white elephant stall? Any books you can let us have, those are welcome too. Mia and the vicar's husband are in charge of books, so pass them along to Mia if you have any.'

'I'm sure I can find something,' he said.

'Excellent. You'll find all the information you need about the fete in the parish magazine.'

'I'll be sure to look.'

He watched them leave. Mostly his eyes were on

Mia Channing; tall and slender, she had a striking elegance about her. When they were out of sight he glanced down to see the peacock staring up at him. 'What?' Owen said.

The bird just stared at him.

'That's your thing, is it? You stare at people, do you?'

Tilting its head, the bird intensified his beady-eyed expression.

Smiling, Owen went back inside the house. A few days in the country on his own and he was talking to a peacock called Putin. What next for him?

Retrieving his glass of champagne from the table on the veranda and topping it up, he returned to the sitting room and sat down on the piano stool. He raised the lid of the piano, made himself comfortable, flexed his fingers and began to play, knowing from the outset that he wouldn't be able to do the music justice. Rachmaninov's Concerto No.2 was not for the faint-hearted, or for a piano that had recently come out of storage and had only just been moved into its new home. Nonetheless, he was in the right frame of mind to give the first movement (the Moderato) his best shot. His mother had only ever known it as the music used in one of her favourite films, *Brief Encounter*, and she used to love listening to him practise. She couldn't hear it enough, she would say, which was just as well because it took him a very long time to learn it. Not that he could ever claim he played it as well as he'd like, but whenever he did, he was transported back to being a child and hearing it for the first time, when a tingle had worked its way up his spine and he'd caught his breath in stunned astonishment that anything could sound so incredible.

Within no time, he grew dissatisfied. Just as he feared, the piano hadn't travelled well. He would need to find a piano tuner.

He stared out of the open French windows at the garden and down the sloping lawn to the still water beyond. A heron was standing to attention on the bank; like the peacock, it seemed to be at home here. The sweet sound of birdsong filled the languid air and far away he could hear a woodpecker drilling. These were the sounds he remembered. And music. Always music. And all too often it was Rachmaninov.

He drank some more of his champagne and thought of his visitors that afternoon, in particular Mia Channing. He was just recalling the unusual colour of her eyes when he heard a soft thud on the wooden floor of the veranda, then through the French windows a head appeared. 'Oh, it's you again, is it?' Owen said aloud, thinking that twice now the bird had interrupted his thoughts about Mia Channing.

Putin surveyed him steadily, then took a couple of steps inside.

'Oh, no you don't!'

The bird held its ground.

'*Out!*'

The bird shrugged as though saying, *suit yourself*, and then slowly plodded off.

No more than a minute had passed when a crash from outside had Owen going to investigate.

Putin was standing on one of the chairs with his beak in the neck of the champagne bottle, which was now lying on its side. Seeing Owen, he withdrew his beak and looked up belligerently, as if challenging Owen to stop him.

Owen laughed. 'Go right ahead. Be my guest.'

Back inside the house, he heard his mobile ring.

When he answered it and realized who it was and that the news was good, he grinned with pleasure. 'That's fantastic,' he said. 'I'll expect it tomorrow then. About two. You've got the address and the directions, haven't you? Yes, that's right, The Hidden Cottage, Little Pelham. That's great. Thanks for letting me know. Goodbye.'

He ended the call and, tapping the mobile thoughtfully against his chin, he decided to lock up the house and go for a wander – to Cloverdale Lane, to see where he'd lived thirty-four years ago.

CHAPTER 14

Jensen checked his bank balance online and saw that his fee had been paid on time and without the need for a reminder. He hated sending a reminder; it made him look desperate. And he wasn't desperate. Work was going well, better than he could have hoped for. People seemed to like what he did for them. He worked fast and was reliable; those were his key attributes. The rest was all smoke and mirrors. But not flannel. He never misled a client; he was always honest and direct and very much to the point. Case in point was the job for which he'd just been paid. Originally the travel company that specialized in upmarket escorted tours in Eastern Europe had wanted him to do a patch-up job on their website, but after one look at it he'd told them straight out that the site was a dated mish-mash and needed a massive redesign, that patching and tweaking would only lead to further problems. He told them he could not only provide a problem-free site but one that would be user-friendly and would be guaranteed to bring them in more business. It took them forty-eight hours to be convinced he was right, but then they gave him the go-ahead. Three months later, they were delighted with the new site and were now paying him to manage it.

Getting up from his desk, he crossed from his office to his kitchenette in three short strides and put the kettle on. There was just time for a cup of coffee before he had to collect Madison from school. In preparation for a job this evening Tattie was having her hair and nails done. Occasionally when she didn't have time to go to the salon to get her hair styled into what she called the classic Marilyn smooth-glam-wave look, she wore a wig, but she preferred to do the job properly. She didn't like short cuts. Or cheating people. 'I don't want people to feel I couldn't be bothered,' she would say. 'They want star quality and that's what I'm paid to give them.'

Pleasing people was important to Tattie. As was laughter. She said there wasn't enough of it in the world. Jokes and amusing anecdotes came so easily to her. She was irrepressibly upbeat, endlessly positive, always able to find something good to say about a person. Being so resolutely optimistic, her glass wasn't so much half-full as full to overflowing. There really wasn't a pessimistic bone in her body. He had never met anyone like her before.

There were times when he could believe that her spirited personality was rubbing off onto him, grinding away at his rock-solid propensity always to think the worst. He once said to her how ironic it was that she impersonated a woman who lost herself to self-doubt and depression when she herself was the opposite. 'I've had my moments, JC,' she said. 'Oh, I've definitely had my moments. We all have. No one's immune. But when you've learnt how to be happy, you just know the alternative isn't worth a dime.'

'Can you teach me the trick?' he'd asked, half-joking, half-serious.

She'd smiled. 'Already working on it, JC.'

He had feared her opinion of him might have altered after his birthday – after she'd seen the way he and his father behaved around each other – but all she'd said was that it was a shame when two people couldn't get along. His taking her to Medlar House had in many ways been a test, to let her see how his father brought out the worst in him. But there had been no judgement from her, no condemnation, only acceptance. And he loved her for that.

Love. He could scarcely believe it, but it was true: with miraculous and implausible speed she had made him feel something he didn't know he was capable of feeling. It was as if she had opened a door that had always been there, but for which he'd never had a key. Walking through that door was like entering a world that was both familiar yet wholly unfamiliar.

To his even greater surprise, having Madison in his life was an unforeseen bonus. She was great. But not at all like her mother. Much more of a worrier, she doubted her ability at times and hated to be the centre of attention. 'She takes after my father,' Tattie had told him, 'a smarter man never lived, but he's an anxious, shy man.'

The mug Jensen was now drinking his coffee from had been Madison's birthday present to him – on one side was a picture of him pulling a face and on the other there was a photo of Madison with Tattie. 'She organized it all herself,' Tattie had explained with happy pride. 'She found the photos on the computer, went to the shop and paid for it with her own money.'

Jensen had been touched that a nine-year-old who had known him for so short a time had gone to such trouble. He'd promised her he'd always use it while he was working, that no other mug would do from now on. She'd then told him to close his eyes, that she had another surprise for him. '*Ta-daar!*' she'd sung out, revealing a birthday cake. 'I made it,' she'd said, 'at Lauren's.' He could see her lower lip wobble when she'd said her friend's name and he had quickly distracted her with a thank-you hug. Only an hour beforehand she had been crying on the sofa with him because she was losing her best friend. His experience in dealing with distraught children was equal to his knowledge of astrophysics and so all he could do was put an arm around her and let her cry. That was how Tattie had found them when she returned from the shop with the milk she'd gone for. He could tell that Tattie was shocked by the news, but more so because, as she later said, she'd have thought Lauren's mother might have at least hinted that this was on the cards.

When he'd blown out the candles on his birthday cake, having been instructed to make a wish, he'd wished for Madison to find a new friend after Lauren and her family had moved away. He was no expert on these things, but he was sure Madison was the kind of girl who needed a close friend. He hadn't been like that as a child; he'd been a bit of a loner. Although when he thought about it, his sister Eliza had been the nearest thing to a best friend for him when he'd been growing up.

The ringing of his mobile on his desk interrupted his thoughts. It was his mother.

The mothers at the school gate, together with a smattering of dads, nannies and grandparents, were now quite used to seeing him there and no longer gave him the wary who-the-hell-is-he? eye. He didn't blame them. He knew he didn't look like one of them, a bona fide relative or paid child carer. But that was OK. Fitting in had never been his thing.

Hovering at the back of the group and listening through his headphones to Morrissey singing he'd go out if he only had something to wear, he felt a tap on his arm and turned to see Lauren's mother. He stopped Morrissey mid-flow, took off the headphones and let them hang around his neck. Five days had passed since Madison had learnt that Lauren's family was moving away and

Heather had gone to great lengths to apologize to Tattie about keeping it from her. Apparently it was a secret and she couldn't tell anyone about Ross's new job, it was all very hush, hush.

'Hi, Jensen,' she said, 'Tattie busy?'

'She's at the hairdresser's preparing for a job.'

'What's it tonight, then?'

'A corporate do; she's presenting prizes to a bunch of salesmen of the year. Before I forget, she wanted to know if it's still OK for Madison to have a piano lesson after school tomorrow?'

'Yes, it's fine, no problem.'

The bell rang and within seconds a noisy swarm of children appeared in the playground. Jensen spotted Madison and Lauren bringing up the rear deep in conversation, matching bags slung over their shoulders, their socks sagging identically.

Their goodbyes said, Jensen and Madison turned left to walk home and Heather and Lauren turned right to go in search of their car.

'Any homework to do?' Jensen asked as they walked along the street, Madison's warm and slightly sticky hand in his.

'Just some spellings to learn. Will you help me?'

'Of course.'

'Is it a sleepover night?'

'Yes. Is that OK with you?'

She looked sideways at him. 'Why do you always ask that?'

'Because, you know, I don't want to be in the way.'

Making no comment on this, she said, 'Can you make one of your special breakfasts in the morning before I go to school? Some porridge would be nice.'

'Consider your order placed, mademoiselle.' He put on an exaggerated French accent. 'And would the pretty mam'zell care for brown sugar, honey or syrup with her porridge?'

She giggled and added a little hoppity-skip to her step. 'Syrup, please.'

They walked on to the end of the street and he paused outside the shop where they often stopped to pick up something for tea. 'Do you have any bananas at home?' he asked.

She shook her head. 'Only apples.'

'Let's get some; I'm in the mood for a fried banana sandwich. How about you?'

Her eyes lit up.

They were sitting at the table, their plates empty, the sweet smell of cooked banana overlaid with cinnamon filling the kitchen. Jensen had Madison's spelling list in his hands and Madison had her eyes closed; she did it to help her concentrate.

'Right, here we go,' Jensen said. '*Accept.*'

'A.C.C.E.P.T.' she responded, sounding each letter carefully and without hesitation.

'*Except.*'

'E.X.C.E.P.T.'

'*Excited.*'

'E.X.C.I.T.E.D.' Madison opened her eyes and

looked at Jensen. 'Lauren was excited today,' she said.

'Oh yes. Why's that?'

'She's going to see her new house on Saturday. She's going for most of half-term. She's really excited because she'll be living nearer her grandparents and will be able to see them lots more than she does now.' She pursed her lips. 'I wish I had grandparents I could see more often.'

What on earth was he supposed to say to that? 'Do you wish you were back in America?' he asked carefully.

She gave his question some thought. 'Mmm . . . sometimes I do. But mostly not. Maybe when Lauren's gone I will more.'

'That's understandable.'

'But if I was in America I'd miss you.'

'I'd miss you too.'

'Would you? Would you really?'

'Yes really.'

'You could come with us.'

He smiled. 'Let's get back to the spelling test, shall we? *Expect.*'

She closed her eyes. 'E.X.P.E.C.T.' She opened her eyes again. 'Wouldn't you want to come with us?'

'It's not quite as simple as that. *Expand.*'

This time she didn't bother to close her eyes. 'E.X.P.A.N.D. Adults always say things aren't simple. They like things to be complicated and difficult.'

'I'm not sure it's a matter of choosing things to be complicated or difficult. Life just often is.'

'Only because grown-ups make it that way.'

He smiled again. 'That's certainly true of some people.'

'Do you love Mum?'

Wow, he thought, where did that come from? 'You're not meant to ask personal questions like that,' he said, keeping his voice neutral and his expression bland, 'it's against the rules.'

'*See!* You're making things difficult. It's very easy, yes or no?'

'OK, I give in, you're right, it is easy.'

'So?' She pinned him with a laser-strength gaze from behind her glasses. 'What's your answer?'

'Yes, I do love her.'

Madison smiled and nodded slowly, like suddenly she was the wisest person on the planet. 'That's good. Have you told her you do?'

'Not in so many words.'

'Why not?'

'Because . . .' He swallowed.

'Because what?'

'Because I'm an idiot.' He tapped the table with his forefinger. 'Come on,' he said, 'spellings. *Surprise.*'

'S.U.R.P.—' She stopped. 'Surprise isn't on the list.'

He smiled. 'I was teasing you because I have a sort of surprise for you. But we need to check with Mum first.'

'What is it? Tell me!'

'How would you like to go away for a couple of days?'

'Where?'

'To meet my mother.'

'Really? Will we stay in the village Mum told me about, where you used to live? Will we see the peacock? And real thatched cottages?'

'Better than that, there'll be a fete, which you'll be able to join in with.'

'Cool.'

It was good to see her smile.

CHAPTER 15

Friday afternoon and sitting in the executive lounge at Brussels airport, Jeff was in a foul mood. He knocked back the last of his red wine then went over to the complimentary bar to get a refill.

When he returned to his seat, Pierre-Yvres had reappeared from the gents. Pete, as Jeff liked to call him to his face (or Poncy Pete behind his back), was one of the legal whizz kids from the office in Zurich and the thought of having to sit next to him during the flight to Dubai and then spend the next three days working with him was reason enough to hit the Merlot. Poncy Pete didn't drink. Poncy Pete didn't crack jokes. Poncy Pete didn't talk about anything other than work and the challenges of the global economy. The man had no life outside of work – he lived like a monk as far as Jeff knew – and could make watching paint dry seem like an extreme sport.

Poncy Pete on top of everything else was not what Jeff needed. Ever since last weekend he'd been feeling pretty much rubbed up the wrong way, then, due to a legal tussle over a new contract with one of their biggest customers in the UAE, he knew there was nothing for it but to give up his bank holiday weekend and fly to Dubai. As a consequence he felt peeved and left out, knowing that everyone was going to be at home, all having fun without him.

He'd phoned Mia last night and she'd told him that there would be a houseful over the coming days – for some reason she'd got it into her head to invite Jensen and his girlfriend plus daughter to come for the village fete. Then apparently, once Daisy and Eliza got wind of this, they said they'd also come. 'I think they're keen to meet Tattie's daughter,' Mia had said, 'especially if she's going to figure largely in their brother's life.'

'You really believe that?' he'd said. 'You don't think this is just his way of making a point with me?'

'What do you mean?'

'Come on, Mia; by parading this Tattie and her daughter in front of us, he's rubbing my nose in what I did all those years ago when you were first pregnant. You know he's never really forgiven me for that.'

'You've said some ridiculous things over the years, but that is the most ridiculous. Jensen genuinely cares about Tattie. And her daughter. Oh, by the way, Eliza's bringing her boyfriend as well for the weekend.'

Aware that Mia had deliberately and not so subtly changed the subject, he said, 'What boyfriend? I didn't know she had one.'

There had been a pause from Mia's end and then: 'Why don't you take a moment to think why that might be, Jeff?'

'If you're referring to that boy she brought home from university, I stand by my comments. He wasn't good enough for her.'

'And you'd know who is?'

'Hang on, why are we arguing?'

Mia had sighed. 'I don't know.'

I know exactly why, he'd thought later when he'd rung off. He had questioned Jensen's sincerity when it came to that girlfriend of his. Rule No.1 – he must not *ever* question or criticize Jensen.

After speaking to Mia he'd tried ringing Daisy, but there'd been no answer from her. He'd left a message on her voicemail to call him back. He had wanted to clear the air with her, to apologize for his reaction to her announcement about going to Australia. Perhaps he had handled things badly, but it was shock. He was still in a state of shock at her comment that she needed to get away from him as far as possible. How could she have said that, even if it had been a heat-of-the moment remark?

He was now hoping that a bit of reverse psychology might make her change her mind. He knew how these things worked: keep making a huge deal of it with her and she'd be even more determined to go. Instead he would go along with everything, make out that all he wanted was for her to be happy and if going to Australia made her happy, then so be it. What he needed to do was make the prospect of being so far away from home lose some of its shine for her, make her see what she'd be giving up.

She hadn't rung him back, though.

Poncy Pete nudged him and pointed at the screen; their flight was being called.

Not long after they'd taken off, and with another drink in his hand, Jeff's thoughts returned to Jensen. Was he really serious about this American girl and her daughter? What if the girl decided to go back to America – would Jensen go with her? And how would Mia feel about that? Perhaps then she would know how he felt about losing Daisy to the other side of the world. He almost hoped it came to pass, just so Mia would stop trying to sound so reasonable while at the same time make him appear so unreasonable.

He wasn't being unreasonable. He really wasn't. He just wanted things to be how they used to be a long time ago. A very long time ago when, frankly, the only problems he had to face were those at work, when he could return home and think how lucky he was. God, when was the last time he'd thought that? When was the last time he hadn't felt there was some family crisis to deal with?

When he'd married Mia he'd been tired of living the single life; he'd genuinely reached the stage when he was ready to settle down, to have something true and lasting in his life. Seeing his son – the son he'd previously tried not to think about too much – ill in hospital had given him a massive jolt. All at once he'd felt this huge wave of responsibility. He'd been shocked at the extent of his feelings for a child he didn't know, but suddenly all that had mattered to him was taking care of Mia and their son. Of being with them and making them happy.

When he told Mia how he felt she warned him to go slowly with Jensen, that he mustn't push things with him too fast, that Jensen wouldn't be able to love him overnight. In contrast Jeff had fallen in love with Mia all over again; she had blossomed into a truly beautiful young woman. He was crazy about her and was determined not to lose her by stepping out of line and doing anything wrong, particularly when it came to Jensen. He knew that if he was going to win Mia, he had to win over his son. But it was hard going at times; Jensen didn't always take kindly to having him with them. But when there was something he wanted, Jeff wasn't one to be thwarted by a bit of jealousy and he worked steadily away at gaining his son's trust. And Mia's approval.

It had been curiosity on his part that had caused him to see her again – he had been intrigued to see how she was, and to see what kind of child they had created. The only explanation he had for this change of heart was that he'd recently moved back to the Bristol area, having spent the last three years working in Leeds. His father had also just died. They hadn't been close, far from it – his parents had divorced when he was seven years old and contact with his father had been minimal – but his unexpected death had got Jeff thinking about unfinished business.

He wasn't one for self-analysis, never had been, never would be, but he had been ready to acknowledge that Mia was unfinished business. Some might say that it was a case of him deciding to do the right thing. He disagreed. It wasn't about a guilty conscience getting the better of him; he'd never felt guilty. Mia had made her choice to keep the child and he had made his choice to support her financially, so what was there to feel guilty about? Up until then, he hadn't told anyone, not even his mother, that he had a child. Why complicate matters by bringing her into it? had been his reasoning. To his surprise, and without wasting any breath on the hows and whys, his mother had immediately got in touch with Mia and became a hands-on grandmother, which he'd never truly understood as she hadn't been a particularly hands-on mother when he'd been growing up – her style of parenting had been to leave him very much to his own devices.

To this day he would defend every one of his actions as being true to himself. He had sincerely believed himself to be too young to take on the responsibility of fatherhood. Had he married Mia when she was pregnant as a student, he knew it wouldn't have lasted between them; he would have soon grown restless and bored of domestic life and consequently left her. And though he wasn't around in person to help, no one could ever accuse him of not providing financially for Mia and Jensen.

When they were married he did everything and more to make life perfect for them as a family. That included trying to mend the rift between Mia and her mother. A colder and nastier woman you couldn't wish to meet. She had disowned Mia when she was pregnant and didn't speak to her again until Jensen was two years old, and that was only because her husband managed to convince her to do so. It wasn't until some years later that she learnt that her husband had defied her and had secretly been in touch with Mia, wanting to be sure that she was all right. According to Mia, relations were cool but cordial from then on but then when she told her mother that Jeff was back in her life and they were getting married, the barmy old bat refused to speak to Mia again, claiming that she was a fool to think that the marriage would ever work; a leopard and his spots was quoted.

So Jeff went to see her, to persuade her that he had changed and wanted only the best for Mia, but she wouldn't let him over the threshold, just over-dramatically slammed the door in his face. They didn't speak to her ever again. Perhaps most hurtful of all for Mia was that the first she knew of her father's death was not from her mother, but from a solicitor. The woman couldn't even do that much for her daughter.

The ghastly woman had died four years ago, never having met Eliza or Daisy. There was no touching death-bed reconciliation, no final apology or request for forgiveness, just a last smack in the face when Mia was informed by her mother's solicitor that the proceeds from the sale of her house and what money she had was to be donated to an animal rescue shelter. The bitch of a woman hadn't even liked animals. She hadn't liked anything in life. God knew how she and her husband had ever got it together to create Mia.

Thinking of the unnecessary anger and bitterness Mia's mother had been consumed by for all those years, Jeff thought of his own anger this last week and how Daisy hadn't returned his call. He promised himself the first opportunity he had in Dubai, he would ring Daisy and put things right.

CHAPTER 16

With a hectic day behind her, Mia tidied up and ran the vacuum cleaner round the showroom; it would be one job less for her to do when she opened again on Tuesday, when there would be a rush of returns. This particular bank holiday weekend was a busy time for weddings and from the moment she had opened the barn that morning there had been a constant stream of customers collecting hats and fascinators for the weekend, some having had a panicky last-minute change of mind about what to wear and consequently wanting a different hat. There had also been a number of people dropping in with books for the fete tomorrow, some of the shabbier paperbacks she recognized from last year's fete.

The showroom locked, she crossed the garden and let herself in at the back door. The telephone was ringing. She hoped it wasn't one of the children calling to say they would be late or, worse still, calling to say something had cropped up and they couldn't make it now. She was looking forward to having everyone here again, except this time, with Jeff away in Dubai, they would be guaranteed a tension-free weekend.

She had rather guiltily seized on the opportunity that Jeff's unexpected trip had presented her with and had asked Jensen if he'd like to come and stay for the weekend with his girlfriend and her daughter. From there, things had escalated, with Eliza saying she would come with Greg and then Daisy had announced she'd join them. What was more, late last night after Jeff had called, Daisy had asked if she could bring her flatmate, Scott, seeing as he would be at a loose end for the weekend.

Happily it wasn't one of the children on the telephone with bad news; it was a man, a man whose voice Mia didn't recognize. Not at first at any rate, not until he said his name and a mental picture popped into her head of the amused expression on his face when she and Georgina and Muriel had called on him; he had clearly been playing them at their own game, assessing them as much as they were assessing him.

'Oh, hello,' she said. 'How are you? How are you getting on with your unpacking?'

'I'm fine, thank you,' he replied, 'slowly getting there with the unpacking. Look, I hope you don't mind me ringing you like this, but it's about the fete tomorrow. I've found some books I don't need any more and wondered if they might be of use. If so, I could drop them off.'

'Oh. Well. Yes. Yes, of course.'

'Would it be all right if I called in now?'

'*Now?*'

'If it's a bad time I could leave it until later.'

'No, no, now would be better. Later I have a houseful.'

'You're sure? I don't want to be a nuisance.'

'No, really it's fine. Well, I'll see you in a few minutes, then. Bye.'

'Hold on, I don't know where you live.'

'Oh, don't you? But you have my phone number.'

'I found that from the parish magazine you and your friends gave me earlier in the week.'

'Oh, right. Well, in that case, I'm very easy to find: Medlar House, next door to the church.'

'The vicarage, you mean? Or what used to be the vicarage?'

'That's right.'

'OK, I'll be with you shortly. And I promise not to keep you. I know a busy woman when I hear one.'

Mia ended the call, hoping she hadn't sounded overly brusque. Or overly stupid. She could hear the less than inspiring words '*oh*' and '*well*' echoing in her ears. Had she really been so abysmally inarticulate and repetitive?

While she waited for Owen Fletcher to arrive, she went upstairs to see to Eliza's bed. Nothing had been said, but Mia had made the discreet assumption that Eliza and Greg wouldn't want to sleep apart. If she'd got that wrong, Greg could stay in Daisy's old room. Meanwhile, Jensen and

142

Tattie would sleep in Jensen's old room and Madison would be in the spare room next door. For privacy Mia had thought of giving them The Gingerbread House – as Daisy had called the conversion of the outbuilding into a small cottage, which they'd had done at the same time as the barn showroom – but had decided that if Madison went to bed early and on her own, it wouldn't be right or fair for her to be separated from the house. Instead, Mia had decided to put Daisy and Scott in The Gingerbread House.

Jensen had said he hoped the weekend might cheer Madison up as the girl had just heard that her best friend was moving away and she was upset. The fact that Jensen wanted to do this for Madison flew in the face of Jeff's perpetually poor opinion of their son, an opinion, Mia sadly had to admit, Jensen did little to disprove more often than not.

She hadn't mentioned anything to Jensen, but she had a potential fete buddy in mind for Madison tomorrow. Beth – Joanne and Randall's daughter – was the same age and coincidentally her best friend had moved away recently, so with this in common, the two girls might just hit it off. Unless, of course, Madison was painfully shy, in which case she might not want to be more than two paces away from her mother's side. Which would be a shame.

Eliza's double bed now made, Mia looked round the room. It had changed very little since Eliza had left home. Mostly because it had been as spartan as a cell when it had been occupied. A quiet, intense girl, Eliza hadn't been the kind of teenager to cover her walls with boy band posters. Unlike Daisy, who had had a crush on just about every pretty-boy pop star going; everywhere you looked on her walls there had been a naked, hairless male chest. There had also been a lot of glitter; Daisy had been mad about the stuff, using it to decorate cards she made, old Barbie dolls, ribbons, her nails, her hair, and her clothes. Pink. Gold. Silver. Purple. Green. The stuff had got into every nook and cranny imaginable. If she looked hard enough, Mia was sure she'd find a sparkle or two in the pile of the carpet. Then somewhere along the line Daisy had moved from decorating her nails glittery pink to painting them black. That was when she discovered the Anne Rice vampire novels. Soon after, it was all things *Twilight* and experimenting with goth-chic and slamming doors when she couldn't get her own way. Then the doors stopped being slammed and Daisy took to staying in her room. With hindsight, it was the ominous lull before the storm.

Mia was straightening the curtains at the window when, from downstairs, she heard the doorbell.

'Books,' Owen said, holding out two carrier bags. 'As promised. And also as promised, I shan't keep you.'

'I'm sorry if I sounded rude on the phone earlier,' she said, 'but I'd just finished work and was thinking where to start before my children arrive; they're home for the weekend.'

'You have children?'

'Three.'

'Are they away at school?'

'Goodness, no, they're much older than that. My oldest had his thirtieth birthday last weekend.'

Owen shook his head in disbelief. 'Not possible.'

She smiled. 'I assure you it is.'

While she put his bags down on the floor behind her, Owen sneaked a look further into the hall and stairway, glimpsing an elegant antique console table against one wall with a lamp and mirror above and on the opposite wall two delicately painted water-colours. Everything looked very clean, very tidy, very polished.

It was a far cry from when his mother had briefly cleaned here for the then vicar and his wife and five children and two dogs. He remembered his mother saying that not one of the family had worked out how to open a cupboard or drawer. Nothing had ever been put away. Boots, caked in mud, had been dumped wherever the owner felt inclined to remove them. Wet towels, dirty clothes, toys, books, used mugs and plates and chewed bones and ominous stains on the carpet had been left for her to deal with. In contrast, the house today – if the rest matched the refined elegance of the hall – would be as pleasing to the eye as the current owner was. Owen couldn't imagine this woman allowing so much as a stray hair to interfere with her orderly décor, or for that matter, her equanimity.

'I feel bad that I'm not being as hospitable as you were on Monday and inviting you in,' she said, 'but I have so much to do.'

'That's fine,' he said easily, 'I quite understand.'

Her hand was on the door. 'Will you be around tomorrow?' she asked. 'At the fete?'

'I wouldn't dream of missing my first social engagement here.'

The door began to move towards him. 'I'll look out for you,' she said.

Back on the pavement, Owen looked to his left, towards the green where he saw Bob Parr at the top of a ladder outside the shop; he was tying some bunting to a telegraph pole. Bob saw him and waved. Returning the wave, Owen stood for a moment in the evening sunshine taking in the bucolic scene of old-world charm and beauty. In readiness for the fete the village was festooned with flags and bunting and almost every house, including the Fox and Goose, was now decorated with a hanging basket filled with pretty flowers. Medlar House also had matching hanging baskets either side of the front door and Owen found himself wondering if Mia Channing had done them herself or if she had bought them ready-made. He wondered also about her having a thirty-year-old son. That really had surprised him.

He walked home, deciding not to take the main road as he had before, but to take the footpath between Medlar House and St George's. According to the Ordnance Survey map he'd bought, combined with his memory, the path would lead him up the hill, curving round towards the allotments. He would then be able to cut through the woods – the bluebell woods as he remembered them being called – and dropping down the hill in a westerly direction, he would then come to the perimeter of The Hidden Cottage. It was the route he had taken as a child when he'd visited and had become friends with Gretchen and Lillian Lampton.

It was Gretchen who had opened the door to him that day when he'd plucked up the courage to knock. At first he'd been petrified and had let out a gasp of shock when the door had opened. They'd been right at school: witches did live here! Gruesomely ugly witches. So horrible he could hardly bring himself to look at this one. Her face was hardly a face at all, a sort of squashed face, the features blurred together with a mouth that was pale and almost flat, as if her lips were missing. She was dressed entirely in black, a dress that had no real shape, and her hair was hidden beneath some sort of turban. She looked old, all except for her eyes, which were dark and strong and looked so much younger than the rest of her. He couldn't see her hands; gloves hid them. No, not gloves, but peculiar cotton mittens. She was leaning on a walking stick; it was wooden and knotty. All this he observed in a heartbeat. But if there was one thing his mother had drummed into him, it was manners, and it was politeness that he fell back on as he stood rooted to the spot, too scared to move.

'Hello,' he said, his voice scarcely more than a wobbly squeak, 'I'm sorry to disturb you, but I just wanted to say . . .' His words trailed off. Just what had he wanted to say? He looked at the woman's wooden stick and wondered if she might beat him with it. 'I wanted to say how much I like your garden,' he forced himself to say. 'And the lake,' he added for good measure. 'The lake is the best bit.'

She stared at him, her strong dark eyes unblinking.

He tried to think of something else to say, but couldn't. And then he remembered the music. 'And I like the music that comes from inside the house. I've never heard music like that before.'

Still staring at him, still leaning on the stick, she said, 'Strictly speaking it's not large enough officially to be classed as a lake, but I'll let that inaccuracy pass since you seem a polite enough young man. What's your name?' Her voice wasn't what he'd expected. It was normal. Not croaky or scary. Just perfectly normal. But posh. Oh, it was definitely posh.

'Owen,' he said, trying to make his own voice sound more refined and grown up. 'My name's Owen Fletcher.'

'Good afternoon, Owen Fletcher, it's good finally

to meet you properly. Lillian and I have watched you often.'

'You're not cross that I've been coming here, then?'

'It might have been courteous for you to ask permission, but I shan't hold that against you. Would you like to come in and meet Lillian? She's curious to meet you and it would brighten her day. We seldom have visitors. We're not the sociable sort.'

She shuffled aside to let him in.

He hesitated. Stranger danger, his mother's voice warned in his ear. But then he heard music starting up and he stepped inside, thinking that his mother was wrong; it wasn't strangers he had to be frightened of, it was the danger that lurked in their own home that was the real threat.

Putin was waiting for him on the lawn when he got back. He had that look on his face again, the disapproving one that said, *What have you been up to?*

Ignoring the peacock, Owen went down to the jetty; he fancied having a play in his new toy – a twelve-foot wooden clinker rowing dinghy built of mahogany and oak and finished with natural oil and varnish. He had been out in it every day since it had been delivered. He loved to row around the lake, checking out the wildlife and the state of the banks and deciding what work needed to be done in the way of getting the undergrowth under control and cutting down trees that had grown too big. There were times when he lay in the boat with the sun on his face and drifted with not a care in the world, just thinking how happy he was.

He thought that now as he untied the rope from the mooring post and stepped into the boat and pushed it away from the jetty.

Pulling on the oars, he hoped his next new toy would be delivered in the morning – a sit-on mower. The lawn was badly overgrown and needed to be sorted out sooner rather than later.

As did things between he and Nicole. He'd actually managed to get a text out of her this morning, a brief message saying she'd been busy with work all week. He knew that she was always busy with her job as a head-hunter, but he wasn't fooled; her silence meant one thing and one thing only. He'd texted back to say he'd ring her this evening. Part of him wondered why he should bother. If they each really cared about the other, surely this situation – and the prolonged silence from her – wouldn't have arisen. He couldn't speak for Nicole, but as far as he was concerned, and without him consciously realizing it, their relatively short relationship must have reached a critical stage: its natural end.

He'd done a complete circle of the lake when he decided now was as good a time as any to make that call to Nicole. Pulling the oars in and resting them either side of him, he let the boat slowly drift towards the bank and took his mobile out from his jeans pocket.

It was a while before she answered and when she did, he could hear music and chatter in the background.

'Hi,' he said in his best affable tone.

'Hello, who is it?'

'Nicole, it's me, Owen.' Come on, he thought, don't play games, you know perfectly well who it is – my photo would have shown on your screen when the phone rang.

'Hi,' she said flatly, 'it's not really a good time; I'm out with the girls.'

'Shall I try later?'

There was a pause. 'Hang on a minute and I'll see if I can find a quiet spot.'

With a loud rustling in his ear, he waited for what seemed an age and when eventually he heard her asking if he was still there, he said, 'Yes, I'm still here. How are you?'

'Oh you know, it's been one of those weeks, manic at work.' Her voice had a dull, uninterested edge to it. Normally she sounded so animated and upbeat.

'Is that why you didn't answer any of my calls?' he asked.

His question clearly took her by surprise. 'Actually, Owen, no, that's not the reason. Guess what is?'

'You're still cross with me, is that it?'

'Cross? Not even close. I'm furious. I just don't understand how you could do what you did to me. And all behind my back. I thought you were one of the decent guys. Now I know better.'

He could have tried arguing that he hadn't set out to do anything to her directly, but he couldn't see the point in labouring a point he'd gone over many times already. 'So how long are you going to stay furious with me?' he asked.

When she didn't reply, he said, 'Look, I can see it from your point of view, really I can, but why don't you come here for the weekend and we can talk properly. There's a fete on in the village tomorrow, it'll be fun, and I'm sure once you see the house you'll fall in love with it and understand why—'

'I'm busy this weekend,' she interrupted him.

He took a deep breath. 'And will you be busy next weekend?'

'I might be.'

'Nicole,' he said with great patience, wondering why he'd just suggested she come for the weekend, 'we're both too old to play childish games. If you want to end things then let's just get it over and done with.'

'You know what, Owen, that's the first sensible thing you've said since you bought that bloody stupid house. I hope you'll be very happy there all on your own. Goodbye.'

The line went dead in Owen's ear. He slipped the phone back in his pocket and tried to decide whether he was relieved or disappointed. He picked up the oars and, after pushing the boat away from the bank, he concluded that all things considered, he was relieved. Because let's face it, if Nicole had really mattered to him, he would have shared his dream with her about coming here to The Hidden Cottage. She had every right to be angry with him; he hadn't been fair with her. And if he was absolutely honest, he hadn't really missed her since he'd arrived.

He sighed and in the fading light, the only sound the steady swish of the oars, he rowed thoughtfully back to the jetty.

CHAPTER 17

Madison opened her eyes and lay very still. With butterflies fluttering inside her stomach, she felt like she did when she woke on Christmas morning or her birthday. It was a sort of muddled feeling of happy excitement and nervousness, because what if the day didn't turn out as well as she hoped? Mum said she worried too much, that she should trust her feelings of happiness more. She tried to. She really did. But whenever she looked forward to something, there was always that little voice in her head telling her something would go wrong and spoil the day.

They had arrived here last night and everything was just as Mum had described it – the pretty village, the cottages with their funny straw roofs and the big house where JC used to live and which was the colour of creamy fudge. On the way they'd stopped off at a train station to pick up one of JC's sisters – Daisy – and her friend, Scott. It was a bit of a squash in the back of the car, and pressed against the window, she had noticed Daisy next to her touching Scott's hand every now and then.

The way she did it made it look as if it was a secret touch, as if no one was supposed to see. Madison didn't think they were just friends.

That's how Mum and JC used to be, until one morning Mum had said, 'Madison, I've got something important to tell you and I hope you'll be OK with it. The thing is, JC and I are more than just friends.' Well, *durr*, like that wasn't obvious!

Mrs Channing, JC's mother, had been waiting for them at the house and she wasn't at all what Madison had expected. She had pictured her like Grandma Barb, sort of rounded and cuddly with a big loud laugh and always rushing about trying to do a hundred things at the same time. But Mia – that was what she said Madison must call her – was tall and beautiful with long dark hair and eyes that were the colour of bluebells. She spoke with a soft, gentle voice and all evening Madison couldn't stop staring at her. She was embarrassed to remember that at one point in the evening she had wanted to put her hand out and touch Mia, and the silly thing was, she didn't have a clue why.

JC's other sister, Eliza, didn't arrive until quite late, when they had almost finished eating, and she didn't seem very happy. Apparently her boyfriend was supposed to come as well but he couldn't make it. Eliza was the only one of the two sisters who looked a bit like JC, and that was really only because she had the same golden-brown hair as he did. Daisy's hair was dark like Mia's, but nowhere near as long – she had it cut short, just below her ears.

Thinking how nice everyone had been last night, she thought how great it would be if JC married Mum, because if that happened, his sisters would be aunts to her, and Mia would be her English grandmother. And lying here in this big comfortable bed, in this pretty bedroom with its little fireplace and pale peach curtains and white dressing table and stool, and with its own bathroom, she couldn't think of anything she'd like more.

She thought of the conversation she'd had with JC when he'd been helping with her spellings and when she'd asked him if he loved Mum. She hadn't asked Mum if she loved JC back because she was worried to ask the question in case Mum said she didn't. That would be awful.

From outside she heard the strangest of noises. She sat up, reached for her glasses on the bedside table, pushed the duvet back and went over to the window and parted the curtains. Down on the road, directly in front of the house, she saw the peacock Mum had told her about. She watched him hop up onto the pavement and then after pecking at nothing in particular, he stretched his neck and let out a long and very loud noise that sounded nothing like any bird she knew. How strange that a bird could look so good but sound so horrible.

She got back into bed, taking from the bedside drawer her diary and pencil case. Using her Saturday pen – the sparkly gold one – she began writing.

Awake early and sitting up in bed, Eliza was working on her laptop.

She had a presentation to give on Tuesday and had yet to finish preparing for it. If Greg had been here with her, she would probably have left it until Monday, but he wasn't and so she might just as well make good use of the time available. Besides, working stopped her dwelling on her disappointment that Greg's busy schedule had once again ruined their weekend plans.

Eliza knew she shouldn't let it get to her, but she'd been so looking forward to seeing Greg; now it looked like she wouldn't see him for at least another fortnight. It was one miserable disappointment after another. Before she'd met Greg, her work would have been all the distraction she needed when she was feeling down, but these days it simply wasn't enough. Seeing her brother with Tattie and Madison, and realizing she had never seen him happier, made it worse for her; it made her miss Greg even more.

With Putin making his usual early-morning racket outside, she returned her attention to her laptop and her presentation, determined that there would be no Death by PowerPoint on her watch. She had done it enough times to know how to avoid producing a generic and hellishly boring presentation and was frequently complimented on the ones she gave, especially for the complete lack of techno fluff employed. Less is more, was her motto. Too many people made the mistake of believing that the latest piece of techno-wizardry with all its dynamic bells and whistles was the answer to getting a point across. Seldom was this true. Over-animating was one of her pet hates, along with an overload of drop-downs and sound effects, which might seem impressive but which ultimately did nothing but divert attention.

An hour later she could hear voices, showers being run and doors opening and closing. She checked the time: eight thirty, time to get up.

She was about to shut her laptop when her email box pinged. She clicked it open, hoping it would be a message from Greg. She did a lot of that. It was the same with her mobile – whenever it rang with a call or a text, she always experienced a thrill of expectation that it would be Greg.

The email wasn't from Greg – why would it be when it was three thirty in the morning where he was in New York?

Instead it was from Simon, one of her colleagues in the office. She and Simon had joined Merchant Swift as graduates at the same time and they had always worked well together. They had been informed this week that they'd been assigned a new project, to head up a team to build an internal computer system for a private healthcare company. Its headquarters was in Milton Keynes, and since that was where she and Simon would have to spend most of their time during the course of the job, Eliza was tempted to ask Mum if she could stay here at Medlar House. The prospect of weekly stays in hotels had long since lost its allure for her and the thought of some home comforts was quite appealing.

She read Simon's email.

Morning, Charlie Chan, he'd written, using one of his nicknames for her, *thought you might like this.* He'd sent her a link to a YouTube clip showing a piglet wearing a purple wig and a bikini miming to Lady Gaga singing 'Born This Way'.

Rarely did a day go by without Simon sending her a humorous link; heaven only knew how much time he spent trawling the internet for them. She watched the video and sent a quick message back and then went for a shower.

When she returned, there was another message from Simon.

Hope your bank holiday weekend's got off to a good start AND YOU'RE NOT WORKING!

Of course I'm not working, she replied.

Quick as a flash, his response pinged.

Channing, you are the worst LIAR in the world! Why else would you be looking at your laptop? Switch it off and go outside and play!

How well he knew her.

She dried her hair, got dressed, drew back the curtains and looked down onto the sunlit garden and in particular at The Gingerbread House, where the curtains were still drawn.

CHAPTER 18

At two o'clock, after the time-honoured crackle and whistle of tannoy static, the Reverend Jane Beaumont declared Little Pelham's village fete open. Shortly afterwards, the brass band started up with a jaunty rendition of 'Is This the Way to Amarillo?' and as people started milling around, Daisy leant in to Tattie and said, 'We should have got you to open the fete as Marilyn. You'd have brought some classy razzle-dazzle to the occasion.'

Tattie smiled and plucked a daisy from the grass where they were sitting on the green and added it to the daisy chain she was making. 'I think there's plenty of razzle-dazzle here already. It's all so perfectly quaint and English. Everyone looks so happy and relaxed.'

'It's relief,' Jensen said, 'relief that the event hasn't been rained off, or we're not forced to stand around in a force nine gale.'

Tattie gave him a playful flick with her hand. 'You're such a cynic, JC.'

'Not so. I'm a realist.'

'So, Tattie,' Scott said, 'what's the strangest opening you've ever had to do?'

She selected another daisy and considered the question. 'Well, there was a new car showroom in Knightsbridge which I was invited to open and that was certainly strange because a wealthy Saudi thought I was for sale as well as the cars. He was adamant that I had to be a part of the deal he wanted to strike. "No Marilyn, no car," he kept saying.'

'What an arrogant perv,' Jensen said with disgust. 'I'd have kicked his arse all the way into next week if I'd been there.'

Tattie put her arm through Jensen's and rested her head against his neck. 'I love it when you talk all tough,' she said in a girly voice, with a flutter of her eyelashes that was pure Marilyn.

Laughing, and unconsciously mirroring the other girl's body language, Daisy slipped her own arm through Scott's. Realizing her mistake, she went to correct it, but Scott clamped her arm with his and she knew that to remove it would only attract more attention. And anyway, she thought, it's going to come out this weekend, so why not go with the flow? But aware that her brother, who missed nothing, was staring at her with a telling expression in his eyes, she said, 'Madison seems to be having a good time, doesn't she?'

They all looked over to where Tattie's daughter was helping Mia and the vicar's husband on the bookstall.

'She certainly is,' Tattie said, 'and your mum's a total star with her.' She smiled warmly at Daisy and offered her the daisy chain necklace she'd been making. 'For you. You can't be called Daisy and not wear your namesake.'

'Oh, thank you.' Slipping it over her head and looping it around her neck, Daisy looked at Scott. 'How do I look?'

He smiled. 'Like a proper daisy princess.'

She returned his smile. God, how she loved him! And how she couldn't wait to escape to Sydney where she could start a new life with him. Away from her father. Away from his interference and disapproval. Because he would disapprove of Scott. She knew it. No man would ever be good enough for her. Certainly not one who was ten years older.

'Come on,' Jensen said, springing to his feet, 'let's rock on over to the coconut stall and say hello to Muriel. Mum says she's itching to meet you.'

Tattie looked up at him. 'Why, to see if I'm good enough for you?'

'Nah, to see if you've got a screw loose.'

'Why's that?'

'Because you consort with the likes of me.'

'Daisy,' Tattie said with a frown as she got to her feet, 'why does your brother have such a perpetually poor opinion of himself?'

'He's not alone,' Daisy said, 'we all have a poor opinion of ourselves; it's a Channing trait.'

'Yeah, all except for Dad,' Jensen muttered.

They made their way across the crowded green, dodging the children running around in their fancy dress costumes, passing the plant stall where Eliza had been roped in to help Georgina, and on towards the coconut shy, which Muriel was in charge of running.

'Aha!' she exclaimed when they approached. 'And who do we have here, none other than a brace of handsome young 'uns. My, don't you all look fit and well! Come on, then, Jensen, introduce me to your lovely girlfriend.'

'Tattie,' Jensen said, 'say hello to Little Pelham's Mafia boss, Muriel Fulshaw, and be careful what you say or you'll find a horse's head on your pillow in the morning.'

Muriel tutted and held out her hand. 'Ignore him. Ask anyone round here; I'm an absolute sweetheart. Good to meet you, my dear. I've heard wonderful things about you from Mia.' She then turned her attention to Scott and looked enquiringly at him.

Quick to pre-empt matters, Daisy said, 'This is Scott, my flatmate.' Well, she could hardly introduce him to Muriel as her boyfriend before explaining the situation to Mum, could she? But the sooner she did, the better – it was all getting so awkward. Poor Scott, she had promised him last night that she was going to talk to Mum this morning after breakfast, but annoyingly she hadn't been able to get her alone.

The handshaking over with, Muriel said, 'Now,

Daisy, what's this I hear about you hightailing it off to Australia?'

'Goodness, word spreads fast.'

Muriel laughed. 'We have an excellent news network here; everything gets reported.'

'What can I say?' Daisy replied with a shrug. 'It's all true what you've heard.' And quickly changing the subject, she said, 'We've come to win a coconut.'

'I should jolly well hope so. It's three balls for a pound. Who's going first? How about you, Tattie?'

'Go on then, I'll give it a go. Is there any particular technique I have to use?'

'Any technique you like,' Jensen said, handing over some money, 'but knowing Muriel, she's probably superglued the coconuts on to the posts and only a wrecking ball will knock them off.'

'Jensen Channing, that's a terrible slur on my good name. I shall have words with you later.'

Tattie took aim, and surprising them all, expertly threw the wooden ball as if she was pitching a baseball, even drawing her knee up to her chest. To everyone's amazement, she knocked one of the coconuts to the ground with a resounding crack. They cheered loudly and she high-fived them all. When she scored another direct hit and a second coconut fell, their raucous cheering attracted passers-by to stop and watch her take aim with the third ball. Unbelievably a third coconut was sent flying and the crowd that had gathered cheered enthusiastically and gave her a round of applause.

'In all my years of doing this, I swear that's a first,' Muriel said, gathering up the fallen coconuts. 'What do you do, play for the New York Yankees in your spare time?'

Laughing, Tattie said, 'Put it down to a misspent youth. But I feel bad taking three – just give me the one coconut.'

'Very sporting of you,' Muriel said approvingly. 'Who's next, then? One of you boys going to rise to the challenge?'

Scott and Jensen looked at each other. Scott said, 'Our reps are on the line here, mate.'

'I'll give it a shot,' Jensen said. 'I've no shame in losing to a world-class champ.' He handed over some more money to Muriel, lined himself up, aimed, and missed.

And missed again.

And again.

The crowd, which had grown, clapped and cheered in sympathy. Jensen took a bow. 'Over to you, Scott,' he said.

'Go on,' Daisy urged him. 'You can do it.'

His first shot went wild. As did his second, but his third had the coconut wobbling and the crowd audibly held its breath, but it remained stubbornly in place and he too received a round of applause for his effort.

Smiling, Muriel offered the balls to Daisy. 'It's girls against boys now,' she said. 'Give 'em hell, kid!'

'Oh, but I'm worse than useless,' Daisy said, taking a step back.

'You can't be any worse than your brother and boyfriend,' someone shouted out from the crowd. Blushing at the word *boyfriend*, Daisy took the balls from Muriel. To her astonishment, her first ball made contact, but not enough.

'More welly,' encouraged Scott at her side.

Her second ball missed entirely.

'Come on, Daisy,' urged Tattie. 'One for the girls. You can do it.'

And incredibly she did. Her third ball knocked a coconut clean off its stand. *'Yay!'* she yelled ecstatically, flinging her arms around Scott and kissing him. When she let go, Jensen was looking at her with a raised eyebrow. She met his gaze and knew that he *knew*. 'Don't say anything to Mum,' she said quietly. 'Not until I've spoken to her.'

He gave her one of his classic none-of-my-business shrugs.

Owen loved the sound of a brass band; there was nothing like it. The tone and volume of the instruments got him right in the pit of his stomach. He stood for a moment in the warm sunshine happily listening to the medley of Beatles songs being played.

Around him people were smiling, chatting, laughing, eating and drinking, all having a good time. He searched amongst the faces for any he might recognize, but drew a blank. He'd been here a week now, and while he hadn't exactly made himself that visible in the village – he'd only been to Parr's twice and had yet to set foot inside the pub – he had wondered if anyone would come calling to say, 'Hey, I remember you.' But no one had. Which was fine. It was highly likely that anyone he had known thirty-four years ago had moved away, just as he had. And really, when he thought about it, he hadn't known that many people, just a handful of kids from school and Gretchen and Lillian Lampton.

Whenever he looked back to that day when he'd summoned the courage to knock on the door of The Hidden Cottage, he remembered it as a day when his life changed. Not that he had articulated that precise thought when he was a boy, but as the days passed and his visits increased, he'd known that the time he spent with Gretchen and Lillian was special.

Confined to The Hidden Cottage as they were, the two women had created their own little world in which they lived and he, while everybody else was kept out, had been allowed in to their sanctuary to be a part of their lives. He discovered that all those times he had sneaked into their garden and sat by the lake listening to the music coming from the house through the open window, they had been covertly observing him from behind net curtains.

They had previously had trouble from a number of older boys in the village – things thrown at their windows, names called through the letterbox, the usual vile things children get up to when they sense a helpless victim – but Gretchen and Lillian had decided he was different. Intrigued by the solitary boy sitting in their garden, they had wanted to know more. So they had lowered their guard and awarded him a privilege that no one else had ever been granted. He felt honoured and special. And it became their secret. They never said he wasn't to tell anyone about his visits; it just seemed implicit, and besides he hadn't wanted to tell anyone because whenever anything good happened to him, it always seemed to be taken away. His father saw to that. Consequently he had learnt that it was better to keep quiet, to keep things hidden. Even from his mother.

That day when he'd first stepped inside The Hidden Cottage, Gretchen had slowly led him into the room where music was playing. The first thing he noticed was a large piano in front of the French windows overlooking the garden. He had never seen a piano like it before – there was so much of it and it looked so expensive, not like the battered upright thing they had at school for assembly on which Mrs Beck bashed out their morning hymns.

'This is my sister, Lillian,' Gretchen had informed him, going over to turn down the music. 'She's by far the nicer of the two of us.'

In front of him was a woman dressed almost identically to Gretchen, even down to the white cotton mittens. She was sitting in an upright chair and while her face wasn't as bad as the other woman's, it still wasn't right. Her grey hair was patchy and thin, like some of it was missing. 'Hello,' he said politely, 'my name's Owen.'

She smiled and patted the rattan stool next to her. 'Come and sit down so I can get a proper look at you.' He dutifully sat on the stool and looked curiously about him. The walls were lined with shelves, packed with books, hundreds of them, maybe thousands. Other than in a library, he'd never seen so many. His gaze fell onto the record player and the disc that was spinning. 'Music,' he said, 'there's always music playing here. That's one of the reasons why I've been coming.'

The two women looked at each other. It was difficult to know exactly what the exchange meant because their faces weren't like normal faces and so their expressions didn't really show. But he sensed he'd said something significant.

'Music has been our life,' Gretchen said, going slowly over to the piano. She touched it lightly with a mittened hand. 'We used to play all the time.' She sat stiffly on the piano stool and as if it was much too heavy for her, she carefully lifted the lid. But she didn't touch any of the keys.

'We played all over the world,' Lillian said next to him. 'We'd been playing individually for some years and then we became a double act. We even had a record made. We taught as well. You're quite unusual to like classical music at so young an age.'

170

'I didn't know I did until I heard it here,' he said.

'When we watched you through the window, we could see you swinging your legs perfectly in time to the music. Do you play an instrument?'

He shook his head. 'No, but I've started singing in the choir at school.'

'That's good. Let me see your hands. Hold them out.'

He did as she said.

'Mmm . . .' she murmured thoughtfully, 'nice long fingers; you have a good reach.' Then: 'Would you like to have a go on our piano?'

Gretchen turned round. 'Lillian, do you really think that is such a good idea?' Her voice was sharp and she looked not at her sister, but at Owen with her strong dark eyes, as if appraising him.

'I'd like him to try,' Lillian said. 'What's the harm in that?'

A shrill cry from a child behind him made Owen start and brought him back from the past.

He looked around the green with its colourful stalls and cheerful faces. With hindsight he saw that it would have been a mistake for Nicole to come here today. A city girl through and through, she would probably have gone out of her way to rubbish the fete. She would have looked around her and dismissed it as rustic nonsense and condemned the village as hicks-ville. Which would have totally ruined it for Owen. No, things had definitely worked out for the best.

In front of the big oak tree in the centre of the green, he recognized Georgina standing behind a table of plants. There were two small boys with her, one dressed as Superman, the other as Spiderman, along with a rather serious-looking girl in her mid-twenties who was dealing with a customer. Georgina saw him, gave him one of her bright smiles and waved. He waved back and strolled over, noting that two stalls further on was the bookstall.

'Hello there,' Georgina said merrily as the two boys ran off, nearly colliding with a woman and a pushchair. 'You made it then?'

'Of course. How's business going?'

'Not bad. Can I interest you in some plants for your garden? Or what about some runner beans? I grew them myself from seed.' She held up a tray of five-inch-high seedlings. 'Six plants for a mere three pounds.'

'A bargain, I'm sure. Trouble is, I haven't got as far as figuring out what I'm going to do with my garden yet.'

'You could grow these in a biggish pot with some canes. They wouldn't be any trouble; all you'll need to do is keep them well watered and fed regularly.'

How could he say no? 'All right, I'll take them, but on the proviso that if they start to misbehave, you'll be on hand to sort them out.'

She beamed. 'It would be a pleasure.'

He handed over a five-pound note. 'Now all I need is a pot and some canes.'

She held out his change. 'You'll need some compost as well. I've got some canes I could give you.'

'Thanks, but I wouldn't want to gain a reputation for being a scrounger. Keep the change; add it to the coffers.' He inclined his head towards Superman and Spiderman, who had joined a queue for ice-creams. 'Are they your boys?'

'They are today.'

'And tomorrow?'

She laughed. 'Depends on their conduct. I might put them on eBay. Have you met Mia's eldest daughter, Eliza?' she added when the customer whom the girl had been serving had left them.

'No, I haven't.'

'Eliza,' Georgina said, 'this is Owen Fletcher, the new owner of The Hidden Cottage.'

He held out his hand and, discerning no real similarity in her features with her mother, he said, 'I gather you're home for the weekend.'

'That's right. How are you liking Little Pelham?'

'I'm liking it a lot. People have been very welcoming.'

'You mean nosy?'

He laughed. 'Better to be talked about than ignored, wouldn't you say?'

'The way I heard it from Mum was that the Little Pelham Mafia paid you a call.'

'They did indeed.'

'Owen used to live here when he was a boy,' Georgina said.

'Yes, I heard that too from Mum. What made you come back?'

'To fulfil a long-held promise that I would live here again one day.'

'In that case, I hope it lives up to your expectations.'

'I'm sure it will.' He turned back to Georgina. 'Can I leave my runner bean plants with you until the fete's over?'

'Certainly,' she said. 'I'll put them under the table for safe-keeping.'

'Thanks. And now I'd better circulate and spend some more money. See you.'

To the sound of the band now playing 'Mack the Knife', he moved on to the next stall, giving the piles of assorted junk no more than a cursory glance.

The bookstall was inundated with customers; they were lined two-deep along the length of the two trestle tables.

'Hello,' he said, after he'd managed to attract Mia's attention. 'You look busy.'

'I am. I've lost both my helpers and suddenly the world and his wife have descended upon me.'

'I could give you a hand, if you like?'

'Really?'

'Don't worry; I am capable of adding up and counting out change. I'm not as stupid as I look.'

174

She smiled. A real sun-coming-out-from-behind-the-clouds smile. 'You're a lifesaver,' she said.

And you, he thought, are quite simply one of the most beautiful women I've ever met.

CHAPTER 19

'We're going to make a den down by the brook – do you want to come?' The boy asking the question had a front tooth missing and was dressed as a cowboy with a toy gun pushed into his belt and a hat tipped sideways on his head with a fringe and a silver badge on it.

Madison looked uncertainly from him to Beth. She didn't really want to go. She was happy here, sitting on the grass in the sun and talking to this girl with her messy curly hair and freckled face. She had appeared at the bookstall with her mother and after she'd spent ages slowly hunting through all the books for one on the solar system and not found anything, Mia had asked Madison if she wanted to go off and explore the fete with the girl whose name was Beth, and who Madison had realized was one of the few children here who, like her, wasn't wearing a fancy dress costume. Mum had given her some spending money earlier, but Mia had insisted on giving her some more. Beth had taken her round the stalls, stopping off first to buy some cupcakes, which they'd eaten straight away. Then they'd had a go on the tombola and

Beth had won a jar of hot chilli sauce and Madison had won a bottle of aftershave, which she was going to give to JC. On the white elephant stall, Beth had bought a bookmark and Madison had bought a fluffy pink rabbit. She hadn't decided yet whether to keep it for herself or to give it to Mum. Lastly they'd bought themselves an ice-cream, which they were now eating while sitting on the grass.

'What do *you* want to do, Madison?' Beth asked her.

She shrugged. 'You go if you want. I'll stay here.' She knew what boys were like; when they asked if you wanted to join in with one of their games, all they really wanted was someone to boss around and show off in front of.

Beth looked back at the boy. 'That's OK, Michael, we'll come and see your den later, when it's finished.'

When he'd gone, Beth said, 'They're always making dens and they're never any good. And they *always* end up arguing over whose fault it is that it doesn't work.' She licked at a dribble of ice-cream that had trickled down the cornet and onto her thumb. 'They can be very childish at times. Is that your mum over there?'

Madison turned to where Beth was pointing and saw her mother with JC and Daisy and Scott. JC was behind Mum with his arms around her, his chin resting on the top of her head as they stood listening to the band; they were moving ever so slightly to the music, almost dancing. 'Yes,' she said, 'that's my mum.'

'She doesn't look like the other mothers here; she looks like someone off the telly. Is she famous?'

Madison smiled with pride. She loved the fact that Mum stood out from everyone else, that she was special. It made her feel a bit special as well. 'Not really,' she said. 'But she has been on the telly.'

'Cool. How long are you staying here?'

'We go home on Monday.'

'Are you doing anything tomorrow? If you aren't, you could come and play at my house. I could show you my new telescope.'

'That would be nice. But I'll have to check with Mum. What do you use your telescope for?'

'To look at the stars, of course.' She then smiled. 'Don't tell anyone, but sometimes I use it to spy on people.'

'That sounds fun.'

'It is. But you really mustn't tell anyone; Mum and Dad would be cross with me if they knew.'

Happy that Beth trusted her enough to confide in her, she said, 'I promise.' She carried on licking her ice-cream, thinking what a brilliant time she was having.

The band had finished playing and people had spent all they were going to spend and were drifting away, some home and some over the road to the Fox and Goose.

Richard, the vicar's husband, had never returned, his services permanently required on the tombola to fill in for Ray Coombes, who'd tripped over and broken a toe – 'That'll teach him to wear those awful sandals of his,' his wife had said – and so Mia had been glad of Owen's help. 'You can leave whenever you want,' she'd told him, feeling guilty that he'd found himself roped in for more than he had bargained on, but he'd said he was enjoying himself and lending a hand was as good a way as any for him to meet people. He had chatted with everyone in a relaxed and engaging manner, effortlessly making friends and fitting in. One or two of the older members of the village said that while they would never have recognized him, they did remember his name, and his parents. Mia had overheard the words 'bad lot' and 'bully' being guardedly muttered in respect to Owen's father.

With no one around, and seeing that some of the other stall holders, including Georgina and Eliza, were packing up, she said, 'Owen, I doubt we'll get any more customers now, so you can go if you want; you've been more than generous with your time.'

'That's OK, I'm not in any hurry to get away. What happens to all the books we haven't sold?' he asked, looking at the tabletop wreckage.

'The really old books will go for recycling and the rest will go to the PTA to sell at the school fair next month.' She bent down and pulled out two boxes from under the table, then another two.

'I'll help you box them up,' he said.

'There's no need; I can manage.'

'I'm sure you can, but never let it be said that I'm the kind of man who doesn't see a job through.' He took one of the boxes from her. 'Do you have a system – paperbacks separated from hardbacks, or everything in together?'

'Everything in together will be fine,' she said. 'I'll sort them out later.'

They'd packed away all of the books and handed over their takings when Mia saw Daisy and Scott crossing the green in her direction. She hadn't said anything yet to her daughter, but Mia hugely suspected that there was more to Daisy and Scott's friendship than they were letting on. She had thought it when she had watched them getting out of Jensen's car last night – it was the way Scott had taken Daisy's weekend bag from her and slung it over his shoulder along with his own and fallen in step alongside her. On the face of it, it was nothing, but to Mia's eye there had been an innate intimacy to what he'd done; it had been the act of an established partner.

Watching the two of them approach, it was obvious to Mia now that Scott had everything to do with Daisy wanting to go to Australia, and she had no problem with that. Scott was a decent and level-headed man; yes, he was a lot older than Daisy, but maybe that was what she needed, someone to keep her grounded.

'Anything we can do to help?' Daisy asked cheerfully, now in front of the bare trestle tables.

'All done, thanks,' Mia responded. 'Have you met Owen?'

Smiling at Owen, Daisy said, 'No, but my sister and I saw you in the shop last Saturday. I see Mum's press-ganged you into helping before you've even found your feet here.'

'Hey,' Mia joked, 'that's not true; all I said was that if he didn't help me I'd put his name down to help Muriel next year.'

Owen laughed. 'I may only have been here a week, but my survival instinct told me which was the better option.'

Jensen and Tattie then appeared, along with Madison and Beth, the two girls looking like they'd been friends since forever. 'I've had an idea, Mum,' Jensen said. 'To save you cooking tonight, why don't we have a Mr Wu takeaway?'

'Brilliant idea,' Eliza said, coming over to join them. 'Put me down for a broccoli and ginger beef stir-fry. I'm starving, I haven't had anything to eat all afternoon.'

'What about you, Madison?' Mia asked. 'Do you like Chinese food?'

'I love it. Noodles are my favourite.'

'That's settled then. Beth, if it's OK with your parents, do you want to join us?'

The girl nodded eagerly and smiled at Madison.

'What about you, Georgina?' Mia called over to her friend. 'Fancy a Chinese tonight? Looks like we've got a party brewing.'

'It's the best offer I've had all day, but sadly I'll

have to pass. I've just been talked into a sleepover, so I'll be rustling up pizza and chips for four hyperactive boys.'

'Oh, poor you, good luck with that!' Then feeling that it would be rude not to include him, Mia turned to Owen. 'You're welcome to join us if you'd like.'

He hesitated. 'I wouldn't want to intrude on a family occasion.'

'You won't be intruding. It'll be my way of thanking you for your help today and for repaying your hospitality last Monday.'

'In that case, how can I say no? What time do you want me to come?'

'Come for six thirty.'

Later at Medlar House, while the others were out in the garden, Daisy finally managed to get her mother on her own in the kitchen; she was laying the table for supper. 'Mum, why don't you sit down and I'll make you a cup of tea?'

Her mother stopped what she was doing. 'Why do I have the feeling that offer comes loaded with subtext?'

Despite her nerves, Daisy forced herself to laugh and went over to the kettle. 'It's not that rare I offer to make you a drink.'

'It's rare enough to make me know that you have something on your mind.'

The kettle filled, Daisy faced her mother. Scott had suggested he be with her for this, but she'd wanted to do it alone. She knew that too often in her life she had relied upon or hidden behind others, although in many ways she was doing exactly the same thing again – telling Mum first so she could be the one to break the news to Dad. She took a deep breath. 'The thing is, Mum, Scott and I are, well, we're—'

'More than just friends?' Mia interrupted her, her head tilted to one side, an eyebrow raised.

Daisy stared at her, shocked. 'How did you know? Did Jensen say something?'

'I didn't know for sure, but I definitely had a feeling about the two of you. Why did you think Jensen might have said something? Did he know already?'

'He guessed earlier today. Not that I made it that difficult for anyone to guess. Do you mind?'

'About you and Scott? No. But presumably he's the reason you want to move to Australia. Why didn't you tell us that straight away?'

'Come on, Mum, it's Dad; you know what he's like. Can you imagine his reaction to me being in a relationship with a man who's ten years older than me?'

Her mother sighed and sat down. 'So what now? You sneak off to Australia without telling him about Scott? Is that the idea?'

'You sound cross.'

'Not cross, love, just tired of it all, the constant secrecy in this family. We don't seem capable of being honest with each other. Why is that?'

Daisy pulled out the chair opposite her mother and sat down. 'It's not you, Mum. You must never think that.'

'But it is me who you expect to break this latest round of news to your father, isn't it? Is it serious between the two of you? I mean, really serious?'

'Yes,' she said. 'He's asked me to marry him. And I've said yes. I love him, Mum. I really do. I know you probably think I'm only twenty-three and that I'm too young and—'

Her mother reached across the table and took her hands. 'Daisy, that isn't what I think at all. And seeing you with Scott I can see that he's good for you.'

Daisy could feel her eyes filling with tears. 'He is, Mum, and I know it will work between us. It's always worked between us, ever since I moved in with him. You see, we've lived together as friends, and we've lived together as . . . as a couple, so we know it works. It's not like we don't know one another.'

Her mother smiled and squeezed her hands.

'What I wanted to do,' Daisy continued, 'but Scott wouldn't let me, I wanted to wait until I was in Australia and then tell you and Dad about Scott. Which I know would have been wrong.'

'I'm glad Scott was sensible enough to talk you out of that.'

'He is sensible, Mum, and he'd never do anything to hurt me. He understands me. He knows what I'm like. But Dad's never going to think well of

184

him, is he? He'll never approve. Or of any decision I make without his input.'

'He certainly won't if you sneak off to the other side of the world without telling him the truth.'

The kettle began to boil. Daisy got up, but her mother said, 'Stay there, I'll do it.'

Watching her make the tea, pouring water, dunking teabags, stirring in milk, Daisy wondered at her mother's calmness – nothing ever seemed to faze her. Years ago that trademark stillness of hers used to drive Daisy mad and she would deliberately do whatever she could to force Mum to lose her temper. Feeling so relentlessly stirred up as a teenager, she had despised Mum's seemingly unnatural composure, had taken it for submissiveness. Now she knew better; it was strength. Real inner strength, the kind Daisy wished she had. Because really, she was nothing but a coward.

Putting the mugs of tea on the table and sitting down again, Mum said, 'You said Scott's asked you to marry him – do you have a date in mind for the wedding?'

'No. But when it happens, it will be in Australia. I'm sorry if that's a disappointment to you.'

'Is Scott stipulating that?'

'We've agreed it between ourselves. It's how we do things, Mum. We're not like you and Dad, with Dad making all the decisions.'

Mum looked at her with a small frown. 'Is that how you see it?'

'Isn't it *exactly* how it is? What choices does he ever give you?'

'I didn't go to Brussels with him. I chose to stay here.'

'But the point is, he wasn't prepared to consider your feelings when he was offered the job; he just went ahead and accepted it. It's the way he is – he has to be in control of everything. I've never been able to do anything without him wanting me to do it *his* way.'

Taking a cautious sip of her hot tea, she watched her mother closely. It was a long time since she had spoken so bluntly about Dad. When Mum spoke, the question took Daisy by surprise. 'Are you absolutely sure Scott is giving you the choice to stay here and you're not just going along with what he wants?'

'Trust me, Mum, Scott is nothing like Dad. And I really don't want to stay here; I want to go to Australia. We'd have a completely different life there. A better life.'

'It's a big step you're taking, especially as you've never been there before. It all seems to be happening in such a rush.'

'It doesn't feel that way for us. In fact it doesn't seem to be happening fast enough. I finished work yesterday, by the way. For good.'

'You've handed in your notice?'

'I gave a week's notice last week. I can't tell you what a relief it is knowing I'll never have to sit in that miserable office ever again.'

'Does your father know?'

'No.'

Her mother looked at her steadily, the small frown once again creasing her forehead. 'So when do you want me to tell your father all this? When he gets back from his trip?'

'Would you? I know I should do it myself, but I can't look him in the face and say the words. I just can't bear the thought of him going ballistic. He'd find every reason he could to convince me I don't know what I'm doing and that Scott isn't right for me.'

'In all probability he's going to do that anyway.'

'But you'll be able to calm him down.'

'You're joking, right?'

'Please, Mum. Try. For me.'

'OK, I'll do my best. But no promises. You know your father's a law unto himself.'

Daisy put her mug of tea down and went round the table to hug her mother. 'Thanks, Mum. You're the best.'

When she was sitting down again, the frown was gone from her mother's face and in its place was a happy smile. 'I suppose congratulations are in order, aren't they? My youngest daughter getting married; that's quite a big deal you know. Are you going to tell the others this weekend while you're all together?'

'Can I? Tonight?'

'Why not?'

'Dad will be cross that he was last to hear, though.'

Her mother shrugged. 'Let's cross that bridge when we have to. For now it's your moment; you enjoy it. We'll celebrate with some bubbly and a Mr Wu takeaway. How does that sound?'

'It sounds great.'

CHAPTER 20

With a bottle of red wine in hand and with Putin following behind him, Owen set off down the garden towards the lake. The bird seemed in a subdued mood; he hadn't let rip with a single screech or once fanned out his tail feathers in a showy look-at-me display since Owen had arrived home from the fete. His head now kept permanently low, he gave the impression of sulking, as if he resented Owen going out for the evening. 'You're always out these days, you treat this place like a hotel,' he imagined the bird muttering.

Owen skirted the lake and after he'd located the gap he'd purposely made in the dense tangle of rhododendron and hawthorn bushes and slipped through it, he looked back at Putin, who had stopped some yards away. Fixing his beady eyes on him, the bird gave Owen an imperious stare.

'No need to wait up for me,' Owen said happily.

Dropping down into the woods, the air softly weighted with the smell of wild garlic, he stood for a moment to admire the haze of bluebells caught in the shafts of sunlight streaming through the trees. He felt the same emotion as he had yesterday evening when he'd walked back from Medlar House after dropping off the books with Mia, an uplifting sense of being exactly where he should be.

A short while later, he took the steep incline and, emerging from the woods, climbed over the stile and joined the public footpath where he was faced with the choice of taking the path to the right, down towards the church and Medlar House, or going straight on to the allotments – that's if they were still there.

He decided he just had time to make a detour and minutes later he was pleased to discover that the place, just as he remembered it, was a hive of activity in the warm spring evening, with people working on their plots. He spotted Muriel Fulshaw filling a watering can from a green plastic water butt in front of a shed and went over to her. 'Hello,' he said, 'I missed you at the fete this afternoon.'

'Ah, hello there! Yes, I wondered what had happened to you. Thought perhaps you'd chickened out and stayed away.'

'No fear! I was helping Mia on the bookstall for most of the afternoon.'

'That sly old Mia, she gets all the best help!' Looking at the bottle of wine in his hand, she raised an eyebrow. 'Is that for me?'

'Sorry, 'fraid not. I've been invited for a Chinese takeaway at Medlar House.'

'Lucky old you. And if Mr Wu is on the menu,

190

you're in for a treat. He's the best thing about Saturday nights round here.'

'Why's that?'

She wagged a finger at him. 'You obviously didn't read the parish magazine very closely; Mr Wu is a travelling Chinese takeaway and Saturday night is when he rolls into Little Pelham. He parks his van near the green and while people wait for their orders to be cooked, they either stand around chatting or go into the pub for a drink and come out when their food is ready. It's all marvellously convivial.'

'Sounds like a perfect arrangement. Well, I'd better push on; I mustn't be late. I just stopped off to see if the allotments still existed.'

'Not so fast! Seeing as you're here, there's someone who'd like to meet you, someone who remembers you from when you were a boy.'

'Really?'

'Come with me and I'll introduce you.'

She led him to the other side of the allotments, to a plot that had a small greenhouse attached to it. A man dressed in work boots, knee-length shorts and a ripped sleeveless vest was digging industriously; his head was shaved and the biceps of his tanned arms were pronounced and extensively tattooed.

'Joe,' Muriel said, 'this is Owen. Owen Fletcher.' She turned back to Owen. 'This is Joe Coffey.'

The other man stopped digging, straightened up and, leaning on his spade, he looked at Owen hard.

191

Owen stared back at him. 'Joe Coffey, as in Joe Coffin?' he said uncertainly, conjuring up the name from the past but not the face.

The other man suddenly grinned. 'Bloody hell, mate, it really is you, isn't it?'

'You mean you actually recognize me?'

'Yeah, something in the eyes there and the mouth. Anything recognizable about me?'

Owen struggled to think of something. But drew a blank. It was a bit like when he'd stood outside his old house in Cloverdale Lane – the exterior hadn't really meant much to him; it was what was inside his head that counted. 'Sorry,' he said, 'obviously my memory isn't as good as yours.'

Joe laughed. 'No worries, I suppose being practically bald doesn't help, does it?'

Owen laughed as well. 'Not much.'

'Bit unfair, though – you look much younger than me. How d'yer manage that?'

'You've caught me on a good day.'

'I seem to recall you always were a polite sod. Unlike me. I was always getting into trouble, shooting my big mouth off. I've just heard from Muriel here that you've bought The Hidden Cottage and moved in last weekend.'

'That's right.' Smiling at Muriel, Owen added, 'I'm surprised you've only just heard.'

'Joe's been away,' Muriel informed him, 'otherwise he'd have known before now, make no mistake about that.'

'I've been working for a cousin of mine up in

Yorkshire for the last eight days,' Joe explained. 'Only got back late this afternoon.'

'Right then, boys,' Muriel said, 'seeing as you two are getting along so famously, I'll leave you to it.'

When she'd gone, Joe shook his head. 'It's so weird seeing you again. I haven't thought of you in years.' Then, just as Muriel had, he spied the bottle of wine in Owen's hand. 'So where are you off to?'

'I've been invited to supper at Medlar House.'

'Have you now?' Leaning in, his voice lower, Joe said, 'Take it from me, that Mia's a bit of all right. Can't say as I like that husband of hers much, but there's no accounting for taste. And there I go again, shooting my mouth off. You married?'

'I was.'

'Same here. She left me for a tree surgeon last year. Again, no accounting for taste. Children?'

Owen shook his head. 'No.'

'I've got two teenage lads; they live with their mother just down the road in Yardley Hastings, so at least I get to see them regularly. Look, why don't we meet for a drink and have a proper chat and catch up? And if there's any work you need doing on the house, look no further; I'm your man. You can find me here most evenings. Failing that, I'll call on you. If that's OK?'

'It's more than OK; I look forward to it. For now, I'd better get going, I don't want to blot my copybook.'

'See you then.'

Husband, Owen thought as he walked away.

Mia was *married*.

For some reason he had assumed that she was divorced. She wore no ring and at no stage in any of their conversations had she referred to a Mr Channing. There had certainly been no sign of him at the fete this afternoon.

When he reached the end of the footpath – between St George's and Medlar House – Owen looked across to the green where a van was parked on the road with the words *Mr Wu* emblazoned on it; there was a small queue of people extending from the open hatch.

He turned sharply left for Medlar House and, ringing the doorbell, he wondered if the husband Joe didn't think much of would be joining them for dinner. For no rational reason he hoped not.

CHAPTER 21

Madison was in bed but she couldn't sleep; she had too much whirring around inside her head. She'd had the best day ever. And tomorrow was going to be just as good, she just knew it.

While they'd been eating their Chinese takeaway this evening, they'd all been invited to go and see where Owen lived – a house called The Hidden Cottage, and it had a lake with a boat. He'd said it wasn't a very big lake, that they weren't to get too excited. He'd also said that she could have a go in the boat with him if she wanted. Beth as well. He'd even said she could have a go on his piano, that he'd had it tuned the other day and needed an expert like her to try it out. She just couldn't believe how amazing it was being here with JC's family.

Something else had happened while they'd been eating: Daisy and Scott had told them that they would be getting married.

'Married?' Eliza had said. 'But you're not . . . I mean . . . I thought you were just friends.'

JC had laughed. 'I think that was the general

idea, Eliza; they were throwing us off the scent. Welcome to the family, Scott. I hope you have a good sense of humour and a tough skin, because man, oh, man, you're sure gonna need it.'

Madison didn't know what JC had meant by that, but she'd secretly smiled to herself, because she'd known that Daisy and Scott weren't just friends.

Everybody was then hugging and kissing Daisy and Scott and Mia asked JC to open a bottle of champagne she had in the fridge. Even Madison and Beth were allowed a few sips and everyone said things like, congratulations, and I hope you'll be really happy, but then Eliza said, 'Have you told Dad?' The laughter instantly stopped and the room went very quiet. It was odd because it felt as if the lights had suddenly been turned off. It was Mum who broke the silence by asking when Daisy and Scott thought they'd get married. They'd said they weren't in a hurry, but probably some-time next year.

Remembering all the talk of weddings and stuff, and thinking how excited everyone had been, Madison hoped that she might be asked to be a bridesmaid. Lauren had been a bridesmaid last year and she'd said it had been brilliant fun.

Turning onto her side, she realized that this was the first time she had thought of Lauren since getting here. She wondered if Lauren had thought of her today. Would she be jealous of Madison's new friend, Beth? Perhaps it would be better if

Madison didn't mention anything about it when she was back at school.

When Beth's father had arrived to take her home after supper, Beth had told him about them being invited to The Hidden Cottage and had asked if Madison could go home to their house for tea afterwards. 'Please say yes, Dad,' she'd said, 'please, please, *please*!' He'd laughed and said he couldn't think of a reason why not. He was then introduced to Owen and had ended up staying for a drink and it was really late by the time he and Beth left.

It was like they'd had the most amazing party that had gone on for the whole day. She felt like she'd been here for a week and not just one amazingly fantastic day. She wished they didn't have to leave on Monday, that they could stay for the whole of half-term.

Dressed in her pyjamas and sitting on the edge of her bed, Eliza had just tried ringing Greg, but he must have switched off his mobile. She had checked her emails but there wasn't a message from him. Not even a hurried two-line message as he sometimes did.

She had never missed him as much as she did now. She knew why, it was seeing Daisy and Scott and Jensen and Tattie all loved up. Seeing them so happy had the effect of making her feel horribly left out. It would have been lovely if Greg had been here today; it would have been the perfect opportunity for him to meet her family, to be a part of it. And without the pressure of having Dad around.

It was an awful thing to say, but it always felt like they were more of a family when Dad wasn't with them. His very presence put them on edge. To put it bluntly, he was a disruptive force amongst them. Mum didn't exactly defend him, but she wouldn't come right out and condemn his behaviour. She said that all families had to make allowances for each other and Eliza supposed that was what they'd been doing for years.

She put her laptop to one side and, knowing that Mum was in the kitchen tidying up, she went downstairs to see if there was anything she could do to help. She had told her mother about the new project she would be working on in Milton Keynes and had broached the subject about staying here during the week. Mum had been all for it.

'I thought you were in bed already,' her mother said when she saw Eliza.

'I was just checking my emails. What can I do to help?'

'I'm almost finished; just the last few glasses to put in the dishwasher. You can put the kettle on if you like. I'm more than ready for a cup of tea. How about you? Anything more to eat or drink?'

'A piece of that chocolate cake you bought at the fete would be nice.'

Her mother smiled. 'I'll keep you company and have a slice as well.'

When everything was put away and their tea was

made and poured out, they sat down. Eliza knew she shouldn't be eating cake on top of what she'd eaten for supper, that it would go straight to her hips and thighs, as did just about everything else she ever ate, but she wasn't in the mood to care. She had long since come to terms with the glaringly obvious: that she was never going to have Mum's elegant slim build, unlike Jensen and Daisy who had both inherited those particular genes. Unfortunately for her, she took after Dad's side of the family and there wasn't a damned thing she could do about that.

'It's a shame Greg couldn't have joined us for the weekend,' Mum said.

Eliza looked up from her plate. 'Yes,' she said, 'it is. I wish he'd been here.'

'You OK? You seem a bit down.'

Eliza took another bite of cake. It wasn't often that she and Mum had these moments together, moments that, if she were honest, she wasn't entirely comfortable with. She was no good at girly heart-to-heart sessions; they'd never held any interest for her. But give Mum her due, she never forced her into saying more than she wanted to say. Tonight, though, Eliza felt differently; she had a great urge to talk. She wanted to say out loud what she was thinking, if only to be rid of the worry it was causing her. 'I wish I was better at relationships, Mum,' she said. 'I don't think I know how to behave in them.'

'Now what's put that thought into your head?'

'It's the frustration of not seeing Greg.'

'But last weekend you said his being away so much suited you, that it gave you your space. What's changed? Is it Greg?'

'No, it's not him, it's me.'

Mia tutted. 'Why do we women always do that? Why do we always blame ourselves by saying "it's me"?'

'But it's true. I knew when Greg and I started seeing each other what it would be like and I was happy with that. What really gets to me is that I've never been a needy person, and suddenly that's exactly what I've become. I hate it. And I hate not hearing from him. I hate the disappointment when he has to cancel flying over.' She stared across the table at her mother, shocked and relieved that she had poured it all out in one go.

'Missing the man you love doesn't make you needy,' Mum said.

'It's how I feel,' she said, conscious that whereas her mother's voice was gentle and reassuring, hers sounded pathetically whiny, 'and I despise myself for it. I should be stronger, I should be able to cope and—'

'Eliza, there are no *shoulds* in this. It's the most natural thing in the world to want to be with the person you love. Have you discussed this with Greg?'

'Absolutely not! If I do that, it's guaranteed to frighten him off.'

'Not necessarily. But you know, there's always

the danger that you could be giving him mixed messages.'

'In what way?'

'He could interpret your apparent coping with the situation as a sign that you don't care for him as much as he cares for you, that you're happy with the status quo. In turn he might be playing things cool so as not to scare you off.'

Eliza sat back in her chair and fiddled with the cuff of her pyjama top. She hadn't thought of it that way. Could it be possible that she'd been giving out the wrong signals to Greg? 'You really think I should be completely honest with him?' she said.

'Yes I do. So often it's not what we say but what we *don't* say that causes all the trouble in a relationship. If you want the relationship to work with Greg, you have to tell him everything you've just told me.'

'But what if it frightens him off?'

'Then he isn't right for you.'

'You make it sound so simple.'

'Oh, Eliza, it's anything but simple, but sometimes we make things needlessly hard for ourselves.'

They drank their tea and when Eliza had finished her slice of cake and resisted the temptation to help herself to more, she said, 'When are you going to tell Dad about Daisy and Scott? I presume she's asked you to break the news to him, rather than do it herself.'

'She has and I don't know whether to ring him or wait until he gets home.'

'Either way, I wouldn't like to be in your shoes when you do tell him. Or Daisy's. What about the age gap? Does that worry you at all, Scott being ten years older?'

'No, not particularly. I've thought for a long time that Daisy would probably be attracted to someone a good deal older than her.'

'You mean a father figure? Isn't that borderline creepy?'

'Relationships come in all different shapes and sizes. And,' she added with a smile, 'remind me again of the age difference between you and Greg.'

'Yes, but that's different; I'm the sensible, more mature daughter, therefore that's what I would look for in a potential partner. Interestingly, I've never thought of Jensen as the marrying kind, but seeing him with Tattie and Madison has made me change my opinion.'

'I agree. Tattie clearly makes him very happy. And Madison is a delight. It's been lovely having her here.'

'You'd be a step-grandmother if they married,' Eliza said with a yawn that suddenly crept up on her.

Mum smiled. 'And on that terrifying thought, let's call it a day. Come on, time for bed.' She stood up and took their plates and mugs over to the dishwasher. 'By the way, it was kind of you to help Georgina today. She was very grateful.'

'No problem. I enjoyed myself. As I think Owen did with you on the bookstall.'

'Yes, it was a good way for him to meet people. I think he's going to fit in well here. He certainly seems to have the right attitude.'

Stifling another yawn, Eliza kissed her mother on the cheek. 'Goodnight, Mum, and thanks for the chat.'

'Sleep well, darling.'

Mia locked the back door, turned out the lights and went upstairs. She stood in the dark at the open window in her bedroom and let her mind turn over the events of the day.

It was strange, but as her children were each reaching a major milestone in their lives – committing themselves to relationships and therefore growing away from her as was only right – she had never felt closer to them.

She looked down at the garden, to the barn and The Gingerbread House where a light glowed through the curtains. She thought of Daisy's act of pretending she and Scott were nothing more than friends and wondered how on earth she was going to break the news to Jeff in a manner that would minimize the fallout.

And would Jeff be right when he inevitably claimed that Daisy was too young to contemplate marriage? Or would it be the making of her, being in a permanent and steady relationship? Certainly no previous boyfriend had made sufficient impact on Daisy for her to so much as talk of love, never mind marriage. In fact, to Mia's knowledge, there had been no boyfriend who had lasted more than a month or two. The normal process had been for Daisy to say that she was seeing someone and then a week later to say it was over – this usually coincided with Jeff pestering to meet the boy in question.

Pushing aside her anxiety at telling Jeff about Daisy and Scott, she thought of Eliza and immediately felt another layer of anxiety wrap itself around her. She couldn't remember the last time Eliza had asked her for advice and she wondered now if she had said the right thing. What if honesty drove Greg away? What if Eliza then blamed Mia for losing the man she loved? No, she told herself firmly, it had been good advice. As she'd told her daughter, if honesty scared Greg off, then he clearly wasn't right for her.

She drew the curtains and went over to the bed, where she undressed and slipped on her nightdress. She then went into the bathroom and started to remove what little make-up she was wearing. She was patting her face dry after washing it when her thoughts turned to tomorrow and Owen's invitation to spend the afternoon with him. 'Are you sure about us all descending on you tomorrow?' she'd asked when she saw him to the front door after dinner, and he'd been thanking her for a great evening. 'You're quite at liberty to change your mind; we'll be quite a rabble.'

'I wouldn't have invited you if I wasn't sure,' he'd said. 'Goodnight then. Oh, and thank you for the torch. I should have thought to bring one with me.'

'That's all right. Take care.'

Getting into bed and switching off the light, Mia hoped Owen wouldn't have a change of heart overnight. There was something irresistibly enchanting about The Hidden Cottage and she was looking forward to seeing it again.

CHAPTER 22

'Owen, my friend, it's your lucky day! A quick jog along the A428 and I could be with you in the proverbial blink of the eye.'

'At the speed you drive I can believe it.'

'And you're sure it's OK for me to stay the night?'

'What's this, consideration from you, Rich? You're not having a midlife crisis, are you?'

'Nah, that's more your thing. Is there a decent pub in the village where we can go for lunch? Or should I, this side of civilization, try and pick something up on the way?'

'Not only is there a pub here that serves food, but we even have electricity, and there's a rumour that we'll be hooked up to the internet before too long.'

'Yeah, OK, funny man. Now how about you leave the wit to me and you go and get that guest room ready? Hey, and be sure to put a heart-shaped chocolate on my pillow.'

'I will, so long as you promise to behave this afternoon; I have friends coming.'

'Anyone I know?'

'No. These are *new* friends, hence the need for you to conduct yourself in an orderly fashion.'

'Not a chance in hell of that happening!'

They chatted for a few minutes more and after they'd ended the call, Owen smiled, pleased at the prospect of seeing Rich. They'd been friends since they were twelve years old and couldn't have been closer had they been brothers.

When Owen's father had been alive, he had forced the family to live a nomadic existence, uprooting them every time he fell out with an employer and lost his job. On his death, Owen and his mother were at last not just free of the tyranny of the man, but free to live a life that wasn't based on fear and secrecy. This meant that they could settle in one place and stop looking over their shoulders for fear that they had been found.

They were living in Basildon when they heard the news that Ron Fletcher was dead, that he had been living rough and had died of hypothermia. There had been no tears shed or words of remorse uttered from Owen's mother, only the promise that from now on there would be no more moves; they would be putting down roots – their days of taking flight were behind them. Trusting her, and believing they were now going to stay long enough in one place to make it worth his while to make a friend, Owen had allowed himself to get to know Rich, who was in the same class at school as him. Initially Owen had been wary, but after Rich had told him

207

about his father running off with the babysitter and not leaving a penny for the family, only debts, Owen had lowered his guard and confided in him about his own father. Very soon they became the best of friends, as did their mothers, who, both in the same boat, joined forces and started up a cleaning agency together.

All these years on, there wasn't a thing Rich and Owen didn't know about each other. What had always bound them together was the need not to turn out like their fathers and as a consequence they'd had a hunger to earn a ton of money. Whereas most of their contemporaries at school hadn't given a damn about exams or studying, Owen and Rich saw it as a way out of not exactly dire poverty, but a distinct lack of funds. Owen had his eye on going to university, but at sixteen Rich left school and went to work in the city as a trader assistant. By the time Owen had made it to LSE to study Economics and was paying his way by playing the piano in hotel bars, Rich was earning obscene amounts of money as a trader in his own right – it was Rich who put a word in for Owen at the bank where he worked when Owen graduated. In Owen's second year at university, Rich suggested he move in with him, since he'd just bought a two-bedroom flat. It was in that same year that Owen started going out with a fellow economics student he'd recently got to know at university; her name was Bea.

Rich had never been married; he frequently

claimed he'd never met the right woman. 'You mean nobody's been mad enough to take you on,' Owen would counter-claim. But Rich had just phoned from Cambridge implying he was there because of a woman. 'I'm not saying any more than that,' he'd said when Owen had demanded more information. 'You'll have to wait until I'm there for all the details.'

In turn Owen would have to tell Rich about Nicole. Although the person he actually wanted to talk about was Mia. There was something about her that intrigued him. He barely knew her but the more time he spent in her company, the more time he wanted to spend getting to know her.

Last night at Medlar House he was conscious that, whoever Jeff Channing was, he didn't seem to be much missed. In fact, the family seemed perfectly complete without the man. It reminded Owen of him and his mum – it had always felt right when it was just the two of them. When Dad had been present, they weren't themselves; they'd been guarded and in fear of the next verbal or physical outburst.

Owen would be the first to say that no one should define themselves by constantly referring to their partner, but he still thought it was odd that Mia hadn't previously mentioned her husband. And what about the absence of a ring? It was the first thing he'd looked for when he'd arrived at Medlar House last night, and lo and behold, there was a gold band on Mia's left hand. He'd swear it hadn't been there before. There again he hadn't mentioned anything about Nicole. But a four-month relationship didn't really compare to a marriage.

Before they'd gone to order their food from Mr Wu's van on the green, Mia had caught him looking at a family photograph. Pointing to the man at the centre of it, he'd said, 'Your husband?'

'Yes,' she'd replied. 'Jeff's away for the weekend; he'll be sorry to have missed you this evening. What can I get you to drink?'

That was the only reference she made to Jeff Channing. Which should have no more importance to Owen than what the weather was doing in Outer Mongolia, but it was another thing about Mia that intrigued him.

During the evening he'd watched her interacting with her family, particularly with the girl called Madison. There had been a quiet intensity to her when she spoke to the child, a way of making Madison feel that in that moment nobody interested her more. He could see it in the encouraging smile she gave Madison, the tilt of her head, the gentle warmth that exuded from her and which seemed tangibly to touch the girl. As absurd as it sounded, he had wanted to be on the receiving end of such focused attention.

A mind so rife with thoughts about a married woman was clearly not good. Thank God Rich was coming to stay. Ten minutes in Rich's company and he'd be brought back down to earth and put firmly on the straight and narrow again.

*   *   *

It soon became apparent that Rich wasn't in any fit state to bring Owen back down to earth – his own head was stuck way up in the clouds.

'I've finally met her,' he said after he'd arrived and had demanded a full tour of the house, garden and lake before settling on the veranda with a beer. 'I've met the future Mrs Lancaster, although of course she might well want to keep her own surname. I'd have no problem with that. No problem at all. Or she could combine the two. A double-barrelled wife is fine in my book.'

'*Whoa*, slow down, fella!' Owen said with amusement. 'Start at the beginning if you don't mind.'

Rich's face now took on the expression of a man who couldn't wait to tell his story. 'Her name's Catherine Carter and the moment I laid eyes on her, I knew. I just knew that the search was over. She's the woman I'm going to marry.'

With an excited gleam in his eye, Rich then went on to explain that he'd met Catherine in London three weeks ago at a mutual friend's dinner party and that they'd hit it off straight away. Phone calls, emails and text messages followed, along with dinners out and then she invited him to join her for a charity ball in Cambridge last night, which her parents had a hand in organizing.

'You've met the parents already?' Owen managed to interject.

'Her brothers as well. I've been thoroughly checked out.'

'So how come you're sitting here with me? Why aren't you still in Cambridge with her?'

'She's spending the day with her family and visiting an elderly relative. I'm going back to Cambridge tomorrow and then we'll head home for London.'

'And why are you so certain she's so right for you?'

Rich shrugged, then drank some more of his beer. 'I can't put it into words, I just know.'

'Do you think she feels the same way?'

He shrugged again and his expression became serious. 'I don't know. Not for sure. And that scares the crap out of me. I mean, what would she see in a bloke like me? She's gorgeous, and I'm, well, let's be frank, in a Shrek lookalike competition, I'd walk it.'

Owen smiled. He'd never known his friend to doubt himself or his ability. Not during any of the financial crises he'd lived through, or even back in 1987 when Black Monday saw 50 billion wiped off share values, had Rich wobbled. Owen had always joked that his friend's nerves weren't made of steel; they were crafted from tungsten carbide. But now it looked as if Superman had met his kryptonite.

They walked down into the village to the pub for lunch. Steak and chips ordered at the bar, along with a bottle of wine, they went back outside to the front of the pub and sat down at a table overlooking the green. The Parrs were there and gave Owen a friendly wave. As did another couple he recognized from the fete yesterday, but whose names he couldn't remember.

Owen poured their wine and decided it was his turn to fill Rich in on what he'd been up to since moving to Little Pelham. He told his friend about Nicole.

'Do you want my honest opinion on that?' Rich said.

'I'd expect nothing less.'

'I was always worried that she was only interested in you because of your financial situation.'

'Not my good looks, then? I'm gutted.'

Rich laughed. 'Sorry to burst that bubble of yours. But seriously, and more importantly, you're happy coming back here? It doesn't remind you too much of your father?'

'Oh, it was always going to do that. But the good memories far outweigh the bad ones.'

'You've got to admit, not that I'm siding with Nicole, it is bloody odd what you've chosen to do.'

Owen took a sip of his wine. 'It had to be done. When I saw that the house had come on the market, I had to buy it. And if it doesn't pan out, I can always sell up and move on somewhere else.'

'Do you think that's likely?'

Without realizing he'd done it, Owen's gaze had moved from the right to the left of the green, taking in the thatched cottages opposite before coming to rest on Medlar House. 'Who knows?' he said.

'How about the locals – anyone remember you?'

'A few, but it's the name they remember. Or rather, my father's name. I met someone yesterday I'd been at school with, not that I recognized him, but then we weren't what you'd call close friends thirty-four years ago.'

Rich turned and looked straight at him. 'And when you've had your fill of pottering about the new homestead, what will you do then?'

'I thought I might grow a beard.'

Rich looked at him over the top of his sunglasses. 'And when you've done that, what then?'

'I haven't made my mind up completely.'

'Which suggests to me you have something rattling around inside that head of yours. A new business venture perhaps?'

'There is something, but I'm not going to tell you what it is yet. All I'll say is that it won't be about making money. I've got enough to live comfortably for the rest of my life, I have no desire to flog myself like I used to.'

Rich smiled. 'A bearded altruist – who'd have thought it?'

Their food arrived and after they'd got themselves sorted with salt and pepper, mustard and vinegar, they got stuck in and minutes later they both agreed that the steak was excellent. Rich topped up their glasses. 'Tell me about the people who are coming this afternoon. Proper natives or incomers like you?'

'Not natives, but well established—' He broke off. Over to his right, hurtling down the lane with three carousing kids onboard and a noisy gang chasing behind, was the racing sofa he'd seen the day of his arrival.

Rich followed his gaze and laughed out loud. 'Bloody hell! That looks fun.'

The sofa came to a halt in the same place Owen had seen it run aground before and as before the children tumbled out onto the grass.

'Is it a village tradition?' Rich asked. 'Did you do it when you were here as a child?'

'Sadly no.'

'I'm telling you now, Owen, I have to have some of that action before I leave.'

Forty-five minutes later, their lunch eaten and paid for, it was all arranged. Having helped the children push the sofa back up the hill they were now being instructed on how best to ride it. The advice was enthusiastically given but wholly conflicting. Rich, however, was beyond listening; he just wanted to hit the thing fast and furious, like he did whenever they skied together. It said much of their friendship that skiing was the only time they pitched themselves against each other. Yet as they took up their positions, with Rich acting as lead man, Owen had the feeling that had they had another sofa to hand, they would have raced one another to the finishing line on the green.

Being so much bigger and heavier than the

children, it took all of the motley crew to get the sofa off the starting blocks. 'Come on, you guys,' Rich yelled at them, his head down, 'get your backs into it!'

And boy did they ever. Suddenly the sofa was shifting at speed, careering down the lane at a hell of a lick. Holding on tight, they hurtled faster and faster, cottages and tiny front gardens little more than a blur. Above the deafening noise of sofa wheels on tarmac, Owen could hear the cheers of encouragement from the kids running behind them. As they approached a bend in the narrowest part of the road and he and Rich instinctively leaned to the right, banking hard, they picked up even more pace and Owen began to wonder at the wisdom of what they were doing. This was madness on an unprecedented scale; they were too old for this kind of caper. But at the same time, he was enjoying the colossal rush of adrenaline.

God knew what speed they were doing when they hit the green, but suddenly they were catapulted out of the sofa and were flying through the air with equal speed. With an almighty thud, Owen landed on top of Rich and they both let out a shout that was part relief and part elation.

'You OK?' Owen asked his friend when he'd caught his breath. Some of the children had gathered around them; the others were righting the sofa.

'I will be when you get your foot out of my groin,' Rich replied in a strangled voice.

Laughing, they disentangled their legs and arms

from one another and rolled onto their backs on the grass. Owen could hear clapping. He turned his head towards the pub and saw that people were on their feet and leaning against the balustrade of the decking area. 'My reputation here has either just been made or destroyed,' he said.

Rich sat up and rubbed his shoulder. 'I don't suppose anyone took a picture of us, did they?'

'Give it five minutes and it'll be on YouTube,' Owen said with a laugh. Then glancing over towards the church and the clock on the tower, he saw what time it was. 'Uh-oh, we need to get home and plump up the cushions ready for my guests.'

'Don't suppose you could plump up my arse, could you? I think the stuffing's been knocked out of it.'

On his feet now, Owen put a hand out to Rich. 'Come on, old man, shift it.'

'Don't you want another go?' one of the boys asked.

'Ask us again when we've recovered,' Rich groaned as they limped across the green.

CHAPTER 23

While Owen poured drinks and passed them round on the veranda, Rich took up his God-given role as jovial *bon viveur* and regaled everyone with an exaggerated account of their sofa escapade.

'Heedless of life and limb and to the detriment of Owen's dignity, I was the one who talked him into it,' he told the group when he'd finished, 'so I must insist that if there are any accusations in the village of disreputable behaviour, they have to be laid fairly and squarely at my door and not Owen's.'

'To hell with any accusations,' Scott said. 'Jensen, I vote we get our own two-man bob team together and have a go ourselves.'

'Oh, no you don't,' Daisy said, swiping him playfully on the shoulder, 'I'm not having you coming to any harm when we have so much to do for our move to Sydney.'

Getting up from where they had been sitting on a blanket on the lawn, Madison and Beth approached the veranda. 'Owen,' Madison said, 'can we have a go in your boat now, please?'

Owen turned to Tattie. 'Is that OK with you?'

'Sure. But, girls, no messing about. You do exactly as Owen tells you. Right?'

Madison rolled her eyes and wobbled her head from side to side. 'Yes, *Mum.*' Next to her, Beth giggled.

'Or perhaps I should come with you, if you're not prepared to take me seriously?' Tattie said in a stern no-nonsense voice.

'Oh, Mu-*um.*'

'Don't worry,' Owen assured Tattie, 'I'll keep a good eye on them.' Then to the girls, he said, 'I'm the captain, OK? You do as I say at all times. And the first thing you have to do is give me a salute as befits my high-ranking position.'

He showed them how and they copied him perfectly, just managing to suppress a couple of sniggers.

He looked over to Rich. 'You're in charge up here. Keep the drinks flowing and the stories about me to the minimum.'

Rich laughed. 'Aye, aye, Captain Haddock.'

Owen led the girls down to the wooden jetty. 'Right,' he said, pulling the boat towards him, 'I'll get in first and then I'll help the two of you in.'

They nodded obediently and after he had them settled side by side on the seat at the stern, he untied the rope from around the post and pushed the boat away from the jetty with one of the oars.

'Is the water very deep?' Madison asked, once Owen had started to row.

'It varies,' he said. 'In places, nearer the bank, it's really shallow, about knee-high.' He pointed over towards the island. 'But there, it's much deeper and would probably cover the top of your head, which is why you mustn't do anything that might tip the boat over. Can you both swim?'

'Yes,' they said simultaneously.

'But not very well,' Madison admitted. 'I can only do one length of a big pool.'

'I'll let you into a secret,' Owen said. 'When I was your age I couldn't swim at all. It wasn't until I was thirteen that I learnt. It was Rich who taught me.'

'If I don't lean over too much, can I put my hand in the water?' Beth asked.

'Of course.'

'Is Rich your boyfriend? Is he going to come and live here with you?'

Owen laughed at Madison's question, mostly for the matter-of-fact way she'd asked it. Children today were so different from when he was growing up, so much more worldly. 'No,' he answered. 'Rich is my oldest friend. We were at school together. Would you like to go over to the island and see if we can find the heron who's a regular visitor here?'

On the jetty with his mother, having removed his shoes so he could dip his feet into the water, Jensen took a long, satisfying swig of his beer, then tipped his head back to enjoy the sun on his face. 'Thanks, Mum,' he said, turning to look at her.

'What for?'

'For this weekend. For making Madison feel so welcome. And for cheering her up.'

She smiled back at him. 'I haven't done anything.'

'You made it possible. Trouble is, I reckon it's going to be difficult to prise her away.'

'Do you have to rush back so soon? Can't you stay on for a few more days?'

'Unfortunately not. Tattie's got some bookings and I've got a client to meet on Tuesday.'

'That's a pity. But – and I know this is a long shot – as it's half-term you could always leave Madison here and come back for her later in the week. I'm sure Beth would love to see more of her. That's if Madison would like to stay on without her mother; she might not want to.'

Jensen laughed. 'Are you kidding? She's already been on at Tattie. Apparently Beth wants to have her for a sleepover so they can stay up late and do some star gazing.'

'Then why not see what Tattie says? But I'd quite understand if she felt she couldn't leave her daughter with someone she hardly knows.'

'You two talking about me?'

They both turned to see Tattie behind them. Jensen held out his hand, inviting her to sit next to him. 'Mum's come up with a genius idea.'

'But are you sure you'd manage?' Tattie said when Jensen had explained. 'You've got work to factor in.'

'I'll manage. Besides, I think Madison would enjoy helping me, don't you?'

'Look, Mum! I'm rowing!'

They looked over to where Madison was rowing towards them. '*Yay!*' Tattie called back to her with a wave. 'You go, girl!'

Jensen pulled out his mobile from his jeans pocket to take a photo. 'Hold it right there, Madison,' he called to her. 'Big smile. You too, Beth and Owen.'

Laughing, Tattie said, 'What do you mean, smile? She hasn't stopped smiling since she got here.'

The pictures taken, Jensen put his mobile away. 'So what do you think about Mum's offer?'

'I think it's a brilliant idea. But are you absolutely sure, Mia?'

'Yes, it'll be fun having her around. She's a real credit to you. You should be very proud of her.'

'I'd like to take the credit, but the truth is, she's a credit to no one but herself.'

Jensen put his arm around Tattie. 'Take the compliment or take the consequences.'

'What consequences?'

'You get pushed into the water.'

'Oh yeah, and what kind of example would that give Madison and Beth?'

'It would teach them to accept a compliment.'

Mia laughed. 'I'll leave you to bicker it out.'

She was on her feet when Owen brought the boat alongside the jetty.

'We saw a heron on the island,' Madison said excitedly. 'It had the longest legs and when it flew off, its wings were like *so* big.' She spread her arms out wide to show just how big and accidentally

222

biffed Beth on the nose. 'Oops, sorry,' she said and for no reason that Jensen could fathom, the two girls started to laugh.

'Oh no, they've reached the giggling loopy stage now,' Tattie said, 'which means it's time to get them back on terra firma.'

'Chuck us the rope, Owen,' Jensen said, now on his feet.

The dinghy securely tied, Owen passed Beth to Jensen, followed by Madison. Still laughing, and at Owen's instruction, the girls ran off up the garden to ask Rich for a drink.

In the peace and quiet they left behind them, Owen said, 'Anyone else care for a spin around the lake? How about you, Mia?'

'Oh, no, let someone else have a go.'

'Go on, Mum. Why not?'

'Yes, Mia,' joined in Tattie, 'you've done nothing but chase after us; it's time for you to enjoy yourself. Hang on, I'll go and get your glass of wine topped up, then you can really kick back.'

Jensen helped her into the boat and by the time she was seated, Tattie had returned with her refilled glass and a can of San Miguel for Owen. Throwing the rope to Owen, Jensen waved them off. 'Have fun,' he said, his arm around Tattie.

'I could get used to this,' Tattie said with a happy sigh as they watched Owen pull on the oars.

'Used to what?'

'This idyllic lifestyle. It's just so unbelievably perfect.'

Jensen turned and kissed her. 'Then maybe we should think about getting out of London. *Together.* You, me and Madison.'

She looked up into his eyes. 'Could we?' she whispered.

'We can do anything we want. *Anything.*'

And standing there in the arms of the woman he loved, the sun shining down on them, Jensen had never felt happier or surer about a thing than he did right then.

CHAPTER 24

As Owen rowed them away from the jetty, Mia saw that further up the garden Rich and Scott were kneeling on the long grass so that Madison and Beth could climb onto their backs. Daisy then began pointing where they had to stand and indicated the opposite side of the garden where, with one hand raised in the air, Eliza stood in front of a sprawling rhododendron bush vibrant with pink flowers.

'Looks like a race of some sort is about to start,' Mia said.

'I guarantee Rich wins,' Owen said, pausing with the oars and holding them against his legs.

'Ready, steady, *GO!*' Daisy shouted in a voice so loud Jensen and Tattie turned to see what was going on.

Sure enough, Rich was first to reach Eliza and as soon as Madison had slapped her hand against Eliza's, he was heading back to Daisy and singing 'We Are The Champions'. Bouncing on his back, her head bobbing wildly up and down, Madison waved to her mother and Jensen who joined in with the laughter and happy cheers. The clamouring exuberance of their antics on the lawn contrasted extravagantly with the serenity of the lake.

'You know your friend well,' Mia said.

Owen laughed. 'I certainly do. Rich always plays to win.' He started rowing again, each stroke creating a shower of droplets that fell like sparkling diamonds in the bright sunlight.

Leaning over the side of the boat, Mia let her hand trail in the cool water. With the sound of birdsong filling the air, she closed her eyes and listened contentedly to the languid splish-splash of the oars. Then aware that Owen had stopped rowing, she opened her eyes and found he was staring directly at her. Self-conscious, she sat up straighter and shook the water from her hand.

'What were you thinking just then?' he asked. 'You looked very relaxed.'

'I was thinking how wonderful this is. If I lived here I don't think I'd ever want to leave.'

'I feel much the same.' He started rowing again, taking them round to the back of the small island that was densely overgrown with trees and bushes. She twisted her neck and saw that the house was now out of sight.

Once again Owen stopped rowing and letting the boat drift, he pointed to the island. 'You'll probably think I'm crazy, but I want to build a summerhouse on it. Call it a folly, if you will, but I want it to be a symbolic place of escape.'

Imagining how good it would be to have her

own island to escape to, Mia cast her gaze about her. 'Isn't all this escape enough?' she said.

'Can you have too much escapism?'

The boat turned slowly so she was now facing into the sun. She put a hand to her brow to shield her eyes to look at him. 'Needing somewhere to escape implies that you feel trapped or that you're running away from something. Are you?'

'That would be an obvious conclusion to reach, but strange as it may seem, I'm not. Actually what I'm doing, and I've only recently realized this, is that I'm actually running *to* something.'

'Do you know what it is?'

Seconds passed, during which he seemed lost in thought. 'Yes,' he said simply. 'Yes I do.' He began rowing again, inviting no further comment, leaving her instead with the tantalizing wish to know more. But sensing he might think she was prying, she let it go. 'What other plans do you have for the lake?' she asked, playing safe with a less personal question.

'Just lots of general maintenance and perhaps I'll have a new jetty installed,' he answered. 'I don't think I need to do anything about attracting more wildlife; it seems to be doing well enough without my interference.'

Watching a dragonfly skimming the surface of the water, she said, 'I've lived in the village all these years and while I knew of the house, I had no idea just how beautiful it was here.'

'Missing what's right under our noses is often the way, isn't it? I used to sneak in here as a child.'

'Really?'

'I'll tell you about it one day.'

'Not now?'

'No. Another time.'

She laughed. 'You're a very infuriating man, you know that, don't you? You feed me these intriguing little titbits only to leave me wondering.'

He laughed too. 'I'm just trying to make myself sound more fascinating than I really am.'

Oh, I think you're plenty fascinating, she thought. Determined to learn something more about him, she said, 'So how come you've moved here on your own? Being such a *fascinating* man, I can't believe you don't have a significant other in your life.'

'Ah, well, therein lies another story. There was somebody, but Friday night, after I'd dropped the books off for the fete with you, she blew me out. Not that the two things are connected,' he added with a short laugh.

'Oh, I'm so sorry. Now I feel awful for blundering in like that.'

'No need to apologize. It was my own fault; I acted selfishly and deserved what I got.'

Thinking he didn't seem the selfish kind – but then nobody knew better than she did that appearances could be deceiving – Mia said, 'Were you together for long?'

'Not really, we only met in January. So no hearts broken. Just one of those things.'

Wondering if he was putting a brave face on the break-up, or if he genuinely wasn't bothered, Mia sipped some more of her wine. Then staring into the distance, to the far side of the lake where a fallen tree was lying half-submerged in the water, she found herself hoping that Owen wouldn't tidy the lake up too much, that he would allow nature to add her own unique charm.

'Tell me about Mr Channing.'

She looked at him, surprised. 'What do you want to know?'

'I'm curious to know what sort of man he is. I'm also curious why you don't wear your wedding ring all the time.'

Glancing at her left hand and her wedding band, she said, 'But I do.'

'No you don't, not all the time.'

'Goodness,' she said, instinctively on her guard and affecting an air of amused nonchalance, 'what strange things are of interest to you. Are you sure you don't have too much time on your hands?'

Without answering her, and using just the one oar, he steered the boat round the curve of the bank, narrowly missing an overhanging tree branch. When they were some way clear of the branch, he stopped rowing and with his eyes fixed on her, he said, 'I wish there was a way of saying this that wouldn't cause offence, but the trouble is, I find everything about you is of interest to me. You're a very interesting woman.'

She tensed. 'If this is what passes for fun for

you,' she said in a quietly measured voice, 'I don't think you should say any more.'

'You think I'm teasing you?'

'I think it's possible that you've just been dumped by your girlfriend and now you feel the need to reinflate your squashed ego by flirting with the first woman to hand.'

'Ouch,' he said with a frown. 'You don't think you're being overly sensitive to what was meant as a compliment?'

She met his gaze full on. 'Was it meant as a compliment?'

'Yes. A risky one, I'll admit. But I really meant no harm by it. All I wanted to do was . . . oh, hell, I don't know what I hoped to achieve. But it certainly wasn't this. You look so incredibly angry with me.'

His sincerity both touched and alarmed her. A sloppy drunken flirt with predictable chat-up lines she could deal with, but a sober and contrite man whose company she enjoyed was a different matter. Especially as lurking not so very far beneath her innate sense of propriety was a stirring of something that had no right to be stirred. As if reminding herself of its presence and significance, she looked down at her wedding ring. 'The reason you saw me without my ring,' she said, feeling compelled to make the point, 'was because I was bitten on my finger last weekend by a gnat and the ring was rubbing against the swelling and making it worse.'

He glanced at her hand. 'Is it better now?'

'Yes, thank you,' she said. This was good. Now he was behaving himself; now there'd be no more silly talk from him.

'I'm sorry,' he said. 'Not for your finger, but for offending you. Although, I am sorry about your finger as well. Very sorry. Bites are nasty things. I once had a mosquito bite on my nose. My God, you wouldn't believe how awful I looked. Children would laugh and point – they were the brave ones; the terrified ones ran off screaming into the night never to be seen again. I was reduced to walking around with a bag on my head like the Elephant Man.'

A small laugh burst out of her. Followed by another.

'You find the single most humiliating moment in my life funny, do you?'

She laughed some more.

'You're a cruel woman.'

And you're a very dangerous man, she thought when she had her laughter under control.

'I'm going to be perfectly honest with you,' he said, his face now serious. 'When I moved back here, I told myself to expect the unexpected, but never did I think I'd meet someone as unexpected as you.'

She stared at him helplessly. What could she possibly say? 'I'm sorry if I've given you any cause to think . . .' her words trailed off.

'To think what?'

She thought of her conversation with Eliza last night. 'If I've given you any misleading signals.'

'You can put your mind at rest on that score; the fault is all mine. But just so you know, I'm not some sort of lecherous philanderer. Far from it. I really don't make a habit of making declarations of this sort to women I've only just met. And I apologize unreservedly for upsetting you. Just accept that I'm an idiot who can't keep his mouth shut when he should. Will you promise me something?'

She nodded.

'For the sake of my self-respect, which has just reached an all-time low, will you try and forget we ever had this conversation?'

'Forgotten as of now,' she said with as much conviction as she could manage.

It was an out and out lie. She knew she wouldn't be able to forget what he'd said. Because already the siren voice of temptation was whispering in her ear – *What would it take to believe he was serious and do the unthinkable?*

It wasn't often that Owen could reduce his friend to stunned silence, but he certainly had now. An hour had passed since his guests had all left and so it was just the two of them sitting on the veranda. In silence.

Finally Rich spoke. 'Just to clarify matters,' he said, 'forty-eight hours after breaking up with Nicole you're coming on to another woman, and not just any woman, but a married woman who is a neighbour. What. The. Hell. Were. You. Thinking?'

232

'All right, no need to labour the point that I cocked up spectacularly. I get it. It was a stupid thing to do.'

'Stupid doesn't come close, Owen. You might just as well pack up now and leave because you've completely blown your chances of being happy here. How soon before Mia tells someone what you said and word goes round? More to the point, what's to stop her from telling her husband?'

'She won't.'

'Oh yeah? How can you be so sure?'

Owen shrugged. 'It's just a feeling I have. She doesn't seem the sort to go running to her husband. Or to indulge in tittle-tattle. Especially about herself.'

Rich gave him a withering look. 'You'd better hope you're right or your days of being happy here are seriously numbered.'

Owen stared morosely down the garden to the lake. Rich was right on all counts. And the worst of it was he really couldn't explain what madness had taken hold of him. All he knew was that something extraordinary had happened when he'd been alone in the boat with Mia. He knew that attraction could hit at any time and in the strangest of ways, but never before had he felt it as powerfully as he had when Mia had tilted her face up to the sun and closed her eyes. Such a simple and spontaneously innocent gesture, but one that had stopped him in his tracks. And led him to sitting here in total misery.

How was he ever going to convince Mia that he wasn't the contemptible chancer she clearly now believed him to be? Oh yes, she'd behaved impeccably for the rest of the afternoon, but not once did she look him in the eye again. Frankly, she looked like she couldn't wait to get away. And who could blame her?

CHAPTER 25

As far as Jeff could see he might just as well be invisible – nobody listened to a word he said, never mind cared about his opinion. To cheer himself up, he decided he'd get a newspaper from Parr's and then settle himself in the garden with a beer. He'd get a pork pie as well. He hadn't had one of those in ages. That would definitely hit the spot.

But when he pushed open the door at Parr's and found the place chock-full, he was hit with yet a further blast of annoyance. Because there, at the front of the queue holding everyone up while Windolene Wendy fawned over him, was Owen Fletcher. It was about a month since he'd moved here and there seemed to be no escape from him. All Jeff heard these days was Owen Fletcher this, Owen Fletcher that. He couldn't talk to anyone in the village without being told what a great addition he was to Little Pelham, how he'd rolled up his sleeves and mucked in at the fete; how he'd given Georgina a hand with a problem she'd had with her computer; how he'd made a generous contribution to the village hall fund to put in a new toilet and modernize the kitchen. Closer to home, the man had even offered to give Tattie's daughter piano lessons when she was around. And if Jeff had heard it once about Owen bloody Fletcher's sofa-racing antics, he'd heard it a million times. The man was clearly a show-off. The kind of man who went out of his way to attract attention to himself, to enhance his image and social standing for his own ends. He'd soon learn that that sort of behaviour wouldn't wash. Not in the long run. People might be taken in now, but they would soon tire of him. That's if the more astute members of the village weren't already seeing through his act of Mr All-Round-Nice-Guy.

Jeff had only spoken to Little Pelham's newest inhabitant on one occasion, three weeks ago when he'd returned from his trip to Dubai, when he'd bumped into Owen Fletcher outside the DIY shop in Olney. He'd spotted the green E-Type with its pretentiously personalized number plate of OWE1, and seeing its owner about to open the driver's door as Jeff pulled in behind, he had decided to approach and introduce himself. 'Ah, so you're Jeff Channing,' the man had said.

'The one and only,' Jeff had said back. 'How are you liking village life? Not too quiet for you?'

'No not at all; it's suiting me very well.'

'I suppose you knew what to expect, having lived here as a boy.'

'More or less.'

'So what do you do? What's your line of work?'

'I do as little as possible. I sold up my business and came here to live as stress-free a life as I can manage.'

Smug git, Jeff had thought when Owen had driven off.

He thought the same now as he joined the queue to pay for his paper and pork pie and watched Owen through the window where he was now outside on the pavement talking to Joe Coffey. Apparently they'd been at school together here in the village and Joe was building a summerhouse for Owen up at The Hidden Cottage. Jeff wondered how that was going down – old school pals and one of them now working for the other. If Owen wasn't the thoroughly irritating man he was – a supposed paragon of altruism – Jeff would warn him that Joe had a habit of over-charging for any work he did. But in this instance, Joe could rip the client off as much as he wanted.

'All right, Mr Channing?'

Jeff turned away from the window and realized that he was now at the front of the queue and was on the receiving end of Wendy's sugary-pink smile. 'That's a nice new range of pork pies we're doing,' she said, indicating the pie in his hand. 'Only just started with them last week, but they've been flying off the shelves. You won't be disappointed, I guarantee it.' Wendy had one of those grating accents that in Jeff's opinion made her sound a bit simple. She pronounced new as *noo* and every time she said it, he itched to correct her. He never did though. Adopting the friendly voice he always did with her, he said, 'Morning, Wendy, how are you?'

'Couldn't be better,' she beamed. 'Anything nice planned for the weekend,' she asked, 'other than having Jensen home?'

'Having him home is pleasure enough,' he lied.

Joe had disappeared when Jeff shut the shop door behind him, but now Muriel was deep in conversation with Owen. 'Jeff!' she called out. 'Owen's just come up with a marvellous idea.'

'Oh yes,' Jeff said. What now? Had the man discovered a cure for cancer? 'What's that then?' he asked.

'It's about the talent show,' Muriel said, 'Owen's suggested an excellent way to bring it bang up to date. Go on, Owen, you tell Jeff.'

Owen smiled. 'I just thought that maybe you could rebrand the evening and call it Little Pelham's Got Talent.'

Perfect, thought Jeff, talk about a god complex – now he thought he was Simon bloody Cowell! For the last few years Jeff had been the compere for the annual show, the most important role in his view; it was he who kept the evening from sliding into chaos, and who occasionally, when the acts were really poor, generated the most laughs. 'I wasn't aware that it needed updating,' he said.

Muriel laughed. 'We all need updating now and then, Jeff. Right, I'll be off then. Have a good weekend you two. Cheerio.'

Left standing alone with Owen, Jeff said, 'I think

you'll find that some of the longstanding stalwarts of the talent show are more resistant to change than Muriel.'

The man gave a maddening little shrug. 'It was just a suggestion. Nothing more. The last thing I'd want to do is tread on anyone's toes. Are you on your way home?'

'Yes.'

'Me too. I'll walk with you.'

Jeff forced himself to smile, all matey geniality.

They fell in step and walked in the direction of Medlar House. 'What's the latest on Daisy's move to Australia?' he asked.

In a single stroke, Jeff's forced air of smiling matey geniality was gone. Who the hell was this man to enquire about Daisy? How dare he poke his nose into what was entirely a private matter. 'Nothing new to report,' he said coolly, grateful that they had now reached Medlar House.

He was just turning in to the drive when Owen said, 'Tell Madison I'll see her tomorrow morning. That's if she still wants a lesson.'

Tell her yourself, Jeff thought as he went round to the back of the house. What was he now, a ruddy messenger boy?

Parked next to the barn there were two cars he didn't recognize, probably hat customers for Mia.

In the kitchen he put the bottle opener into his pocket, helped himself to two bottles of beer from the fridge and went back outside, to the area of the garden at the side of the house that

239

wasn't overlooked by the barn or The Gingerbread House.

Sitting in the sun, his beer opened, his newspaper unfolded, he bit with determined relish into the pork pie. This was more like it. This would help to get his weekend back on track. God knew he needed something to improve his mood. Because ever since he'd returned from his trip to Dubai everything had gone downhill.

He still couldn't believe that Daisy had lied to him. That she had been lying to him for some months. All that rubbish about her wanting to go to Australia as some kind of adventure she felt in need of had only been half the story.

Marriage. Unbelievable. How could she even contemplate marrying a man ten years older than her? A man they hardly knew. And to think that Jeff had thought he could trust Scott to take care of Daisy, to look out for her. How wrong he'd been.

The shock of what Daisy had done – keeping the truth from him, and such a truth! – cut so deep that he hadn't been able to bring himself to speak to her for several days. When he'd thought he could trust himself to speak without losing his temper, he'd called her from Brussels. 'Sweetheart, I just don't understand why you kept this from me,' he'd said. 'Why did you do it? Is it because deep down you know it's wrong, that you know you're making a huge mistake?'

'Dad,' she'd said, 'I'm sorry it's happened the

way it has, but I didn't tell you because you always think you know what's best for me. You never trust me to make my own decisions.'

'That's not true. Not true at all. But listen, if you have to go to Australia, go, just don't rush into getting married. Take things slowly. One thing at a time. And if it doesn't work out in Sydney, you can come back. No one will say, "I told you so," I promise you.'

'Please, why don't you try listening to me, Dad? I'm not rushing into this. It's not like Scott and I are getting married overnight. I know what I'm doing and that it's right for *me*.'

'You thought starving yourself to death was the right thing to do not so long ago.' As soon as the words were out, he'd known he'd blown it.

'Cheap shot, Dad,' she'd said, 'even by your standards.' She'd then hung up on him, before he'd had a chance to apologize.

Kicking himself, he'd hit redial, but she hadn't answered. She didn't later that evening either. Nor the next day. That was nearly three weeks ago. Too ashamed, he hadn't admitted to Mia what he'd said, saying only that Daisy was refusing to speak to him. Mia's advice was to give Daisy time and space, which seemed to be her panacea for all family problems.

It wasn't just Daisy's betrayal that upset him; it was Mia's as well. She had known for some days about Daisy and Scott and not told him. 'I didn't want to tell you over the phone,' she'd said.

'Knowing how it would upset you, I thought it would be better to tell you when you were home.'

Yet more rubbish. She had deliberately withheld the information from him, had deliberately excluded him from the single most important decision of Daisy's life, a decision that would lead to her making the biggest mistake of her young life. And it was a mistake. He knew it. Marriage shouldn't ever be rushed into. That was why he'd taken his time with Mia – he simply hadn't been ready. He didn't believe anyone was ready until they were nearer thirty than twenty. Marriage when you were too young could only ever end in divorce. No one knew what they really wanted until they'd got some life experience under their belt.

He sighed and took a long draw on his beer. He wished he knew what the hell it was Mia wanted these days. OK, they'd had their moments in the past when they'd had their disagreements, but as far as he could see she seemed intent on pulling in the opposite direction for no good reason other than to be difficult. First her refusal to move to Brussels with him, and now this Daisy and Scott business.

He screwed up the paper bag that had contained his pork pie and drank some more of his beer, thinking how behind his back everything was suddenly changing, with no one seeking his opinion on the matter. It was as if he didn't count.

For the last fortnight Eliza had been spending

Monday to Thursday living back at home while she worked on a new project in Milton Keynes and now Jensen and his girlfriend had some half-baked notion to leave London and move to Little Pelham. They were here now for the weekend, staying in The Gingerbread House while house-hunting.

During dinner last night Tattie had been full of talk about wanting to give Madison a more child-friendly upbringing than the one London could offer. There had also been much talk of the convenience of their work enabling them to live out of London; all they needed was the internet and a reliable train service. To Jeff's ears it sounded like a lot of head-in-the-clouds thinking.

Mia seemed to think this latest turn of events put paid to his theory that Jensen was merely using Tattie to get back at him. He wasn't convinced. He wouldn't put anything past Jensen, not when the boy had a history of lying and stealing from him. Whenever he reminded Mia of the credit card Jensen had taken from his wallet to rack up a bill over the phone for three hundred quid's worth of computer games, she always said the same: 'He was sixteen, Jeff. He was young and not thinking straight and he's apologized many times over to you for what he did. Now let it go.'

Jensen could apologize till his last breath and Jeff wouldn't let it go, for the simple fact he didn't believe his son was capable of a genuine act of contrition when it came to him.

Something else Jeff didn't understand was Mia's disproportionate fondness for Madison. It was a mistake for them to get too attached, because when – not if, but *when* – it all went pear-shaped, it would be harder still for the girl to cope with the break-up if she saw Mia as a surrogate grandmother.

He couldn't help but think that for all Mia's eagerness to analyse a problem into submission, in this instance he seemed to be the only one who was evaluating the situation and seeing the mess that lay ahead. But since no one was asking him for his opinion, all he could do was sit back and let them comprehensively screw things up. He supposed then they'd come crying to him to sort it all out.

He shook his head. His weekends weren't supposed to be like this. When he'd taken on the job in Brussels he'd imagined he would arrive home on Friday evening and have Mia all to himself – that life, now that the children had left home, would be all about the two of them spending time alone together and enjoying themselves. Not for a second had he thought he'd be vying for his wife's attention, squeezed out by a blasted nine-year-old girl.

Nor did he imagine that Daisy would be refusing to speak to him.

Where had it all gone wrong?

And why was it only he who could see things so clearly?

CHAPTER 26

While washing up their lunch things, Daisy glanced every now and then over her shoulder to where Scott was stripping the bookshelves in the sitting area. Her visa was now sorted, their flights were booked, but watching him carefully place their things into packing boxes, which would be shipped to Sydney ahead of their departure, made the move seem so much more of a reality. They were really going.

As the days passed and their leaving date grew ever nearer – only thirty-three days to go now – Scott's excitement grew exponentially. He would be the first to say that he had thoroughly enjoyed his time in England, but Daisy knew that Australia was home for him; it was where his roots were, where his family was and the friends he'd grown up with. She liked knowing that she was soon going to be a part of that world, a world that was his and which he assured her she would love. But really, she would be happy wherever she was, so long as she was with Scott.

The last of the cutlery washed, she pulled the

plug out and let the water drain away; she dried her hands and slipped on the engagement ring Scott had surprised her with two weeks ago. 'I was going to wait until we were in Sydney,' he'd explained, 'and, you know, make a big symbolic thing of it, get down on one knee and formally ask you to marry me. I had it all worked out, I was going to take you for a cruise around the harbour and pop the question.'

'What made you change your mind?'

He'd grinned. 'I couldn't wait.'

'I'm glad you didn't,' she'd said. 'Go on, put it on my finger for me. Do it properly.'

Looking at the solitaire ring now, and turning her hand so the diamond twinkled in the light coming through the window, she experienced a thrill of anticipation for the life that awaited her. All the baggage she'd carried, she would leave behind. It was her chance to start life afresh, to be the person she wanted to be.

'Hey, look what I've just found,' Scott called to her. 'I wondered where it had got to. Do you remember I said I couldn't find it last Christmas?'

She turned to see him holding a snow globe – contained within it was an Aussie-style Santa wearing sunglasses and cut-off shorts and carrying a surfboard on his shoulder. An old friend of Scott's in Sydney had sent it to him when he'd first moved to England. 'Make sure you pack it safely,' she said with a fond smile. 'Fancy a cup of coffee?'

'That would be great.'

Filling the kettle, she had an unexpectedly vivid memory of the moment she stopped believing in Father Christmas. She had been seven years old and it was the start of the Christmas school holidays and she, Eliza and Jensen were with Mum shopping for new fairy lights. Seeing the entrance to Santa's Grotto at the local garden centre, Daisy had pestered to be taken inside, but Mum had said they didn't have time. Though suspecting it wasn't the real Santa in the garden centre grotto, Daisy was clued up enough to know that you didn't come out empty-handed – the previous year she'd been given a pack of felt tip pens. Eager to see what was on offer this year, she pestered until Mum finally raised her voice and told her to be quiet, at which point she began to cry.

Until then Eliza and Jensen had been doing what they always did, rolling their eyes and looking bored. When her crying grew louder, Jensen taunted her with a nasty laugh, which was invitation enough for Daisy to kick him on the shin. He'd glared at her – he never hit her back, because if he did, Dad would go berserk – but Eliza had come to his defence, as she usually did, and said, 'You always have to spoil everything don't you? And if you weren't such a stupid cry-baby, you'd know there's no such thing as Father Christmas, so there's no reason for you to go into the grotto where it's just some silly old man in a silly red suit wearing a silly fake beard made of cotton wool

247

giving out silly presents made in China.' Ten years old and her sister had sounded so infuriatingly grown up.

With people now looking on at them, Daisy had instantly stopped crying and said that of course she'd known all the time that Father Christmas didn't really exist. No way was she going to let her brother and sister think she didn't have a Scooby Doo about anything, or that she wasn't as smart as them.

In contrast to that crystal-clear memory, she couldn't remember the exact moment when she stopped believing in the myth that was her father, or to be precise, when she stopped worshipping him. She supposed it had crept up on her, a slow realization that he wasn't the perfect superman she'd believed him to be. Or wanted him to be. Hand in hand with that realization came a gradual sense of disappointment, combined with a massive awareness of her frustration that she could do nothing in her own right, nothing that wasn't fully endorsed by Dad. She had felt utterly trapped, like a butterfly kept in a glass jar. As she'd later learnt through the help of a counsellor, she had made herself ill as a way to seize control, to release herself from the glass jar. But, of course, all she'd done was replace one trap with another.

Her father's words – *You thought starving yourself to death was the right thing to do not so long ago* – had hit her as physically as though he'd struck her. She had hardly been able to bring herself to tell

Scott what he'd said and had only done so because he was so concerned for her – apparently she had been shaking and the colour had literally drained from her face when she'd ended the call. Furious, Scott had insisted she switch off her mobile for the next twenty-four hours so that she couldn't be further upset or bullied into talking to Dad. The following morning he had been all for speaking to her father himself, but by then she had calmed down and said that they would speak to him together, just not now; she wasn't ready. She knew she was being a coward, but she couldn't help it. Scott had suggested she tell her mother what Dad had said, in the hope she might be able to talk some sense into him, but Daisy didn't want to drag her mother into it. This was strictly between Dad and her; it wasn't Mum's problem. They had spoken quite a bit on the phone in the last few weeks, and Mum had asked her straight out what had gone on between her and Dad, but she'd kept quiet, knowing that if she told Mum the truth, it would only lead to more trouble.

Nearly three weeks on and Daisy knew, for her own sanity, and for Mum's sake, that she had to put things right with Dad before she left for Sydney. To do that, she had to find the courage to talk to him.

The weird thing was, and she couldn't really get her head round this, was that while at times Dad made her feel stifled and angry by his over-powering love for her, a part of her still wanted to please him and gain his approval, just as she had when she'd been little.

She might not be able to fully comprehend why that was, but what she did understand was that her father's refusal to accept her as an adult stopped her from being the person she wanted to be. Only with Scott did she feel that she was truly herself. As he'd once said, love was supposed to set you free, not hold you captive.

'You OK?'

She turned away from the kettle, which she'd forgotten all about plugging in and found Scott standing behind her. 'Just thinking,' she said.

He smiled that slow, reassuring smile of his, the one that always made her think everything was going to be all right.

CHAPTER 27

Sunday morning and Eliza was at Heathrow airport. The arrivals hall was surprisingly busy, given that it was so early, only a quarter to seven.

Serene's flight from Singapore was due in the next ten minutes, and factoring in the time it would take for her friend to pass through passport control and retrieve her luggage, Eliza reckoned she just had time to satisfy her rumbling stomach with some breakfast. She queued for a croissant and a cappuccino, eschewing the bucket-sized option in favour of a normal cup, and found a table that gave her a view of a screen with its rolling flight information.

Being here made her think of Greg, of the travelling he did and the many airports he passed through. She knew from the little she did that air travel was not in the slightest bit fun or exciting when it was done on a regular basis. During his last visit Greg hadn't been his usual self and had fallen asleep on the sofa while she'd been getting supper ready. He'd been sleeping so soundly she hadn't had the heart to wake him and so had eaten her supper alone and watched the television with the sound turned down low. When he'd finally woken, he'd apologized, saying that he was shattered. She'd kissed him and said, 'That much was obvious.'

That had been last weekend and for the two nights that he'd stayed with her there had been a subtle tension between them, a strain that left her feeling flat and disappointed.

He'd left early Monday morning, shortly before she'd caught the train for work up in Milton Keynes with Simon. 'So how was your weekend with Lover Boy?' Simon had asked her after he'd returned from the buffet car with a paper carrier bag of coffee and shortbread biscuits. With her virtually paranoid need to keep her private and work life separate, Simon was the only one at work with whom she discussed anything remotely personal.

'I've told you before, don't call him Lover Boy,' she'd said. 'His name's Greg.'

'Ooh, snappy, snappy,' Simon had replied, passing her coffee and biscuits to her. 'Does that mean it wasn't a good weekend?'

'It means if you had any sense you'd back off and leave me alone.'

'In that case you'd better have my biscuits as well as yours; you need sweetening up. No way am I spending the day working with you when you're in such a foul mood.'

'My mood was fine until you started on at me. Now drink your coffee and be quiet.'

'Bossy as well as snappy. I can see I'm in for a helluva day. I'm so glad I'm not stuck in a hotel all week with you.'

'I never knew you could be so annoying.'

He smiled. 'Yeah, you did; I'm the one big constant in your life. So for the sake of our excellent working relationship, tell me what Lover— I mean, Greg did at the weekend to upset you.'

Reluctantly, just to get Simon off her case, she'd explained. 'It's my fault,' she'd said quickly, not wanting to appear as though she was whingeing, 'I know it is. We spend so little time together, that when we do, I expect too much.'

'Long-distance relationships aren't the easiest,' Simon had said, stirring his coffee. 'But the guy needs to shape up, in my opinion; you deserve better. Tell him straight, Eliza, you're a woman with needs that need satisfying. Some old bloke dozing on the sofa ain't gonna cut the mustard. No, siree. You need to find someone your own age.'

'A little louder,' she'd hissed. 'I don't think they heard you four coaches up.'

Checking the screen – Serene's flight had just landed – Eliza had since decided that for all Simon's flippancy, he was basically saying the same as Mum: she had to make her feelings clearer to Greg. And if they did take their relationship to the next level and planned to be together more permanently, which one of them would move to be with the other? She really couldn't imagine giving up her job, but if push came to shove, if it was that or lose Greg, she would do it.

Thinking about Greg, she dug out her iPhone to check her emails, to see if he'd sent her a message. He'd been on his way yesterday afternoon to San Francisco for a meeting with a new start-up company. To her delight, he'd been in touch. She read his email and smiled – *You know you're in San Francisco when the stranger in the lift with you says he has eight body piercings. And none of them visible. ? Hope your weekend with your friend is going well. X*

She put her mobile away, finished her croissant and thought how much she was looking forward to seeing Serene. It was a shame her friend's visit would be so short, but it was very much a last-minute arrangement with Serene managing to squeeze a few days out of her busy itinerary to see Eliza on her way to Barcelona for a trade fair.

Her coffee finished, Eliza went to find herself a good vantage point from which she would be able to spot Serene's arrival. She had just slung her bag over her shoulder when she did a double take. Telling herself she was imagining things, she stared across the concourse to where a steady stream of arrivals was spilling out, some of them looking around for a familiar face or a placard with their name written on it, the luckier ones meeting with an immediate hug and a kiss from a loved one. You are *so* imagining things, she told herself again.

But she wasn't. It *was* him!

Almost as if her feet had registered this knowledge before her brain, she began moving towards him, dodging around people and trolleys laden with luggage, her gaze fixed on his face as he stared straight ahead, unaware of her and her joy at seeing him so unexpectedly. He must have had a last-minute change of schedule and was actually planning to surprise her. A pity she was going to spoil his surprise, but what were the odds of her actually being here in the airport when he flew in?

She was close enough now to call out his name and she was on the verge of doing so when a small child rushed forward. 'Daddy!' the little boy shouted, flinging himself at Greg's legs with such force he took a step back. 'Steady on there,' Greg laughed, 'or you'll have us both over.' He leant down and picked the boy up and kissed him. 'Have you been good while I was away?'

The boy nodded solemnly, his eyes wide. He was impossibly cute. 'I've been very good, haven't I, Mummy?'

Eliza's heart was pounding wildly, her mouth was dry, and a voice was screaming inside her head, *No, no, no, this can't be happening!* She wrenched her gaze from Greg and looked at 'Mummy', who was now leaning in for a kiss and a hug. She was a pretty, petite woman with a glossy

255

bob of dark brown hair, the same colour as the boy's, and there next to her was a pushchair with a baby fast asleep in it.

Eliza felt physically sick. And having been rooted to the spot with shock and disbelief, her feet once again took charge and she backed away, a hand clasped to her mouth. Her eyes brimming with tears, she stumbled through the crowd, bashing blindly into people, not caring that they were tutting or giving her filthy looks.

She saw the sign for the Ladies', burst through the door and locked herself into one of the cubicles. She retched and retched and when it was over, she flushed the toilet and leant back against the door clammy and weak with exhaustion. She squeezed her eyes shut. He was a father. And very probably a husband. Why? Why had he done it? All those lies. All those times they'd lain in bed together and he'd said he loved her. What had it all been about?

From somewhere she could hear the sound of a phone ringing. It took her a while to realize it was her mobile. She grabbed it from inside her bag and her immediate response was to hope it was Greg calling her. The thought was enough to make her sick all over again.

But it was Serene. Oh God, she'd forgotten all about her! 'I've arrived,' her friend said.

'Sorry,' she managed to say, 'I'll be with you in five minutes.'

'Fine, no worries.'

She rang off quickly and unlocked the cubicle door. She went to the row of basins and splashed water onto her face, summoning all her willpower to compose herself.

She was drying her face with a paper hand towel when the door opened and a child's cheerful sing-songy voice said, 'Will Daddy help me build my marble run when we get home?'

Eliza froze.

'Perhaps not straight away,' a woman's voice replied, 'but later on, when he's had a little nap and recovered from his long flight, I'm sure he will.' Leading him towards a cubicle, the woman – 'Mummy' – caught Eliza's eye and smiled.

Eliza saw a flash of rings on her wedding ring finger and wanted to die.

Of shame and humiliation.

Of abject misery.

Unable to return the smile, she wrenched the door open and shot outside, terrified that if she stayed in there a second longer she would blurt out what a bastard Daddy was, that he was the very worst kind of man, that he didn't deserve such a sweet little boy.

She turned the corner practically at a run and went slap into Greg who was minding the pushchair. He looked directly at her and his face dropped. Then the colour rose to his cheeks and the full extent of his horror was plainly visible. 'Eliza,' he said faintly.

'Quite the happy family man, aren't you?' she

said, glancing at the pushchair. 'I've just seen your son and presumably your wife in the toilets.'

'I— I . . .'

'What? You can explain? Now this I have to hear.' She suddenly felt scarily calm.

When he didn't say anything, not even to deny the woman was his wife, just looked nervously over her shoulder, she felt a surge of powerful anger course through her. And knowing she would never get this opportunity again, she struck him hard on the cheek with the open palm of her hand. He never saw it coming and recoiled, and if it was possible, he looked even more shocked.

'You vile, cheating, lying bastard,' she said, aware that a couple of teenage lads a few yards away were getting a good eyeful.

'Go on, love,' one of them said, 'whack him again and I'll take a picture.' The lad held up his mobile phone. Nothing was private any more. Not even a humiliating break-up.

'Eliza, don't,' Greg said. 'Please don't make a scene.' The pleading desperation in his voice was pitiful, and made her wonder what she had ever seen in him.

'You're not worth the effort,' she said, as he manoeuvred the pushchair containing the sleeping baby so that it was between them. 'You're beneath contempt.'

She walked away, then hesitated and turned back. 'Oh, and you had better come up with a good explanation for your wife as to why you now have a slap mark on your face. But knowing what a first-rate liar you are, I'm sure you'll think of something.'

The adrenaline still pumping through her, she went to find her friend.

CHAPTER 28

ollowing a busy weekend with Jeff at home and Jensen, Tattie and Madison staying while house-hunting, Monday had been equally hectic for Mia.

With the wedding season in full swing and Ascot just around the corner, Mia hadn't had a moment to herself from the minute she'd opened the barn at nine o'clock until now, just gone three. A new delivery of hats had arrived in the middle of the morning and with no more customers booked in, she took the opportunity now to deal with the paperwork from her supplier. Making a copy of the invoice, she then filed the original away for her accountant and the copy for her own records. Next she had a number of phone calls to make, including one to Bev her cleaner who'd left a message saying she wouldn't be able to make it this week, due to an emergency dental appointment. Bev was Wendy Parr's cousin and while she was reliable and efficient, Mia knew the woman was a shocking gossip and so she was always circumspect in what she said when Bev was around.

Being circumspect was something Jeff needed to learn. Which was a massive understatement. Shortly before Jensen and Tattie and Madison had left for London, Jensen had told Mia that he'd had a chat with Daisy and had got out of her why she was so upset with Dad. Horrified, Mia had waited until they were alone and then she had tackled Jeff.

'Don't look like that,' he'd said. 'I know I shouldn't have said it, but I did. And the more I think about it, the more I stand by the truth of my words.'

'And what precisely would that be?' Mia had said, struggling to keep her anger from igniting.

'That Daisy's track record shows she's not known for making the best of decisions.'

'She was ill, Jeff! Do you still not understand that after all this time? Whatever decisions she made during that period in her life were not those of a happy and well-balanced young woman. She was desperately unhappy and it was our doing. *Our* doing. We failed her.'

'Oh, here we go, another round of blame distribution. Why do you always do that?'

'Because I still feel guilty that I didn't see the signs, and I always will. Don't you feel guilty at all?'

'If you remember, I was busy travelling—'

That was the point of ignition, when her anger flared and she had to walk away from Jeff for fear of doing or saying something she would regret.

His adamant refusal to accept that he played any part in Daisy's anorexia was beyond her comprehension. Whenever they got near discussing the issue, something Jeff was loath to do, it was she who always ended up feeling solely responsible. He might not come right out and say the words, but the implication was there and ensured that yet another layer of guilt was added to the load she already carried. Transference of guilt, it was called, and Jeff was a master of it.

An hour later, satisfied that everything was in order, paperwork and phone calls made, along with displaying the range of new hats, Mia awarded herself the rest of the day off. She was checking the diary to see what appointments she had for tomorrow and the coming days, when she heard the door open. She looked up to see Owen and her heart quickened.

'Not intruding, am I?' he asked.

'Not at all,' she replied, doing her best to mask her surprise, to appear perfectly at ease and normal. In the weeks since he had invited them all to The Hidden Cottage, other than spotting him driving by in his car, this was the first time she had seen him. She knew from general talk in the village that he'd been busy doing all the things that everybody does when moving into a new house, but she had wondered if the reason their paths hadn't crossed was because he had been avoiding her. Perversely her disappointment at not seeing him again had outweighed her relief at not having to confront the Awkward Moment between them. Just as she had known it would, that scene in the boat with him had played on her mind and had left her still undecided whether he was just a cynically shrewd man who'd detected she was unhappy in her marriage and would therefore be an easy conquest, or if he had meant what he'd said. The two scenarios were equally unsettling.

He closed the door and came in. 'So this is where it all goes on,' he said, looking about him. 'I'm impressed.'

'Thank you. Are you looking for a hat for a special occasion?' she joked.

He smiled. 'Funnily enough, no.' He approached the counter. 'I've brought this for you. It's your torch, the one you lent me the night of the fete when I came for dinner. I meant to give it back to you before, but I forgot. Then I forgot about it again yesterday when Tattie and Jensen brought Madison for her piano lesson. And for the record, you were right when you said I would need it; that road really is pitch black late at night.'

She put the torch to one side and was about to say something when he said, 'I've also come to apologize. I behaved badly the last time I saw you and I've come to the conclusion that the only way I can rid myself of the whole embarrassing memory is to tough it out and prove to you that I'm not the man you think I am.'

She couldn't help but be charmed by his

approach. 'And how do you plan to go about that?' she asked.

'I'd like to invite you to come and see something with me. After which I'm hoping that you'll review matters and hopefully think well of me again. On the basis that you thought well of me in the first place, before I made such a monumental prat of myself.'

'What if I said you didn't make a prat of yourself?'

'Then I'd think you were being extraordinarily kind and polite.'

The phone on the counter rang, making Mia start. 'Sorry,' she said, 'I'd better take this.'

'Go ahead.' He turned away tactfully.

She picked up the receiver. 'Mia's Hats,' she said: it was a customer enquiring about opening hours and how to find the barn. While she gave the woman the information she needed, Mia watched Owen moving about the barn. He came to a stop in front of one of the displays and picked up a hat – it was the one Madison had called a flying saucer when she'd helped Mia on Saturday, just as she had when she'd stayed on at Medlar House for a few extra days during half-term. To Mia's surprise, Owen put the fuchsia pink hat on his head, looked at himself in the mirror, then turned around to show her, at the same time pulling a face and striking a pose. Trying not to laugh, she carried on giving directions to the woman on the phone.

'Sorry,' he mouthed at her. He removed the hat and put it carefully back on the stand. As he stood sideways on to Mia, with sunlight pouring in on him through the large picture window, she observed his profile – the clean-shaven chin, the straight nose, the short dark hair that was greying slightly just above his ears. He was dressed in old jeans that had grass stains on the hems and a navy-blue T-shirt that showed off his broad shoulders as well as a pair of deeply tanned arms. *What would it take*, that wily treacherous voice of temptation reminded her, *to believe he was serious and do the unthinkable?*

'I shouldn't have done that,' he said when she finished the call. 'Now your estimation of me has gone down even further. If that's at all possible.'

'Shall we just accept that you've hit rock bottom and start afresh?'

He smiled. 'That sounds more than generous.' He came back to the counter. 'Can you spare me an hour right now to come and see something special? Please say yes; I'm like a child with a new toy and desperate to show it off. And there isn't anyone else I can ask.'

'Well, if you're scraping the barrel of social contacts that desperately, how could I say no?'

They took the footpath between Medlar House and the church, followed it up towards the woods where they left the path that was lined either side with a froth of cow parsley and entered the cool of the leafy shade.

'The bluebells have all gone over,' Owen said as they stood at the top of the rise, 'but the wild garlic is still putting on a good show.'

Seeing the dense carpet of lacy white flowers laid out before her, Mia breathed in with pleasure the softly tangy air. 'It's lovely,' she said quietly and then fell in step beside him as they descended the slope that was cushiony-soft under foot.

'Any news from Jensen today on the cottage they're hoping to rent?' he asked. 'Madison was so excited yesterday morning when she was telling me about it. I got the full story on the bedroom that would be hers and the garden where she's going to have some hens. Did you know that she plans to bring me eggs in exchange for piano lessons?'

Mia laughed. 'Yes, the dear girl has it all worked out. As for news, I haven't heard anything from Jensen today, but hopefully that's a good thing. I expect they're busy organizing all the necessary references and giving notice on their flats in London. I still can't believe they're really doing it, though, moving to the village. It's all happening so fast.'

He turned his head slightly towards her and with the dappled sunlight falling across his face, said, 'Looks like all roads lead here right now. It must be fate.'

She smiled evasively and changed the subject. 'It's extremely kind of you to give Madison piano lessons. She says you're very patient with her, and that you play brilliantly.'

'Not brilliantly, not by any stretch of the imagination.'

When they reached the boundary of his land, there was a person-sized gap in the hedge and Owen guided her through. With her back to the wood, she faced the lake and watched a pair of swallows swoop in the clear blue sky. She listened to the sound of sweet birdsong and the faraway call of a cuckoo and experienced the heady sensation of having escaped into another world. It was a bittersweet feeling and one that made her chest tighten with myriad emotions.

'Right,' he said, 'if you feel you can trust me, I'd like you to close your eyes and only open them when I say you can.'

Wanting to prove that she did trust him, she did as he said and allowed him to lead her by the hand. 'No cheating,' he said, as if reading her mind when she was tempted to take a sneaky peep. 'Just a few more steps to go.'

'You're not going to push me in the lake, are you?' she asked as she cautiously made her way over the uneven ground.

'As if I'd be so ungentlemanly.'

They came to a stop.

'You can open your eyes now.'

She blinked in the brightness of the sun. Then she saw it. '*Wow!*' she said. 'That's quite something.'

'You approve?'

She smiled. 'Very much so. But it's so much

more than a summerhouse. It's . . . it's, I don't know what to call it.'

'According to the manufacturer, it's a pavilion, which sounds ridiculously pretentious and grandiose, doesn't it?'

'Not at all. Is this what Joe's been helping you with?'

'Yes, he's done a fantastic job. We finished it last night.'

'You helped build it?'

He laughed. 'I wouldn't go so far as to use the word "build" in relation to my input. I basically did what I was told, fetching and carrying and following very precise and very simple instructions. Would you like to take a closer look?'

He rowed them across the lake, the golden June sunlight bouncing off the water and dazzling Mia's eyes. They were greeted at the island by none other than Putin, who shattered the still air with one of his notorious shrieks.

'What are you doing here?' Owen asked the peacock as he stepped out of the boat and tied the rope around the remains of a chopped-down tree. 'I thought I told you this was private property? Now *scram!*' Putin stared back at Owen with a look of total disdain, making Mia laugh.

'Do you always talk to him like that?' she said.

'I hate to admit it, but yes. In return he tries to intimidate me with an evil-eye stare. Give me your hand.'

She did as he said, but the boat gave a disconcerting wobble as she placed one foot on the dry hard ground and with her weight caught between the two, the boat began to slide away from the bank. She let out a startled cry and immediately Owen's arms were around her and clasping her tightly. 'I'm not normally so clumsily inept,' she said, embarrassed.

'You landlubbers are all the same,' he said casually.

But there was nothing casual about the way he was staring at her, or the way he was making no attempt to release her. The very air between them seemed to vibrate with tension and she felt a flash of alarm as her body sparked with the impulse to do something very wrong. Oh God, make him let go of me, she thought. Because right now, she was incapable of doing anything other than staying locked in his embrace.

As if reprimanding them, Putin let out a deafening shriek and they both jumped and then laughed; the moment diffused. Letting go of her, Owen bent down to the water's edge and pulled on a length of string that was tied to a tree root. 'Would you join me in christening my new hideaway with a glass of wine?' he asked, retrieving a bucket containing a bottle of Sancerre that had been cooling in the water.

'How very organized you are.'

'Wait till you see just how organized.'

He led the way and through the open doors of

the pavilion she saw that it was furnished with a pair of Lloyd Loom chairs, complete with cushions. In front of the chairs was a table and on it were glasses and a wicker picnic hamper. He caught her looking at the table. 'I know what you're thinking,' he said, taking a towel from the hamper and drying the bottle.

'You do?'

'That this all seems overly presumptuous, that I was arrogantly cocksure of myself that you'd come.'

'And were you?'

He shook his head. 'Quite the reverse. But I erred on the side of optimism. It's what I always try to do. Better to hope than not, don't you think?'

She looked at him hard. 'Owen, will you promise me something?'

'What?'

'That this isn't all part of some elaborate game you're intent on playing? I want you to be honest with me.'

He put the bottle down and came over to where she was standing hesitantly in the doorway. No more than a few inches from her, his perfectly clear hazel eyes seemed to trace her every feature, her every line, her every wrinkle. Oh God, she thought, a woman her age should never be exposed to such close scrutiny.

'I promise you faithfully I'm not playing any kind of a game with you,' he said.

'Good.'

CHAPTER 29

As Mia looked at him with her astonishingly beautiful eyes, Owen felt something deep inside him squeeze and then squeeze some more. He also felt compelled to kiss her but knew he mustn't. He'd promised himself that he would behave faultlessly, that if he managed to persuade Mia to come here today, he wouldn't put a foot wrong; there would be no repeat of that afternoon in the boat. He needed to know that he could make amends for that day, that she could be comfortable around him.

'Come and sit down,' he said. 'I'll pour you a glass of wine.'

His back to her as he opened the bottle of Sancerre, he said, 'It's four weeks since you first visited me here with Muriel and Georgina. Hard to believe that a whole month has passed, isn't it?'

'Do you feel settled? Or is it too soon to tell?'

'I feel more settled than I've ever felt anywhere. I felt it my very first night here.' The wine poured, he handed her a glass. He sat in the chair next to her and listened to the call of a faraway cuckoo while watching a cloud of gnats dancing over a patch of glistening water.

'So what have you been up to since I last saw you?' he asked. 'Apart from applying to the local council to have me evicted on the grounds of un-neighbourly conduct,' he added with a smile. 'I've half-expected an angry mob of villagers turning up here waving pitchforks at me.'

She smiled too. 'I've been too busy with work and family matters to make any complaints on that score, so you can rest easy. And if you're wondering if I told anyone what you said to me that day, I haven't.'

'That's a relief. So, family matters, what does that constitute? Problems?'

'There are always problems,' she said with feeling.

He stretched out his legs in front of him, drank his wine thoughtfully and watched her raise her glass to her lips. Lips that he very much wanted to kiss. He cleared his throat and looked away. 'Serious problems?'

'I hope not. But we always seem to be dealing with some family drama or other. It's a Channing trait.'

She sounded anxious. And tired. 'Would it help to talk about it?' he said. 'I'm told I'm a good listener.'

She shook her head. 'If I start, I probably won't be able to stop. And I'm sure you must have better things to do with your time than listen to me.'

'I have plenty of free time, remember? I'm a man of leisure. Which I don't think your husband approves of. He gave me a very resentful look when I ran into him recently and he asked me what I did.'

'Take no notice. It's just his way.'

'He seems a very forthright sort of man. Does he make you—' Owen stopped himself short, reminded himself sharply of his promise to behave.

'Does he make me what?'

'Happy?' *Damn!* What was the matter with him? Why, having gone to the trouble he had, couldn't he sit here and enjoy her company without interrogating her on her marriage? Anyone would think he was obsessed! Which he was, God help him. He had done his damnedest to get her out of his head by avoiding bumping into her, just as Rich had advised him, but it hadn't worked.

'Why do you want to know?' she asked at length, his question having provoked an abrupt and drawn-out silence that made the warm afternoon seemingly hang suspended in time.

'Because I want to get to know you. I want us to be friends.'

'Georgina and Muriel are my friends but they've never asked if Jeff makes me happy.'

'Big difference,' he said, floundering for a suitable answer. 'I'm a man and we ask different questions.'

She let out a laugh. He might have expected it to be a scornful laugh, but it wasn't. He looked

273

at her. There was no sign of scorn in her face either.

'I know what you're getting at,' she said, 'but since you don't know us as a couple and you've exchanged no more than a few words with Jeff, I don't think you can really comment on my marriage.'

'True. But I'm an outsider looking in and from the little I've seen, I get this feeling about the two of you. And your children. When you're with them you seem complete as a family unit, just the four of you.' He was about to go on and explain that he knew what he was talking about based on his own upbringing, but was interrupted by the sight of Putin suddenly launching himself off the ground and disappearing into the branches of a tree. 'I'd never thought about it before,' he said, 'but until I made Putin's acquaintance I think I just assumed that peacocks couldn't fly. They don't look built for it.'

'They're like pheasants; they tend to glide rather than fly any real distance.'

'So I've discovered.'

They both sipped their wine and stared up into the branches where Putin gave the impression of hiding from them. Or perhaps he was spying on Owen, checking that he didn't do anything foolish?

'There was a time when we were happy,' Mia said quietly. 'Very happy.'

Keeping his voice as subdued as hers, sensing anything else would stop her from opening up to him, Owen said, 'When did it change?'

'When Daisy came along. Jeff actually delivered her when she was born and was instantly besotted with her. I'm afraid he's guilty of having a stronger bond with her than with Jensen and Eliza and of spoiling her.'

'Why do you think that happened?'

'Who really knows? It's that inexplicable dimension to human nature, what makes us fall in love with one person and not another.'

'I didn't think parenting was supposed to be like that.'

'It shouldn't be, but in Jeff's case it is. I don't think he sees anything wrong in having a favourite child; he would tell you that he's merely being honest and that the rest of us aren't.'

Owen took a few moments to consider her admission. 'And there really is no way of explaining to Jeff that his thinking is flawed?'

'Oh no. Because what you have to know about Jeff is that he's incapable of confronting the emotional realities of family life. Or married life, come to that.'

'To you and your children's credit, they seem to get along well enough with each other. There don't seem to be any divisions.'

'Not now there aren't. The turning point was when Daisy was ill with anorexia; Eliza and Jensen were wonderful with her. They instantly put the past and their differences behind them and tried to support her while she was recovering.' Mia turned her gaze directly on him. 'I warned you that once I started talking I wouldn't be able to stop.'

'And I said I had plenty of time, so don't worry. Do you think you'll always stay married?'

'I have till now.'

'That's really not answering the question, is it?'

'You've never had a family. When there are children involved, it's no longer just about two people and their needs.' There was a sadness in her voice now. Regret too.

'I wanted a family with my ex-wife, Bea,' he said. 'I wanted it very much. Unfortunately I wasn't able to keep my end of the bargain in that respect and it became a contributing factor to the breakdown of our marriage.'

'I'm sorry. I had no idea. But then there's such a lot about you I don't know.' Her violet gaze intensified. 'Tell me some more. Tell me about you and Bea and how you met and how you fell in love and how you knew that she was the woman you wanted to marry.'

And so he did.

He'd just finished telling her how painful it had been for them both to admit that the marriage wasn't working in the way it should when Mia looked at her watch and let out a small cry. 'Oh! I had no idea it was so late.' She rose from her chair. 'I'm really sorry, but I have to go. Eliza will be arriving any minute, if she hasn't already.'

Disappointed their time together had come to an end, Owen followed suit and stood up. Beside him, she looked out at the lake, which was now bathed in the roseate glow of the early evening sun. 'It's so perfect here,' she said, as if seeing the view for the first time.

Keeping his voice light, he said, 'It's perfect with you here.'

She slowly turned her head and met his gaze. She was silent for a moment. A very long moment. Finally she said, 'Owen, I can't make a complicated situation worse by adding yet more chaos to it.'

'You could always simplify things.'

'I know that. But right now my family needs me.'

He frowned. 'Are you sure it isn't *you* who needs your family? To hide behind?'

'Why would I want to do that?'

'To make life safe. It takes courage to change things, as I've discovered.'

'Please don't call me a coward. You have no idea how much strength it's taken to live the life I have. Or the sacrifices I've made.'

Owen thought of his mother and the many sacrifices she had made when she was married. Oh yes, he knew all too well the strength it took to stay in a bad relationship. 'Actually,' he said, 'I can imagine it. Come on, I'll take you home.'

CHAPTER 30

Mia refused Owen's offer to accompany her home. Parting from him at the edge of the woodland, she slipped through the gap in the hawthorn and rhododendron bushes and plunged into the cool shade. She was sorry to leave The Hidden Cottage, particularly the lake and the island. While there, wrapped in the quiet and soothing seclusion, she had felt isolated from the rest of the world, as if she had fled Medlar House and was free of all its ties and commitments. It was why she had opened up to Owen. She had felt safe to do so. As he'd said himself, he was an outsider and she'd trusted him not to talk to anyone about what they'd discussed.

Despite what he thought, she had never hidden behind her children – rather she had always put their happiness and welfare before hers, wanting stability and security for them. And now Jensen and Daisy were happier than she had ever seen them and, together with their partners, were building the foundations of a shared future. Eliza's relationship with Greg might not be as advanced, and who knew what would come of it, but for now

Mia was happy that her serious-minded daughter had discovered the value of having something in her life other than work.

Birdsong pealed like bells ringing out from the trees, and hurrying through the wood, Mia thought of Daisy's newfound contentment and her spirited determination to create a new life. It was a dangerous thought, but she found herself thinking that if Daisy was brave enough to free herself from what had gone before, could she not do the same? Could she not now put the past to rest and accept that sacrificing her own happiness as a way to make amends for being a bad mother and failing Daisy had to stop? The guilt would always be there, just as she'd told Jeff last night, but surely enough was enough. What purpose did it serve to go on punishing herself by staying with Jeff? Had the penance changed anything? Had it given her any comfort?

Plenty of women in her situation would have left Jeff years ago, but plenty would have stayed. Many years ago, Mia's father had secretly confided in her that it took courage to leave a bad marriage, but equally it took courage to stay. He had been talking about his own marriage, which had been far from happy. 'Anyone who doesn't understand why,' he'd told Mia, 'simply doesn't understand the complexities involved.'

She emerged breathless from the footpath between the church and Medlar House and saw a taxi. All thoughts of herself were immediately banished the moment she saw Eliza. Her first thought was that her daughter was ill; she looked as if she didn't have the strength to stand.

Her second thought was to wonder who the young man was who was paying the taxi driver. With various bags slung over his shoulders, along with a case at his feet, he wore an expression of immense concern, especially when he turned and put a hand to Eliza's back, as though to support her. Was this Greg?

All this Mia noticed in as much time as it took to cover the few steps from the footpath to the entrance to Medlar House. Close up, she could see that Eliza had been crying; her face was blotched and swollen with tears.

'Eliza!' she said, alarmed. 'What's wrong? What's happened?'

Eliza's answer was to lean heavily into Mia's arms and cry.

It wasn't until they were in the house that Mia got anything coherent out of Eliza – how she'd gone to the airport yesterday morning to meet Serene and had run into Greg and . . . and his wife and children. Only then did Mia realize the man with them in the kitchen, who had removed his suit jacket and tie and was silently making himself useful at Mia's instructions by making some tea, was Eliza's work colleague, Simon.

'He lied to me, Mum,' Eliza sobbed, her voice painfully thick with tears. 'Everything he ever said was a lie. And the worst of it is, I believed him. I believed every word.'

Mia held her daughter close, rubbing her back, letting her get it all out.

'I thought he loved me. I should have known better. No one will ever love me. I'm fat and I'm ugly.'

'That's not true,' Mia soothed her. 'Not true at all. And I never want to hear you say anything like that again.'

'But it *is* true,' she wailed. 'I know it is. But for a short while I believed it wasn't. That's what hurts so much. I was so stupid.'

'You weren't stupid,' Simon said, coming over to the table and placing a mug of tea in front of Eliza. 'He was a lousy bastard who conned you. He's probably done it before and will do so again. And I swear if I ever meet him, I'll make sure he can never do it again. I'll tattoo the words "Cheating Husband" on his forehead!'

Hearing the anger in his voice, Mia looked at Simon gratefully. 'Come on, love,' she said to Eliza. 'Drink some tea.'

'I just don't understand why,' Eliza said miserably. 'Why did he have to use and humiliate me this way? What was I, a game to him? A cheap bit of easy fun? Was he laughing at me behind my back the whole time?'

Sadness and real anger flowed through Mia, and unable to bear for her daughter to feel that she'd been used, she said, 'Perhaps he cared for you deep down. Perhaps he was waiting for the right time to leave his wife for you?'

'You don't lie to the person you love,' Eliza said hotly, snatching a tissue from the box Mia had placed on the table. She wiped her eyes roughly, blew her nose and for a moment seemed to regain her composure. But then her swollen bloodshot eyes filled with fresh tears once more. 'If you had seen his family, Mum. His . . . his son was such a beautiful little boy. How could he do it? How could he cheat on his family like that? I just don't understand it. I don't think I'll trust another man ever again.'

Later, while Eliza was soaking in the bath at Mia's insistence and Simon was upstairs in the spare room changing out of his work suit, Mia had unearthed a lasagne from the depths of the freezer. This was now in the oven and with some frozen peas in a pan ready to heat through, she was setting the table in the kitchen and thinking of Eliza, how hurt and angry and horribly disillusioned she was. Time would eventually heal her – it always did – but for now the poor girl was in real pain and wouldn't be able to see beyond her heartbreak for a very long time yet.

From behind her, Mia heard footsteps. She turned to see Simon, dressed now in jeans and a T-shirt. He looked thinner and much younger than before, practically boyish, as if he'd shed a layer of grown-up maturity when he'd removed his suit. Though he looked nothing like her son, he reminded Mia of Jensen. Something in the body language, the casual youthfulness.

'Anything I can do to help?' he asked, pushing his hands into the back pockets of his jeans. He had a faint discernibly northern accent.

'Thank you, but I've got everything under control,' she said, adding some sprigs of mint from the garden to the saucepan of peas. 'Would you like a beer?' she asked. 'Or a glass of wine? Or something else?'

'Thanks, a beer would be great.'

While she sorted a drink for him, she said, 'Everything OK in your room? Anything you need?'

'It's more than OK and way better than the Travel Lodge where I'm booked in for the week. Sorry if I've put you to any extra bother. I didn't mean to invite myself to stay, I just wanted to see Eliza safely home.'

Mia passed him the opened bottle of beer and a glass. 'It's no trouble,' she said. 'And I'm extremely grateful you took care of Eliza the way you did.'

'It was nothing any good friend wouldn't do for her.'

'How long have the two of you worked together?' Mia asked.

'I joined Merchant Swift as a graduate the same time as Eliza, so since forever. Well, that's how it feels at times. Don't get me wrong, I enjoy work, but I'm not like Eliza; I don't live for it. She's the real deal when it comes to platinum membership of the corporate highflyer club – I just tag along in her wake.'

'I'm sure that's not true,' Mia said. 'Did you ever meet Greg?'

He shook his head. 'No. The guy was never around. Supposedly he was always out of the country. Now we know different.'

'Indeed we do. When did Eliza tell you about bumping into him at the airport?'

'This morning. I knew there was something wrong when we caught the train up to Milton Keynes together. She looked awful; dead pale and like she hadn't slept for a week. I'd never seen her look like that before. I knew about her old school friend coming to stay the night, and that she was really looking forward to it, so at first I thought maybe they'd knocked back a few too many Baileys together. When I teased her about having a hangover, she suddenly lost it and started crying.'

'Oh, poor Eliza. How did she get through the day?'

'Being the uber-pro she is, she threw herself into work. I suggested she claimed she was ill and came here, but she wouldn't hear of it, so somehow she held it together, but then when we'd finished and we were packing up our things, she fell apart. No way was I going to let her go off on her own in the state she was in.'

'That was very kind of you.'

He shrugged and drank some of his beer. 'As I said before, it's what any good friend would do. I'm just glad she let me help. She's not very good at that. She sees it as weakness, I think.'

Mia swallowed back a lump of sadness. 'You're right,' she said, feeling suddenly very fond of this intuitive young man. 'She's always been that way; ever since she was little she always had to be so fiercely independent.'

'I sort of guessed that much.'

With her eyes shut and her ears submerged beneath the water, Eliza lay in the bath listening to the amplified sound of her breathing. At the same time she pictured her tears sliding into the water, slowly adding to the volume until finally the bath overflowed.

Married.

A husband.

A father.

It didn't matter how many times she said the words, the shock didn't lessen. If anything it multiplied and she felt worse.

But trust Mum to try and make her feel less upset by saying that maybe Greg did love her, that he was waiting for the right time to leave his wife. She didn't blame Mum for saying that; she was just desperate to find a way to make Eliza feel better. To lessen the pain. To make her feel less worthless and used.

If any of that theory was true, why hadn't Greg shared it with her? She would have understood. She would have given him time to sort things out. But no. He was a coward. A cowardly, lying, cheating adulterer. Nothing he could say would ever make her think well of him again. And the proof of his guilt was that he hadn't been in touch. Not a single text, phone call or email. Nothing. Only the resounding silence of his guilt.

Last night, when she had been beside herself with tearful rage, Serene had said that she should speak to Greg again. That the only way she would ever feel the matter was truly closed – for her, not him – was to have one last conversation with him. 'Otherwise you'll have endless imaginary conversations inside your head and drive yourself crazy,' her friend had said.

Serene's last words to her this morning, when she'd left for her flight, were: 'You must make a list of all the things you want to say to Greg. Then in a fortnight's time, insist that he meets you. You might not get the answers you want, but if you don't do it, you'll always regret that you didn't have the courage to face him.'

For now Eliza knew she wasn't strong enough to do that. If she were to be in the same room as Greg, she would disintegrate and she couldn't allow that to happen. Never again would she allow herself to be so weak.

CHAPTER 31

Tuesday afternoon. The school bell had rung more than fifteen minutes ago and JC still hadn't come to collect her.

This, Madison planned to say to Mum, was exactly why she needed to have a mobile phone. 'I would only use it for emergencies,' she would say, as she had already said about a hundred times, to which Mum always said, 'No dice, missy, you're too young to have your own mobile; you'd only do something silly with it, like lose it or break it.'

But she wasn't too young; there were plenty of children her age who had one. And anyway, she was way more sensible than Mum. Who was it who lost her mobile on a train last year? Mum, that's who! And who was it who dropped her new mobile and cracked the screen? Mum, that's who!

Madison could see Mrs Tyler coming over to check on her. Mrs Tyler had a big mole on her chin with a yucky thick hair sticking out of it and it didn't matter how often she told herself not to look at the mole, Madison's eyes were always drawn to it. 'No sign of your mother, then?' Mrs Tyler asked.

Madison shook her head. 'Mum's working today; Jensen's coming for me.' She didn't really understand why, but Mum had told her always to use JC's proper name to a teacher. Something about making him sound more official.

'In that case, be sure to wait here,' Mrs Tyler said. 'No going off on your own. I'll be back in a minute or two.'

Madison watched Mrs Tyler go back inside the school building. She knew the way home perfectly well, and she knew where the spare key for the front door was kept, but she also knew that to walk home alone would send Mum crazy-mental. And she'd probably go crazy-mental at JC too for being late.

But where *was* JC? He'd never been late before. Dropping her PE bag to the ground where her other bag lay, she switched from one hand to the other the painting she'd done in Art, and looked at her watch. JC should have been here precisely nineteen minutes ago. Around her were a few other children waiting to be picked up. She was glad she wasn't the only one still waiting.

Lauren and her mother had hung about for a bit, but they couldn't stay any longer because they had to dash off for Lauren's violin lesson. When Madison thought about it, Lauren was always dashing off somewhere. Yesterday at the school gate her mother had said to Mum that she'd be glad to get out of London, when their pace of life would slow down. 'I know exactly what you mean,'

Mum had said. 'We're looking forward to it as well.'

Lauren and her family were leaving London next week, way before the end of term. Mum and JC said that if everything fell into place, it wouldn't be long before they too would be leaving and moving into the lovely little house they'd found at the weekend. It had the cutest name: Lily Cottage. Mia had told them that if anything went wrong, they could always stay in The Gingerbread House until they found somewhere else.

Everything was happening so fast. It was like a dream. The best ever dream. Especially as yesterday Mum had spoken to the head teacher of the school in Little Pelham and heard there would be a place for Madison in September. Not only that, but just like with Lauren, it was all arranged for Madison to leave ahead of the end of term here and spend a couple of days in her new school before it closed for the summer holidays.

It was weird, but Lauren seemed to be turning the whole thing into a competition. She kept going on about the enormous garden she was going to have and how they'd only be a short distance from the sea and that her new bedroom would be as big as their classroom. Madison knew she was exaggerating, but that was OK. What wasn't OK was that Lauren had looked at the photograph JC had taken of Lily Cottage and described it as tiny, no bigger than an iddy-biddy dolls' house. 'Is that it?' she'd asked. 'But I thought you'd be getting something bigger like we are.' Hurt and annoyed, Madison had put the photograph away, thinking that she wouldn't miss Lauren one little bit when she was living in Little Pelham. And anyway, she had a new friend now: Beth.

Madison looked at her watch. Again. JC was now twenty-three minutes late. And she was the only one left to be picked up. Now she was worried. What if something had happened to him? What if he'd had an accident? What if he'd had his head-phones on and had crossed that busy road by the corner shop without looking?

Suddenly breathless and all hot and sticky, she tried to stop the thought going any further. JC had to be all right. Because if he wasn't, if some-thing bad – something *really* bad – happened to him, then they wouldn't move to Little Pelham. The thought of anything horrible happening to JC made her stomach flip with panicky fear. She hated it when she felt like this, when one minute she felt brilliantly happy and the next she felt sick and scared. That was the trouble when you wanted something too much; the more you wanted it, the more chance there was that you would lose it.

That was how she felt about JC. He was the nearest she had ever had to a father. Just recently she had come close to calling him Dad. She didn't know how he would react if she did, or what Mum would say, but he really was like a proper dad to her. She probably saw more of him than Lauren saw of her father; he didn't ever collect Lauren from school.

Madison had never known who her father was, or even what his name was. Mum always said it wasn't important. Not that they ever talked about it. Why should they? Mum was right; all that mattered was the people Madison already had as family and they were Mum and Grandma Barb and Grandpa Tom; they were her family. Well, that's how it had always been until now. Now it was different. Now there was JC.

When they moved to Little Pelham, there would be no more sleepovers for JC – he would be with them all the time. Just like a real family. And there would be Mia to see every day. Maybe not *every* day, but quite often. And that was a nice thought. It was always nice being around Mia. She was so beautiful. But in a quiet, calm way that made Madison feel all warm and happy. She had lovely eyes, sort of purply-blue, which didn't sound at all lovely, but they were. And she let Madison help in her hat shop; she didn't treat her like a silly baby who couldn't be trusted.

But none of that would happen if something bad happened to JC. Why wasn't he here? Where was he? She looked at her watch. He was now thirty minutes late.

From behind her she heard the sound of Mrs Tyler's bossy voice. 'Madison, I think you'd better come in and wait in the after-school club now.'

But then two things happened at the same time. Mrs Pearson, the school secretary, came hurrying over and JC jogged in through the school gate. 'Madison, I'm really sorry,' he said. 'I got held up with a work thing.'

She was so relieved to see him, to know that he was all right, tears pricked at the backs of her eyes and she threw herself at him. 'I thought something terrible had happened to you,' she said, her face buried somewhere in his stomach.

'Hey there,' he said, bending down to look her in the face, 'nothing bad is going to happen to me, I've got hidden powers; I'm Mr Invincible.' Then straightening up, he said to Mrs Tyler, 'I did call. I left a message with the school secretary to say I was running late. The message was passed on, wasn't it?'

Realizing that she'd forgotten all about the painting she'd had in her hands, Madison picked it up from where it had fallen on the ground next to her bags. At the same time, Mrs Pearson stepped forward. 'That's what I came to tell you, Mrs Tyler. I was looking for you earlier, but I couldn't find you.'

'I was in the staff room, of course,' Mrs Tyler said. She looked cross as she spoke to Mrs Pearson, but when she turned to JC, she smiled, and it wasn't her usual closed-mouth smile – this was a big smile that showed her large uneven teeth and made lots of wrinkles around her eyes. It also made the mole on her chin look even bigger. 'Sorry about the mix-up there,' she said in a voice very different from her usual bossy one. It was like she was trying to be extra specially nice to JC. 'But happily you're here now,' she added. 'See you tomorrow, Madison.'

'I think she fancies you, doesn't she?' Madison said when they turned out of the school gate.

JC laughed. 'It's my curse in life for all women to fancy me; it's my devilish charm and good looks.'

Madison laughed. She liked it when JC talked like that. Mum called it his Oscar Wilde voice. She slipped her hand into his and tried to match his long strides. Today he was wearing a faded black Converse trainer on one foot and a dark green one on the other. He had a different combination for every day of the week and he never broke from the pattern. Mum said he was like her and the coloured pens she used to write her diary. Kindred spirits, she called them. Which was a fancy way of saying they liked the same things.

'Sorry again that I was late,' he said. 'My mother phoned with some bad news and then a very annoying client called and wanted me to fix a problem right away.'

'Why's he so annoying?'

'First, because he's rude and arrogant, and second, he made me late for you. And that's unforgivable.'

After a boy on a bicycle had swerved past them on the pavement to avoid a bus that had stopped to let off some passengers, Madison said, 'What's the bad news from your mother? It's nothing to do with our cottage, is it?'

'No, don't worry about that. I spoke to the agent this morning and everything's just fine. And here's the deal: any worrying to be done, you leave it to me, OK? You stay right out of it.'

She smiled. 'OK. So tell me about Mia. What's happened? She's all right, isn't she?'

'What did I just say about worrying?'

'But I'm allowed to care, aren't I?'

'Right, I see you're in one of your smart moods.'

'I'm always in a smart mood. It's what makes me so unique and special.'

He smiled. 'No argument there. Well, it's a bit complicated, but my mother wanted to tell me that my sister Eliza is upset about something.'

'What kind of something?'

'Her boyfriend turned out not to be a very nice man at all. He'd been lying to her about who he was.'

'Why did he do that?'

'Some men are like that. They like to lead a secret life.'

Not really sure what JC meant, she said, 'Did Eliza love him?'

'I think she did.'

'That's sad then.'

'You're right, it is. And it's wrong. People shouldn't tell lies.'

They passed the corner shop and were crossing the busy road – the road junction where Madison

294

had pictured JC being knocked over by a car – when she thought of something important. 'We don't need to mention you being late for me to Mum, do we? It wouldn't be a bad lie to forget about that, would it?'

He stepped over a humungous pile of revolting dog mess. 'No,' he said, 'I'll tell her.'

'But she'll be cross with you and I don't want you to get into trouble. And it wasn't really your fault, was it?'

He squeezed her hand. 'She has every right to be cross with me. No secrets, Madison. That's the rule I have with your mother.'

'Do you have the same rule with me?'

'Sure I do.'

'Good. So tell me why you and your dad don't like each other.'

'*Whoa!* Where did that come from?'

'I watched the two of you at the weekend and you hardly spoke and when you did, you had a look in your eyes.'

'What kind of look was that, Sherlock?'

'Like you were cross with him and wished he wasn't there.'

'My, you were being observant. What about my father? Did you notice anything particular about him?'

She gave this some thought. 'He seemed annoyed most of the time, and then there were times when he didn't seem to fit in. Or as if he didn't want to join in.'

'How very perceptive of you.'

'Do you think he didn't really want us there?'

'Anything my father says or does, you mustn't ever take seriously. That's another rule. OK?'

Aware that JC hadn't answered her question properly, she said, 'So why don't you like each other?'

He shrugged. 'It's more a matter of not really getting on that well. That's the way it is in some families.'

Which was what Mum had said last night when Madison had asked her the same question.

They were home now and as JC put the key in the lock and opened the door, Madison decided not to ask any more questions. When they were living in Little Pelham, she'd soon find out exactly what was going on. It was all going to be so brilliant when they moved there.

CHAPTER 32

The following day, finishing work early so he could avoid the worst of the traffic, Jensen was on his way to Little Pelham. Tattie had encouraged him to make the trip; she seemed to think he might cheer his sister up. He wasn't totally convinced, but he was willing to give it a shot. In fact before Tattie had said anything he had already decided – after Eliza hadn't returned any of his calls or messages – to see her. His sister's unprecedented silence told him all he needed to know: she was in a bad way.

For all Eliza's smartness, she wasn't that worldly, not when it came to relationships at any rate. No way would he have said anything before but from what she'd told him about this Greg character, Jensen had had his doubts. It had been all those last-minute cancellations that had done it.

If there was one thing he hated, it was dishonesty. Those who lied and cheated were pretty low down the food chain in his book. Which was why he'd told Madison that there could be no secrets from Tattie when they'd been walking home from school yesterday. It was partly this principle of his that made the sparks fly when he was around his father. He hated having to bite his tongue when he was in his presence. He wanted to be honest. He wanted to confront his father and tell him exactly what he thought of him, that he was an egotistical idiot who expected the world to revolve around him.

In common with most egotistical men, Jeff Channing had a profoundly polarizing personality and over the years it had brought out the absolute worst in Jensen, made him instinctively want to challenge and defy his father at every turn.

It hadn't always been like that, though. Jensen could actually remember a time when Dad had been fun and impulsive, springing amazing surprises on them. One school holiday he'd stopped off at the travel agent on the way home after work and announced that they were off to Disney World in the morning. Another time, he'd announced they were going on holiday to Mauritius the following day. The downside was that Mum would be in a flat spin trying to get the packing done while the rest of them crowded excitedly round Dad trying to get a look at the travel brochure and the hotel they'd be staying in.

Dad had always had what you'd call a 'big personality' and when you're a young child that can work, but as you get older you begin to feel the rub of it and it becomes an embarrassment. Most fathers know to back off, but Dad hadn't. He'd flexed his 'big personality' even more to assert his central role, but not in a good way. He became borderline tyrannical and would lose his rag far more than he used to, especially if Daisy was involved and claimed that she had been treated unfairly by Jensen and Eliza. Whenever Jensen pointed out that Daisy was lying, Dad would fly off the handle and say that there was only one liar in the family and it wasn't Daisy.

It got to be a regular claim from Dad that he was treated with more respect at work than at home. 'Then why don't you stay there?' Jensen had muttered one day. For which he'd received a stinging clip around the ear. Mum, who'd never once smacked them, had been furious and later Jensen had overheard her asking Dad to apologize to him, but Dad had said hell would freeze over before he'd do that. Things went from bad to worse after that, with Jensen never missing the chance to tell his father that a man who could leave his nineteen-year-old girlfriend when she was pregnant didn't deserve his respect.

Yet for all the ill-feeling Jensen felt towards his father, Madison's questions yesterday had brought him up short: his behaviour was no example for a child to witness. Tattie had hinted as much for a while now, but he had shrugged the hints off, believing he could maintain a certain level of pretence whenever Madison was within hearing of him trying to be civil to his father.

Clearly he'd failed. And that bothered him. As Tattie had said in bed last night, if they were to live in the same village, the rancour had to be curtailed. 'I don't want Madison drawn into your history,' she'd said. 'I know exactly why you do it and what makes you do it, but if the move is going to work for us, you have to work on polishing your social skills with your father.'

Jensen smiled at her choice of words. Social skills. Good one, Tattie. But then she could always do that. She could always make him smile. And laugh. 'I'm not asking you to be best buddies all of a sudden,' she'd said, 'but you could try to be the better man. Because, beneath it all, JC, you *are* the better man.'

He wanted to believe her. But he wasn't sure it was true. That's what he hated most about being back at Medlar House when his father was there – he became as bad a person as Jeff Channing and that really wound him up, provoked him to go on the attack.

But he was determined to try and change. He'd do it for Tattie and for Madison. Because as much as it surprised him, he felt he was letting them down if he didn't change. The bottom line was, he wanted to create a better life for the woman he loved and for her daughter.

If anyone had told Jensen that he would return to Little Pelham to live, he would have said they were crazy. No way, he would have said. Under no circumstances would he intentionally put himself within spitting distance of his father on a permanent basis. Absolutely not. But Tattie and

Madison had changed all that. Being back in the village with them he had seen the place through different eyes, and caught up in Tattie's enthusiasm for adopting a vastly different lifestyle, he had seen how perfect it could be for them as a family. Work-wise they would both be able to operate from home just as they already did, and the commute to London would be easy. Of course, it didn't have to be Little Pelham they moved to – there were any number of options available – but the combination of the good reputation of the school for Madison, the familiarity of the village for him, along with having Mum so close by, all added up to a no-brainer situation.

He had no experience of children, but he knew a great kid when he saw one, and Madison was definitely a great kid. She might not have her real father on hand, or grandparents nearby – although she now had Mia – but she had a mother who adored her and Jensen knew how that felt.

When he and Tattie first got together, Tattie had made her position very clear. 'Don't ever think of coming between me and my daughter,' she'd told him. 'If you can't live with the knowledge she'll always come first, you'd better go now. If bullets are flying, and there's only one person I can protect, she's the one I'll take the bullet for. Got it?'

He'd got it all right. Some might say it was an uncompromisingly harsh thing to say to a new boyfriend, a guaranteed deal-breaker, but he had respected her honesty. Holding his hands up, as though in surrender, he'd said, 'Believe me, I'd walk away if I imagined you thought differently.'

He'd been shocked yesterday how upset Madison had been when he was late to pick her up from school. Shocked but also touched that she cared about him, and he liked that. What was more, he liked being needed by Tattie and Madison. It was a surprisingly gratifying feeling.

An hour later, he pulled onto the drive of Medlar House and parked alongside his mother's VW Golf. He switched the engine off. While driving here and reflecting on his father he had also thought of his mother. He and Mum had always been incredibly close. The bond between them was just about as strong as it could be. But that wasn't surprising, given that for the first few years of his life it had been just the two of them. While there was no way he could remember everything about that time, it had left its mark on him in all sorts of ways, one of which was that he was extremely protective of his mother and hated to see her caught in the crossfire of Dad's anger and frustration that nobody did things the way he wanted them to be done.

But something else that had left its mark on him was that he knew how it felt suddenly to have to share your mother with a stranger. Which was why he'd been so careful with Madison; he hadn't wanted her to feel like he was muscling in and pushing her out. When Dad had popped up unexpectedly in their lives – when Jensen had been ill in hospital – his abiding memory was of wondering when this stranger would leave, so it could be just him and Mum again.

He let himself in at the back door and called out to his mother.

'Up here,' she answered him.

He dumped his bag in the hall and took the stairs at a run, just as he always had as a teenager and with his father's admonishing words ringing in his ears. 'Watch the carpet why don't you, it cost a ruddy fortune!'

'Up here' proved to be his old bedroom. Mum was making up his bed. He went over and kissed her cheek. She was wearing perfume and she smelt summery, of flowers. 'You don't have to do that,' he said, 'I'll do it later.'

She smiled and reached for a pillowcase. 'Almost done,' she said. 'I seem to be making and unmaking beds all the time these days. Not that I'm complaining. I'm glad that you've come; it will mean a lot to your sister. I haven't told her you were coming. I thought it would be a nice surprise.'

He thought she looked and sounded tired, a bit strained. Perhaps it was worry for Eliza. He took the pillowcase from her and began stuffing the pillow into it. As he did so he had a sudden vision of age and infirmity creeping up on his mother. Then of her not being around any more. It was an appalling thought, an inconceivable thought, and one that he simply couldn't deal with. He could not conceive of a world in which his mother no longer existed. A world in which her gentle manner didn't soothe him into a better mood, or when she could effortlessly rebuke him with one of her quiet grave stares.

'What's the latest on Eliza?' he asked, clearing his throat to loosen the sudden tightness in it.

'She didn't go to work today. Simon told them she'd come down with a bug. She's in the shower now.' His mother glanced at her watch. 'And Simon's due back any minute. I insisted he stay with us, rather than a soulless hotel. It seemed the right thing to do.'

'Fair enough. What's he like?'

She smiled. 'Perfect for your sister. Only she doesn't realize it.'

Intrigued, Jensen tilted his head. 'You're going to have to fill me in.' The pillow sorted, he tossed it on the bed and put his arms around his mother, gave her one of his trademark massive hugs that lifted her off the ground.

She smiled when he put her down. 'It's going to be good having you living back here again,' she said.

'Oh, you'll soon be sick of me. Come on, downstairs and tell me all I need to know before talking to Eliza.'

While Simon helped Mia clear away after supper, Eliza sat outside with Jensen in the gathering twilight.

'Simon seems nice,' Jensen said.

'He is,' she replied. 'We've always worked well together. He's been very good to me, has more than gone the extra mile in covering for my ineptitude this week. I owe him.'

'Never been anything between the two of you, then?'

She turned and looked at him. 'What do you mean?'

'You know, in a non-work-colleague way. No special water-cooler moments between you?'

Eliza tutted. 'Just goes to show how poor your powers of observation are. Simon's *so* not interested in me.'

'He *so* is, little sis.'

'And you, big bro, couldn't be more wrong.' She lowered her voice, even though there was no danger of them being overheard out here in the garden. 'Simon's gay; I'd have thought you'd have managed to work that out for yourself.'

Jensen laughed. It was the first time anyone had laughed around her since Sunday morning at the airport. But for some reason, her brother appeared to be laughing *at* her. 'What's so funny?' she asked, feeling cross.

'Take it from me, Simon is *not* gay.'

'He is too.'

'Eliza, you're hopeless.'

She looked at him indignantly. He was smiling now. 'Why's that then?'

'OK, so tell me what makes you think he's gay.'

'It's perfectly obvious; he never talks about any girlfriends, or even girls in general for that matter. And look how he is with Mum, helping her with the slightest thing. He's in there now washing up, for heaven's sake!'

'That's the sum total of your critical analysis, is it? The guy's too helpful and never talks about girls.' Jensen shook his head in what she considered to be a very irritating manner; it made her want to thump him. 'Honestly,' he went on, 'for someone who is so smart, you can be remarkably stupid.'

'And you can be remarkably annoying,' she snapped. Now she did thump him. On the arm. Hard. Like they used to when they were children and were giving one another dead arms.

'Go on, thump me again,' he laughed. 'Get it fully out of your system.'

She raised her hand again, but then dropped it. She could feel her cheeks burning. 'Why are you being so horrible to me? You said you'd come here to cheer me up and all you're doing is making fun of me.'

He put his arm around her shoulders, tried to pull her close. But she wouldn't yield to him. He said, 'Let's call it the art of misdirection, because for a short while, I took your mind off Greg the Bastard, so you could at least thank me for that. If it helps, you can take out your anger with him by using me as a punchbag. Nothing like some good old-fashioned violence to make you feel better.'

It was on her lips to say she didn't think she'd ever feel better again, but then she realized that compared to this time last night, she did indeed feel less manic.

It was dusk-dark and what little light there was made black silhouettes of the trees and The Gingerbread House at the far end of the garden. A few birds were still chirruping farewell to the day. Sitting here like this with Jensen, as they had many times before as teenagers, she felt a clearing of the miasma that had fugged her brain since seeing Greg at the airport. She welcomed the moment of clarity, sensing that it would be fleeting, that all too soon it would be lost and she would be dragged back into a debilitating state of wretchedness.

She had woken this morning leaden with inertia and incipient tears. She hated feeling so pathetic and so full of self-pity. Never before had anything reduced her to this awful mess. She was unrecognizable to herself. All her energy had gone, the slightest thing left her exhausted, and she just wanted to sleep and sleep.

Work could not be further from her mind. And that scared her. Really scared her. She had to pull herself together. There could be no more days like today, when the sum total of her achievements had been to have a bowl of soup with Mum at lunchtime and then spend the afternoon in her pyjamas on the sofa, mindlessly watching the telly until her eyes were gritty and she had grown tired of the inexorable game shows, property searches and cookery programmes.

Finally when she could take no more, she had switched off the television and determined not to give in to the increasing paralysis of her mind, she had hauled herself to her feet. 'I will not allow that man to make me feel this way,' she had said aloud. With an unexpected burst of energy, she had feverishly gathered up the sodden tissues that she had cast around her, thrown them in the bin and gone upstairs for a shower. No sooner was she out of the shower than the lethargy returned and she lay on her bed and gave in to another bout of furious and pitiful tears, thinking of the utter pointlessness of it all. And by 'all', she meant life. Just what was the point of it when it could be so bloody awful? When it could be wrecked in a single moment?

Now, as she rested her head against her brother's shoulder, she thought how weary she was. She was only twenty-six years old but felt more like a hundred and six and that every day of her life so far had been a waste, because nothing in it had prepared her for what Greg had done to her. Whenever she thought of his wife's face at the airport – in particular her friendly smile and the affectionate way she had spoken to her son – Eliza wanted to squeeze her eyes shut with sickening shame. How dare Greg turn her into the kind of woman who could have wreaked such wanton destruction on a family.

Eliza had noted that Jensen, who never said anything he didn't mean, had not added his voice to the highly implausible theory that maybe Greg had cared for her all along and was waiting for the right time to leave his wife. She loved her brother for that, for his unequivocal honesty. 'Thank you for coming,' she said to him now.

'Thank *you* for hitting me. It's a long time since I've had a dead arm.'

In spite of everything, Eliza smiled into the growing darkness. It gave her the courage to say: 'It seems so obvious now; all the signs were there that Greg was lying to me. The absences, the times I couldn't contact him, the sudden changes to his itinerary. I was blind to every one of his lies. The truth was staring me right there in the face, and I never once saw it.'

'No,' Jensen said firmly. 'No hindsight crap. Don't you dare go beating yourself up with it.' She couldn't see if the expression on his face had changed, but she heard his voice soften when he went on to say, 'What was it about him that you loved?'

She sighed. 'The way he made me feel.'

'Which was?'

'That I mattered. That I counted for something.'

It was a few seconds before Jensen said anything. 'I get that,' he murmured. 'I really do. If it makes any difference, you've always mattered to me.'

She swallowed. 'You to me as well.'

The birds had squawked their last notes of the evening now and in the shadowy indigo light, the silence wrapped itself around Eliza as tangibly as her brother's arm.

'We're changing, aren't we, Jensen?' she said quietly. 'You, me, and Daisy. She phoned me today, said Mum had been in touch and told her about Greg. She told me to jack in my job and run off to Sydney with her.'

'Not such a bad idea. Could you do it?'

Eliza shook her head. 'What and leave you?'

'Wherever you were in the world, I'd always be here for you, you know that.'

'Stop it; you'll make me cry again. Just as I was beginning to feel almost human.'

He gave her shoulder a small squeeze. 'Another tear from you, and I'll be forced to give you a dead arm.'

She smiled. 'You and Tattie, you have something special, don't you? Something true and lasting.'

'I hope so.'

'Aren't you sure?'

'I'm so sure of it, I'm scared of losing it. Of cocking it up.'

'You won't.'

'Track record says otherwise. Relationships have never worked out well for me.'

'This time it's different for you. I know it is.'

'Don't say that. Don't tempt fate to have the last laugh.'

* * *

Later, when he was in bed, Jensen spoke quietly into his mobile phone to Tattie. 'I love you,' he said. 'I just wanted you to know that.'

'I love you too, JC.'

'And I love Madison as well. I love us being a family.'

There was a pause.

'What's wrong?' Tattie asked.

'Nothing. I just want you to know how much you mean to me. Before I met you, I was a bit of a loner, a screw-up; nothing ever seemed to go right for me. But you changed that. I took one look at you and it was as if I knew you already. It was like some kind of amazing recognition. Am I making any sense to you?'

'Yes. Lots of sense. And so as you know, you're the real deal for me. The whole enchilada with extra cheese on top. I love you, JC. I wish you were here so I could show you just how much.'

He smiled into the phone. 'Keep that thought until I get back tomorrow.'

When they'd ended the call, Jensen switched off the light. It's going to be OK, he thought. Nothing bad was going to happen. Out in the garden with his sister, he'd had a passing moment of fear and doubt, that life was going far too well for him.

CHAPTER 33

At The Hidden Cottage, with the French doors wide open to let in the cool night air, Owen was playing Brahms's Concerto No. 2.

The Allegro Appassionato was his favourite movement of the concerto and as he always did whenever he attempted it, he heard Gretchen and Lillian instructing him to approach the piece as their much-loved hero Daniel Barenboim had played it. 'One day, when you're old enough and have the necessary skill,' Gretchen had told Owen, 'you must play it with fire in your belly. You must fill the melodic phrasing with sensual artistry. And there must be majesty to your playing! Never forget that. There must be no half-measures. You must give it your all.'

The irony was they'd never taught Owen to play it; he'd been much too young even to think about attempting such a challenging composition, not when it was considered to be one of the most difficult concertos to tackle. At that young age he may have had raw talent, which Gretchen and Lillian had seized upon and tried to nurture during that twelve-month period of living in Little Pelham, but it wasn't until he was a lot older that he first attempted it with any seriousness. But the two women had frequently played their beloved recording for him, placing the scratchy old LP on their turntable and talking him through Barenboim's technique and impressing upon him that Brahms Piano Concertos 1 and 2 were two of the greatest compositions ever written for piano and orchestra.

All these years on and he could still hear the passion in their voices when they spoke of music, of truly great music. Their zeal and heartfelt emotion had stripped away their age and the awful scars they bore from a horrific fire they'd been lucky to survive. He had never had the nerve to ask them how they'd come to be so badly scarred, but one day, out of the blue, Lillian, the quieter of the two sisters, had told him about the hotel in Stuttgart where they'd been staying while on a recital tour in Germany and which had been the target of a freak arson attack.

It was a miracle that only a dozen people had perished in the fire that had quickly spread to the surrounding buildings, she'd told him. Like many others their lives were changed for ever that awful night, and for the two sisters, their hands and upper bodies horrifically burnt, it meant their musical career and nomadic lifestyle were over and when eventually they were well enough to travel, they returned to England to start a new life for themselves. From what Owen had understood, they hadn't had financial concerns – they were ladies with what his mother had referred to as a genteel background. Or what his father would call 'born with a bloody great silver spoon in their stuck-up gobs'.

After a decade of living in London, they had moved to The Hidden Cottage shortly before Owen encountered them, having moved there to live quietly and unobtrusively. 'We're not great mixers,' Gretchen explained to Owen. 'We prefer our own company, given that others find us so monstrously disagreeable to look at.' She further explained that The Hidden Cottage, with its wholly appropriate name, had seemed perfect for them as a place in which to settle, away from prying eyes, away from blatant and offensive stares and remarks. They went to great lengths to preserve their privacy, rarely opening the door to callers, employing a cleaner and a gardener-cum-handyman from outside of the village and ordering in anything they needed by way of food and household requirements. Apart from their GP, Owen was the only other person they had allowed over the threshold. They had granted him the extraordinary honour and privilege to enter their private world, to be a part of their sanctuary.

When Owen reached the end of the second movement, he relaxed his shoulders, dropped his hands to his lap and let out his breath. A passable rendition, he decided. Good, but, of course, not a virtuoso performance. Not even close. He wondered what Gretchen and Lillian would make of his playing. More to the point, what they would make of him being here in their house. Two questions to which, sadly, he would never know the answers.

He let out his breath again, flexed his fingers and stretched his spine, tilting his head from side to side, loosening the muscles in his neck. He got up and went and stood at the open French doors. Apart from the light spilling out from behind him, the garden was in darkness and all was quiet. Very quiet. It was one of the many things about living here that he enjoyed, the profoundly enveloping silence. Particularly at night when Putin wasn't around to make his infernal racket.

Funnily enough there had been no sign of Putin since two days ago, when Owen had invited Mia to come and see the newly built summerhouse. The last sighting Owen had had of the stroppy bird had been when he'd said goodbye to Mia at the gap in the hedge before she'd hurried back to Medlar House. Putin had given Owen a look of scorching disdain and then hustled off into the bushes, his head down as if he couldn't bring himself to pass comment. 'I've done nothing wrong,' Owen had muttered at the bird.

The look Putin shot back at him seemed to say, *Not yet you haven't.*

Owen had always considered himself to be a man of principle, but that conviction was in serious jeopardy now. He could pretend all he wanted that he respected the fact that Mia was married, but he knew that the slightest encouragement from her and he'd have an affair with her. He'd do it in a blink of an eye and, what was more, he'd claim there was nothing wrong.

Man of principle? Man of straw more like it.

And as if to prove how weak he was, he gave in to the need he'd experienced ever since she'd left on Monday to speak to her again.

He'd already added her landline number to his list of contacts and so he scrolled through and tapped her name. Listening to the ringing sound in his ear, imagining it echoing round Medlar House, it dawned on him what time it was and he hastily terminated the call. It was too late to bother Mia.

Was he bothering her?

Would telling her how much he'd enjoyed her company on Monday constitute bothering? Come off it, he told himself; she would see right through that in an instant.

But then he thought how much more of a bother it would be for her to hear the telephone ring and not reach it in time, for her to be left wondering who it was, to worry that it was one of the children in trouble.

He rang her number again, determining that he had to put her mind at rest that it was only him. But the second he heard the ringing tone, he doubted the wisdom of what he was doing. What if somebody else at Medlar House answered the phone? What if Jeff had arrived home unexpectedly?

OK, he told himself, he should hang up. His was one of those infuriatingly withheld numbers, so no one would know that it was him calling. End of problem.

'Hello,' said a cautious voice in his ear. Cautious *and* worried. And hushed.

'It's only me,' he said, his voice emulating her hushed tone.

'Did you try calling a few seconds ago?' she asked.

'Yes,' he said. 'Sorry, I suddenly realized how late it was. Is it too late to talk? Did I wake you?'

'No, I was just in the bathroom.'

'You sound tired.'

'Well, it is *quite* late.'

'No, I don't mean that kind of tired. I mean anxious-tired.'

'It's a long story.'

'I'm not going anywhere; tell me. Unless . . . unless I'm being a nuisance and you'd rather go to bed.'

'That's all right, I'm in bed now.'

He bit back a smart alec reply, kept his mind focused on the tension in her voice. Not her body. Definitely not her body. Or what she might or might not be wearing. Was she a silk nightdress sort of woman? Or did she prefer a cotton T-shirt? Or maybe she slept naked?

317

'Are you still there?'

He swallowed. 'Yes, still here.' He looked out at the garden, stared up at the stars shining brightly in the dark night sky. 'So tell me what's been going on at Medlar House to make you sound so tense.'

'It's poor Eliza. It turns out that the man she was seeing was playing away from home; he's married with two small children. He's been lying to her the whole time. She's absolutely devastated. I've never seen her like this before.'

'The no-good bastard.'

'Quite.'

And there we have it, Owen told himself. That's the reality of an affair. People get hurt. They get badly hurt.

CHAPTER 34

In Brussels it was an oppressively muggy evening. With the air-conditioning on, and stripped down to his boxers and a T-shirt, Jeff was propped up in bed talking to Mia on the phone.

It had been a long week, nothing but meetings and hassle; tomorrow was Friday and he was looking forward to going home. Or rather he *had* been looking forward to going home for a quiet and relaxing weekend until Mia had told him about Eliza having some kind of breakdown over that boyfriend of hers; apparently he'd been leading her a merry old dance. Men were crafty devils when they wanted to be. And he should know – he'd played a few tricks in his time.

Having heard quite enough about Eliza, he said, 'Mia, she'll get over it.'

'Is that all you have to say?'

'What else can I say? Or do you expect me to track the man down and give him an old-fashioned thrashing? Is that what you want? Because if that would help, if you really think it would make Eliza feel better, just say the word and I'll do it.'

Pointing the remote control at the television screen, Jeff changed the channel. The company paid the rent on this apartment, but whoever the owner was, he had tricked it out very much as a fantasy bachelor pad. Which, if Jeff was honest, was what had attracted him to it. Why not? Mia had made it plain she didn't want to move to Brussels with him, so why shouldn't he indulge himself in something she would never condone, such as a fifty-four-inch flatscreen television in the open-plan living area, as well as the same sized one here in the bedroom on the wall opposite the bed, which gave him access to as many channels as there were grains of sand in the Sahara desert. On the ceiling above the bed was a mirror and at the foot of the bed there was a drinks cabinet that slid up and down at the touch of a button on a separate remote control, and which also controlled the air-conditioning and the blinds at the windows. Many a night he'd lain here in this large empty bed and pondered what activities previous occupants had got up to.

Down on the street below, he heard a car horn blaring and in his ear he heard his wife say, 'It would just be nice if you showed that you cared.'

He rolled his eyes and dragged a hand across his face. 'Of course I care,' he said. 'But realistically what can any parent do?' He wished now he hadn't rung home. What was the point when all he got was an earful of narky criticism? And always, *always* it was something to do with the children.

320

Were they ever going to grow up and live their own lives? Although, while he hated the idea, this much he'd say for Daisy: at least she had the guts to think about doing something on her own.

'Look,' he said, 'when I was Eliza's age I wasn't running home to my mother just because some relationship hadn't worked out.'

'No,' came back Mia's voice. 'You'd dumped me and your son and were doubtless shagging for England!'

Shocked at her outburst, Jeff opened his mouth to retaliate and then shut it. No, he told himself, don't go there. But what the hell had brought that on from Mia? Why was she so damned touchy all of a sudden? 'Why are we arguing?' he asked. 'I see little enough of you as it is and now I can't even phone you without getting a bucketload of grief. Can't you sort Eliza out on your own? I mean, it's not as if you told me this when it happened. You knew all this about Eliza on Monday evening; it's now Thursday. I'm always last to hear anything these days.'

'I tried ringing you several times but all I got was your voicemail.'

'I've been busy. You have no idea what my life is like here, just how many bloody balls I'm juggling with. And then you throw in another, telling me that Eliza's upset and somehow expect me to wave a magic wand and make it all better. I'm good, Mia, but I'm not Superman. And since when has Eliza ever asked me for help?'

'She doesn't ask anyone for help. That's her trouble. This is the first time in her life that she's found herself out of her depth and she can't handle it. It's completely unknown territory for her.'

Jeff picked up the other remote control and watched the drinks cabinet slide into view a few inches from his feet. 'Sad fact of life,' he said into the phone, 'Eliza's going to have to learn how to roll with the punches, and the sooner she learns that the better. She needs to toughen up. I can't make things like this go away for her.'

There was a lengthy silence and for a moment he thought perhaps the line had gone dead. 'Mia,' he said, 'are you still there?'

'It would be different if it was Daisy,' she said. 'You wouldn't be saying she has to toughen up, would you? You'd be threatening all sorts on someone who'd treated her as badly as this Greg has treated Eliza.'

He inhaled deeply and shifted down the bed to help himself to the bottle of Jack Daniel's he kept there along with a couple of glasses. 'Daisy's different,' he said, choosing his words carefully. 'She's more sensitive. Besides which, I'm the one she's always turned to. That's the way it's always been. You had Jensen and Eliza and I had Daisy.' As soon as the words were out, he waited for Mia to fire back with – *And look what a fine job you've done with Daisy, she's not even talking to you!*

He'd decided that when he was at home, at the weekend, he would ring Daisy. What was more, he would arrange to go and see her in Luton. He'd apologize face to face and he'd even be nice to Scott. He'd do everything that was expected of him. He might not like her decision to go to Australia and marry this man, but he knew that if he was to have any chance of making things right with Daisy, he had to pretend to give her his blessing. Then in all probability, when she realized she didn't have a fight on her hands, the appeal of Scott and the life he was offering her would wear off. Deny a person what they want and they want it all the more. Hand it to them on a plate and suddenly they don't want it any more. Basic stuff, really.

'But that's not how families should be,' Mia said, surprising him that she hadn't said what he'd expected her to. 'Normal parents don't differentiate between their children; they love them equally and treat them equally.'

Surreptitiously unscrewing the top of the Jack Daniel's bottle, he said, 'It's not about treating them equally; it's about treating them according to their individual needs. Now, Mia, for two seconds can you forget about the children and let me tell you why I've called?' And with a bit of luck, he thought, it would take the edge off her bad mood. 'We've been invited to Monte Carlo. A slap-up all-expenses-paid jolly. A German client is having a company jamboree and a few of us from Rieke Hirzel, the chosen few,' he added with a chuckle, 'have been invited, plus partners.'

'When?'

'It's a bit short notice: July 9th and 10th.'

'Hmm . . . those dates ring a bell for some reason. Yes, I know what it is, it's when I've got the—'

'Whatever is booked, unbook it,' he interrupted her. 'I guarantee this will be much more fun.' Then realizing he'd made another gaffe, that this last remark wouldn't improve Mia's current mood, he hastily said, 'I'll see you tomorrow evening. Usual time. And please, Mia, can we have the house to ourselves? No kids. For once I want a weekend when I have you entirely to myself. I miss you.' He waited for her to say she missed him, but she didn't.

CHAPTER 35

Muriel's dinner parties were legendary and not for the faint-hearted.

While she would be the first to say that she was a terrible cook, what she lacked in culinary expertise she more than made up for with her ebullient hosting skills and generous hand when it came to anything poured from a bottle with an alcohol content. Her generosity with aperitifs, dinner and dessert wines, port and a little something to ease the digestion ensured – unless you were the designated driver and therefore could abstain with total impunity – that rarely did a guest leave with all their senses fully functioning. But as her guests usually arrived on foot they could, on the whole, look forward to a lost morning the following day.

Mia had long since learnt to pace herself and on this occasion she was making doubly sure that she didn't drink too much, worried that if she did she might reach a tipping point and lose her temper with Jeff. Since he'd arrived home last night and she'd told him in bed that Muriel, very much as a spur-of-the-moment suggestion, had invited them to dinner, thereby denying him the peaceful Saturday evening he'd wanted, he'd been in a childishly sulky mood, made worse when she had said Georgina and Owen had also been invited. 'Oh, I get it,' he'd muttered bad-temperedly, 'Muriel's trying to play Cupid and wants us to play along, does she?'

'Something like that,' Mia had said noncommittally, switching off the lamp on her bedside table and hoping to bring an end to the conversation.

Annoyingly Jeff had had other ideas and had gone on at length about Georgina being a fool to get involved with Owen Fletcher. 'I mean, what is the fascination with the man?' he'd asked. 'Every time I go into Parr's, Wendy is all over him like a rash and Muriel's just as bad. I'm surprised she isn't trying to snag him for herself instead of encouraging Georgina to go after him.'

Adding insult to injury, Mia had told Jeff this morning at breakfast that she wouldn't be going to Monte Carlo with him as she had a photographer for a women's magazine coming to take some pictures for an article on small businesses run by women for women. The arrangement had been made more than a month ago and she was actually quite excited about Mia's Hats featuring in the magazine. She had no intention of cancelling or postponing the photographer for the sake of a couple of days spent in the company of a crowd of high-spirited strangers, albeit in the south of France. She'd been on enough of these corporate all-expenses-paid trips to know that there was only so much small talk she could make to a roomful of boisterous, self-satisfied men and their overdressed – or underdressed – wives and partners.

'Now then!' Muriel boomed as she herded them into her dining room. 'Owen, you go on my left and Georgina, yes, you go next to Owen. Jeff, I want you on my right where I can keep an eye on you and enlist your help as and when required. So that leaves you, Mia, to sit between your good husband and Georgina. Sorry, nothing I can do about the girl/boy thing; we're a man short. Story of my life,' she added with a hearty bark of uninhibited laughter, the product of two colossal gin and tonics already consumed. She clapped her hands. 'Righty-ho, sort yourselves out. I need to attend to my witch's cauldron in the kitchen or there'll be no starter.'

At Muriel's departure, Owen pulled out Georgina's chair for her and, smiling her thanks, she sat down.

At Mia's side, Jeff rolled his eyes, drained his gin and tonic with a rattle of ice cubes, and pulled out Mia's chair with a perfunctoriness that left her in no doubt what he was thinking. She may well know exactly what her husband was thinking, with an intuition born of old, but she had never felt more emotionally disengaged from him.

Georgina was looking exceptionally pretty this evening, having swapped her usual cargo-style trousers, trainers and baggy T-shirt for a mint-coloured dress from Monsoon with a matching bead necklace and a pair of strappy sandals. 'Doesn't look like I'm trying too hard, does it?' she had whispered to Mia when she had been last to arrive in a fluster of nervous excitement. 'You look lovely,' Mia had assured her. Georgina had confessed to Mia and Muriel the other day that since she'd been widowed, Owen was the first man to whom she had felt remotely attracted. She'd even admitted to having an extraordinarily erotic dream about him. 'I think it's awakened something lethal in me,' she'd giggled.

'Oh, we've all had that dream about Owen,' Muriel had joked. Then more seriously Muriel had said that Georgina should leave it to her to play Cupid.

So here they all were, with Muriel poised with Cupid's arrow. And watching how solicitous and charming Owen was with Georgina, compared to how boorish Jeff seemed to be deliberately behaving, Mia felt a pang of longing for Monday afternoon, when Owen had rowed her across to the island and they'd sat in peaceful isolation from the rest of the world. So blissful had it been she had relaxed and simply allowed herself the pleasure of talking to him in a way she couldn't with anyone else. He had been right when he'd said he was a good listener. He'd been a good listener again a few days later when he'd called her late at night. She had been surprised to hear from him, but not so surprised as to feel unsettled by his call.

She thought again about that afternoon with him at The Hidden Cottage and how, when she had walked through the woods, she had questioned what purpose it served to continue punishing herself by staying with Jeff. It had seemed almost inevitable that, having briefly and tentatively, maybe even selfishly, considered her own future happiness, she should then find Eliza at home and in need of her help. It was a classic example of what she'd tried to explain to Owen – the strength and pull of family ties and that you could never be free of them. Not that she would ever want to be.

She listened to Georgina asking Owen how the runner beans she'd sold him at the fete were doing and had a sudden mental picture of Georgina at The Hidden Cottage and Owen rowing her across the lake to the island. From nowhere she felt an appalling and shameful flare of jealousy. It made her throat clench and her mouth go dry. Shocked, she reached for her wineglass and put it to her lips, realizing too late and to her acute embarrassment that it had yet to be filled.

Next to her Jeff laughed loudly. 'You'll have to excuse my wife,' he said to Owen. 'Mia's always in a hurry to get a drink down her.'

Had he always had such a crude laugh? Mia wondered miserably as Owen glanced at her, further adding to her discomfort.

Georgina smiled brightly – but then everything about her this evening seemed twinkly bright and radiant. 'It's you, Jeff,' she said cheerfully, 'you'd drive any poor girl to drink.'

'What's that about a drink?' bellowed Muriel from the kitchen.

'It's Mia,' Jeff shouted back at her, 'she's got a real thirst on her tonight.'

'Then for the love of God, pour her a glass of wine. There's plenty of it on the sideboard behind you. Choice of red or white. All open. Pass them round. And, Owen, perhaps you'd do the honours with the candles. There's a box of matches on the window sill.'

Jeff twisted round in his seat and reached for a bottle of each, and continuing with the joke while at the same time playing to the gallery with a theatrical wink, he said, 'Will these two bottles be enough for you, darling?'

Not nearly enough, Mia thought. Oh, not nearly enough.

'You sentimental old thing, Muriel,' Jeff said later when they'd consumed the hottest mulligatawny soup Owen had ever tasted, and Muriel – flush-faced from the kitchen – reappeared in the dining room with a squeaky-wheeled hostess trolley, loudly demanding space to be made: 'Gangway, gangway!'

'Sentimental,' she repeated, crashing the trolley against the sideboard and upsetting one of the dishes on the top deck. 'How so?'

'We had Frank Sinatra earlier; now we have this cheesy medley. Michael Bublé, isn't it?'

Brandishing a carving knife in one hand and a long-pronged fork in the other, Muriel snorted. 'Philistine! I'll have you know this is Harry Connick, Junior.'

'Whoever it is, it's as schmaltzy as hell. You're not trying to get off with me, are you?'

'Hah! Do I look stupid? No offence, Mia.'

Mia waved the comment aside. 'Please, offend away.'

'Well, if it's not me you're trying to seduce, it must be Owen.'

Knowing exactly what Jeff was up to and what Muriel might hope would be the outcome of this perfectly orchestrated evening, Owen said, 'Shucks, Muriel, we've been found out. Now we'll be the talk of the village.'

She laughed. 'Good-o! It's a while since I've been the centre of any salacious gossip.' Again she brandished the carving knife and fork in the air as though she was conducting Harry and his band herself. 'Right then, roast beef,' she said. 'I'll warn you now, it's rare, so no whinging about any blood on your plate.'

While they all watched her attack the slab of meat, Owen stole a glance across the candlelit table at Mia. She looked like she was having the worst evening ever. But then he wasn't having such a good one either. He knew he was being set up with Georgina and while he liked her, they would never be more than friends. But how to make that irrefutably clear without causing any offence? He'd

331

never been in a situation like this before, so wasn't sure of the ground rules, but he knew enough to know that he would have to tread carefully. Little Pelham was a small village and doubtless a number of well-meaning people had already put a conveni- ent two and two together and the last thing he wanted was to cause Georgina any embarrassment or disappointment. He had contemplated lying to Muriel, saying he was busy tonight, but that would have only meant a postponement of the evening to a more convenient date for him.

From the CD player came the opening notes of Harry Connick, Jr singing 'The First Time Ever I Saw Your Face'. Not realizing that he was still staring at Mia, Owen suddenly found his gaze locking with hers in the candlelight, and in what seemed like an abrupt and unnatural silence around the table, he was held transfixed by the intensity of her expression and by the lyrics of the song playing – *I thought the sun rose in your eyes, the moon and the stars were the gift you gave to the dark and the endless skies, my love.*

He swallowed and wrenched his gaze away, just in time for Muriel to pass him a plate of barely cooked meat. 'Mm . . . That looks good,' he mustered faintly.

'I must say, Georgina,' Jeff said, raising his glass to her with a wink, 'you're looking rather gorgeous this evening.'

'Thank you,' she said, with a coy bob of her head.

'And what about me, Jeff? Aren't I looking rather gorgeous?'

Jeff raised his glass to Muriel. 'Muriel,' he said, 'you are as enchanting as ever. And that, I have to tell you, is a very brightly coloured dress you're wearing, very eye-catching.'

'It's to keep me awake,' she said.

'It's keeping us all awake!' Jeff laughed.

When they'd added vegetables and potatoes to their plates and something that Muriel assured them was gravy, Owen sensed that he was about to come in for his share of attention from Jeff.

'So, Owen,' Jeff said, after taking a lengthy swallow of his wine and draining his glass, 'how are you passing your time here in Little Pelham? With not working, I'd imagine you must be bored.'

'Not at all,' he said easily, 'I'm loving the freedom of living each day as it comes. Keeping my choices limited and simple – it's a refreshing change for me.'

'That's all very well in the short term, but in the long term a man needs more than that or he'll go mad. A man, the hunter-gatherer of our species, needs something concrete in his life, or his existence means nothing.'

'Are you being sexist, Jeff?' Muriel said stoutly, refilling his glass. 'Are you saying the same rule doesn't apply to us women?'

'Oh, don't get on your high horse, Muriel. I'm merely stating the obvious that Owen is going to have to do something before too long, or he'll lose his identity as a man and be out of step with the world. Or worse,' he added with a chuckle, 'become a menace in the village. A man with too much time on his hands is never a good thing.'

'Jeff, please, leave Owen alone,' Mia said. 'You don't have a clue what you're talking about.'

'Hey, I'm just saying how it is, that's all.'

'It's good of you to be concerned about my welfare and my sense of who I am,' Owen said, 'but I think I have it pretty well covered.'

'Of course you have,' Georgina said warmly.

'Personally I think it's terrific we have some new blood in the village,' Muriel said, filling Georgina's glass, 'particularly a strapping young chap with time on his hands. It means he can get stuck in and help with whatever needs doing. We're always short of volunteers, as well you know, Jeff.'

Jeff groaned. 'Come on everyone; lighten up. Hey, I know, why don't we take it in turns to try and think of a new career for Owen? What do you think, Owen? Will you let us do that, you know, just as a party game?'

Oh, this he had to hear. 'OK,' Owen agreed, 'why don't you go first? What do you see me doing in the future? What role do you have in mind for me? Apart from village idiot, as,' he paused and gave Jeff a direct stare, 'if I'm not mistaken that post is already filled.'

Muriel roared with laughter and slapped Jeff on the shoulder, making him spill his wine on the tablecloth. 'Jeff, I do believe you've been outplayed at your own game. Bravo, Owen! I knew this evening would go with a swing. Anyone for more beef? There's plenty of it.'

As was to be expected, Owen was assigned the task of seeing Georgina safely home.

Having thanked their host, the four of them set off down Cloverdale Lane and, more than a bit wobbly on her feet, Owen placed a hand under Georgina's elbow. When they reached the main road, Jeff and Mia wished them a good night and predictably, Jeff – who looked very nearly as unsteady on his feet as Georgina – put a clumsy arm around Mia, pulled her roughly to him, and slurred, 'You be good, you two.' He wagged a finger at them. 'And if you can't be good, at least keep the noise down.' The dumb unoriginality of his comment had Mia turning away from him, but it set Georgina off with a fit of giggles.

Owen slowly steered his charge across the green and up the hill towards her cottage on School Lane.

'Thish is svery kind of you,' Georgina said in a deafeningly loud voice, crashing the quiet still of the night – the clock on the church tower showed five minutes to one. Ahead of them, Owen saw a man coming towards them; he didn't recognize who it was, but he was obviously taking his dog for a late-night walk; amusingly he was carrying a mug with him and was drinking from it. 'Hello, Georgina,' the man said as they drew level. 'Had a good night out have you?'

She giggled and swayed towards him. 'A slovely night, shank you, Sjohn. Have you met Owen?' She flung a hand at Owen's chest with unexpected force. 'Owen, thish is Sjohn. Sjohn, thish is Owen.'

'Hi,' John said with a good-humoured smile, 'good to meet you.'

'You too,' Owen said.

Then raising his mug at the pair of them, the man pressed on, following his yellow Labrador down the hill, the way Owen and Georgina had just come.

When they reached her cottage, Georgina rummaged in her bag for her keys. 'They're shere somewhere,' she said. 'I . . . I know I put them in. I wouldn't have left the house un . . . unslocked.'

'Do you have a babysitter inside looking after the boys?' he asked. 'Could she let you in?'

She shook her head. 'They're schtaying the night with um . . . with Molly . . . oh, what the heck?' And holding her bag, she turned it upside down, shaking its contents onto the doorstep. Her eyes wide, she then looked at Owen as if thinking this hadn't been such a clever idea. She then started to laugh like a child, or rather to laugh like a very drunk woman.

He carefully sat her on the low stone wall in front of her cottage, and in the dark gathered up her things – a mobile phone, a packet of tissues, some used tissues, a strip of paracetamol, a purse, some odd coins, an item of feminine hygiene, a hairbrush, a biro, a packet of seeds, a shoelace, a shopping list, a plastic Smurf figure, a handful of fluff-covered sultanas and lastly, and most useful of all, a bunch of keys.

After a few tries, he found the right key and opened the front door. By which time Georgina had fallen asleep with her head resting against the wall of her cottage.

'Georgina,' he said in a low voice. *'Georgina.'*

No response. She was completely sparked out.

With nothing else for it, he placed his hands under her arms, lifted her to her feet and somehow managed to get her inside, hoping all the while that no one was peering out from the cottages opposite and misinterpreting the scene.

CHAPTER 36

The next morning, despite how annoyed she was with Jeff at the way he had behaved at Muriel's, Mia's priority was to get him in the right frame of mind to apologize to Daisy, to make things right between them. What would be the point in expressing her feelings about last night anyway? It would only antagonize Jeff and he'd claim, as he always did, that she was exaggerating, or make that other perennial remark of his, that she lacked a sense of humour.

As soon as he left the house to drive to Luton, Mia rang Daisy to tell her that he was on his way. 'He'll do things clumsily,' she said, 'but try and be patient with him; just let him get the words out. He really needs to do this. So do you.'

'I know, Mum. And thanks. For everything.'

'For what?'

'For trying to make things right all the time. It can't be easy. Not with the way Dad can be. And . . . and I don't think I've always been the easiest of daughters for you.'

'Nonsense.'

'Nice try, Mum, but I know it's been tough for you. Too often you've been caught in the middle.'

Why, thought Mia, when five minutes later she rang off, was it only now, when Daisy was moving to the other side of the world, that they seemed to be creating the kind of mother and daughter relationship she had always hoped to have with her youngest child? Parting with Daisy was going to be such a wrench.

She then phoned Eliza to see how she was. Adamant that she had things to do in London, and promising that she would take it easy, Eliza had caught the train back with Simon on Friday to spend the weekend there. 'I'll be with you again on Monday evening,' she'd said. 'It'll be business as usual then. It has to be.' While it had been good to hear Eliza sounding more positive, Mia was still anxious about her.

With no answer from Eliza's mobile, Mia left a message and wondered what to do next. After seeing Daisy, Jeff was going straight on to the airport to fly back to Brussels, so the rest of the day was her own.

She contemplated going over to the barn to prepare the VAT paperwork for her accountant, but she couldn't face it. Next she contemplated tackling the weeds in the garden, but the sky was overcast and it didn't induce any desire in her to garden. There was a pile of ironing that needed tackling, but again she couldn't summon the enthusiasm.

Admit it, she told herself, everything else is a distraction from the one thing you really want to do, which is to go and see Owen.

It was true. It was that look he'd given her during dinner at Muriel's. She couldn't stop thinking about it. It was the last thing she'd thought of before falling asleep and the first thought she had woken to this morning. She had wanted to believe she had imagined it, but she knew she hadn't. It had been real.

Just as real as the shameful jealousy she'd felt of Georgina. Not only at the table, but when Owen had walked her home. Was he the kind of man to take advantage of a woman who'd drunk too much and stay the night?

She shuddered at the thought, torn between wanting to hate Owen if he had, but wanting to believe he was better than that.

But what if he'd looked at Georgina in a new light during dinner? She had looked so pretty last night. Surely she couldn't blame Owen for being attracted to her?

Oh, but she could when the truth was she wanted him for herself. There, she'd said it. No more pretending. Some genuine honesty from her for a change. And the acknowledgement that she couldn't go on like this. She couldn't spend the day torturing herself with thoughts of Owen and Georgina. Jealousy was the least productive emotion a person could feel, and despising herself for succumbing to it, Mia knew she had to resolve matters. If not for her sake, then for her friend. If Owen had any intention of getting involved with Georgina, he had to be told that he had no right looking at Mia the way he had last night.

No, she told herself. No self-righteous indignation to justify what she was about to do. She mustn't kid herself that she was doing this for Georgina's sake. She had to be honest and admit that she was attracted to Owen and couldn't bear the thought of him with another woman.

Twenty minutes later, filled with resolve, she set off for The Hidden Cottage, opting to eschew the main road and take the footpath as she had with Owen on Monday. The sensible thing would have been to ring him, but the conversation she had in mind needed to be done face to face.

Feather-light rain was just beginning to fall when she turned into the footpath. It was the first rain they'd had in over a week and she considered going back for an umbrella, but decided against it.

When she emerged from the bluebell wood and slipped through the gap in the hedgerow, the rain was coming down in earnest. She started towards the house, crossing the wet lawn and with her foot on the first step up to the veranda, she heard music – piano music – through the French doors that were ajar. She pictured Owen sitting at the piano, deep in concentration, his hands moving over the keys. It was an image that not only reminded her of the intense expression on his face in the candlelight last night, but made her feel she was eavesdropping on a private, almost intimate moment. It had the immediate effect of calming her, of making her take a deep breath.

She took the remaining wooden steps up to the veranda as silently as she could. Out of the rain now, she inched yet closer to the French doors. But then beneath her the wooden floor gave a loud creak. The music stopped abruptly. 'Putin, is that you?'

She stepped in front of the doorway. 'No, it's not Putin,' she said. 'It's me.'

'*Mia!*' Owen rose from the piano and came to her, throwing wide the doors.

Seeing the obvious delight on his face at the sight of her, she felt a thrill of pleasure run through her. 'What was that you were playing?' she asked. 'It was lovely.'

'It's called "How Peaceful",' he replied, 'or sometimes it's known as "How Beautiful". Rachmaninov dedicated it to his wife Natalya at a particularly happy time in his life.'

Then for the longest moment he simply stared at her, and all she could do was stare back at him, unable to tear her gaze away from the compelling expression in his eyes. Caught, just as she had been last night.

'You're soaked,' he said at last.

She looked down at her clothes, which she realized were indeed quite wet. 'So I am. How clever of you to notice.'

A small smile parted his lips. 'Sharp as a pin, me. Not that I'm not pleased to see you, but why are you here?'

She steeled herself. 'I wanted to talk to you.'

'Then you'd better come inside.'

Inches apart, the air potent with anticipation between them, she hesitated. She knew that jealousy had driven her here and if she stepped over that threshold she really would do *the unthinkable*. But it was too late to turn back. The overwhelming compulsion to touch him, to hold him and kiss him was too great.

When she didn't respond, he put a hand to her cheek and touched it lightly. 'Mia,' he said, 'I promised you before that I wasn't playing a game with you. Nothing's changed.'

Oh, but it has, she thought. *I've* changed.

There was a look of great purpose in his face now, as though he had made an important decision. The pressure of his hand resting against her cheek increased and it was all she could do not to throw herself into his arms. With the merest of movements, she turned her head until her lips brushed against the palm of his hand. She heard his sharp intake of breath and then in one fluid movement he drew her to him and kissed her.

CHAPTER 37

The combination of rain, poor visibility and roadworks meant Jeff had no choice but to crawl along at a snail's pace on the M1. Which gave him plenty of time to prepare what he wanted to say to Daisy, as well as reflect on last night.

Normally he enjoyed an evening with Muriel and Georgina; he liked to spar and flirt in equal measures with the two of them, but Owen-bloody-Fletcher's presence had stymied the atmosphere of the evening. The man was that slippery he could cause his very own oil slick. Every opportunity he got, he managed to make himself the centre of attention. For the life of him, Jeff didn't comprehend why Muriel and Georgina, and Mia for that matter, couldn't see the man for what he was, a whopping great fake, a smarmy smooth operator who would probably end up causing Georgina to make an embarrassing fool of herself over him.

Mia had been in a singularly odd mood the entire evening and things hadn't improved at home when they were in bed. Fair enough, he'd been a bit drunk, but not so drunk as to be incapable, which was what Mia accused him of when he'd tried to kiss her.

Luck was finally on his side when he managed to park his Merc on the street two doors down from Daisy's flat. He suddenly felt nervous. He had to get this right. He absolutely must not let his temper get the better of him. He was here to build bridges. He was here to show Daisy that he loved her, that nothing was more important to him than her happiness. When he'd texted her yesterday afternoon to ask if he could come and see her this morning, he'd dreaded her saying no, or worse still, hearing nothing from her at all.

He hastened along the pavement in the rain and buzzed the intercom. A disembodied voice – that of his future son-in-law – instructed him to come on up.

Disappointed that Scott was here, he took the stairs with grim determination. He would have preferred to have this conversation without Scott around, but clearly that was not to be.

He was waiting for Jeff on the landing. 'Daisy's just gone out to the shop to get some bread for lunch,' he said.

'What? No Sunday roast?' Jeff quipped, taking in the ripped jeans, the bare feet, the sleeveless T-shirt, the unshaven chin and the general air of a man who simply wasn't good enough. Who was this nonentity to presume he was good enough to look at Daisy, much less marry her?

'We thought soup and sandwiches would be OK,'

Scott said, ushering Jeff inside the flat and closing the door. 'The thing is, we're out for dinner tonight and we didn't want—'

'You're packing up,' Jeff interrupted, looking round at the packing boxes in the small space. The main pieces of furniture were still in evidence, such as a shabby old sofa and an armchair, a set of shelves, a television and a coffee table, but the rest of the room had been emptied of its contents – the shelves were stripped, as were the walls. *This is really happening*, he thought. *Daisy really is leaving me*. The thought pained him to such an extent, he felt like he'd been punched in the chest. He clenched his fists and turned to face the person who was responsible for causing this pain. 'My wife tells me that you've booked your flights.'

'Yes, that's right.'

The man's casual manner incensed Jeff. 'And you didn't think it appropriate that you should ask my permission to marry my daughter?' he said. 'Or to ask if I minded you dragging her off to some God-awful place in Australia?'

'I'm not *dragging* your daughter anywhere, Jeff.'

This was too much. '*Jeff?*' he repeated. 'Since when did I say you could call me Jeff?'

The other man rolled his eyes and pushed his hands into the back pocket of his jeans. 'OK,' he said with a shrug, 'so that's the way you're playing it, is it? Fair enough. I can play it that way as well. But be very clear on this point, *Mr Channing*: I love your daughter. All I want to do is spend the

346

rest of my life with her, taking the best care I can of her. And while we're speaking so bluntly, I'd say the best thing Daisy could do is to get as far away from you as she possibly can, because you're bad news for her. You've done nothing all her life but screw her up. And from what she tells me, you've done a bang-up job of trying to screw up your other kids as well.'

Jeff stared at him in disbelief. 'Finished?' he asked, his voice gruff with scarcely controlled fury.

'Yeah, I'd say I'm about done.'

His fists even more tightly closed, and fighting hard to stop himself from ramming one into this bastard's smug face, Jeff heard a key turning in the door behind them.

Daisy took one look at her father and Scott and knew straight away that something was wrong. Oh God, she thought when Scott looked at her, but didn't quite meet her eye. What now? And why had she thought it would be a good idea for the two of them to have some time on their own together? She should have sent Scott to fetch the bread. She should have spoken to her father on her own.

'What's been going on?' she asked, clutching the loaf of bread to her chest while closing the door behind her and wishing she were the other side of it.

'We've been sharing a few pleasantries,' Scott said.

Dad snorted. 'More like you were shooting your bloody great mouth off.' He stepped towards Daisy. 'Daisy, I don't think you have any idea the kind of man he really is. He's accused me of things that beggar belief. And if he's been filling your head with this rubbish, then you shouldn't have anything more to do with him. He's . . . he's brainwashing you. He's manipulating you, turning you against me. Can't you see that?'

Her heart sank and she felt a wave of familiar impotency. 'Dad, I don't know who you're talking about, but it's not Scott. Scott would never make me do anything I didn't want to, truly he wouldn't. Why can't you see that? Everyone else does.'

'You mean everyone else has been taken in by him!'

'Stop it, Dad! Just stop it. Please. You said in your text that you wanted to come and apologize, but you haven't, have you? You're only here to try and make me change my mind. You just can't help yourself, can you? You have to keep controlling me.'

'Daisy, believe me, I came in good faith to say I was sorry. And I am truly sorry for what I said, but please hear me out. You and I, we've always had a special bond. Think about it. Haven't I always been there for you? Every milestone in your life, I was there for it. Your first steps, your first day at nursery and then school. I never missed a play or a concert you were in. OK, once or twice I was late, but I was there, Daisy. And why?

Because I loved you. Because you meant more to me than anything else in the world.'

Daisy looked at her father and felt herself being swallowed up by a huge crushing wave of defeat. And sadness. She knew that her father loved her, knew too that in his own way he had always wanted the best for her. That had he been able to give her the stars and the moon, as he'd told her so often as a child, he would have done so.

The crushing wave began to close in on her and she felt the strength to fight her father drain out of her. But then she looked at Scott and remembered what he'd said at breakfast. She had to do this. She simply had to do it or her life would always be the same; she would always be a child. 'Dad,' she said, 'you loved me too much. You tried to make me into something I could never be. You're doing it now. You have to let me go. You have to trust that I can make my own decisions.'

'But you're not, are you? You're letting this . . . this man decide your life for you. He's got you so under his thumb you can't see things clearly.'

Still clutching the loaf of bread to her as if it was a shield, Daisy stepped away from her father and went and stood next to Scott. 'Please don't ever talk about the man I love in that way, Dad. If you do, I swear I'll never talk to you again. Please don't make me do that.'

CHAPTER 38

'I'm not the kind of man who has casual affairs with married women,' Owen said. 'I don't want you to get the wrong idea about me.'

They were lying in bed, on their sides with Mia's back against his chest, their bodies curved together, a natural fit. Her coming here today had totally surprised him. He still couldn't believe she was actually here in his bed. When he'd kissed her for the first time and she had kissed him back leaving him in no doubt how she felt, he'd taken her by the hand and led her wordlessly inside the house and upstairs. If at any stage she had hesitated he would have stopped, but she hadn't.

'And I've never cheated on my husband before,' she said, 'so it's a first for both of us.'

Winding her silky-smooth hair around his fingers, he said, 'I kept looking at you last night and wondering how on earth you've put up with that man for as long as you have. Did you ever love him?'

'Yes. Even when he left me, I still did.'

'Most women's love would have turned to hate at that point.'

350

'I've never hated anyone. I especially didn't want to hate the father of the child I was carrying. What purpose would that have served? I don't hate him now either. I might not like him at times, but hatred doesn't come into it.'

He kissed her neck and thought about what she'd told him earlier, about bringing up Jensen on her own for the first few years of his life. He thought how tough that must have been for her. He chose his next words with care. 'Weren't there other men you dated who might . . . whom you might have married?'

'I was hardly a catch with a young child in tow. And anyway, all my time was taken up with looking after Jensen and trying to hold down a job.'

'What work did you do?'

'I was employed by a cosmetics firm to translate their sales brochures into French. It was convenient in that I could do it at home, but it was slow and laborious work that I could only do when Jensen was in bed. I talked my way into the job, made out my level of French was a lot better than it really was; trouble was I then had to meet that standard. The pay was awful, literally by the word. I'd have earned more stacking shelves in the local supermarket. I might even have met someone, but stuck at home burning the midnight oil meant my social life was non-existent.'

She turned onto her back and looked at him. 'I did love Jeff when I married him. Please don't think it was merely a marriage of convenience. He was different then.' She looked thoughtful. 'But then so was I.'

'What made you realize your marriage wasn't working?'

'When I realized that habit and duty had replaced any real feelings of affection. I kept telling myself that it could still work, that with a bit more effort it could be better. Or it could be enough.'

'Bea and I did the same. We were surrounded by the fruits of our success, but the one thing we'd failed at, our marriage, we both refused to acknowledge. Although Bea was brave enough in the end to do it. If it had been left to me, I think I would have just carried on pretending it was no more than a temporary glitch.' He raised himself up onto his elbow and kissed her. 'What made you come here today?'

'It was the look you gave me during dinner. And jealousy.'

Knowing exactly the moment to which she was referring, he said, 'Hey, you can't hold me responsible for that, that was all you. My God, the scorching way you looked at me I thought I was going to burst into flames. Or at the very least Muriel's beef was going to get cooked.'

'Not true!'

He laughed. 'So what were you jealous of?'

'Georgina. She looked so pretty and I was scared that you might view her differently. After all, she's nearer your age.' She frowned. 'I don't like being older than you.'

He traced a finger along the curve of her mouth. 'A couple of years' difference, that's all. It's nothing. And you can forget about me being attracted to Georgina. I like her, but nothing more, and so as you know, in case she mentions it at any time, she tried to kiss me when I took her home.'

'Did she? Oh, poor Georgina.'

'I just hope she was too drunk to remember what she did. And before you ask, I didn't kiss her back.'

'I was imagining something far worse. I had this awful fear that you might have stayed the night with her.'

'Why on earth would you think that?'

'It's not that much of a stretch. You're a single, commitment-free man; you can go to bed with whomever you want.'

'From the day I met you there's only been one woman I wanted to go to bed with, and that's you.'

'I don't believe you.'

'OK, I'm exaggerating. But I did mean what I said in the boat that day when you came here with your family. I really didn't expect to meet someone as unexpected as you when I moved here.'

Her expression suddenly serious, she said, 'Are you absolutely sure this has nothing to do with your girlfriend ending things with you? You're not just using me to—'

He pressed a finger to her mouth. 'If things had been right with Nicole, I would have wanted her here with me. But it didn't work out that way.' He picked up Mia's hand, the one that bore her wedding ring, and kissed her fingertips, one after the other. He wanted to ask what happened next between them, but decided they'd talked enough. He brushed his lips against hers, lightly at first and then deeply. She kissed him back with equal strength, her hands sliding over him, pressing him to her. He shifted his position and placing his hands either side of her, her legs and arms wrapped around him, he looked down into her face, his eyes on hers. The intense expression in them made his heart thud and his breath quicken. At once nothing mattered more to him than this moment, his wanting her, her wanting him. The desire she instilled in him was electrifying. Before, when he'd brought her upstairs and undressed her, tossing aside her wet clothes, they'd tumbled onto the bed and made love in a frantic and breathless hurry. Now he held himself in check, wanting to be more measured, to explore her body more, to get to know it and to discover what pleased her. He wanted her to be in no doubt what she meant to him. This was no passing fancy on his part; this was so much more than a mere affair. He knew it with all his being.

After they'd made love, they slept. When Mia woke, it was to feel Owen's arms around her, his lips gently kissing the nape of her neck.

'It's still raining,' he said.

'So it is.'

'Are you hungry?'

'Starving,' she said.

'Me too. I'll go and get us something to eat.'

'I'll come with you.'

'Don't you trust me to do it alone?'

She turned and faced him. She kissed him on the mouth. 'No,' she said, 'I don't want to be apart from you.'

'Not even for ten minutes?'

'Not even for five.'

He held her close.

Down in the kitchen, wearing Owen's shirt, Mia sat on a stool and watched him putting a snack together on a tray. She couldn't take her eyes off him, and not just because he was dressed in only a pair of boxer shorts, enabling her to admire his strong, muscular physique. Everything he did fascinated her, every little movement, every little gesture. All of it she took note of, as if committing it to memory – the way he tilted his head from side to side as he decided what to put on the tray; the way he clicked his tongue when he'd made his decision; the way he suddenly turned and smiled at her. Perched on the stool, bringing her knees up to her chin and hugging them, she felt so happy and carefree. Young, too. Ridiculously young. The thought made her suddenly laugh out loud.

'What's the joke?' he asked.

She threw her head back and flung her hands

in the air. 'I feel so happy. Like I could dance around the room. It's as though I'm a little drunk.'

He came to her and, scooping back her hair from her face, he kissed her. 'That's how I always want you to feel.'

'Drunk?'

He smiled. '*Happy* was more what I had in mind.'

Back upstairs in bed they ate and talked some more.

'How long can you stay?' Owen asked.

'I'm yours for the rest of the day. Just so long as I leave when it's still light. I don't fancy cutting through the woods in the dark.'

'I could drive you home.'

'You could. But we might be seen.'

'We were seen last night.'

'You know what I mean. The two of us seen alone together is bound to cause more interest than if we're part of a group.'

'I know,' he said. 'It's just that I don't want to sneak about and turn what I feel for you into something cheap and grubby.'

'I don't want that either.'

'Then leave him, Mia.'

She swallowed. This was it. Once she said these words aloud there would be no going back. 'I plan to,' she said. 'But please don't push me too hard. It's what Jeff's always done. Or more specific-ally, it's what I've allowed him to do.'

'Don't ever compare me to your husband,' he said with feeling, 'I'm nothing like him.'

She could see that she'd hurt him. 'I'm sorry, I didn't mean it like that. But you have to let me do things my way. When Daisy's gone to Australia and when Jeff's recovered from the shock of her going, I intend to ask him for a divorce.'

'When did you decide this?'

She glanced at her watch. 'About an hour ago.'

He looked at her, staggered. 'Wow, I didn't see that coming. You are full of surprises today.'

Feeling a bit dazed, she smiled. 'It feels good.' She leant in to kiss him. 'But it's important to me that I do things in the right order and for the right reasons. I don't want anyone, especially my children, to think badly of you. Which means for now I don't want anyone knowing about us. We must be careful. Do you mind?'

He reached for her hand and laced his fingers through hers. 'I understand,' he said. 'I'll be patient.'

A week. Seven whole days since Eliza had been at the airport waiting for Serene and discovered the humiliating truth about Greg.

A week. A lifetime. It was as good as the same thing.

What shamed her most, apart from the debilitating self-pity she had been consumed by, was that she had been unable to function properly at work. Work had always come first for her and no matter how bad she'd felt, she'd never allowed anything to keep her away from what needed doing. Taking time off because she couldn't stop crying was anathema to her.

Now, however, she was trying to make up for lost time. It was Sunday afternoon and she had spent the greater part of the day working on the client progress report that needed presenting the day after tomorrow. With it now finished to her satisfaction, she tidied away the empty packet of Kettle crisps and two cans of Red Bull that had constituted her lunch, and awarded herself a small pat on the back. A job well done.

But as she tried to cram the rubbish into the overflowing bin and realized that it just wasn't going to fit, and what was more that the contents of the bin stank, anger flashed through her. She looked around her small kitchen, which was usually immaculate, but today looked a hideous mess: dirty plates, bowls and mugs piled in the sink, a pan left on the hob that she hadn't bothered to soak after cooking scrambled eggs in it for her supper last night, crumbs scattered over the work-tops, and a used teabag lying in a revolting brown puddle on the draining board.

Was this what she had been reduced to? Living in squalor? No more! It had to stop. Pushing her sleeves up, she got on with putting the kitchen to rights.

When it was all done, having expected to feel a righteous glow of satisfaction, all she felt was a sense of pointlessness. What was the point in any of it? Why bother about the kitchen? Moreover, why slave away on her day off to prepare a report that would be read by the client and then probably have coffee spilled over it and thrown away?

No, she told herself. There was a point. Her work was important. What she did counted. It mattered. And as if to prove there was value in everything she did, she immediately set about her next task with speed and efficiency.

The ironing board in position, the iron switched on, she fetched the overflowing washing basket from the airing cupboard. Ironing, like everything else in her life, was usually a well-ordered activity that was slotted into her busy schedule at a specific time, enabling her to keep on top of everything. It was how she had always been. Boarding school had taught her that: to run her life smoothly and efficiently and according to a strict timetable.

She soon slipped into a steady rhythm with the iron – collar first followed by the sleeves and the back of the blouse and then the two front panels. It was mindless but in its familiar ordinariness, it was strangely comforting. Before long she had a dozen immaculately pressed blouses – all identical – ready to put away. Simon often teased her about the uniformity of her work clothes, and if he was ever to see her work wardrobe, where there was nothing but these blouses and a row of black and charcoal-grey skirts and jackets, his worst suspicions about her would be confirmed – that she was woefully uptight and suffered from some kind of OCD. Which might well be true, but if it was, it stemmed again from her school days and she didn't have a problem with that. She was who she was. Why pretend otherwise?

In contrast, Simon was probably the most relaxed person she knew and, of his own admission, threw on the first thing to hand in the morning. Unlike her, he didn't do his own laundry – he used a firm that collected and delivered his washing once a week. He had urged her to do the same, saying she could spend her time better, having fun. He was always saying things like that, that she should be more like him and have more fun in her life.

All finished, she switched off the iron, placed it on the worktop to cool down, put the ironing board away and began carrying the blouses through to her bedroom and her work wardrobe, which was her one and only guilty pleasure – her *secret* guilty pleasure. She hung the blouses on the rail and fine-tuned the hangers so that everything was evenly spaced. Below on the floor of the wardrobe, her black work shoes – comfortably flat or with a sensible low heel – were equally perfectly placed; she hated things that didn't line up exactly. Anything out of kilter jarred with her.

With everything in order, she stood back as she always did to admire her efforts before closing the wardrobe doors. But as before, she experienced no satisfaction of a job well done. Instead, she felt a chilling sense of futility. Staring at the rail of clothes that dominated her life, she then opened the smaller wardrobe to the right where she kept her non-work clothes, and which she kept in the same neat and precise order.

The difference, however, could not have been more acute, and as she stared at the few things she possessed for a life outside of work – ancient jeans, loose-fitting jogging bottoms, a couple of baggy tops and some seen-better-days trainers – she tried to remember when she'd last bought herself something to wear that wasn't for the office. Surely she must have bought something special for when she was seeing Greg? But she hadn't, she realized. Because . . . because they had never been anywhere special together. Always he had come here for what he called a nice home-cooked meal, saying he wanted to be with her – alone with her – that he didn't want to waste a precious moment of their time sharing her with other people.

Liar! she wanted to scream. *Liar. You didn't want anyone to see us because you were cheating on your wife! All I ever was to you was a quick and easy shag on the side!*

Her heart was pounding, and the room seemed to shrink around her until all that she could see, summed up in the miserable contents of this small wardrobe, was the stark reality of her pathetic existence. Was this it? Was this her life? Was it even a life?

Choking back angry tears, she returned to the wardrobe that contained her suits and blouses and in a wild fury of helterskeltering emotions she began yanking the hangers off the rail, flinging jackets, skirts and blouses over her shoulder. Exhausted and with tears streaming down her face, she finally sank to the floor and buried her face in the pile of clothes.

Later, when she woke with the pain of something poking her in the ear – a coat-hanger – she looked about her at the heap of tangled clothes. I'm going mad, she thought.

She let out a groan at the sound of the doorbell.

Ignore it, she told herself.

The bell sounded again.

And again.

Reluctantly she got to her feet and went to see who it was.

'Simon,' she said in surprise when she opened the door, 'I thought you were at some music festival with your brother.'

'I was. I just got back and thought I'd come and see how you were. I tried ringing, but there was no answer.'

'I was having a nap,' she said, which was partially true. A comatose nap.

'Can I come in?' he asked.

It would have been appallingly unreasonable to say no, so she nodded and let him in. He had never been to her flat before and she watched him look curiously around as she led him down the narrow corridor towards the sitting room.

'Having a sort-out?' he asked, peering in at the open doorway of her bedroom.

She followed his gaze and blushed furiously, not just at the state of her room, but at the memory of what she had done. Recalling the madness to which she had succumbed was a mistake and she suddenly felt a resurgence of wretchedness. She battled the tears that were threatening to overcome her again but it was no good.

The next thing Simon was holding her and she was crying her heart out once more. This time, though, she was crying not for what Greg had done to her, but for what she had done to herself. For what she had become.

When Mia let herself in at Medlar House, she could hear the answering machine beeping: someone had left a message.

It was Daisy, and she was upset. Jeff's visit had not gone well. Oh, for heaven's sake, what had he done now?

CHAPTER 39

Back in Brussels, having had time to think about what had happened that afternoon in Luton, Jeff's mind was made up: he was going to stand firm.

Mia was on the phone, just as he knew she would be once she'd spoken to Daisy. She was trying to convince him, yet again, that he was wrong. Wrong! *Him?* Unbelievable. But he didn't care what clap-trap she came up with, he had no intention of giving in to her. Not this time. Not when he was in the right. What was more, he was bloody sick of being told that he was the difficult one, that he needed to tread warily and be more sensitive.

What really riled him was that no one had any respect for him or ever stopped to think how he felt. Was he supposed to have no feelings? My God, when he thought about what he'd done for his family! And what did he get in return? Nothing. A big fat nothing.

Well, no more. From now on he was not going to be manipulated by accusations of unreasonable behaviour. And for the record, if anyone deserved to be labelled unreasonable, it was Mia. Never did she see things from his point of view. She always took the children's side in any dispute. Just as she was doing now. Would it kill her, just once, to stand by him?

Stand by him, what a joke! She disagreed with him at every turn, had been doing so for some time now. No wonder the kids behaved the way they did with her as an example.

'If you really love Daisy, you'll climb down and apologize to her and Scott,' she said now.

'I'll apologize when that rude specimen of a boyfriend has apologized to me. And please don't ever use that phrase to manipulate me.'

'What phrase?'

'If you really love Daisy.'

'Oh, Jeff, can't you see that all you have to do is—'

'You weren't there, Mia,' he cut her off. 'You don't know what that sod said to me. He accused me of messing Daisy up. *Me!* I mean, come on, it's perfectly obvious that he's brainwashed her, turned her against me, got her to believe that I'm practically the devil incarnate. And what am I supposed to do meanwhile – stand back and not react? Well, let's see what the reaction is when the Bank of Daddy withdraws its funding!'

'Has Daisy asked you for any money?'

'Not yet. But I guarantee she will do soon. Probably when she gets to Australia and realizes she's made a mistake and wants to get the first flight home.'

'You don't think, after the way you've gone about things, that she'll stick it out just to prove a point to you?'

'I know Daisy. This is another of her phases, like that time when she became a vegetarian; that lasted for all of three weeks if I remember rightly.'

'Jeff, she was ten years old.'

'Doesn't matter how old she was, it's just another example of her believing in something for all of two minutes. This is the same. She's convinced herself she's in love and has got swept along in what she imagines will be a more exciting way of life. It's nothing but a dream.'

'If that's the case, why not let her enjoy the dream while it lasts? Why be so cruel and want to prick her bubble?'

'Cruel? Oh, that's rich! I'm doing what countless times in the past you told me I should have done, which is not to pander or give in to her whims. I'd have thought after Eliza's recent experience you would be the last person to advocate anyone living in a fool's paradise for the sake of a moment's pleasure.'

'There are no certainties when it comes to happiness. But from what I've seen of them together, Scott makes Daisy happy. Haven't you noticed a change in her?'

Remembering how Daisy had stood with Scott's arm around her and asked him to leave before he upset her any more, Jeff said, 'I'll say I have. And not a change for the better.'

'I distinctly recall you saying that you liked Scott when Daisy moved in with him,' Mia said. 'You thought he was a decent and responsible man who would keep an eye on Daisy. What changed your opinion of him?'

'If you'd heard what he said to me you wouldn't be asking that. Just once, Mia, it would be nice if you trusted my judgement and gave me your backing. When was the last time you ever agreed with me? Because for the life of me, I can't remember you doing so.'

'This isn't about us, it's about you and Daisy repairing the damage between the two of you.'

'Actually, you're wrong, this is very much about you and me. It's about us as parents standing firm together. And while we're on the subject, don't you think we should have been told something about Daisy's prospective in-laws? Right now, we know nothing about them. We have no idea what sort of people they are.'

'Daisy's spoken to them. She says they sound nice.'

'Is that it? That's the sum total of the information we have on them, that they're *nice*?'

'What would you rather – that they were horrible?'

'You know what I mean.'

'Yes,' she said, 'I know exactly what you mean. So what happens next?'

'You know what? I don't care. I'm washing my hands of the whole damn thing. Daisy can go to Australia and make the biggest mistake of her life and I'll just wait here until she's ready to admit she got it wrong and comes home. As you've told me so often, I've been too soft and lenient with her, and now she's going to have to learn a lesson the hard way. Now, if you don't mind, I've had quite enough for one day. I'm going to have a shower and go to bed. Goodnight.'

CHAPTER 40

Other than driving to Olney to the DIY store or the nearest big supermarket, Owen had hardly stirred from Little Pelham since his arrival, and so it was with a strange sense of reluctance that he was leaving the peaceful seclusion of The Hidden Cottage. He couldn't pinpoint precisely what was making him feel uneasy, but it was there all the same, a small, inchoate nagging doubt.

It was Friday morning and he was on his way to Virginia Water in Surrey, where he would be spending the weekend with Bea and her new family. Thankfully their divorce hadn't divided their friends and so Bea had invited Rich, along with his girlfriend, Catherine; Owen was intrigued to meet the woman who had made such an impact on his old friend.

Bea had moved to Virginia Water when she and Steve had married; it was unknown territory for Owen, a place he knew only by name and what he imagined it to be – classic high-end Surrey stockbroker belt. With Wentworth on the doorstep, it was perfect for Bea these days as she had caught the golfing bug from Steve. It was through golf that they'd met. Having taken up the game just as their divorce was being finalized – as something to take her mind off 'things' – she had met Steve while having a lesson. Owen could still remember how animated she had been when she'd relayed the encounter to him, and then how equally mortified she had looked. 'Oh my God,' she'd said, 'that was horribly unfeeling and inappropriate of me. I'm sorry.' He had told her he was happy for her. That was the mark of their relationship, he supposed: first and foremost they'd been friends.

With Mia it was different. Right from the start Owen had felt a startling attraction for her, which he still couldn't really explain. It was not unlike the effect The Hidden Cottage had on him; a natural magnetism.

Following her surprise visit last Sunday, Mia had come to him every day since, apart from Monday when Eliza had stayed the night at Medlar House. As soon as she finished work, she would walk through the woods and he would be waiting for her in the usual place, by the gap in the bushes. Greedy for her company, he had tried to persuade her to stay the night with him, but she wouldn't for fear of village tongues wagging or a member of her family ringing late at night, not getting an answer and wondering where she was.

Yesterday she had managed to finish work early and he'd planned a surprise for her. He'd rowed them across to the island, where he'd cooked a supper of trout wrapped in foil on a campfire. 'This is too heavenly for words,' she'd said as they watched the sun slowly sink in the sky. 'I feel as if this isn't really happening to me, that I'm dreaming another person's life.'

He'd taken her hand but hadn't said anything. Everything that was on the tip of his tongue to say would have sounded clumsy or clichéd; silence had seemed better. He'd decided there would be plenty of time to tell her how he felt, that even though they had known each other for such a short time, he knew that he was falling in love with her.

Forty minutes into his journey, he stopped for fuel and called Mia on her work number in the barn. He knew that if he left it till this afternoon to speak to her she would be busy – today was when she had the photographer coming to take the pictures for the magazine article.

'Good morning, Mia's Hats,' she said in a friendly but business-like tone. He could hear talking in the background.

'I'm sorry to be a nuisance,' he said, 'but I just wanted to hear your voice; I'm missing you already. Has the photographer arrived?'

'No, but everyone else has.' Her voice was lower now, almost inaudible.

'Does that mean I can't tell you how beautiful you are and that I wish I'd kidnapped you for the weekend so that we could spend the whole of it in bed together?'

'Um . . . well, yes, that's no problem at all. I can fit you in on Monday for a morning appointment if that suits you.'

He smiled into the phone. 'God, I love it when you talk dirty, Mia.'

'Eleven o'clock then,' she said after a moment's hesitation, 'would that be convenient?'

'Would that be for an all-day appointment? Because I guarantee what I have in mind will require plenty of time.'

'An hour is normally sufficient, but if you like we can play things by ear.'

'An hour? I don't believe it! Short-changing me already! We'll have to discuss that when I'm back. Now, my darling, to save your blushes, I'll get off the line. Good luck with the photo shoot. And, Mia?'

'Yes?'

'This last week has been incredible. *You're* incredible.'

Another hesitation. 'That's . . . that's perfect. I . . . I look forward to seeing you. Goodbye.'

An hour and a half after Owen's phone call the photo shoot for Mia's Hats was well under way. Mia had now posed for the camera so often her face had assumed a stiff falseness that was making her jaw and mouth ache. Part of the problem was that she kept thinking of what Owen had said on the phone and the memory of it made her want to laugh out loud. She was filled with relief when the photographer finally said that she could relax and asked for the first of the models to come forward.

Originally there had been no mention of any hats being modelled but then two days ago Mia had received a call from the editor of the magazine saying it would be nice to have some shots of hats actually being worn. Muriel and Georgina, who had posed for the website in the past, eagerly offered their services but then yesterday the editor had called again and requested that girls of a more youthful appearance pose for the camera.

'Blooming cheek,' Muriel had muttered when Mia had explained the situation to her and Georgina. Mia had then enlisted Daisy and Tattie to help, who thankfully were both free at such short notice. She'd also asked Eliza, but she'd been working in the London office this week, apart from Monday when once again both she and Simon had stayed at Medlar House. Eliza claimed to be feeling a lot better, but Mia could see for herself that she was still very fragile. It upset her profoundly that there was nothing she could do to make the pain go away for Eliza.

It also made her feel guilty about her newfound happiness with Owen, and then, of course, there was the guilty deceit that was never far from her thoughts. To placate her conscience, she told herself the deceit would only continue for a short while. She had been so angry with Jeff on the phone last Sunday evening that she had very nearly told him there and then that she wanted a divorce, but she had held back – she didn't want to do it when she was angry. It had to be done properly, calmly and rationally.

How Jeff would react was anybody's guess, but that was something Mia wasn't going to dwell on. All she knew was that there was nothing he could say or do to make her change her mind. She had backed out once before; it wouldn't happen a second time.

But that was in the future. For now her main concern was his adamant refusal to speak to Daisy unless she apologized to him. As Mia had pointed out, Daisy was so very much his daughter – having inherited his stubbornness – an apology from her was unlikely to be forthcoming any time soon. It was beyond Mia's comprehension that Jeff could hold a grudge against the one person in the world who mattered most to him. 'I don't know how you do it,' Owen had said when she'd told him the stance Jeff was now taking, 'don't you ever want to completely lose your temper with him?'

'I'm too used to suppressing my emotions when it comes to Jeff,' she'd said. 'Staying in control is perhaps how I've stayed sane.'

'You lose control with me,' Owen had said with a smile, 'when we're in bed together.'

She had blushed at his comment. 'That's because you make me feel different about myself,' she'd said. And goodness, how he did! He was such a considerate lover, gentle and thoughtful but at the same time highly passionate and sensual. In turn that increased her desire for him and she gave herself to him entirely and uninhibitedly.

Yesterday he'd asked if it would be arrogant of him to suggest that maybe she became her true self when she was with him. Lying in his arms, she'd kissed him and said, 'I'd say it was a very perceptive insight on your part.'

A burst of laughter brought about a swift change of direction to her thoughts and watching her youngest daughter laughing and joking with Tattie as they struck up various poses for the photographer, Mia thought how wonderful it was to see Daisy so happy and relaxed. The poor girl had gone through so much but in this moment, right now, and despite her father's awful behaviour, she looked more light-hearted than Mia had ever seen her. Jensen had made much the same observation when he'd last seen his sister and agreed that perhaps it was only now, now that she was leaving them, that Daisy was becoming the person she was meant to be. Freeing herself from her family, and all that went hand in hand with that – principally the role she had been cast in – she was no longer carrying the weight of expectation she had grown up with, that of trying to be the daughter Jeff had wanted her to be.

But as happy for Daisy as she was, Mia knew that when the day came to say goodbye at the airport it would be truly heart-wrenching. All she could do was concentrate on the future – the regular chats on Skype and emails and hopefully the trips she would make to Australia to see her daughter. As Daisy said, the world was a much smaller place than it used to be, Australia wasn't really that far away.

Yesterday Muriel had joked that while Mia and Jeff were losing a daughter to the other side of the world, in exchange they were gaining a daughter-in-law and a ready-made grand-daughter. Mia had no idea if marriage was on the cards between Jensen and Tattie, but secretly she hoped it might be. Perhaps it was a quaint notion these days, but she liked the old-fashioned idea of a wedding. She suspected Madison might like it too.

At the photographer's instruction, Daisy and Tattie had now swapped hats and were posing individually for the camera. The pair of them were born to it, Mia thought with a smile. She looked over to where Madison was thoroughly absorbed in a puzzle book. She really was such a delightfully easy child to have around.

Another word search done, Madison closed the puzzle book and watched Mia watching Mum and Daisy. The more she got to know Mia, the more she could see that JC was a bit like her. It was the way he would quietly stand back and watch people, just as Mia did. Which was something she liked to do as well.

It was a shame JC wasn't here with them now but he was busy back in London finishing something important with his work. Madison should really have stayed behind with him and gone to school, but Mum had said that it would be all right for her to have the day off, that no one would really mind, given that she was leaving school before the end of term anyway.

JC had suggested that Mum drive his car here this morning and pick up Daisy on the way and so long as he managed to finish whatever it was he had to do, he would catch the train tonight and join them for the weekend. Tomorrow they were going to go and see their new house again – Mum wanted to check the measurements for the bedroom windows so that she could make new curtains. Then in the afternoon Madison was going to see Beth and have tea with her.

Every time she thought of the new life they would have here, she felt a warm, tingly glow of happiness. But always, always, *always*, she then felt a prickle of doubt and she would worry that it wasn't going to happen, that something would go wrong and spoil everything. Whenever she told Mum this, Mum said that there was nothing to worry about, that nothing was going to go wrong. But Madison wasn't fooled by her certainty, because it was just the sort of thing that mothers had to say, wasn't it?

CHAPTER 41

'B ut—'

'No buts, Channing. Everything's arranged, so you absolutely cannot say no. All you have to do is trust me.' He came round to her side of the desk, where she'd been gathering up her things to go home, and held out his hand to her.

'I don't understand,' Eliza said. She stared blankly at Simon's hand and then at his face.

'You will. Now just for once in your life allow someone to do something for you.' He slipped her laptop bag off her shoulder and hooked it over his own.

'What on earth's got into you, Simon?'

'Nothing but the decision to give you a couple of days of proper relaxation. Is that so very bad?'

'But I was going to work over the weekend.'

He tutted and shook his head. 'I know you were. But to hell with work! You're not a drone; it can keep until Monday.'

'But I can't just—'

He tutted again. 'What did I say about no buts? Come on, let's get going; time is of the essence.'

Suddenly she was being dragged out of the office

she shared with him and he was taking her at speed towards the corridor and the lifts. Thank God there was no one else around to witness this spectacle, she thought. 'Where are you taking me?' she demanded when they came to a halt.

He pressed the button and immediately the doors opened. He pulled her inside. 'Somewhere you'll unwind. Somewhere mobile phones, laptops and iPads are banned. And yes, Eliza, such places do exist in the world.'

She pulled a face at him as the doors closed, realizing then that they weren't alone; there was someone else in the lift with them – a smartly dressed woman Eliza recognized from the law firm on the floor above theirs. The lift began to make its descent and her face reddening with embarrassment, Eliza turned away and in the stark overhead light she caught sight of herself in the mirrored wall and almost recoiled with shock. Surely that haggard stranger with the sickly, washed-out face and the bruised arcs beneath her eyes wasn't her? Did she really look that awful? And oh God, what had happened to her hair? When had she last washed it, never mind been to the hairdresser and had it cut?

The lift doors opened. Simon stepped back and allowed the other women to go first. And as if suspecting she might make a run for it, he took hold of Eliza's arm again. 'Anyone would think I was a prisoner by the way you're manhandling me,' she said irritably.

'An interesting choice of word,' he said, 'because that's what you've become, a prisoner, and of your own making.'

'What's that supposed to mean?'

'It means you need a break. You're worn out. Not just with what Greg did to you, but with what you're doing to yourself. You can't make the pain go away with working crazy hours and pushing yourself to the brink. Not if I have anything to do with it.'

She swallowed. 'I don't know what you're talking about.'

'By the end of the weekend I hope to have disabused you of any more of that absurdly delusional talk.'

On the busy street he hailed a cab directly outside the office building on Shaftesbury Avenue. He pushed her in the back and after he'd spoken to the driver, he got in beside her. She opened her mouth to say that she really didn't appreciate being pushed around, when he shook his head. 'Not another word,' he said. 'I mean it.'

Rich whistled. 'Right, so you ignored everything I said. You've now officially turned yourself into a home wrecker.'

'I haven't!'

Looking up from where she was piping pale blue icing onto Matthew's first birthday cake, Bea said, 'Is it serious, Owen? Do you think she'll really leave her husband for you?'

'I don't want her to leave him because of me. She must only do it if it's right for her.'

Rich held out his glass for a refill from Steve. 'High ideals, mate,' he said, 'but I'm not so sure things really work like that, do they? Wouldn't she have left him before now if things were as bad as you say they are? Sounds like she might be stringing you along.'

Owen exchanged a glance with Bea. She smiled at him. 'Do you want to tell old smarty-mouth here, or shall I?' she said. 'That these things aren't as cut and dried as he thinks they are.'

'What?' Rich said, looking about the kitchen where they'd gathered, now that Matthew had finally settled upstairs.

'You tell him,' Owen replied. 'Then I'll bring his gross insensitivity to his attention.'

'So this is how it can work, Rich,' Bea began. 'Even when the two people in a marriage know it's over, they can often be bound to each other by fear of the unknown, or sometimes they've simply become accustomed to the way things are and accept it. Or,' she said, continuing with the job of piping the cake, a frown of concentration creasing her forehead, 'they hang in there because they still care about each other, or care about what they once had. That's right, isn't it, Owen?'

'Oh, I get it, you're talking about you two, aren't you?' Rich said.

'Give the boy a banana,' Owen said drily.

'Hey, can I help it that I'm late to the relation-ship party?'

'Then stop giving advice,' Bea said. 'Heaven help Catherine, is all I'll say on the matter,' she added with a smile. She straightened up to admire her handiwork. 'Oh, hell, I've only put one T in Matthew's name! I blame you for that, Rich, for being such an idiot and distracting me.'

'Plenty of space there to squeeze in another T,' Steve said helpfully, his arm around her shoulders.

Rich leant over and inspected the cake. 'Don't know what all the fuss is about,' he said. 'It's not as if Matthew can read yet anyway.'

Bea flicked a dishcloth at him. 'You really are the most maddening man on the planet, aren't you?'

'Who is?'

It was Catherine, down from having a shower and now changed out of her work clothes. She was much smaller than Owen had pictured – he'd been expecting a fierce, towering Amazonian woman who would keep Rich in order. But pale-skinned with a smattering of freckles across the bridge of her nose, Catherine was slightly built and in her own words, a 'shortie'. She had a good sense of fun and energy.

'I'm afraid that, as ever, they're all ganging up on me,' Rich said to her, while standing to offer his chair. 'The moment you were gone, they turned on me.'

'Ah, diddums,' she said, ruffling his hair and accepting a glass of wine from Steve. 'Nice work with the cake,' she said to Bea. 'Need any help with anything?'

She's entirely the right woman for Rich, Owen found himself thinking: easy-going and not the sort to take any nonsense from him. What's more, she fitted perfectly within their well-established group, just as Steve had. Which, when you thought about it, was a miracle. A miracle too that Owen got on with Bea's new husband so well. He wondered if they would take to Mia in the same way they had Catherine.

He really hadn't intended to discuss Mia in the depth that he had, but out in the garden earlier, when Steve and Rich were trying to extract a giggling Matthew from a complicated baby seat on a plastic swing and Catherine was upstairs, Bea had laughed and said, 'How many men does it take to get a one-year-old out of a swing seat?' Before Owen had answered, she'd gone on to say, 'You don't seem too cut up about Nicole. Is that because you've met someone else?'

'What makes you think that?'

'Because I know you, Owen. Plus I saw the way you reacted when your mobile went off with a text just a few moments ago. The smile on your face gave you clean away. I presume that was her?'

It had been. A few short words to say that she hoped he'd arrived safely.

And so he'd told Bea all about Mia. It had felt

good finally being able to talk to someone about it. Yet at the same time, hearing himself say the words out loud, he'd been forced to acknowledge that the situation had Majorly Doubtful written all over it. Away from The Hidden Cottage – where life had taken on a happy and almost spellbinding dreamlike quality where anything felt possible – being here, in what felt like the real and highly objective world, a proper and open relationship with Mia suddenly felt far from ever happening. It made him want to get in his car and drive back to Little Pelham, to be with Mia and reassure himself that it was genuine between them, that he wasn't fooling himself.

In Monte Carlo Jeff was watching a bunch of straight-faced German and Swiss businessmen fooling themselves that they were hotshot gamblers and that their losing streak would soon be exhausted and any second they'd be back in the game.

Bored with losing money himself and with the grating hushed intensity of the group gathered around the roulette wheel, he went in search of a drink at the bar. The world-famous casino wasn't at all what he'd expected. He'd pictured people enjoying themselves, having fun, breaking out with cheers and clapping when anyone won. It was more like a bloody morgue. No atmosphere at all. The building itself was impressive and there was obviously some serious money being flashed, but really it was all one massive yawn.

In contrast, the bar was busy with people laughing and joking and the atmosphere was much more to his liking. Everywhere he looked there were men dressed in suits like him, but unlike him, they had their wives with them, all dressed up to the nines, all having a great time. He still hadn't forgiven Mia for not coming. She could have easily rearranged things, but yet again she had behaved with scant regard for his feelings.

He scanned the bar for any of his Rieke Hirzel colleagues and drawing a blank, he edged his way towards the far end where he saw two spectacularly attractive young girls looking his way. Homing in on them, noting the tight little dresses that skimmed great curvy bodies, legs that went on for ever and high-rise heels that fuelled all manner of erotic fantasies, they were damned hot and put all the other women present squarely in the shade.

'Room for a little one?' he asked genially. They smiled brightly and made room for him, one standing either side of him. No complaints with that arrangement, he thought. No complaints at all. This was infinitely better than standing around the roulette or blackjack tables. Turning up the charm, he matched the wattage of their smiles with one of his own. 'How about a drink, you two girls?' he asked.

The taller of the two – she was eye to eye with him – lowered her long lashes prettily. She had tousled hair, lots of it, curly and wavy and all sorts of blonde shades. Her face was tanned and well made-up, her teeth perfectly white, perfectly straight. 'A glass of champagne would be divine,' she said with an accent that was as sexy as hell, but didn't sound too French to him. She didn't look French either.

Her friend – also blonde but of the icy variety and with piercing blue eyes and a body that looked firm and supple – put a hand to the sparkly necklace at her throat. No way could the stones be real. There again, in this particular town anything was possible. 'Yes, champagne would be lovely,' she said. Her accent didn't sound local either. Not that he was an expert.

The barman materialized and Jeff ordered a bottle of champagne. No point in skimping, he thought, might just as well go all the way.

Their glasses filled, they clinked them together and delighted with the way the evening was shaping up, he settled in happily for a chat, aware that the barman was watching, along with a few of the punters further along the bar. Let them look. This was a vast improvement on the tedium of earlier.

Finally Jensen had finished the amendments the client had requested to his website and he could get going. The client was a new one and ran a fast-growing yacht charter business based in the Caribbean and Jensen was hoping for a long and happy, not to say financially rewarding, relationship. He saw no reason why this shouldn't be the case; he knew he was good at what he did, that he had a uniquely creative flair. He also had an above-average obsession for detail, which always reassured the client; they could relax in the knowledge that nothing would be overlooked. As with much of his work, the job had come his way via another client. Word of mouth was always the best way.

An hour later, with a sandwich and a packet of cheese and onion crisps bought on the concourse at Euston Station and plugged in to Thom Yorke's *The Eraser*, he watched the information screen, waiting for it to tell him that his train was ready to board. Annoyingly there was a delay, something about a signal problem. When he was actually on the train and it had set off, he'd ring home and let them know he was on his way.

'OK, Simon, you can relax now.'

'I can?'

'Yes. This is lovely. All of it. And I'm sorry I was so grumpy with you before.'

He smiled. 'I thought there was a moment in the cab when you were going to hit me.'

Eliza looked across the white-clothed table and smiled back at him. 'I thought I was going to as well.'

'What stopped you?'

'Good manners. That and the fact I didn't have the energy.'

He raised his wineglass to her. 'That's because you've been running on empty.'

387

She drank from her own glass and mentally acknowledged that he was right. Acknowledged too that she was just beginning to relax and was grateful to Simon for going to such trouble to bring her here. After the cab had dropped them off at his flat, he'd told her to get into his car and not ask any questions. Resigned and crabby, she had sat in silence and listened sulkily to the music he had selected as he drove them out of London. At some point, after she'd seen signs for Bishop's Stortford and Stansted, she had fallen asleep. When she woke, it was to the sound of Simon telling her they'd arrived.

Out of the car, she had looked up to see an old building in front of her; it loomed over them in the dark. On the other side of the car, subtly illuminated, was a large pond. 'Where are we?' she'd asked.

'Welcome to Suffolk and the Millhouse Spa and Hotel,' he'd replied. 'Your weekend of recuperative pampering starts now.'

While she had stood in the reception area in a daze taking in the flagstone floor, the oversized armchairs placed either side of a cavernous fireplace, the glass vases of flowers and newspapers neatly placed on a long oak table, he had dealt with the business of checking in. From what she could overhear, they were expected.

They were shown upstairs where, in the eaves of the mill, she was shown into her room and introduced to a colossal bed and a freestanding bath. Minutes later, wondering what on earth she was going to do here, Simon tapped on her door.

'Checking to see if I've done a runner?' she said to him.

'No, checking to see if everything is OK. Is it?'

Suddenly overcome with myriad emotions, one of which was knowing she'd behaved badly, she said it was perfect and gave him a small hug.

Now, thanks to room service, they were having dinner in his room, which was next door to hers. The food was delicious, as was the wine. 'I don't deserve you as a friend,' she said.

'That's not what you thought when I confiscated your phone and laptop. You called me a fascist.'

'I've calmed down since then.'

'Thank God for that, Channing.'

'I'm serious, though, Simon,' she said. 'I really don't deserve a friend like you.'

'I totally agree. I don't know why the hell I put up with you. You're a bitch to work with and a right pain in the arse the rest of the time.'

Shocked, she said, 'Am I that bad, really?'

He sucked in his breath and gave a little shrug. 'Let's just say that description fits you on a good day.'

A smirk appeared on his face and the penny dropped. She threw her napkin at him. 'You pig!'

He laughed. 'You're such an easy target; you take everything far too seriously. You've got to lighten up.'

'I hate you.'

'I hate you more.'

★   ★   ★

Jeff drained the last of his champagne and, seeing that the bottle was empty, he said to his two companions, 'How about another?'

The girl with the many shades of blonde hair, whose name was Angelique and who was from Venezuela – her friend, Crystal, was from Bucharest – squeezed his arm, leant into him and whispered in his ear. He'd been wondering when they'd get down to it. He'd been on enough business trips to know the score. No way would a pair of young girls like these two be interested in chumming up with a bloke like him unless there was a financial arrangement involved. The whole time they'd been knocking back the champagne Angelique had given him her full attention, but Crystal's gaze had wandered constantly as she worked the bar, checking for other potential punters.

The transaction agreed, the three of them left the casino and he led them to his hotel a short distance away. It was years since he'd cheated on Mia, but tonight he decided he'd do it in style.

Daisy pulled into the car park and slipped into a space where she hoped her brother would see her. No way was she going to get out of the car to meet him when it was raining so hard.

Tattie had said she would collect Jensen from the station, but since she didn't know the way, it had seemed more sensible for Daisy to go. 'Are you sure?' Mum had asked. 'I'm quite happy to do it.'

Taking the keys for her mother's Golf, she'd said, 'No, no, I'll do it. This way I get out of having to clean up after supper. See you in a tick.'

'Drive carefully,' her mother had called out to her, forever the voice of caution. 'It's just started to rain.'

She'd only been waiting a few minutes when she spotted Jensen. She pipped the horn to attract his attention. He looks well, she thought as he loped along in the rain, his long strides wholly familiar to her. As a child she had tried to imitate the way he walked, thinking that it would make her look as cool as him, but he had derided her for it, had called her a stupid, unimaginative copycat. She had hated him for that and had paid him back by sneaking into his bedroom and breaking the Walkman he'd got for his birthday.

Children could be so needlessly cruel to each other, she thought. When she and Scott had children, she would make sure they were never nasty to one another. But then their circumstances would be different; her children wouldn't have the emotional baggage she and her brother and sister had been saddled with.

She looked again through the side window as her brother was almost level with the car and was glad that things had changed between them. Things had changed a lot recently. Some things for the better and some things for the worse.

Dad. He represented the latter category. But she'd stopped caring. She was going to Australia to marry the man she loved and Dad would just have to sort out his feelings about that on his own. Tough love, that's what that was about.

'Thanks, Daisy,' Jensen said when he'd slung his bag onto the rear seat and got in beside her. He smelt of cheese and onion crisps and coffee and damp hair. 'Sorry I'm so late. How did the photo shoot go?'

'It was fun. We got the photographer to take some pictures of us all together, with Madison as well. Not for the magazine, but for us to keep as a memento of the day. It was Mum's idea, something for me to take to Australia. A shame Eliza wasn't with us – it would have been nice to have her in the photos as well.'

'Not me then?'

She laughed. 'It was strictly a girls' day. And a regular gabfest thrown into the bargain. I haven't laughed so much in ages. Tattie's fab. You've done well there, Jensen. You be sure not to lose her.'

'I'll do my best.'

They were on the A509, the rain really coming down now, when Daisy's mobile rang.

'It'll be Scott,' she said cheerfully, trying to reach her bag that was on the floor behind her seat. 'He'll be ringing to say goodnight.'

'Very sweet, but you can call him back later when we're at home,' Jensen said.

Ignoring him, she released her seatbelt and tried

again to reach her bag. 'Got it! It's OK, I'll only speak to him for a couple of seconds.'

'Law breaker,' Jensen muttered as she put the phone to her ear.

'Spoilsport,' she replied with good humour, pulling a face at him. 'Hiya, Scott,' she said.

Jensen turned his head and did his best to tune out of his sister's conversation. He suddenly felt tired. His eyes were dry and itchy from staring at his computer screen all day. He had a headache as well. Maybe Tattie was right and he needed glasses.

He closed his eyes and wished his sister would get off the phone, not because he was particularly law-bound, but because Daisy wasn't the best of drivers; it had taken her three attempts to pass her driving test and then five weeks after passing she'd gone out in Mum's car and driven it into a lamppost, claiming that it had been a simple case of mixing up the accelerator with the brake pedal.

Above the noise of the rain hammering on the roof of the car he listened to the swish of the windscreen wipers. One – maybe both of them – was beginning to judder against the glass; the rubber was shot. Tomorrow he'd get a new set of wipers for Mum and change them for her.

Thinking of tomorrow, his thoughts turned to the rented cottage they would be going to have another look at and which they would soon be moving in to. Everything was fixed in London for them to leave and Madison's excitement was growing daily. Tattie was getting pretty excited as well and had all sorts of plans for their new life here, one of which was to turn herself into a domestic goddess. 'I swear I'm gonna learn to cook, JC – you'll be real proud of me!'

'I'm real proud of you already,' he'd said, mimicking her accent.

Aware that his sister was still talking to Scott and that he could hear something pinging, Jensen fought to open his eyelids and tell her what he thought about her so-called 'couple of seconds'. But from nowhere a high-pitched scream had him jolting in his seat and he snapped his eyes wide open.

In an instant terror filled him and as he instinctively put his hands up to defend himself, all he was aware of was the insane brightness of the lights coming towards them.

CHAPTER 42

Madison woke with a start.

Straight away she knew that something was wrong. She hadn't meant to fall asleep – she'd wanted to stay awake to see JC when he arrived. Mum had promised she would send him up to say goodnight as soon as he got here. But he hadn't been up to see her, had he? She would have woken if he had.

She put on her glasses and peered at the alarm clock on the bedside table, and with the help of the light from the streetlamp outside coming through the gap in the curtains, she could see that it was almost half past eleven. She pushed back the duvet and padded across the soft carpet to the door that was ajar. Lights were on downstairs. She stepped onto the landing, leant over the balustrade and heard voices.

Low voices.

Not happy voices, but worried voices. And it was Mia and Mum talking. *Only* Mia and Mum.

She strained to hear more but there was definitely no sound of Daisy's voice. Or JC's.

Then she heard the sound of a car. *JC!*

She sped back to her bedroom and stood at the window. Through the gap in the curtains she looked down onto the street where it was pouring with rain and saw a police car. It had stopped directly outside the house. A policeman got out from the driver's side and then a policewoman from the other side. They looked up at the house and Madison realized two things at the same time: that the policeman had seen her and that her heart was beating so fast her chest felt like it might explode.

This was bad. The police didn't arrive late at night with good news. Only bad news. Something had happened. Something very bad.

CHAPTER 43

Owen watched Mia carefully managing her grief. Dressed entirely in black, her face set in an implacable pale mask of grim determination to get through the day, she looked utterly exhausted, as if she had experienced every level of harrowing tiredness and was now functioning as nothing more than an automaton.

He hadn't planned to come here to Medlar House, had only meant to attend the funeral service as a mark of respect and then discreetly slip away. But walking out of the packed church with Georgina, he'd found himself being swept along with everyone else heading this way. When he'd hesitated on the pavement, Georgina had touched his arm and said, 'Please come. It's better that people do.' In a lighter tone, she'd added, 'I'm worried that we might have over-catered and I don't want poor Mia left to eat Muriel's sandwiches for the rest of the week.'

So here he was, a glass of wine in his hand, feeling it was a mistake. He couldn't bear to see Mia like this, weighed down with such deep sorrow, her every move and gesture wrought with exhaustion and suffering, and he unable to comfort her. Yes, he could offer his condolences, as he had already, along with everyone else, but that wasn't what Mia needed. Words alone would not get her through this unthinkable ordeal.

He looked about the terrace of the garden where most people had congregated and where Georgina and Muriel were circulating with large trays of sandwiches and bite-sized food. Seeing the way people were tucking in, Owen doubted there would be a problem with anything left over.

It was three weeks since Mia had phoned him that awful, tragic night when he'd been at Bea and Steve's. Choking back sobs, she had told him there'd been an accident and she couldn't get hold of her husband or Eliza. For a moment this seemed to be what mattered most to her. 'They need to know. They need to be here. But I can't get hold of them.' She said it over and over, until he said, 'Mia, I'll drive back now. I'll be there in no time.'

'*No!*' she'd cried, her voice frantic and shrill. 'Please, I don't want you to have an accident as well. I just wanted to . . . I just needed to speak to someone.'

He'd ignored her pleas and had set off immediately, leaving a hastily written note for Bea on the kitchen table, not wanting to wake her or disturb the sleeping household.

He'd driven straight to the hospital in Northampton and found Mia there with Tattie and Madison, all three of them sitting in dazed shock.

If Tattie had been surprised to see him, she had kept it to herself, but then she'd had so much more on her mind. 'What's the latest news?' he'd asked, dreading the answer.

'We're still waiting,' Mia had said.

Now as he stood alone on the terrace, wondering if he could leave without anyone noticing, Owen felt the presence of someone behind him. He turned to see the young man who had sat next to Eliza in church, the one who'd had his arm around her shoulder when she'd followed her parents out at the end of the service, her head lowered as she'd wept. A good friend, Owen had decided. Maybe the one Mia had told him about called Simon, the work colleague. Not the boyfriend who'd turned out to be married.

The young man nodded at Owen in the time-honoured way of breaking the ice and Owen responded by introducing himself, describing his association with the family as merely that of neighbour. 'And you?' he asked.

'I work with Eliza,' he said, 'I'm Simon. I was with her the night it happened.' He pushed his hands into his trouser pockets, shook his head. 'I still feel awful for what I did.'

Intrigued by his comment and sensing he wanted to talk about it, Owen said, 'What did you do?'

'I was trying to give Eliza a special weekend, two days of relaxation – you know the kind of thing: time to get away from it all. I thought it would be the perfect break for her.'

'Doesn't sound like you did anything too awful,' Owen said.

He shook his head. 'I took her mobile away. I told her she had to manage without it. No calls. No emails. No work. But then her mother was desperately trying to get hold of her and there was no way of anyone tracking her down. It wasn't until we were back in London on Sunday evening, when I allowed her to switch her mobile back on, that she knew anything was wrong.'

'You can't blame yourself for that.'

'I do though,' he said grimly. 'I shouldn't have done it. I should have left well alone.'

The regret in his voice and the intensity of his expression told Owen that this young man was no more just a work colleague to Eliza than Owen was just a neighbour to Mia. Glancing round the terrace, he wondered at the lives people led and the amount of pretence that went on.

His suit jacket thrown on the floor, Jeff was lying face down on the bed. He couldn't take any more of the pretence. To hell with the social niceties that demanded the bereaved pulled themselves together for a show of dignified mourning over a fucking sausage roll and a glass of wine. How could anyone expect him to do that when Daisy was dead?

Dead.

Dry-eyed, he let out a moan of gut-wrenching pain and buried his face into the pillow. Three weeks on and he hadn't shed a single tear. He didn't know why. The need to cry was there, but it was as if something deep inside him had shut down.

Three weeks of feeling like this. Three weeks of being unable to accept that she was gone. His little Daisy. His baby. His precious, *precious* baby. He pushed his face harder still into the pillow, wanting it to choke him, to smother the breath out of him. How could he go on living in a world that didn't contain Daisy? What was the point?

And as for that nauseating service he'd been forced to sit through, listening to the vicar dishing out platitude after platitude about the loss of a child never being an easy thing to accept. What the hell would she know about it? How many children had she lost? What gave her the right to tell him how to think and behave?

He drew his knees up, tried to curl himself into a ball, and thought of the superhuman effort it had taken not to throw himself on Daisy's coffin in church and tear the lid off. On the rare times he actually slept, he had the same recurring dream. He dreamt that Daisy wasn't dead, that she'd been put in the coffin by mistake and was calling for him. *'Help me, Daddy,'* she would cry. *'Help me!'*

He hadn't thought he'd be able to go through with the actual burial, but somehow he'd done it. Or he thought he had. He had no recall of it, so God only knew what state he'd been in. He remembered walking back to the house afterwards, though. He vaguely remembered Scott speaking to him and Mia, and introducing his parents, who'd flown over especially from Australia. Apparently they were here to support their son in his grief.

Grief.

What grief would Scott know? He'd known Daisy for hardly any time at all. How could his superficial loss compare to that of a father? And for what he'd done to Daisy – not only turned her against her own father, but caused the accident by ringing Daisy on her mobile – he hoped Scott never knew another moment's happiness. He deserved a life of unending misery.

Down in the garden he could hear the level of noise increasing as guests chattered, filling themselves up with wine and food. If he had the strength, he'd go down there and tell them the show was over and to bugger off to their own lives and leave him in peace.

It was unbelievable what people said at funerals, all mindless small talk, none of it serving any real purpose. And then there were the offensive comments, the ones made by people who seemed to think he should be grateful that he hadn't lost both Daisy and Jensen in the crash. Some were calling it a miracle that Jensen had survived. How could it be a miracle if Daisy was dead and all Jensen had suffered was a broken arm, some cracked ribs and a few cuts and bruises?

No, don't talk to him about miracles and being

thankful. He had absolutely nothing now in his life to be thankful for. If he could turn back the clock, he'd have no qualms in swapping Daisy's life for Jensen's. He'd do it in a heartbeat. In fact he'd do anything to turn back time and have his daughter alive once more. He'd even let her marry that idiot downstairs and give her his blessing to live in Australia. Just to have her alive again. To be able to say he was sorry for the way he'd spoken to her the last time he'd seen her, to tell her just how much he loved her.

He took a deep, shuddering breath and shivering with sudden cold, he wrapped his arms around himself.

He had one other regret. That he had spent that night the way he had. The thought of himself in bed with those two prostitutes, when his precious baby girl had been dying, would haunt him for ever. Was this his punishment for that night?

He heard a knock at the door and then the sound of it opening. He made no attempt to turn over and see who it was.

'Jeff, can I get you anything?'

It was Mia.

'Go away,' he said.

Keeping his eyes shut, he heard her come in and move round the bed. He smelt her perfume, then felt a hand on his shoulder, but he flinched at her touch. 'Leave me alone,' he said. 'I want to be on my own.'

He heard the rustle of her clothing as she moved

away. Then with relief he heard the door quietly shut.

Still shivering, he kicked off his shoes and got under the duvet and tried to sleep, hoping that when he woke everyone would have gone. Or better still, he hoped he never woke up ever again.

The other side of the door, Mia stood very still. She breathed deeply. Very deeply. Very steadily. Her fists clenched at her sides, she willed every last scrap of her physical strength and emotional energy to hold firm, to fight off the urge to slide to the floor and howl out the raw agony of her grief.

Jeff had looked at her this morning when she'd been dressing for the funeral and said, with real disgust in his voice, 'How can you do this? How can you put on your clothes as if this is just another ordinary day?'

'What's the alternative?' she'd replied tiredly. 'We have to get through this day. And tomorrow. And the day after. There's no other way. All we, or at least, all *I* can do, is put one foot in front of the other and hope I can get through it.'

Ever since he'd flown back from Monte Carlo, Jeff had slept in Daisy's old room. That's where he was now. He'd given no explanation and Mia hadn't asked him for one. She knew why he had to be in there: to be close to Daisy, to feel her presence in the few things that she'd left behind after she'd moved in with Scott. He had said that he didn't want anyone else to go in there and again she hadn't questioned this. Just as she had to find a way to get through each day, he had to find his own way to survive this nightmare.

What she did question was his belief that only his grief counted. That anything she or Eliza or Jensen, and in particular Scott, felt was inferior to his loss.

She went downstairs and found Jensen and Madison in the kitchen. Since the accident rarely did Madison leave Jensen's side – she had practically glued herself to him, terrified that something might happen to him again. There were times when Mia wished she could do the same. With Eliza too. She wished she could keep them close, never out of her sight, just as when they'd been babies and toddlers.

When the police had come to the house that night and told her outright that Daisy was dead and the condition of Jensen was unknown, she had been utterly convinced that she had lost them both. Later, at the hospital, when she had learnt that he had survived and that he was going to be all right, she had fallen against Owen and wept anew, but this time with relief. Then she had hugged Tattie and Madison and they had all cried together. It hadn't taken her long to worry how she would ever find the right words to break the news to Jeff when she finally got hold of him.

'You OK, Mum?' Jensen asked her now.

She nodded and gently patted his good shoulder,

resisting the fierce need in her to hold him tight, to reassure herself that he was really still alive, that she hadn't lost him. It was an emotion she experienced every time she looked at him. Three weeks on from the accident and the cuts and bruises and the burns to his face and hands, which had been caused by the airbag, were healing well. His right arm, broken because he'd raised his arms to brace himself against the impact, was in a sling, and his fractured ribs still caused him pain, as did his neck. But the debilitating headaches had stopped and he'd been assured that the brief coma he'd suffered had left him with no long-term ill-effects.

When he'd been discharged from hospital he and Tattie and Madison had moved into The Gingerbread House. Tattie had been wonderful, throwing herself into looking after Jensen and stepping in to run Mia's Hats when it had been beyond Mia's capabilities. She had been a godsend – not just a huge support to Mia and Jensen, but also to Eliza. Jeff had wanted none of her help, though. But then he wanted nothing from anyone. Only retribution, perhaps.

Despite all the evidence to the contrary, Jeff had initially blamed Daisy's death on the lorry driver who had been involved in the accident. But the poor man had not been at fault. According to the statement he'd given the police he had done everything he could to avoid a head-on collision, but for whatever reason Daisy simply hadn't seen him and had driven straight into him. Injured himself, the lorry driver had been the one to alert the emergency services, and again in his statement, he'd described the scene, saying that Daisy had been thrown through the windscreen and that he had believed her to be dead, convinced that no one could have survived such an impact. Jensen's seatbelt had undoubtedly saved him.

Mia blinked hard and put a hand to her mouth to stop her lips from trembling. 'Where's Eliza?' she asked. Again, that protective need to know where her children were. To know they were safe.

'She's in the garden with Mum,' Madison said, turning round from where she was making a mug of tea. Mia watched the girl carefully carry it across the kitchen to where Jensen was sitting in the armchair by the French doors. He'd removed his black jacket and tie and was wearing a crumpled grey cardigan over a white shirt. He hadn't shaved since the accident and his beard accentuated how haggard he was. He'd lost weight, far too much weight for one who couldn't spare it, and he wasn't sleeping well. Tattie had told Mia that he had terrifying nightmares and cried out in his sleep, that he woke shaking and bathed in sweat.

Mia knew that Jensen blamed himself for not being firmer with Daisy, for insisting that she didn't speak to Scott on her mobile. And the seatbelt. He kept blaming himself for that, for forgetting she'd released it to reach for her phone and that he hadn't realized what the pinging sound was; it had been the seatbelt alarm.

But Jensen wasn't to blame for the accident that would scar their lives for ever. If anyone was to blame, Mia was. She had brought this tragedy on them.

Owen saw Mia come out of the kitchen and, watching her spot Tattie and Eliza amongst the mourners, along with Simon, he decided it was now or never to speak with her. Not since they'd been at the hospital had he had a chance to speak to her on her own. There had been no communication between them in the following days and weeks. Nothing.

'Mia,' he said quietly as he intercepted her. 'How are you?' He immediately regretted the question. 'Sorry, dumb thing to ask. You probably feel like hell, don't you?'

'Something like that, yes.' Her voice was low and husky and tugged at his heart. Her gaze was completely blank.

'Is there anything I can do to help?' he said. 'Anything. Name it and I'll do it.'

'There's nothing,' she said. 'Nothing anyone can do.' He suddenly wished he could get her alone and hold her. Just for a minute. One whole minute to let her know that he was there for her.

He hesitated fractionally, afraid of saying the wrong thing. 'I just want you to know, that any time you want to speak to me, you can. It doesn't matter what time of day or night it is, ring me. I mean it.'

For the longest moment she continued to look at him without speaking. Her gaze was so blank he wondered if she'd been prescribed some sort of medication. 'Thank you for coming today,' she said at last. 'It was good of you.'

He tensed. It wasn't that she was talking to him as if he were a casual acquaintance, or worse, a stranger, that scared him, it was the total absence of emotion in her face that unnerved him. The words *catatonic shock* echoed inside his head and he realized that the mask she was hiding behind was in place even for him – even he wasn't permitted to see the depth of her anguish.

'Mia,' he tried one more time, with great gentleness, 'I can't bear to see you like this, suffering so much. Don't shut me out, please.'

She swallowed. 'I'm sorry, but I have to. It's for the best. I told you once before that I couldn't make a difficult situation any more complicated than it already was. Which means . . . whatever we thought we had was a mistake. I should never have done it.'

He looked at her in disbelief, knowing that while her eyes were pools of haunting blankness, his reflected the profound love he felt for her. 'Don't say that,' he murmured.

'You probably won't understand,' she said, 'but I feel as if what I did with you brought this tragedy on my family.'

He tried not to show his dismay. Tried to reason with himself that, shattered by grief, she needed to make sense of a senseless catastrophe. It was a natural human response; there always had to be a reason. 'Bad karma, you mean?' he said.

'Yes.'

He stared at her helplessly. What could he say? Now was not the time to tell her she was wrong. He had to do as she said and allow her to retreat deep into herself. For some people it was how they protected themselves from being hurt any more than they already were. And so he had no alternative but to mask his own feelings and walk away.

Which he did, resisting the urge to say that he was a patient man and would wait for her.

CHAPTER 44

It was September and Madison had been at her new school for more than a fortnight now. She loved it. There wasn't a day when she didn't enjoy being there. Her teacher, Miss Atherton, was brilliant and made all their lessons really fun.

Last lesson today they'd started work on a harvest festival frieze that was going to be put in the main entrance hall, where everyone would see it when they came in. The part she had been given was to paint a picture of a ploughed field with a scarecrow and birds flying above it. She was glad she had something easy to do; Beth had been given a pot of glue and a load of pasta, rice and lentils and asked to make a mosaic picture of a basket with a pumpkin in it. At the end of the lesson, when Miss Atherton had said it was time to put everything away, Madison had helped Beth sweep the floor where most of the rice and lentils had ended up. The frieze had to be finished by next week, which was when they'd be having the special harvest festival assembly, when parents and grand-parents would be invited as well. Madison had been picked to read out a poem she'd written. Mum and JC had said they'd be there and Mia had also said she'd come.

With school over now, Madison and Beth were on their way to Parr's. Friday was the best day of the week for Madison; it was when she was allowed to spend some of her pocket money at the shop on sweets or an ice-cream and then, if the weather was fine, go and sit on the green with Beth. Later she had her piano lesson with Owen. It was just the most perfect day. But then everything about living in Little Pelham was perfect. Mum let her do far more things on her own here than in London, like walking to school without her, although sometimes Mum liked to come with Madison because she enjoyed meeting the other mothers. She was doing less of the Marilyn Monroe work now, preferring instead to spend more time on the eco party bags. She was talking about selling them not just online, but actually having a shop. That would be cooler than cool because then Madison would be able to help her there. Like she helped Mia in the barn.

They had to wait ages at Parr's before they could choose what they wanted as just about everyone else from school had got there ahead of them, including Georgina with the twins, Edmund and Luke, who were *sooo* cute.

At last they were at the front of the queue and Madison was glad it was Bob Parr who was serving them and not his wife. Wendy always stared really hard at you with her eyes all tight and narrow, like she thought you were going to steal something. The more she stared at Madison, the more she felt like pinching something! Beth's mum said Wendy was the worst gossip on the planet and if you wanted people to know anything you just told Wendy and within an hour everyone in the village would know.

Alone in the shop today, Bob was wearing a dark blue apron over a white shirt. It was his new look and he'd started wearing the apron after the shop had closed for three days while it was given a make-over. When it had reopened, Bob and Wendy had put on a small party – Mum had been there as Marilyn Monroe and had officially reopened the shop and had her photo in the local newspaper. That was when Bob had first worn his apron. JC said give it time and he'd be wearing a bow-tie and a straw boater and the price of everything would shoot sky high.

'Hello, girls, what can I get you?' Bob said cheerily. 'Probably not warm enough for an ice-cream today, is it? Looks like rain. How about a mixed bag of sweets with a twist of sherbet thrown in?'

They both said yes and he reached behind him to a shelf where he had a small pile of bags ready made up. They gave him their money, said goodbye and were out on the pavement when they saw that it didn't just *look* like rain, it *was* raining. A group of older boys from school who'd started a game of football on the green were scooping up their school sweatshirts, coats and bags and were leaving. Beth pulled a face. 'Better make a run for it,' she said. They parted at Cloverdale Lane – Beth to go straight on, and Madison to go left. By now it was raining hard, and, passing Muriel's cottage, Madison ran doubly fast, her rucksack bouncing on her back.

When the hill got too steep for her to keep running she pulled her hood over her head and waved at the ginger cat sitting in the window of No. 14 – he was always there when she came home from school. In the cottage next door lived a small white dog called Angus and his owner let Madison play with him in her garden sometimes.

Lily Cottage was almost at the very top of the hill and wasn't as old as some of the other cottages, but Madison thought it was easily the nicest. It had walls the colour of pale honey and in the summer lots of tiny pink roses had climbed up the front of the house, all the way to the bedrooms where pretty flowered curtains showed at the windows. Mum had made them and Mrs Richards in the cottage next door liked them so much she'd asked if Mum could make some for her.

When she got round to the back door, Mum was there with an umbrella. 'I was on my way to find you,' she said, taking her inside and removing her dripping anorak. 'Just look at you; you're wet through!'

'You've been baking again,' Madison said, not

caring one little bit that she was wet, not now that she could see – and smell – the plate of scones on the table. Mum claimed that living in the country had given her the push she needed to learn how to cook properly. Madison didn't really understand why where you lived affected how you cooked, but Mum had definitely got the hang of baking. Her wet things put in the small boiler room, Madison looked longingly at the scones. 'Can I have one before I go to Owen's, please?' she asked.

'That was the general idea,' Mum said with a smile. 'But first, can you go upstairs and tell JC you're home? There's something we want to talk to you about.'

Madison's heart did a double beat. 'Is it something bad?'

Mum looked serious. 'Just go up and get JC while I put the kettle on and lay the table.'

Madison had a sudden and very bad feeling that their lovely new life was about to come to an end and they would have to move back to London, back to a place where she had no friends. Or worse still— But no, she didn't want to think of what could be worse. She still had nightmares about the crash and often dreamt that it wasn't only Daisy who had died.

When she'd been at the hospital with Mum and Mia and they'd been waiting for news about JC, she had felt sick with fear that he was dead. Then when they knew he was OK, she had actually been sick, all over the floor in the corridor. Some of it had splashed onto Owen's shoes. She had been so embarrassed, but the nurses had been really kind and had given her a cup of sweet tea to make her feel better. It was while she was drinking the tea – with Owen looking after her in the waiting room – that Mum and Mia were allowed to see JC. She had been told she could see him the next day, when he would be feeling stronger. She hadn't said that it was already the next day, that it was nearly four in the morning.

At the top of the stairs, giving herself time to think, Madison went into the bathroom. She sat on the loo and thought hard. How had Mum and JC been this morning at breakfast? She racked her brains trying to remember if there had been anything different about them. Mum was a good actress when she wanted to be, but JC wasn't – his face always gave him away – so she focused her thoughts on him. All she could come up with was that he seemed quiet, lost in his own thoughts. But then since the accident he'd been like that a lot. Introverted, was what Mum called it. She said you couldn't survive a crash like that and not become slightly introverted.

There was something else that he suffered from at times; Mum said it was called survivor guilt. It meant that he felt bad that he had lived and Daisy had died. Madison knew it was sad that Daisy had died, but if someone had to die in that crash, she was glad it was Daisy and not JC. She couldn't bear it if JC died. There had been times, very soon

416

after the accident, when Madison had felt angry with Daisy, because everyone knew you weren't supposed to use your mobile phone when you were driving. Everyone knew it was dangerous and stupid and because of Daisy's stupidity JC could have been killed. Madison used to be on at Mum all the time about having a mobile; now she never wanted to have one. Not ever.

She flushed the toilet and washed her hands, tried again to think what it might be that Mum and JC wanted to talk about with her. Was it something to do with her piano lessons with Owen? Had they decided they were too expensive? But they weren't, were they? Owen had said he wouldn't charge anywhere near the proper amount because he wasn't a qualified teacher. Not yet, anyway. He was planning to do a teaching course, though, and maybe that's what Mum and JC were worried about. Maybe they thought that once Owen was qualified his lessons would be too expensive. She really hoped that wouldn't happen. And it wasn't as if Owen needed the money. They all knew that he was super, *super* rich and didn't need to work, that being a piano teacher was something he wanted to do because he liked the idea of teaching others something he loved.

Finished in the bathroom, she climbed yet more stairs, to the very top of the house, to what had once been the loft. The owners they rented the cottage from had turned the loft into a big bedroom with the tiniest bathroom next to it, and it was up here that Mum and JC had their office, where JC did his website work at one end of the room and Mum did her eco party bags at the other.

Her stomach churning with panicky dread, Madison tapped on the half-open door just as Mum had insisted she did in case JC was on the phone.

When Madison's face peered round the door, Jensen stopped what he was doing and took off his reading glasses – he'd only had them a few weeks and he was still getting used to using them. Tattie had been right about him needing to get his eyes tested. 'I'm always right,' she'd told him. 'Get used to it, buddy.'

'Hey, Mads,' he said, using the name she had recently given him the green light to use, 'home from school already? I had no idea it was that time. Good day?'

'Yep, it was fine. Mum said you're to come down and that there's something you want to talk to me about.'

He heard the anxiety in her voice and pushed his chair away from the desk, standing up. 'Don't look so worried.'

'But something's wrong, isn't it?' she said. 'I know it. I always know. Like I knew there was something wrong that night.'

Jensen knew which night she was referring to and said, 'You're the smartest girl I know, for sure, but you don't know everything. Let's go

418

downstairs. There's a hot rumour doing the rounds that your mum's promised us tea and scones.'

Her expression remained glum. 'I don't think I can eat anything, not until you've told me what's wrong.'

He shook his head. 'Nothing's wrong.'

'So why are you and Mum making such a big deal of it?'

'Because it's something important and we, as a family, that's you, your mother and me, have to discuss it.'

'You're not leaving Mum, are you?'

He frowned. 'Now why would you think that?'

'Because it's the one thing I don't want to happen and sometimes when you want a thing really, *really* badly, like maybe too much, it's taken away from you. Look what happened to . . . to Daisy.'

Since the accident it wasn't often Madison uttered Daisy's name, and hearing her do so now, so completely out of the blue, struck Jensen like a physical blow. His heart thudded and feeling lightheaded, as if the blood was draining from him, he steadied himself against the desk. He forced himself not to let his thoughts spiral out of control, not to give in to the panicky tightness in his chest. Breathe normally, he told himself, focus on what was important right now.

The moment passed. He went to Madison and crouching down he took her hands in his, perhaps more to reassure himself than her. She looked at him anxiously.

'I'm sorry I said Daisy's name,' she said. 'It upset you, didn't it? I won't do it again.'

'It's OK, and of course you can mention my sister's name. Just because she's no longer with us, it doesn't mean we can't talk about her.'

'But you see what I mean, don't you, about bad things happening and spoiling everything.'

'I don't have any real answers for you, Mads, other than to say that accidents happen; sometimes there's an explanation for why they do and sometimes there isn't. But we mustn't live in fear. We have to let ourselves believe in the good things.'

She released her hands from his and hugged him. He hugged her back. Then: 'Come on, you lead the way downstairs.'

In the kitchen, Tattie was waiting for them, the table set with plates, pots of jam and cream. They all sat down in their usual places and with a foot bouncing against the leg of her chair, Madison said, 'Can you just get this over with, please?'

Tattie looked at Jensen and he nodded. She said, 'Madison, JC has something to ask you. He's already asked me but I said that it's not just me who can answer the question – you have to as well.'

Her foot still bouncing against the chair leg, Madison looked at Jensen. 'Ask me, then. And if it's do I want to go back to London, the answer is no.'

'London doesn't come into it,' he said.

'What does then?'

He cleared his throat. 'The thing is, I've asked your mother to marry me and she says I have to ask your permission.'

Madison's eyes widened. 'My permission? You mean . . . you mean—'

Both Tattie and Jensen smiled at her.

'We mean that we can't make the decision to get married unless you're absolutely happy with the idea,' Tattie said.

The corners of Madison's mouth lifted and she began to smile. Then the smile got bigger and bigger. 'OMG, that is just so *way* the coolest thing!'

Tattie tapped her wrist and looked stern. 'Speak English, Madison, not this nonsense language of the verbally challenged.'

Madison sniggered and then burst out laughing.

So did Tattie and Jensen.

'Well,' Tattie said when the laughter had died down, 'do we have your permission? And think about your answer; it's very important.'

Madison's answer was to let out a whoop, followed by '*Whoopididdledeedo!*' She then jumped out of her seat and with her hands in the air, she spun round on the spot. '*Whoopididdledeedo!*' she yelled again. Coming to a stop, she hugged her mother. 'I think it's the best idea ever, ever, *ever* in the history of best ideas.' She then came round the table to Jensen and hugged him carefully. It was some time since he'd had the cast removed from his arm, but she continued to be ultra-cautious around him. 'Does that mean you'll be my proper dad now?' she asked.

Jensen looked again at Tattie. Getting the go-ahead nod from her, he said, 'Looks like you're well and truly stuck with me, kiddo.'

'Yay!'

CHAPTER 45

Eliza was late. Not an unusual occurrence, even for a Friday, but this Friday evening was supposed to be different; this particular evening she was supposed to finish work early and be on time.

But as ever, she'd lost track of time in the office and it had only been when she'd heard the sound of a vacuum cleaner approaching that she'd looked about her and seen that the place was deserted. She'd thought of texting to say she was running late, but had decided it would only make her later still.

Taking the lift down, she said goodnight to Malcolm, the building's longest-serving security guard, and like a greyhound released from its trap, she sped off up Shaftesbury Avenue. Infuriatingly no one else shared her urgency – rather they seemed to be deliberately slowing her down by getting in her way. Her frustration escalating, she felt like ramming them with her laptop bag to make them get out of her way. Pavement rage. She'd be the first to go to prison for it!

She checked her watch and wished she hadn't.

She was now forty-five minutes late. Her only consolation was that Simon knew her so well he would wait for her. But today of all days she hadn't wanted to be late for him. It was the least she could do when he'd been such a good friend to her these last few awful months.

The death of her sister had shocked Eliza massively. It was the senseless waste of such a young life that got to her, that and the cruel randomness of it. She was constantly fighting the anger within her that questioned why any of them should bother to strive for happiness when it could be snatched away so brutally. Simon's answer to this was, 'But, Eliza, what's the alternative? Isn't it better to have experienced a moment of happiness than none at all?'

Eliza wondered if poor Scott would agree. At the funeral he'd been in a terrible state, had wept when he'd told Mum that he would always blame himself for ringing Daisy when he did. Mum had merely nodded and murmured vague words of reassurance. But Eliza knew that Dad held Scott responsible and that he had even said he hoped Scott never stopped feeling guilty for what he'd done. It was a wicked thing to say and God only knew how Scott would get over the accident. Eliza genuinely hoped that in time he did, if only because, as Jensen had said, surely that's what Daisy would have wanted. Sadly it was inevitable that now Scott was living back in Australia they would probably never see him again.

Understandably he would want to try and erase from his memory his brief but devastating association with the family.

Forced to stop behind a group of people who were taking up most of the pavement while they consulted a map, Eliza realized that she was now level with the restaurant where she was meeting Simon. She looked through the window at the busy bar area to see if he was there. There was always the chance he was late himself. She was just thinking that he would have texted to let her know if he'd been delayed, when she caught her breath.

She moved closer to the window to get a better look, not quite believing what she was seeing. Transfixed, she watched the way he stroked the girl's bare arm, the back of his hand lightly brushing against her skin. It was exactly how he used to touch her. And the girl was gazing at him just as she had once stared adoringly into his face. The only difference in the situation was that he was doing this out in public for all to see, not sneakily behind closed doors as he had with her. He was leaning in now for a kiss.

Someone bumped Eliza from behind and it had the effect of instantly galvanizing her. Pushing open the door, she went inside. She marched straight up to him and tapped him on the shoulder.

'Hello, Greg, long time no see.' The stupefied expression on his face was priceless. 'How's your lovely wife and your gorgeous little boy?' she asked. 'Oh, silly me, I can't remember whether your second child was a girl or a boy, but then that was probably because you never told me you were *married* and had a *family*.'

Relishing the effect she was having on him – rendering him speechless – and with adrenaline pumping through her, she turned to his pretty companion whose mouth was open in a cartoon-like oval of disbelief. 'Here's my top tip for the night,' Eliza said to her. 'This pathetic excuse of a man,' she prodded Greg's shoulder with a finger, 'is about as real as a politician's promise, so have nothing more to do with him. Take it from me; he's a serial adulterer who will tell you he loves you. Actually, he'll tell you anything you want to hear, and then he'll go home to his wife and children and tell them a pack of lies as well. And I should know, because not so long ago I was stupid enough to be taken in by him. Yeah, I know, I don't look that dumb, do I? But it just goes to show, appearances can be oh so deceiving.'

It was then that she noticed Simon sitting at the other end of the bar and that he was watching her with interest. Had he not been there, she might have been tempted to pick up Greg's glass of red wine and tip it over his head. But that would be overly melodramatic and she didn't want to cause an unpleasant scene for Simon.

Instead she turned back to Greg. 'See that guy over there,' she said, indicating Simon, 'now that's a decent man. That's a man who's kind, honest and genuine. You're not fit to be in the same room as him.' Her voice dripping with loathing, she then turned away in a final show of disgust.

'What was all that about?' Simon said, when she joined him and he stood up to kiss her on the cheek. This was a new feature to their friendship. Now they no longer worked together, things had changed subtly between them.

She took a deep breath as she sat on the stool beside Simon, the rush of adrenaline having now subsided, leaving her breathless and with a racing heart. 'That,' she said with great emphasis, 'was Greg.'

'Was it indeed? And the girl – is she his wife?'

With her back resolutely set to Greg, Eliza said, 'No. Another fool like me.'

An eyebrow raised, Simon said, 'Not any more by the looks of things; she's on her feet and – uh-oh, turn round quick, you'll like this.'

Eliza did as he said, just in time to witness Greg's companion doing what she had decided not to. The noisy swell of the packed bar momentarily quietened as all eyes took in the scene. The same eyes then followed the girl's rapid departure, then Greg's, his shirt and trousers stained dark red. He looked like he'd been shot in the chest.

'I call that a job well done,' Simon said when the entertainment was over and the hush was replaced with the hum and buzz of people resuming their conversations.

'Thank you,' Eliza said. And then: 'Sorry I'm late.'

427

Simon attracted the attention of one of the barmen. 'Being as predictable as you are, I factored in the extra wait time.'

She groaned. 'I knew you'd do that. I'm sorry though, really.'

'Stop grovelling, Channing, it doesn't suit you. Now what would you like to drink? And when we've ordered, you can tell me exactly what you said to Greg. It obviously had the desired effect. And I've gotta say, he looked a bit of a jerk to me. No . . .' he lifted a hand 'sorry – guilty of putting the guy down – he's clearly worked at the whole jerk thing and, fair play to him, he's pulled it off totally.'

Eliza sniggered, suddenly feeling a wave of giddy exhilaration. What she'd just done felt hugely significant.

Their drinks ordered, she gave a word-for-word account of what she'd said.

'And how do you feel?' Simon asked.

She let out her breath. 'I'm OK.'

'Really?'

'Momentously OK. I can honestly say he's history now.' And she meant it. She felt sorry for his wife, but seeing Greg with another girl could not have been a more fitting way to bring about the definitive closure she needed. Not that she had given Greg much thought these last few months. Losing her sister had seen to that. It had given her a fresh perspective on her self-pity. It had made her realize how pathetic she had been to waste so much energy on feeling sorry for herself.

There were so many memories Eliza had of her sister, but recently one in particular kept coming back to her. It was the day after Jensen's birthday when Daisy had said that Eliza had got herself fast-tracked to adulthood at far too young an age. It had always been too easy to dismiss poor Daisy as not having a real grasp on what was going on around her, but really she'd been far more emotionally astute than Eliza.

A great wave of sadness engulfed her at the thought of never seeing her sister again, of never being able to tell her that she'd been right and that Eliza was now determined to change things. She didn't know how exactly, not yet, but she would.

Their drinks arrived with a tray of nuts and olives and, toasting Simon, Eliza said, 'Happy birthday.'

They each took a long sip of their drinks and settled properly into the evening.

'So how're things back at home?' Simon asked. 'Your mum any better?'

'It's hard to say. She's just sort of shut down. Dad's even worse. He's still sleeping in Daisy's old room. There's no talking to him.'

'I guess that was to be expected with how he felt about your sister.'

'I know, but it's the extent of it that worries me. Sometimes when he looks at Jensen or me, I swear I can see him wondering why it couldn't have been one of us who died.'

Simon frowned. 'I can't believe any parent would think that.'

'Don't make the mistake of confusing the relationship I have with my father with that of yours with your father – the two couldn't be more different.' Not wanting to bring the evening down, she changed the subject. 'Hey, I've got you a birthday present.' She delved into her bag and pulled out a small package.

He grinned. 'Oh, Channing,' he said with mock bashfulness, 'you shouldn't have.'

'You're kidding? Late for your birthday dinner and no present? You'd never have spoken to me again.'

'Damned straight.' He took the present from her and gave it an experimental shake followed by a squeeze. 'Shall I open it now?'

'No, keep it for later when I'm not around, then you won't have to fake your reaction. I still have the receipt if you want to change it.'

'As if.' He bent down to the floor and slipped the package inside his work bag. She hoped he did like it; she'd spent ages trying to find the perfect present for him. In the end, knowing his fondness for proper pens, she had settled on a Montegrappa fountain pen. It had cost a fortune, but he was worth it.

'So what's new at work?' he asked. 'Any interesting gossip for me?'

She shrugged. 'Same old, same old. Nothing new or exciting to tell.'

'Hey, it can't be the same old, same old; I'm not there. How's my replacement shaping up?'

'He's a nightmare. Even more untidy than you and he drinks so much coffee and Red Bull he's like an atrociously hyperactive toddler. He's exhausting to be around.'

'Is he any good?'

'He's OK. But not a patch on you.'

Simon speared an olive with a cocktail stick and smiled. 'Do my ears deceive me or is that a compliment from you?'

She smiled. 'It may be the last you get, so make the most of it. How about you? Still enjoying your new job?'

'I am, actually. Although I miss working with you. I liked being the good cop to your bad cop.'

'And there was me thinking I was the brains to your beauty.'

He laughed and she watched him spear another olive. The truth was, she missed working with him and wished at least a dozen times a day that he hadn't been poached by another firm. She missed the ease of the working relationship they'd had, the way they could fill in the blanks for each other. She had been shocked when he'd got on the train with her one morning six weeks ago, when they were finishing off the job in Milton Keynes, and he had confided in her that he'd been approached by one of Merchant Swift's main competitors. She had thought he was happy where he was, that the work suited him; it was still a mystery to her why he'd moved.

Since he'd left a fortnight ago she had been worried that he hadn't really enjoyed working with her, that maybe she was too exacting, perhaps too picky and inclined to find fault. Had she, she'd often wondered, unintentionally forced him to play second fiddle? If she had, she owed him an apology, because she would never knowingly hurt him. He was, she had come to realize, apart from Mum and Jensen, the person who mattered the most to her. Though she could never tell him that. God, no! He'd be horrified, wouldn't he? It was all very well being work colleagues and good friends, but there were lines that absolutely could not be crossed and she didn't want to embarrass him or risk spoiling their relationship.

Something Jensen had got right was that Simon wasn't gay. She'd got that hopelessly wrong. Looking back on it, it now seemed absurd. No wonder Jensen had laughed at her.

During their dinner that night in Suffolk – before they'd got the awful news about Daisy – Eliza had asked Simon about the relationships he'd had. To her surprise, he'd said he'd been involved with a girl for about a year, but it hadn't worked out. 'In the end we just wanted different things,' he'd explained. 'She wanted to go travelling for a year and I didn't. Simple as that. The last I heard from her, she was in Thailand working in a bar.'

'And before that?' Eliza had asked.

'This and that. Nothing special. Why do you want to know?'

'No reason,' she'd lied, 'just wondering.'

Now, feeling bold, probably thanks to her altercation with Greg earlier, she decided to ask Simon the question she'd wanted to ask him ever since he'd resigned. 'Simon,' she said, 'can I ask you something?'

He looked up at her.

'What made you leave Merchant Swift?' she asked. 'Was it me?'

He gave her an odd look. 'Why would you think that?'

'I'm concerned that it was. In Suffolk you teased me that I was a bitch to work with, but I'm worried that there might be some truth in that.'

He rolled the cocktail stick between his thumb and finger, then poked it through a corner of a napkin. 'You were never difficult to work with, not in the way you think.'

'What way then?'

He drank some more of his wine, then looked at her. 'You really have no idea, do you?'

'All I know is that we've always got on really well and if I've done something to hurt you, I need to make amends for it.'

His normally sleepy-looking eyes darkened and she had the weirdest feeling that she had never really looked at him before. Maybe she hadn't, because all of a sudden, as though seeing him in close-up for the first time, she thought how attractive he was with his sandy hair that was styled in the habitually messy way he favoured and the way his mouth always seemed to be turned up in an easy-going smile. But really what she noticed most was that he looked so effortlessly relaxed as he sat next to her, with his jacket and tie off and his shirt unbuttoned at the neck.

'Eliza,' he said, jolting her out of her thoughts, 'you did nothing wrong. It was me. I fell in love with you.'

She stared at him, stunned. 'But you . . . but you couldn't have . . . I mean, with me?'

'With you, Eliza. Most definitely with you.'

'But . . . but you never said anything.'

'How could I? You were all loved up with Greg. I had to keep my distance. I had to hide my feelings for you. If you think about it, I did a bang-up job, didn't I? You never guessed or suspected.'

'Perhaps that's because I'm a dull-witted idiot.'

He smiled. 'Well, there is that.'

'But I don't understand why you felt the need to go and work somewhere else.'

'I thought that if we were no longer work colleagues, and with Greg out of the picture, you might start to view me differently, more like a potential boyfriend, as opposed to a boring old friend.'

Feeling a great rush of affection for him, she said, 'You've never been a boring old friend. Far from it.'

'But is that all I can ever be to you, a friend? Think very carefully before you answer; there's a lot at stake.'

She swallowed. 'I think subconsciously you've been a lot more than just a friend to me for some time. I've missed you so much this last fortnight.'

He moved his left hand along the bar towards her hand, until his little finger was touching hers. 'I've missed you too.' Then, covering her hand entirely with his, he said, 'How about we eat now?'

She nodded. 'It's your birthday; you make the rules.'

'So it is. In which case, I'm officially claiming a kiss before the evening's over.'

CHAPTER 46

Saturday morning and Owen was at Parr's. The last time he'd called in Mia had been here and shielded by customers, he'd had no way of knowing if she had assiduously avoided looking at him or she just hadn't noticed him.

As he added a jar of passata sauce to his basket he heard Bob talking to the only other customer. 'A dreadful, dreadful business,' Bob was saying, 'the change in that poor woman – you just wouldn't credit it. And as for her husband, he's in a bad way.'

Wendy joined in. 'He sleeps in Daisy's old bedroom,' she said with just a little too much relish to her voice, 'has done so ever since the accident.'

Bob shushed his wife, but she ignored him. 'He does too,' she asserted, 'it's common knowledge, everyone knows.'

'Only because you and Bev keep telling everyone,' Bob muttered as the customer left. 'If you ask me, that cousin of yours needs to show some respect and keep her mouth shut. If I was Mrs Channing I wouldn't have a gossip like her cleaning for me.'

Common knowledge might well be an exaggeration, but Owen had heard something similar from Joe, who had been asked by Jeff to install a lock on Daisy's bedroom door. Presumably a lock to keep people out, to preserve the room as some kind of shrine.

By the time he left the shop, having nodded his head at the appropriate moment with Bob and Wendy and agreed with the general feeling in the village that Daisy's tragic death was a crying shame, he felt ashamed for effectively giving gossip the oxygen it needed to spread. But he did it because it was one of the few ways he had of finding out how Mia was.

Another means was through Madison when she came for her piano lessons, and if not directly from the girl herself, then from her mother and Jensen, depending on who dropped her off. Initially, understandably, one of them stayed while she had her lesson, but now that they knew and trusted him, they were happy to leave Madison in his care. When the lesson was over, he would walk her home, or drive her if it was raining hard. She was surprisingly good company, full of chatter about school and her new friends and how much she loved being here in Little Pelham.

Yesterday she had been even more of a live wire and much too fidgety to concentrate on the Grade One exam pieces he was coaching her for in readiness for December when she took the exam. It was very unlike her to make so many mistakes or to be reminded so frequently to soften her wrists and to curl her fingers. They'd given up on the tarantella and moved on to the andante and when things still hadn't improved, he'd decided there wasn't any point in forcing her to play when she wasn't in the right frame of mind. So he'd asked her if there was anything on her mind. And then it had all come tumbling out: Jensen and Tattie were getting married. 'But you mustn't tell anyone,' she'd said, 'not yet. It's a secret. And the best bit is JC's going to be my dad. If I had the choice of all the dads in the world, he'd be the one I'd choose.'

Back at home now and making himself some coffee, Owen thought that if he'd had the chance to choose his father, he certainly wouldn't have got stuck with a vicious bully like Ron Fletcher. A man who thought nothing of lashing out at his wife and child, or threatening two women who had shown a young boy nothing but kindness. A man who sadistically threatened to set fire to The Hidden Cottage with both Gretchen and Lillian inside it. That was the moment when Owen had finally stood up to his father.

Owen had known from the start that if his father ever knew about his piano lessons, he would put an immediate stop to them, as well as to his friendship with Gretchen and Lillian. He would do it on the basis that Owen was getting above himself, which was an accusation regularly hurled at him. As was the claim that Owen's mother spoiled him.

'You're turning him into a cissy!' Ron would shout. 'He's got as much backbone as a wet sock! Look at him, just sitting there like a whimpering dog.'

Anything that smacked of bettering oneself was anathema to Ron Fletcher. Reading anything other than a betting slip was classed as subversive and he proudly boasted that he'd never read a book in his life and had no intention of ever doing so. If he'd been drinking and caught Owen or his mother reading a book, he would snatch it out of their hands and throw it on the fire. That was if he was in a good mood. In a bad mood he'd make Owen rip the pages out one by one. The first time Owen refused to do it, he was belted so hard on the side of his head, his ears rang for a whole day.

For months and months Owen didn't tell his mother about his visits to The Hidden Cottage; he didn't want her to be involved. He knew it was better for her to be in ignorance rather than live with the fear of keeping something from her husband. But then one day, because he hated lying to her, Owen risked it and told her about Gretchen and Lillian. It was pride that made him do it; he wanted to share with her something for which he'd been told he had a talent. Amazed and curious, she then went with him to The Hidden Cottage to meet Gretchen and Lillian, and a friendship struck up between the three women. But it was a friendship that led to the secret ultimately becoming known to Owen's father.

One afternoon, home from work much earlier

439

than usual, Ron Fletcher found the house empty and when Owen and his mother appeared at the back door, having been at The Hidden Cottage, he was waiting for them with a furious look on his face. 'Where've you been?' he demanded. They were never supposed to go anywhere without him knowing their exact whereabouts. Their days had to be thoroughly accounted for; it was a way to screen out any meddling influences. If he could have kept Owen off school, he would have done. If he could have kept them permanently locked inside the cottage, he would have done that as well. He ruled the way any tyrant does, by instilling fear and subservience. He had it down to a fine art and only needed to follow through with about seventy-five per cent of his threats to ensure total obedience.

'Where've you been?' he repeated, his voice weighted with menace, his large bulk filling the small kitchen.

With no ready lie on his mother's lips, Owen had stepped in with one of his own. 'We've been for a walk,' he said, 'up to the allotments.'

'Why?' he rounded on Owen. 'What's up there to see?' To Owen's mother: 'Who've you been talking to?'

His mother, a hopeless liar, had hesitated with a tremble and it was all her paranoid husband needed to know that she was hiding something from him. Owen was sent up to his room and, lying on his bed, his head stuffed under the pillow,

440

he heard the familiar noises of his father carrying out his special brand of interrogation. And then he heard the crying. The awful sound of his mother crying.

The next morning, her bruised face and careful way of moving filled Owen with a burning and shameful anger. It was just the two of them in the kitchen, his father having already gone to work at the farm, but still Owen couldn't say anything to his mother for fear of making things worse. Hadn't he made it worse already by telling her about The Hidden Cottage? His breakfast barely eaten – he'd felt too sick to eat it – he gently kissed her goodbye on the cheek and said just one word: 'Sorry.'

Tears had filled her eyes and she'd said, 'It wasn't your fault. You mustn't ever think it is.'

But all he could think about on his way to school was that he was to blame. He should never have told his mother about Gretchen and Lillian.

Life was full of innumerable shades of regret and wrongly taken paths, Owen thought now as he decided it was warm enough to drink his coffee outside. One never learnt, so it seemed.

Common sense and a fully working moral compass would have made it all too clear that he and Mia were a regret waiting to happen; they should never have embarked on an affair. And he was to blame. He was the principal guilty participant, for he was the one who had encouraged Mia to be unfaithful to her husband. He knew she would never leave Jeff now; Daisy's tragic death would bind them together even more so. From here on, it would be how they would be defined as a couple: the couple whose daughter died in a car crash.

Outside on the veranda, Putin was standing on the top step, as if waiting for Owen. Seeing him, the bird stretched its neck and eyed him in his usual suspicious and belligerent manner.

Pushing his hands into his pockets, Owen looked out at the garden and to the lake. Whenever he pictured Mia, he didn't see the Mia who had leant back in the boat with her eyes closed, or the Mia who had described herself as feeling drunk with happiness, or the Mia who'd lain in bed with him, her eyes luminous with desire. Instead he recalled the Mia the day of the funeral, the Mia with the haunting blankness in her eyes. He didn't think he would ever forget the chilling coldness to her words when she said whatever had taken place between them had been a mistake.

He had reasoned that shock and grief had fuelled her decision, and he still stood by that. But he now reasoned that it would probably never change, because a parent never truly gets over the shock of losing a child. Mia would learn to live with the loss, but she would never get over it. It would always be there for her.

When he thought of what might have been between the two of them, a dull ache pressed heavily on his spirits and he became jittery with a restless energy. He felt it now and knew the best way to rid himself of it was to pour that energy into playing the piano.

Two hours later, when he was all played out and feeling more his normal self, he went to pick some runner beans.

It seemed nothing short of a miracle that the plants he'd bought from Georgina at the fete had not only survived his inexpert care, but had produced an extraordinary quantity of beans. What was more, they were edible. He had picked a large bowlful when he heard a voice. '*Yoo-hoo!*'

'I know that voice,' he said, when Muriel appeared round the corner of the house wheeling her bicycle.

'I should hope you do. And I'm very glad to find you at home in your splendid idyll far from the madding crowd.'

He watched her prop her bicycle against the wall. 'And why's that?' he asked. 'What do you want from me?'

'It's more a matter of what I can do for you,' she said, coming over and inspecting the bowl of beans in his hands. 'Not bad,' she said, turning them over, 'not bad at all for a legume virgin.'

'Praise indeed,' he said with a smile. 'So what is it you can do for me?'

'I'm going to make you a star, Owen Fletcher.'

He laughed. 'Does that mean you're going to lure me onto your casting couch and have your wicked way with me?'

'I certainly hope so. Why else would I have volunteered to be artistic director?'

'My, that's a very grand title.'

'I'm a very grand woman. Here,' she said, after opening a canvas bag and digging around in it, 'this month's parish magazine.' She slapped it on top of the beans.

'Thank you. And would your visit have something to do with roping me in for the talent show?'

'The nail and hitting it on the head springs to mind.'

'Now, Muriel, I have to warn you – this is the bit where I go all coy and say, oh, but I couldn't possibly.'

'Yes, and this is the bit when I twist your arm. Very hard. And in response you say, Muriel, I'd love to participate – where do I sign?'

'Mmm . . . I had a nasty feeling that would be your position. What exactly do you want me to do?'

'Nothing too awful. I thought you could tinkle the ivories for us.'

He looked at her sceptically. 'Just that? Nothing else?'

'Well, you might like to add a few colourful flourishes. Make it a performance, you know, entertain the troops.'

'You mean dress up and make a fool of myself?'

She beamed. 'Got it in one!'

'Are we talking Bobby Crush meets Liberace, by any chance?'

'Owen, it's as if you're a mind reader.'

'And on that bombshell, how about I make us a drink and you can tell me more about the show and what it entails?'

They sat on the veranda and once they had discussed the show – with Owen happily offering his services – the conversation inevitably turned to Mia. It was inevitable because that was what Owen wanted and he deliberately steered the conversation in that direction, wanting Muriel's take on what was currently going on at Medlar House.

'Frankly, I'm worried about Mia,' Muriel said. 'I know it's still early days, but she hardly leaves the house and if she does, it's only to cross the green to Parr's or to go and see Jensen and co.'

'She's working, though, isn't she?'

'Oh yes, and that's mainly down to Tattie stepping in and helping to get things on the move again.'

'What about Jeff? How's he coping?'

'I haven't seen him in weeks, not since he decided the compassionate leave he'd been given served no purpose and went back to work in Brussels. In my opinion it was the best thing he could do. One simply has to get back into the saddle and get on with life. The sooner Mia realizes that, the better.' She waved a hand vaguely about her and added, 'You're probably thinking I sound unreasonable and hard-hearted, but life goes on, it really does.'

'Mia will get there,' Owen said with more certainty than he felt. 'We all need to be patient with her.'

Muriel eyed him over her mug of coffee and he was reminded of Putin looking at him earlier that morning. He suddenly felt dangerously exposed, as if Muriel might know – or suspect – something he'd rather she didn't. Or was he imagining things? Surely Muriel couldn't possibly know anything?

He was relieved to escape her scrutiny when he heard the telephone ringing. 'Excuse me,' he said, quickly up on his feet and shooting inside the house before she could extract a confession from him.

The phone call was from a woman in the village enquiring about piano lessons for her son. He jotted down the details and suggested a time when the mother and son could call in to meet him.

Back outside, not wanting to risk any further beady-eyed looks from Muriel by resuming the discussion about Mia, he leant against the wooden balustrade of the veranda and looked out at the lake. 'That's the third enquiry I've had this week about piano lessons,' he remarked casually.

'The floodgates are opening!' Muriel responded with a hearty bark of laughter.

He turned round. 'A steady trickle, more like it.'

'You wait, you'll have an army of love-struck women wanting to learn before too long.'

He smiled. 'Then you'd better get in quick while I still have a free slot for you.'

She fluttered her eyelashes at him. 'Owen, I like to think you'll always have time available for me. Now remind me, when do you go on that music course in London? It won't interfere with the talent show, will it?'

'It's next month, third week of October, and it's only for one day with the Associated Board of the Royal Schools of Music.'

'I say, now who's throwing grand titles around? But I thought you were talking about a teaching diploma? Surely that can't be done in a day?'

'That comes later.'

'Is it all really necessary when you're getting the pupils by word of mouth already?'

'True, but if a job's worth doing, it's worth doing properly. Besides, I passed Grade Eight a long time ago and feel I owe it to anyone I teach to be fully up to speed on all fronts. Including the theory side of things.'

'I'm intrigued – why did you never follow a career in music when you were younger? Why did you go into business?'

'Back then I was more interested in making money. Money represented security and stability. And I wanted a ton of it. Two tons of it, given the chance.'

'Well,' Muriel said, hauling herself out of the chair and getting to her feet, 'I think we can safely say you achieved that ambition, and some.

But then I doubt you do anything by half, do you?'

Seeing her off, Owen was left with the uneasy feeling that Muriel's remark had been loaded with subtext. But what exactly?

CHAPTER 47

While Tattie walked Madison to school, and before he started work, Jensen went to see his mother, hoping to catch her before she opened up the barn.

The space on the drive where her car used to be parked was empty; his mother was in no hurry to find a replacement. For Jensen, the empty space was a stark reminder of the accident. He could recall very little of the crash, other than blindingly bright lights and the sudden and terrifyingly violent sensation of being crushed. Now and again, often when he was about to fall asleep, his brain tried to fill in the blanks with a kaleidoscope of distorted images and sounds. They could be real, or more likely, as he was inclined to believe, they were the product of his overactive imagination. He had absolutely no way of knowing for sure.

He gave a cursory knock on the back door at Medlar House and let himself in. With no sign of Mum in the kitchen he went looking for her, wondering how she would take the news that he and Tattie were now planning to get married. He was worried that she would think it inappropriate so soon after Daisy's death, but whatever her opinion he had to tell her today because odds on, and despite telling her it was a secret until Mia knew, Madison would probably tell Beth at school and before long everyone would know. Ideally he should have told his mother over the weekend, but with Dad around he'd decided against it. He wanted to share the news with Mum first. On her own.

The impulse to get married had come to Jensen, not surprisingly, after coming so close to his own mortality. When you really had no idea if you were about to experience your final day on earth, you might just as well go for broke while you could, he had concluded. Not the most romantic of reasons to get married, but what counted was that he loved Tattie and wanted to be with her, so why not go the whole way and make things official? When he'd asked her to marry him, it hadn't been a properly thought-out proposal, more a spur-of-the-moment saying aloud what he'd been thinking for some weeks. He'd been brushing his teeth in the bathroom and wiping his mouth on a towel, he had then wandered through to the bedroom where Tattie was reading a cookery book. 'You know what we should do?' he'd said.

'Hmm . . .' she'd responded absently, not looking up from the book.

'We should get married.'

That did catch her attention and giving him one of her long and steady looks, she had asked him why.

'Because I love you,' he'd said, 'because there's no one I'd rather be with for the rest of my life.'

Her face had broken into a smile and she'd said, 'Good answer, JC.'

'And yours?'

'What do you think?'

'I think I'm suddenly too scared to think what it might be.'

She'd pulled him down onto the bed and kissed him. 'Yes, I'd love for you to be my husband. And for me to be your wife.' She'd kissed him again and then laughing, she'd burst out, 'My God, that sounds so grown up!'

'We *are* grown up.'

Suddenly serious, she'd said, 'But we need to discuss it with Madison.'

'Understood,' he'd replied.

He found his mother upstairs in Daisy's old room. She was standing at the foot of the bed in front of a pile of neatly folded clothes. She turned, saw him in the doorway and looked startled.

'I did call out to you,' he said.

'I didn't hear,' she said, her voice no more than a whisper.

'Should you be doing this?' He indicated the folded clothes and the black bin liner in her hands.

'It's got to be done. These are things Daisy left here a long time ago.'

'Does Dad know what you're doing?'

'No.'

'Is that wise? I thought he kept this room locked when he wasn't here.'

'I asked Joe to get a copy of the key for me. And I don't care what your father says; it has to be done. I won't have this room turned into a morbid shrine. It's not natural. It's—' Her shoulders dropped and she closed her eyes briefly. She inhaled deeply, then let out her breath, screwed the empty bin liner into a ball and flung it on the bed. He could see she was close to tears and went to her and automatically put his arms around her. But she flinched and he let go, remembering too late that she couldn't bear to be touched now.

'Mum,' he said, 'don't make it any harder for yourself; sorting out Daisy's old things doesn't have to be done now. There's no hurry. You shouldn't do it alone anyway. I'll help you when the time's right.'

As if suddenly exhausted, she sat down on the bed, her head lowered. He sat next to her. Hanging on the back of the door was not only his father's towelling bathrobe but a selection of ties and a suit in a dry-cleaning bag. Realizing that this was the first time he'd set foot in the room since his sister's death, he didn't know how his father could bear to sleep in here. Seeing Daisy's things, the poignant reminders of her life, Jensen could feel his heart pick up speed and the familiar tightening in his chest. It still didn't seem possible that she was gone, and though he'd never been as close to her as he was to Eliza, he missed her. He missed her simply because she had been his youngest sister, the drama queen of the family, the one who'd caused them the most anxiety. He also missed her occasional moments of insight and advice. The last she'd given him had been that night when she'd met him at the station. Just minutes before the crash, she'd told him how great Tattie was. 'You be sure not to lose her,' she'd said.

He blinked and, clearing his throat, he said to his mother, 'Does it bother you much that Dad still sleeps in here? Is that why you want to get rid of everything? To make him stop?'

'No. Yes.' She took a breath. 'I mean, it's not natural, is it, to want to sleep in your dead daughter's—' Her voice cracked and she broke off. Then: 'He's taken one of her pillows to use in the apartment in Brussels.'

'It's just his way of trying to find some comfort. Don't read too much into it.'

'I don't mind that he hardly talks to me; I can cope with that. In fact I prefer the silence. But what hurts is the accusation that I couldn't possibly understand how he feels because I never loved Daisy the way he did. But then, he's right – I didn't love her like he did.'

'And thank God you didn't,' Jensen said firmly. 'You loved her the normal way a parent loves a child. You and I both know that Dad's love for Daisy wasn't a healthy love; she was smothered by it.'

As if she hadn't heard him, she chewed on her lower lip and said, 'Every morning I wake up thinking, if only I had gone to fetch you from the station that night, if only I hadn't let Daisy drive. I feel so guilty.'

'Mum,' he said softly, 'you have nothing to feel guilty about. Whereas I do. I should have ripped that phone out of her hands and remembered her seatbelt wasn't done up. If I had done that, she'd still be alive today. She'd be in Sydney with Scott planning their new life together. I think that every day. And I think how Dad must hate me for it. Has he said as much to you?'

She shook her head. 'He wouldn't dare.'

'Give it time and he will. What's more he'll eventually say it to my face.'

'But you must ignore him if he does. You mustn't take it to heart. Will you promise me that?'

'No, Mum, I can't promise that. Any more than I can turn back time and make you happy again.' Seconds passed. 'Can I ask you something?' he said.

She nodded.

'Before the accident, I remember thinking that you were happier than I'd seen you in a long while. Were you?'

'I . . .' she faltered. 'I was happy at the thought of you and Tattie and Madison coming to live here.'

'Just that? There was nothing else?'

Her gaze slid away from his. 'Your happiness has always been important to me,' she said.

'And yours is important to me also.' He instinctively went to put his arm around her again, but stopped himself. 'Mum,' he said, 'we've always been so close. We've never hidden anything from each other, have we? Not the important things. You used to say that there was a special intuitive understanding between us. Remember how Eliza banned us from playing Pictionary together because no one stood a chance against us?'

She nodded, but still didn't look at him.

'Which is why I'm going to stick my neck out and ask you why you rang Owen the night of the accident.'

Her face jolted in shock and picking up a pair of Daisy's jeans, she began folding them with exaggerated care. He watched in discomfort her hands shake and hated himself for pushing her like this. On top of everything else, didn't she have enough to cope with?

'I suppose it does look odd now, doesn't it?' she said lightly. 'But the simple answer is I got in a muddle with my mobile and instead of Muriel's number I pressed Owen's. O comes after M – it was an easy mistake, especially given the state I was in. And when he said he'd be there, I was so relieved I . . . I just needed a familiar face at the hospital.' She added the jeans to the pile of clothes.

How many times had she rehearsed that answer? he thought, as once more long empty seconds passed between them.

'Why did you want to know?' she asked at last.

He tried not to feel hurt that she wasn't being honest with him, but he couldn't bring himself to push her any further. What was there to go on anyway? Only his intuition and what Tattie had told him about that night at the hospital when Owen had arrived, coupled with the politely guarded way Owen always enquired after Mia. As far as Jensen knew, Dad didn't know about Owen's involvement that night, and all things considered, he reckoned it would be better it stayed that way.

He shrugged. 'Just curious.' Then remembering why he was here, he said, 'There's something I want to tell you. About Tattie and me.'

CHAPTER 48

Tattie had gone on ahead and saved them both a seat, on the end of the row towards the back. Slipping in next to Jensen – he had insisted on accompanying her – and aware of glances being cast in her direction, Mia sat down and mentally wrapped herself in what she had started to imagine as her cloak of invisibility.

She was only here for the school harvest festival because she'd promised Madison she would come, and to reassure Jensen that she was all right. She wasn't, of course. How could she be? She felt empty, as if the stuffing had been ripped out of her. Simple everyday tasks seemed beyond her at times, such as choosing what clothes to put on in the morning, or what to cook for supper. She would often find herself staring into the fridge not having a clue how long she had been standing there.

Talking to people was an ordeal and other than relying on mechanical small talk when dealing with a customer, she avoided doing it as much as she could. Talking meant listening and selfishly she didn't have the energy to pretend she was remotely interested in anything anyone had to say. 'It's because they care that they want to talk to you,' Muriel and Georgina had both said. What difference did it make if they did care? She just wanted to be left alone. Entirely alone. She didn't even want Muriel and Georgina bothering her. She didn't mean it nastily, she just didn't want to feign yet another emotion, that of gratitude for their support.

Georgina, who'd lost her husband and, in her own words, knew how grief could screw you up, was the most difficult to accept help from. How could Mia accept her support when she was filled with remorse that she'd had an affair with Owen knowing full well that Georgina had harboured hopes of a relationship with him? Although in her typically resilient way, Georgina now joked that she had given up hope of there ever being anything more than friendship between her and Owen.

'I'm clearly not his type,' she had said. 'I can't think why – a frazzled mother with a ready-made family; what more could he want? Oh, and let's not forget how drunk I can get!'

Georgina's sympathetic understanding and humour only made Mia feel worse. And who would think well of her if they knew she felt guiltier deceiving a friend than she did her own husband?

Since Jeff had returned to work in Brussels, his presence and absence from Medlar House were practically indistinguishable. Last weekend when he was home, she had hardly seen him; they each had retreated to different parts of the house – she to the kitchen, or over in the barn, and he to Daisy's old room. He slept in there, worked in there, watched television in there, but mostly, she imagined, suffered in there.

What little interaction they had took place during meal times. She didn't mind. To the contrary, it was a comfort knowing that she didn't have to pretend with him. She could sit at the table in silence and not worry about trying to think of something to talk about. She could almost thank him for not forcing her to behave differently. She felt anchored by the sense of isolation they had each adopted and was grateful not to have to expend an iota of physical or mental energy, of which she had precious little on the best of days. She was relieved too that Jeff clearly wasn't interested in sex. The thought of him touching her made her feel physically sick. She didn't understand why, but she couldn't bear to be touched by anyone else either; even a hug from Eliza or Jensen made her feel uncomfortable.

On a day-to-day basis she felt as if she was fighting an impossible battle against a tide of emotions. Some came and went, but always there was indescribable regret mixed with the raw and aching sadness of losing Daisy, and the endless, endless guilt, that things should have been different.

At the hospital that night, when she was told that Jensen was alive she had experienced what she knew was only natural, what any mother would feel: joyful and tearful relief. But then in its wake, she'd been hit with shameful guilt. How could she feel joy when Daisy was dead?

Aware only vaguely of her surroundings, of parents looking on proudly as their offspring performed and of children fidgeting as they sat cross-legged on the floor at the front, Mia closed her eyes and succumbed to what she had come to think of as an empty moment, when there was nothing to occupy her.

It was during these empty moments – usually at night when she couldn't sleep – that Owen came to her in her thoughts. Sometimes she fought to block out any reminders of him, but other times she gave in and allowed herself to dwell on the bittersweet memories of their short affair. She hadn't yet decided whether she did it to punish herself or out of a longing to derive some comfort from remembering the closeness of their all too brief time together.

It was the intimacy of their conversations, not the physical intimacy, that lingered most poignantly for her: his sharing with her the story of his childhood and his time in Little Pelham when he was a boy and why The Hidden Cottage was so special to him. Their first time in bed together, she had noticed an ugly scar about four inches long on his right shoulder blade. When she'd asked him how he'd got it, he'd initially deflected her question, saying it was nothing. When she'd pressed him, he'd told her and she'd been horrified, could not imagine how any parent could do such a thing.

But no matter how poignant the memories were of those shared times together, Mia knew that she had to free herself from any feelings she'd once had for Owen. She had to cut him out from her life altogether. If she couldn't do that, she was convinced she would become swamped by guilt and self-loathing. And fear. Any loneliness she felt was the price she had to pay. She had to sacrifice her feelings in order to rid herself of her shame, a shame that was all wrapped up in the guilt that she had put herself before her family.

She had told Owen the day of the funeral that she believed she had brought this tragedy on her family and while she knew that he wouldn't be alone in thinking that she was being irrational, these were the undeniable facts: the first time she had planned to leave her husband she had been devastated to learn that Daisy had been making herself profoundly ill, and then once again when she planned to divorce Jeff, Daisy was killed.

There wasn't a day that passed when she wasn't haunted by the belief that she was in some way responsible, that her selfishness was inextricably bound up in the loss of her youngest child. It all came down to the single most important truth: she should have been a better mother; she should have known that something was going to happen.

And for all those who would claim she was wrong, that her wanting to end her marriage had

461

no bearing on the wellbeing of her children, she had this to say: what mother, who loved her children as much as she did, would be prepared to put it to the test and risk the life of another child?

A nudge at her elbow had her flicking her eyes open. She turned to see Jensen looking at her. 'It's Madison's turn to read her poem,' he whispered.

She directed her gaze to the front of the school hall and concentrated on Madison who, to all intents and purposes, was going to be her granddaughter when Jensen and Tattie married. Not so long ago the thought would have pleased her, but now she viewed the girl as another person whom she might love and lose.

Mia watched Madison staring out at the audience, her eyes searching the sea of faces for her mother. Once located, Madison then adjusted her glasses, tucked her hair behind her ears and began reading her poem in a clear, loud voice. Her confidence impressed Mia, especially as she knew that Madison was not the most confident of children, that she frequently let her anxiety get the better of her.

Now that Madison was sitting down on the floor with her classmates and both Tattie and Jensen had relaxed either side of her, Mia once again closed her eyes and thought how proud she was of her son. It seemed that overnight he had truly grown up, had shrugged off all that had gone before. She thought of all those years when she had worried about him, when he was never truly in step with the world, at odds with so much of it, but perhaps chiefly at odds with himself. But now, as Eliza had said, he was fast becoming the lynchpin of the family, holding them together with his quiet, resourceful strength. None of which Jeff saw. For having effectively removed himself from the family circle, he had placed himself beyond reach and beyond any form of consolation.

Jeff didn't know it but he had cause to be grateful to Jensen. Had it not been for Jensen, Mia would have gone ahead and got rid of Daisy's things and invoked heaven only knew what trouble. As it was, Jensen had put everything back in the cupboards and locked the bedroom as though they'd never been there. Several weeks later and Mia couldn't think why she had wanted to do it in the first place; she was glad Jensen had stepped in. It would have only been deeply antagonistic towards Jeff and he was suffering enough without her making it any worse for him. What did it matter if he turned the room into a shrine? If it helped him cope with his grief, who was she to take that away from him? Was it any worse than the time she spent at Daisy's grave in the churchyard next door? Or the way she liked to sit with an old photo album on her lap turning the pages, watching Daisy grow before her eyes and remembering how her smile could brighten her beautiful face?

No, she was glad that Jensen had stopped her from making a terrible mistake. She was glad too that Jensen hadn't questioned her any more about Owen and why it was him she had turned to on the night of the crash. The truth was he had been the only one she had thought would be the source of comfort she needed. With hindsight it had been unwise of her, but she really hadn't been thinking straight and could not have cared less about the consequences. Following that conversation with Jensen, she had decided that even if he suspected something he would never say anything and, so long as she never referred to it, the affair would remain a closed and forgotten chapter in her life.

But try as she might to convince herself that her silence was all that it would take to put Owen behind her, the fear of discovery was still there. What if Owen said something?

Or worse, what if someone else had noticed something and some of the stares she received from people in the village were not of sympathy, but of suspicion?

It was always possible that without someone with whom she could share the secret and her remorse, she had become paranoid. But that, she supposed, was what a guilty conscience did to one. It was probably why so many people confessed and made a clean break of things – to be free of the burden of knowing they had done something very wrong.

Would that ultimately be the only way she too would feel free?

CHAPTER 49

It was a blustery autumn morning and the sky was grey. It looked like it was going to rain. But Madison didn't care. It was the first day of half-term – Saturday morning – and they were flying to America to stay with Grandma Barb and Grandpa Tom. 'It's time for your grandparents to check me out,' JC had joked when they told her about the trip. 'They need to be sure I'm good enough for your mum.'

Grandma Barb had told her all about the things they would do together, and that she'd got Grandpa to repaint the little room that Madison would sleep in and that she was getting the house ready for Halloween. Mum said that Grandma had always gone a bit crazy when it came to Halloween and that she liked to decorate the house from top to bottom with anything that was spooky or shaped like a pumpkin.

Staring ahead through the windscreen, Madison saw a man jogging towards them on the grass verge.

'There's Owen!' she cried out abruptly. Embarrassed by the loudness of her voice in the quiet of the car, she said, 'Can we say goodbye to him, please?'

For a moment she didn't think Mia was going to stop, but then the car slowed and came to a standstill as Owen also stopped. Madison lowered the window, as did JC in the front.

Breathing hard, Owen said, 'You're all set, then?'

JC nodded. 'Yep, we're ready for lift-off. Madison just wanted to say goodbye.'

Owen moved to the rear of the car and smiled at her. 'You be sure to have a good holiday,' he said. 'I'll see you when you're back, and be warned, we have the talent show and your exam to prepare for.' He smiled at Mum and then turned to look at Mia in the front. But Mia wasn't looking his way. She was staring straight ahead through the windscreen. She seemed to be concentrating very hard on nothing in particular. She did a lot of that. Staring into the distance. She never used to, not before Daisy died. Madison also noticed that her hands were gripping the steering wheel, her knuckles showing white and ugly, almost like the bones were poking through. Madison felt sorry for Owen – he seemed to want to say something to Mia, but it was obvious she didn't want to say anything to him. It was as if they'd had a big row and Mia no longer wanted to be friends with him. Madison couldn't think why.

'Well, then,' Owen said, straightening up, 'I'd better let you get on. Safe journey!'

'Bye!' they said at the same time. All except for Mia.

As they drove away from the verge, Madison raised herself up and leant out of the window to wave at Owen. He waved back and again Madison felt sorry for him. What could they have argued about for Mia to be so rude to him?

Mia had been gone for a while when Jeff decided to get up.

Lying in bed, he had listened to her getting ready – the shower running, drawers opening and shutting, footsteps crossing the landing then going down the stairs, the rumble of the kettle boiling, the sound of keys being scooped up, the back door shutting and then finally the sound of his car starting up. *His* car because they'd only just got around to buying a replacement for Mia's old Golf and it wasn't big enough for all the luggage.

Showered and dressed, he went downstairs and found a note left for him by the kettle. *Sorry, no ground coffee, I forgot to buy some yesterday.*

He stood staring out of the window at the leaden sky. Behind him, the clock on the wall ticked inexorably in the silence. It was a loud, ponderous tick. An annoying tick. It was there in the deafening silence of every meal he and Mia now shared. He considered getting a chair and reaching up to the clock and smashing it on the floor, but he couldn't be bothered.

Instead, he pulled on his coat to go in search of some coffee.

On the green, a gust of chilly wind was shaking the leaves from the oak tree, chasing them across the grass. He buttoned his coat and thought how much he now hated Saturday mornings. Monday to Friday, he could get through the days. Work was his salvation. So long as he had that – a full diary, wall-to-wall meetings, endless reports to prepare or read, planes to catch – he knew where he was. It was the long empty hours of the weekend that he couldn't cope with. He had no idea how to fill them, other than burying himself in yet more work and finding ways to avoid talking to anyone. There was nothing he could say to people, nothing that meant anything.

He was no nearer accepting the horror of Daisy's death than he had been back in July when it happened. How could he be? How could he ever get over the loss of his precious daughter? Or his regret that he hadn't resolved matters with her? He felt sick in his heart whenever he thought of the dreadful last words they had exchanged. He had never believed in heaven – he still didn't – but he needed to imagine that Daisy was somewhere better than this bloody awful place and that she knew he was sorry, sorrier than he could ever put into words.

Several times he had stood at the foot of her grave in the churchyard and begged her forgiveness, but not once had he ever experienced any kind of response or relief. And he knew he never would because she wasn't there. He could not bring himself to picture her there beneath the ground, shut in a box, her body decaying, her insides being . . .

He stopped himself short. Enough! Better to picture her in her old room, lying on the bed happily listening to music, magazines and clothes strewn messily all over the carpet. It was why he slept in there, it was the only place he could remember her properly. As she was. His perfect little baby girl.

Yet for all the painful suffering of his grief, he still had not cried. While he could not imagine feeling any worse than he did, he was beginning to fear that he was undergoing some form of delayed shock, that something more devastating than this agony awaited him.

He pushed open the shop door and as the tinkly bell announced his presence to those inside – Bob, Wendy and Muriel – he braced himself for the inevitable sympathetic expressions, the excessively considerate handling of him.

Bob was the first to speak. 'Morning, Mr Channing,' he said in the awkwardly moderated voice he now used to speak to him. 'Looks like autumn's really with us now, doesn't it? I was only saying to Muriel a few minutes ago, I don't know where this year's gone.'

Jeff nodded silently.

From the window where she was arranging a display of pumpkins, Wendy smiled at him. 'Goodness,' she said, her tone almost as sickly as her pink lipstick, 'it'll be Christmas before we know it.'

Adding a loaf of bread into her wire basket, Muriel groaned. 'Oh, please don't remind me, not when I still have so much to do for the show. I'm convinced this year we won't be ready in time.'

Christmas, Jeff thought with a brutal stab of pain. Christmas without Daisy. His first Christmas without her. How would he get through it?

He found the ground coffee he wanted and went to pay for it.

Muriel had got there before him.

'That's all right,' she said, 'you go ahead. I'm in no hurry.'

More kindness and consideration. He wished they wouldn't do it. It didn't help. He didn't want their pity. He'd prefer it if they ignored him.

He had his wallet out of his pocket when Muriel said, 'I was wondering, Jeff, whether you might have given the show any more thought.'

He jerked his head up. 'No,' he said, 'no, I don't think I could possibly—' The words got stuck in his throat and he fiddled with his wallet.

She looked at him, her face unnaturally softened with benevolence. 'It won't be the same without you. You—' She hesitated. 'You don't think it might do you good? You know, give you something else to think about. Something fun. Something to cheer you up.'

He stared at her, summoning the right response. 'Muriel, I know you mean well, but really there isn't anything in this world that could cheer me up.'

Suddenly unable to take another word or expression of their understanding, and terrified he would break down in front of them, he slammed a handful of coins down on the counter. His heart beating fast and desperate to escape, he threw open the shop door with a crash. The bell tinkled loudly as if in protest.

Out on the pavement, he stepped into the road and felt like a truck had hit him. The air knocked from him, he fell to the ground with a heavy thump, conscious only of a man in shorts and a T-shirt above him. When he'd caught his breath he saw that the man was Owen Fletcher and he was bending down, a hand outstretched to help him to his feet. In an instant, the control he'd been struggling to retain welled up inside him and converted itself to furious anger. He pushed the proffered hand away and got to his feet. 'Watch where you're going,' he snarled.

Owen took a step back. 'I'm really sorry,' he said. 'Are you OK? Any damage done?'

To add insult to injury, Muriel with Bob and Wendy in tow now appeared on the pavement, making his humiliation complete. 'I'm fine,' he snapped, before they could fuss over him.

'You forgot your coffee,' Muriel said, holding out the packet to him and looking worried.

Fighting to keep his composure, Jeff took the bag of coffee from her. 'Thanks,' he muttered in a strangled voice.

He set off across the green. Bloody Owen Fletcher, he thought miserably. Why was it whenever he was in that smug bastard's company he felt like punching him hard? There the man was, cruising through life with not a care in the world. It was enough to make him sick.

CHAPTER 50

Owen raised the axe and, swinging it through a perfect arc, cleaved the log in two. He then rearranged the pieces and chopped the two into four.

'Not bad,' Rich said, taking the axe from him. 'Now I'll show you how it's really done. Load me up.'

Smiling, Owen placed a log on the tree stump that now made the ideal chopping block and stood back. 'Ready when you are.'

Rich took his first swing and the blade of the axe dug deep, but the log didn't split. He lifted the axe and the log came with it. 'Must be a sticky bit of wood,' he said, pulling a face.

'Yeah right, nothing to do with being a total rookie.'

'Hey, fella, no dissing me when I've got a dangerous weapon in my hand.'

Owen laughed. 'First rule of woodcutting, leave it to an expert. Here, give it to me.'

'What, and have you gloating for the rest of the day? Not on your life!'

Still laughing, and glad to have his friend here,

he said, 'Trust you to turn a simple task into a championship face-off.'

Two hours later and with the hawthorn trees that Joe had helped Owen to cut down earlier in the week now chopped and piled in the wood store, Owen proposed a beer. The light was fading and the temperature was dropping fast, but still warm from their exertions, the two men sat on the veranda, chinked bottles and sighed deeply and contentedly.

With Catherine away on a girls' spa weekend, Rich had rung yesterday and invited himself for Sunday lunch, and after they'd put away epic amounts of roast beef, roast potatoes, Yorkshire pudding, carrots, and the last of the runner beans from the garden, Owen had declared them in need of some exercise. Eager for another sofa ride, Rich's hopes had been dashed when Owen gave him the news the sofa had been taken away by the council some weeks ago. His disappointment had been short-lived when he'd taken one look at the logs Owen had made a start on already and had rolled up his sleeves with typical enthusiasm. 'Soon have the rest chopped,' he'd declared.

'You're becoming quite the man of the soil,' Rich said now. 'Growing your own food, chopping your own wood . . . what next, I ask myself – self-sufficiency with a pig and a goat in the garden?'

'There are halfway measures, you know.'

'Some hens, then? How about fresh eggs every morning?'

Owen took a long swig of his beer. 'A nice idea, but who would look after them when I'm not here?'

Rich eyed him thoughtfully. 'Thinking of getting away, are you? Bored with playing the country bumpkin already?'

'And there you go again. There really are no half measures with you.'

'Hey, all I'm doing is an honest bit of fishing. I've been here since half past twelve and while I've been happy to hear about your flourishing career as a piano teacher, the one-day course down in London and all about the Little Pelham's Got Talent show, not a word have you said about the married woman in the village here who'd so captivated you. And that's despite my subtle and not-so-subtle hints.'

'I told you ages ago that it was over between us.'

'That was *then*. What about *now*? Has nothing changed?'

Owen ran a hand over his unshaven chin and looked up at the darkening sky. 'No.'

'Come on, give me more than that.'

'There really isn't more to tell. Since the death of her youngest daughter she's avoided me. In a nutshell, and this is my reading of the situation, she associates our affair with being happy and that's an emotion she won't allow herself to feel again.'

'She said that?'

'No. What she actually said was far worse. She's convinced herself it was a mistake and that it brought about the death of her daughter.'

'Right. That twisted old cookie of karma payback. God help you, in that case.'

'Grief makes people behave in a variety of ways; this is her way of coping, I guess. There doesn't have to be any logic involved.'

In the silence that followed, Owen thought of Mia's steadfast refusal to so much as look at him yesterday morning when he'd been out jogging and Madison had wanted to say goodbye.

In contrast to Mia shutting down her emotions – this was what she was doing, according to Muriel – Jeff's emotions had seemed highly reactive when Owen had literally bumped into him outside Parr's. The expression on his face had made Owen think of a nuclear reactor of anger just waiting to explode. It made Owen wonder how the man would behave if he ever discovered about him and Mia.

He couldn't deny there had been numerous times since the day of Daisy's funeral – when he'd witnessed for himself Jeff's grief – that Owen had experienced flashes of guilt for what he had done. Yet it didn't alter how he felt about Mia.

Their relationship had come to an end before it had really begun, but she was never far from his thoughts. Along with the dull ache of their separation and what could have been. He knew he should give up on the idea of there being anything more between them, but he wasn't ready yet to do that. Better to hope than not, he'd once said to Mia.

'Do you think you'll leave here because of what's happened?'

Rich's question took Owen by surprise and he failed to find an answer.

His friend said, 'I know what a sentimental old devil you are. My money's on you now feeling that the happy idyll you've created for yourself has lost some of its charm for you.'

'I never had you down as being so astute,' Owen replied in a carefully neutral tone.

Rich shrugged. 'Maybe you've always underestimated me. So, am I right? Are you going to sell up?'

CHAPTER 51

Hi Eliza,

Good news! My reputation has not gone before me in Maine and Tattie's parents haven't run me out of town. I see now where Tattie gets her frankness from; Tom and Barb are totally straight down the line. They could teach our family a thing or two!

How are you? Not working too hard? You and Simon OK? How's Mum? Have you heard from her? I've only been away a few days, and I know it sounds stupid, but I kind of miss you. It must be the distance.

Take care.

J.

It was a very untypical email from Jensen. Point of fact, before Daisy's death, any email from him would have been a rarity and never would he have put into actual words something that resembled an emotion. But then Eliza was no one to talk; free-flowing sentiment was hardly her forte.

But here was Jensen saying he missed her and for the rest of the day his words resonated with her, right up until she'd finished work and was on her way home. Emerging from the underground into the darkness and rain, and without an umbrella, she shifted her heavy bags on her shoulder and made a dash for it, taking care to avoid the puddles and not to bump into anyone.

Taking care.

There it was again, another reminder of Jensen's email. Hadn't she always done that? Hadn't she always taken the path of care and extreme diligence? Simon said she was the most conscientious person he knew – compulsively conscientious was how he actually described her. He said he was on a mission to change her attitude and to bring some much-needed balance into her life. 'I'm going to turn you into a productive slacker if it's the last thing I do,' he'd said only last night when she'd promised him she'd join him in bed in ten minutes' time. It was an hour later when she finally switched off her laptop and slipped in beside him.

They were still in the early stages of their relationship, still discovering new things about each other. Surprising things at times. For instance, she'd had no idea that Simon was such a fantastic cook. The trouble was, he was a messy cook and used every pot, pan and utensil she possessed and turned her small, normally neat kitchen into a war zone. It drove her crazy. But since she wasn't much of a cook, it wasn't a bad trade-off.

Letting herself in, she was greeted by the smell of cooking. And music. She didn't have a clue what it was, but Simon couldn't be in the flat unless he had something playing. Music appreciation was another thing he was determined to teach her.

She was hanging up her wet coat when he appeared in the narrow hall. 'I know, I know,' she said tiredly, 'I'm late. Again. I'm sorry.'

'Another black mark against you,' he said disapprovingly, 'one to add to the many.' He kissed her, his lips warm and inviting against her cold mouth. 'Come on through and get warmed up. Supper's nearly ready. What?' he said, when she didn't move or say anything.

'Kiss me again, please.'

'Any reason why?'

'Because one of the things I love about you is that nothing ever fazes you.'

He pointed to the front door. 'OK, you can turn around right now and go back wherever you've come from. I don't want this imposter, I want my real girlfriend returned to me, the one who doesn't dish out compliments at the drop of a hat.'

She laughed and kissed him for a very long time. 'Can dinner wait a bit longer?' she asked, tipping her head back and locking eyes with him.

'Bed, Channing? At this hour of the evening?'

She pushed him towards the bedroom. 'You're always telling me to let go and be more spontaneous.'

★ ★ ★

Much later, when they were curled up on the sofa watching an episode of the latest series of *The Killing*, Eliza said, 'Simon?'

'Mmm . . .'

'I've been thinking.'

'Mmm . . .'

'About us.'

He turned and looked at her. 'That sounds ominous. Had I better put Lund on hold?'

She nodded and he pointed the remote control at the television, freeze-framing Sarah Lund against a gloomy Copenhagen skyline.

'So what's on your mind?' he asked.

She suddenly felt unsure of herself. What had seemed so right in her head just seconds earlier now felt a step too far. She sat up straight so that she could look him square in the eye. No point in doing it any other way. 'I was wondering if you'd like to move in on a permanent basis.'

'Permanent,' he repeated. 'As opposed to—'

'As opposed to how we currently go about things, dividing our time between two places. Of course, if you think it's too soon or inappropriate I'd quite understand. It's just a thought. Maybe a not very good thought. Maybe you like things how they are and think why change the status quo.' Oh God, she silently groaned, somebody stop her from making this sound any worse than it did already.

He tilted his head to one side. 'What's brought this on?'

'It makes sense,' she said. 'And would save us

both time and money. I mean, you're here virtually all the time anyway.'

'So it would be an eminently *practical* arrangement?'

'Well, yes. Obviously.'

'Mmm . . . I need to think about that. You see, the thing is, I'm not sure I can commit to that.'

She felt her cheeks redden with regret and embarrassment. How did she always manage to get it so wrong? 'Oh, right,' she said, 'well, like I said, it was probably presumptuous of me to suggest it. Forget I ever said anything.' She nudged his hand with the remote control. 'Go on, let's get back to Sarah Lund.'

But Simon continued to leave the Danish investigator frozen on the screen. 'Eliza,' he said, 'when I say I can't commit to something that's solely a practical solution, I mean that I'd prefer to move in with you for an entirely different reason. Such as I love being with you and hate it when we're not together. So my question to you is: do you want me to move in solely because it's a sensible and practical option, or because you want things to be more permanent between us?'

Realizing the mess she'd made of things, she said, 'You're such a smart arse at times.'

He smiled. 'Go on, Channing, say the words. Get them out. Hear them and know them.'

'Why do you tease me like this?'

'I'm teaching you to express yourself.' He tapped

her leg with the remote control. 'Still waiting to hear you say the words.'

She moved away from him and crossed her arms. 'I've changed my mind. I don't want you to move in now. You'd make my life intolerable.'

He waved the remote control under her nose. 'No Lund until you've said the words.'

With a swiftness that caught him off guard, she snatched the remote control from him and held it out of his reach. 'Hah! Not so clever now, are you?'

With equal swiftness, he leant forward and pinned her down on the sofa. 'Say you love being with me! Say you want things to be more permanent between us!'

'No!' she squealed. 'Never!'

He began to tickle her, making her laugh and squeal all the more. As she wriggled beneath him, begging him to stop, he suddenly raised himself from her and looked down into her eyes, and in a split second the moment changed. 'Eliza,' he said, 'you know I love you, so why would you think I wouldn't want to live with you 24/7?'

She swallowed. 'You might think it would spoil things.'

'What will spoil things is if you keep doubting my feelings for you. You have to believe I would never hurt you like Greg did. I'd never do anything to hurt you.'

'Deep down I know that, but—'

'But what? Either you believe and trust me or you don't.'

'It's not that, genuinely it isn't.' She sat up and straightened her clothes. 'I'm just scared of you seeing the real me and not liking what you find.'

'That's what makes you drive yourself so hard, isn't it? You always feel you have to present a certain image of yourself to everyone, the super-efficient, ultra-professional Eliza Channing.'

When she remained silent, he said, 'That is who you are, Eliza, but you're also totally gorgeous and sexy as hell into the bargain.'

'I'm not gorgeous. I'm at least a stone overweight and as for being sexy—'

He put a finger against her lips. 'Repeat after me, "I, Eliza Channing, am gorgeous and am as sexy as hell."'

'Don't be stupid,' she mumbled against his finger, suppressing a giggle.

He lifted it away from her mouth. 'Say the words.'

She shook her head. 'I can't.'

'Oh, Eliza, you're hopeless. Your perception of yourself is seriously skewed. I wish you could see yourself as I see you.'

She considered his words and thought that she wasn't the only one who needed to modify their thinking. 'I'll say the words if you say something in return for me,' she said.

'Go on?'

'You must stop feeling you did anything wrong the night my sister died. Taking my mobile away from me had no direct effect on what happened. None at all.'

His expression altered and she knew that her suspicions were right, that he did still feel guilty. 'But it did have an effect,' he said with a frown. 'It meant your mother couldn't get hold of you when she needed you most. I know how frantic my own mother would be if she couldn't get hold of me in a similar situation.'

'But there could be any number of reasons why a person can't be reached in an emergency. And how about back in the day when mobiles weren't around?'

His frowned deepened.

'You did nothing wrong,' she said. 'Your heart was entirely in the right place when you took me to Suffolk. It was the nicest thing anyone has ever done for me.'

Later, when they were in bed, Eliza listened to the comforting rise and fall of Simon's breathing. He slept so easily and so soundly.

Lying there in the darkness, listening to the distant rumble of traffic, she thought how glad she was that he had found the courage to make clear his feelings for her. It must have been awful for him to listen to her going on about Greg all that time.

Life, she thought, was full of random moments of chance. Had she not seen Greg at the airport, she almost certainly wouldn't be here now with

Simon; she would probably still be being strung along by Greg and deluding herself that he loved her.

And how different things would be if Daisy hadn't gone to collect Jensen from the station that night. Poor Daisy. Her happiness had been so fleeting.

Whenever Eliza thought of the accident and how miraculously Jensen had survived, an icy chill ran through her. She couldn't imagine losing her brother as well as Daisy. She recalled Jensen's email that morning and his words – *I miss you* – and decided that since she couldn't sleep, she might just as well do something useful.

She reached for her iPad that was on the floor by the side of the bed, but no sooner had she switched it on than Simon stirred. He lifted his head from the pillow and blinking in the glare of the screen, he peered at her through a scrunched-up eye. 'Channing, what the hell are you doing?'

'I'm emailing Jensen. Go back to sleep.'

He groaned and closed his eyes. 'So long as you're not working. Because if I thought you were, I'd have to take steps.'

She smiled and bent to kiss him. 'Beauty sleep, Simon. Get to it.'

'Say hi to your brother from me,' he mumbled sleepily.

Seconds later the steady rise and fall of his breathing had resumed. It would be good when he moved in permanently, she thought. A sudden image of Daisy nodding her approval flashed into her head. *At last you're getting some proper fun into your life,* she imagined her sister saying.

'I am, Daisy,' she murmured. 'I am.'

CHAPTER 52

After days of wind and rain, the sun was shining from a tranquil sky of translucent blue in which small clouds hung like balls of puffy white cotton wool.

Inside the barn all was not so serene. The cause of the hubbub was Georgina's two boys, Edmund and Luke. They were here with Georgina and Muriel to try on their talent show costumes, which Mia had made for them. Although making them was a stretch, all she'd really done was come up with a very simple idea.

'I know I'm in danger of repeating myself, Mia, but this really was a genius idea of yours,' Georgina said as she readjusted the wig on Luke's head.

Muriel was trying to do the same to Edmund's wig. 'Keep still, you wretched little monkey,' she said as he bounced beneath her hands as if on springs.

Luke then got in on the act and he too started bouncing on the balls of his feet. Slipping out of his mother's grasp, he bounced over to his brother. 'Boing! Boing! Boing!' he chanted to the inevitable delight of Edmund, who joined in.

Muriel threw her hands in the air in despair. 'That's it, no treats for you two rascals! I shall eat them all myself.'

The two boys instantly stood to attention and offered up smiles of breathless angelic compliance.

'That's more like it,' Muriel said in the sudden hush. She dug around in her bag and pulled out two bags of chocolate buttons. She held them aloft. 'These are yours, but only if you stand very still and let Mia take some pictures of you. Heaven only knows why, but your mother wants a keepsake of this nightmarish episode.'

They obediently turned to face Mia. Ready with the camera, she hurriedly took as many photographs as she could before they grew bored. She then gave them permission to relax so she could capture their true spirited nature. 'Wave your hands in the air,' she instructed, 'and pull the daftest face you can manage, but keep looking into the camera. That's great. Well done!'

'Well done for being a couple of monkeys?' Muriel roared. 'They can do that in their sleep!' Despite the admonishment, she smiled fondly at the boys and handed over the promised treats.

The two boys fully occupied now, Mia showed Georgina the pictures she'd taken. 'Will they do?' she asked.

'They're brilliant. Thank you so much. Not just for the photos, but for making their costumes. You're a star.'

'It was nothing. Really. And they're the stars, not me. Or rather they will be when they get on the stage; everyone will love them.'

'A couple of real showstoppers,' Muriel said. 'Heaven help us all!'

They turned to look at Luke and Edmund who, dressed as mini versions of Jedward – outrageous hair-on-end blonde wigs, skinny-legged black trousers and black jackets embellished with gold and silver stars – were now sitting on the floor lining up chocolate buttons on their legs and eating them one by one.

'While they're quiet, let's have a look at the magazine you're in, Mia. Are you pleased with how the article came out?'

Putting her camera down, Mia turned to the shelf behind her. She passed the magazine to Georgina. 'Page twenty-one,' she said, but made no further comment on it. She had received the magazine in the post that morning but had barely glanced at it; it was too painful a reminder – the day when the photographer and journalist from the magazine had come here was the day Daisy died. 'I'll put the kettle on, shall I?'

Georgina looked up from the magazine. 'I'd love to stay,' she said, 'but I need to get the boys to Olney for a haircut.'

'Don't forget Stephen's Halloween party,' Luke called over.

'What are they going as?' Mia asked.

'The same as last year: vampires. I've bought

490

them some new blood-tipped fangs and resur-
rected the black capes you made for them last
year.'

'Nothing as scary as Jedward, then,' Muriel said
with a wink. 'What time are you due at the
hairdresser?'

Georgina looked at her watch and her eyes
widened. 'Oh Lord, it's later than I thought. Quick,
boys, out of those clothes – we need to get going.'

After Georgina and the boys had left in a whirl-
wind of frenzied activity, Muriel said, 'If there's
still tea on offer, I wouldn't say no.'

'Of course,' Mia said. Although she would have
preferred to be on her own now. She was exhausted.
She still found the slightest task took all her energy
and powers of concentration. 'Shall we go over to
the house?' she said.

'No, here's fine. I promise I won't keep you long.
I can see that you're shattered.'

Grateful for Muriel's honesty, Mia went through
to the minuscule kitchenette and filled the kettle.
Plugging it in, she suspected Muriel had something on her mind that she wanted to discuss. It
was probably something to do with the talent show.
More than likely Muriel now considered sufficient
time had passed and was about to press-gang Mia
into helping on the night. She had, after all, helped
in all the previous years. Not only that, but because
she'd put together the Jedward outfits for Luke
and Edmund – adapting two pairs of trousers and

black school blazers from a jumble sale and sourcing a couple of wigs from an online joke shop – Muriel would take this as a positive sign that she was coping and moving on. All she was really doing was taking one day at a time. Nothing more. There was no other option.

The tea made, she took the two mugs through to Muriel. 'Is this about the talent show?' she asked.

Muriel shook her head. 'No. Have you and Jeff thought of seeing a grief counsellor?'

Taken aback, Mia took a moment to reply. Finally she said, 'Do you honestly think Jeff would do that?'

'He saw a counsellor once before when Daisy was ill, didn't he?'

'He had a positive reason to do it then, to help Daisy get better. And he only went once and disregarded more or less everything that was said.'

'Have you discussed seeing a counsellor with him?'

'Oh, Muriel, we hardly talk. The few occasions we actually sit in the same room together, talking is the last thing he wants to do. Or indeed what I want to do.'

Muriel tutted and shook her head sadly. 'That won't do.' Her voice was surprisingly gentle.

'You're probably right, but as for Jeff, he's unreachable.'

They sipped their tea in silence.

Looking up from her mug, Muriel said, 'Why

did you think I wanted to talk to you about the talent show?'

'I thought perhaps you'd considered sufficient time had passed for me to pull myself together and help.'

'Would you like to help?'

'Maybe,' she said carefully, 'but I'd hate to commit to something and then not be able to do it.'

Muriel nodded. 'I understand. But what if I put you down to help with refreshments, like last year? That wouldn't be too taxing, would it?'

Mia smiled tiredly. 'All right, I'll do it.'

'Good girl. Everyone will be so glad to have you back in the fold. I know it's selfish of people, but often the only way they can handle another person's grief is to see some visible sign of them getting over it.'

'I know.'

Her tea finished now, Muriel said, 'Well, this won't get the baby bathed; I need to get home. Oh, by the way, I saw Owen this morning. I told him I was seeing you this afternoon and he sent his regards.'

Mia took Muriel's empty mug along with her own through to the kitchenette. 'How is he?' she asked casually, her back to Muriel.

'He's well. But we must do all we can to keep him here.'

Mia turned. 'Why? Is he thinking of leaving?'

'I get the impression that the novelty of living

here might be wearing off. He doesn't seem to have the same enthusiasm as he did earlier in the summer. Oh, I nearly forgot, tell me quickly the latest news from Maine. How's Jensen getting on with his future in-laws?'

CHAPTER 53

While Tattie, Madison and Barb were visiting an old family friend, Jensen was giving Tom a hand raking up leaves in the garden.

'I reckon I'll be doing this from now until December,' Tom said, looking at the dense circle of trees that surrounded them. 'And I know what you're thinking, son – why not put it off until then and do the job in one go? I did that once before and you should have seen the mess those leaves made of the grass.' He laughed. 'I never heard the last of it from Barb. She's a woman who likes things just so. You might have noticed that.'

Jensen nodded in a non-committal sort of way. He certainly had noticed that Barb, just as Tattie had warned him, was a neat freak, but he wasn't about to criticize his future mother-in-law behind her back. Instead he said, 'Madison's pretty particular about her things as well; she never has anything out of place in her bedroom at home.'

Tom chuckled. 'We sure know who she gets that from. But she's a great kid. Bright as a dime. A terrible worrier, though. I'm told she gets that from me, but I never think of myself as a worrier, more a man who likes to know where he stands. How about you, JC? Are you a worrier?'

'I have my moments.'

'How about now? Any worries about getting married? I'm sure I'd have a few doubts if I were in your shoes, it's not for every young man to take on a ready-made family.'

Here was the frank openness Jensen found so refreshing in the Morrow family. There was no beating about the bush for Tom and Barb; they got straight to the heart of the matter. When he'd emailed Eliza saying they could teach their family a thing or two, he hadn't been exaggerating. 'No doubts at all,' Jensen said. 'I've never felt more sure about anything.'

Resting his hands on the handle of the rake and seeming to contemplate his answer, Tom nodded gravely. 'I hope you'll forgive me if you think I'm speaking out of turn,' he said slowly, 'but I believe this is something that needs to be said.'

Jensen tensed, fearing that perhaps this moment had been carefully engineered in Tattie's absence for her father to say exactly what he thought of her choice of husband. Giving the other man his full attention, he thought how different he was from his own father. They were about the same age – late fifties – but that was the only similarity. To say Tom was an imposing figure was a massive understatement. He looked like he could pick Jensen up with one hand and hold him above his head without breaking sweat. He was a giant of a man, built of solid muscle and with a buzz cut that shouted ex-military. Which wasn't the case. He'd spent all his working life as a high school maths teacher – who wouldn't knuckle down to their algebra with him at the front of the classroom? Barb joked – and coaching high-school football. He'd retired early last year for no other reason than he wanted to spend more time with his wife. 'To keep an eye on me, more like it,' Barb further joked.

'I want you to know that Barb and I are very happy to welcome you into our family,' he went on in his surprisingly quiet voice for one so big. 'I was concerned initially about losing our daughter to someone living so far away from us, but we both think you're a fine young man and we couldn't be happier that you and Tattie are getting married. Our only regret is that we won't see more of you all.'

Jensen didn't know how to respond to Tom's unexpected speech. But the man hadn't finished.

'Tattie says you're not close to your father,' he continued, 'that you have a difficult relationship with each other, bad history, she says. Is there no way you can resolve matters? As one gets older, one realizes just how short life can be.'

His throat tight, Jensen said, 'Actually, after the death of my youngest sister, that is something I've recently come to appreciate.'

Tom shook his head. 'Of course,' he said, clearly embarrassed, his brow creased. 'I'm sorry. That was clumsy of me. I'm sorry if I have spoken out of turn, but that's what we do in our family: we speak plainly and honestly and where praise is due, we give it wholeheartedly. And you deserve a lot of praise, son.'

'You haven't spoken out of turn,' Jensen said, 'far from it. What's more, I think you're right; I should try to make some sort of peace with my father. I'd like to do it for Madison's sake, but I don't have a clue how to go about it.'

Tom nodded thoughtfully. 'Where there's a will there's usually a way,' he said.

Yes, thought Jensen. But was his will strong enough to put the weight of history he had with his father behind him?

Mia lay in bed wide awake.

She had been dreaming that it was early in the morning, a beautiful autumnal misty morning, and she had been in the churchyard next door, laying fresh flowers on Daisy's grave. Then hearing music, she had followed its siren-like call to its source, taking the path to The Hidden Cottage. Emerging from the bluebell wood, the music grew louder and ever more compelling. She knew that it was Owen playing the piano and as she skirted the lake and drew nearer to the house she became worried that he would see her. But her desire to listen to the music and to be soothed by it made her want to stay and so she sat on the wooden jetty, her back to the house.

Looking out over the lake, its glassy surface so still and smooth that the sky and surrounding trees were perfectly mirrored in it, the music filled her senses and from nowhere she felt Daisy's presence. Not physically, but in her heart. It filled her with peace and was such an exquisite emotion, tears ran down her cheeks and she cried openly and freely, her head tipped back. With time seeming to stand still, she slowly became aware that the music had stopped and she felt hands, warm and sure, on her shoulders. Welcoming the touch, she turned to see Owen.

That was when she woke up and found that her face was wet with real tears.

CHAPTER 54

With last night's dream still lingering like a soothing aura around her, and as if it was meant to be, Mia bumped into Owen the next morning.

She was in Olney to pay some cheques into the bank, and with that errand done, she moved further along the main street to the dry cleaner's. It was there, as she pushed open the door to step inside to collect Jeff's suit, that she came face to face with Owen on his way out. He looked as startled as she felt, but was the first to compose himself.

'How are you?' he asked.

'Oh, you know, muddling along. You?'

'Much the same.'

The awkward exchange ground to a halt. They both looked away, he to the right, she to the left. When their eyes met again, he said, 'I don't suppose you'd . . .' His words trailed off.

'What don't you suppose?'

'That you'd have a coffee with me?'

He was amazed that she'd said yes and as he carried their tray of cappuccinos through the crowded café to where she was waiting for him at the only available table, he felt nervous. He sat down, slid her coffee towards her, dispensed with the tray and with a sense of foreboding took a mental deep breath, preparing himself for something he really didn't want to hear.

'I dreamt of you last night,' she said softly.

'Really?' Right, well, that certainly wasn't what he was expecting. 'I hope it wasn't a bad dream,' he said lightly.

She picked up the spoon from her saucer, dipped it into the froth of her coffee and stirred it slowly as if not wanting to disturb its surface. 'It was a good dream,' she said. 'But it wasn't just about you; it was mostly about Daisy. I woke up crying from it. And yet . . . and I can't explain why, but it wasn't a sad dream.' She stopped moving the spoon and looked straight at him. 'I'm sorry I ignored you the other day in the car. That was very rude of me.'

Again he wasn't expecting an apology from her. 'You don't have to apologize to me, Mia. I understand. Truly I do. I just wish there was a way I could make things right for you. To make you happy again.'

She blinked, but didn't say anything.

'Did Jeff mention to you that I ran into him that day? Literally. Just outside Parr's.'

She shook her head. 'How did he seem to you?'

'Awful. And very angry. Like a man spoiling for a fight. I think if I'd given him cause, he would have taken a swing at me. Is there any way he could know about us?'

'No. Absolutely not. But . . .' she faltered and put the spoon down. 'But I think Jensen suspects there'd been something between us.'

'He's never hinted as much to me.'

'He wouldn't.'

'What makes you think he suspects something?'

'He said he'd noticed how happy I was before . . . before the accident. He then asked me why I telephoned you that night.'

'That doesn't necessarily mean he knows anything.'

Her expression intensified and as he stared into her violet eyes, Owen was reminded of the strength of his feelings for her.

'I know my son,' she said. 'He never says anything without a reason.'

'What did you say to him?'

'I lied. Something I've never done with Jensen before.'

'I'm sorry you had to.'

'So am I. I'm sorry for a lot of things.' She drank some of her coffee, then looked anxiously about the café, her gaze darting and hovering. She was probably checking to see if there was anyone here who knew her, worried at them being seen together. Drinking his own coffee, he noted the extra lines at the corners of her eyes, the fine strands of grey threaded through her hair, and the weight she'd lost. Grief had changed her but she was still beautiful. She was one of those women who always would be.

Her gaze came back to rest on him. 'I want to ask you something,' she said, 'and I think it's because of the dream I had last night. It's made me think about some things more clearly.'

'Go ahead.'

'For both of our sakes, can we put what we did behind us and be friends? I don't want to go on ignoring you. Ultimately it will only make things worse and people will wonder why.'

He put his cup down. 'Is that what you want?'

'Yes.'

'It wouldn't be better for you if I left Little Pelham?'

She frowned. 'But you can't leave; you've only been here a short while.'

'That's not really answering my question, is it?'

'I wouldn't want you to leave because of me,' she said. 'Not when I know that it was a dream of yours to live here.'

'Maybe I need to have a new dream.'

She blinked and her frown deepened. 'You'd be greatly missed. Only yesterday Muriel said that we must do all we can to keep you here.'

Surprised, he said, 'What made her say that?'

'She has the impression that you've lost some of your enthusiasm for living in the village. Is that true?'

He fixed her with a long, hard stare. 'What do you think?'

Her gaze, almost hypnotic, didn't waver from his. 'I think I'll always wonder how things might have been between us, if . . . if I hadn't lost poor Daisy.'

He leant forward. 'Mia, we could still make it happen.'

'I can't leave Jeff. Not now. He doesn't have anyone else to turn to. I'm all he has.'

It was just as Owen feared. This was what he'd known she would say. There was even something to be admired in her stoicism. It might be misplaced, but she wasn't the kind of woman who would kick a man when he was down.

'What if I said I'd wait?' he tried.

'For what?'

'For Jeff to get over Daisy's death and for you to feel he could cope if you left him.'

'He'll never get over her death. She was everything to him.'

Choosing his words with care, Owen said, 'Do you still feel that our affair brought about Daisy's—?'

She raised a hand to stop him. 'Please don't,' she said, 'don't say the words.'

'I'm sorry. But I sincerely hope you no longer think that. You've suffered enough without torturing yourself by believing something that can't possibly be true.'

Her eyes intense and pleading, she said, 'How can you be so sure it isn't true?'

Without thinking what he was doing, he reached across the table and took her hand in his. 'I can't prove it to you, Mia, but every ounce of my being says life doesn't work that way.'

She opened her mouth to speak but closed it abruptly, snatching her hand away from his. 'Don't turn round,' she said, staring out of the window, her face stricken, 'we've been seen.'

His heart plunged. 'Who?' he asked, resisting the instinctive urge to follow the direction of her gaze.

'Wendy Parr.'

He groaned. Wendy Parr, the woman who could single-handedly spread news faster than Twitter.

CHAPTER 55

Saturday afternoon. While Mia was in the barn with customers, Jeff was feeling restless and in need of some fresh air. He'd drunk too much whisky last night and was paying for it now with a fuzzy head. So he put on his coat and went for a walk.

It was a depressingly damp autumnal day and it wasn't long before he felt the chill of it seeping through him and he headed for home. He was almost back at Medlar House when he decided to stop off at the church, to take a look at Daisy's grave. He hadn't visited for some time, but today he felt drawn to it and as he stood before the grave, he thought of the cause of his hangover. He had got drunk last night – angry drunk – because Mia had asked him if he thought it would help if they were to see a grief counsellor together; apparently Muriel had put the idea into her head. He'd told her straight that it was the last thing he'd ever consider doing and had grabbed the bottle of whisky and taken it upstairs with him.

Why the hell would he see a counsellor? His only experience with counselling had been when Daisy was ill and he'd been subjected to the most offensive and vile accusations. The worst – the very worst any father could be accused of and which he could barely bring himself to recall – was that he had loved Daisy in an unhealthy way, that it was an obsessive love that had led him to *interfere* with her.

He swallowed back the loathsome memory of sitting in that room and being subjected to such a despicable accusation. Furious, he'd stormed out of the session and never went back. Nor did he ever utter a word of it to Mia, or to anyone else. To say the words aloud, even to deny them, would have given credence to them and to his dying breath he would never do that. He'd been made out to be a monster and he wasn't. He was a father who'd loved his daughter. No more, no less.

Choked by the memory, he covered his face with his hands. Then feeling his thoughts would taint his daughter's grave if he stayed there a second longer, he turned and fled. He stopped at the lych gate to catch his breath. His chest tight with a painful stitch, he inhaled deeply and caught the faint aroma of a bonfire burning somewhere. And voices. They were coming from the other side of the lych gate. He recognized one of the women's voices; it belonged to Bev, their cleaner. He pricked up his ears when he heard his name mentioned. Mia's as well. Curious to hear more, he stayed out of sight and held his breath.

'I tell you it's true. Wendy saw them in Olney. *Together*. Bold as brass, holding hands.'

'How long do you think it's been going on for?'

'Who knows? They've obviously been careful.'

'Not careful enough if they're sitting there for all to see in Olncy. But as my mother used to say, there's always someone who sees you when you're up to no good.'

'Too true. It all goes to prove that no one is what they seem. It's Jeff I feel sorry for. The daughter dead and his wife carrying on like that. Now we know the real reason they've had separate bedrooms.'

A car went by, its engine drowning out what the two women said next, but then Jeff heard, 'Mind you, he's a bit of a looker, isn't he? I mean, would you say no to him if he invited you into his bed?'

There was a short burst of crude laughter.

'Would I heck! Hey, maybe we should sign up for piano lessons? Owen Fletcher can tinkle my ivories any time he wants.'

More laughter followed and then the two women said good-bye. Still staying out of sight, Jeff peered round the side of the gate and watched Bev turn to go up the main street of the village while the other woman crossed the road to go in the opposite direction.

His heart thumping wildly in his chest, he stood motionless and understood now why he'd taken such a dislike to Owen Fletcher. It had been instinctive, an innate sense that the man was trouble, the sort of man who would take advantage of a vulnerable grieving woman.

Fury boiled inside Jeff as he thought of Mia in bed with Owen Fletcher; it ripped through his guts with an explosive force. He dragged in a breath then coughed, gasped and retching hard he made it just in time to the stone wall where he threw up in the long grass.

Afterwards, he wiped his acrid mouth with the back of his hand and shuddered, both at the disgusting mess on the grass around him and at Mia's duplicity. How could she do it? And with Owen Fletcher?

Gritting his teeth, he left the churchyard and stepped onto the pavement. He stared to his left at Medlar House. His jaw muscles clenched. He knew exactly what he was going to do next.

Owen was upstairs stripping wallpaper in his bedroom. As much as he disliked the black and purple pattern of the wallpaper the previous owners had favoured – too fiercely boudoir chic for his taste – he did wonder why he was going to the bother of removing it. If he wasn't going to stay, why waste his time and energy on such a futile exercise?

Because the bottom line was he didn't want to sell up and leave. He wanted to stay. He liked it here. He liked his place within the village; it felt right. More to the point, he wasn't a quitter by nature; he liked to see things through.

He tugged on a piece of wallpaper and it came away in a long satisfying strip.

To stay here happily, as he wanted, all he had to do was be satisfied with having Mia as a friend. Surely that wouldn't be too difficult if it meant he could keep hold of his dream?

Gathering up the stripped wallpaper and bundling it into a bin liner, he went over to the open window and looking down at the garden he had a sudden mental picture of himself as a boy, watching the dragonflies skimming the surface of the water while listening to the music coming from the house and thinking how one day, when he was grown up and rich enough to buy whatever he wanted, he would live here. His childhood dream had been to bring his mother to live here, to give her the kind of life he'd felt she deserved. It hadn't exactly worked out that way, but then life rarely went the way one thought it would.

Certainly the day he'd decided he was going to stand up to his father hadn't ended how he had imagined it would. He'd had it all planned in his head, had gone over and over it. He was totally prepared.

Except he wasn't prepared for just how sick and twisted Ron Fletcher was. Several days had passed since his father had beaten out of his wife the truth of where they'd been that day when he'd come home early from work and found the house empty. Nothing further was said on the matter but two days later when Owen arrived for his usual after-school piano lesson at The Hidden Cottage, he was dismayed to find his father there. There was no sign of Lillian, but Gretchen was standing at the open door. Her face was always unreadable, because it was so badly disfigured, but Owen could see the apprehension in her eyes.

'Ah, and here's the boy himself,' his father said in his horribly sarcastic voice as Owen drew near. 'Now I know everything about the big secret you've been keeping from me,' he said, grabbing hold of Owen by the arm. 'And what have I told you before about lying? Liars always get caught out, and you, Owen, have been caught out. What have you got to say for yourself?'

'I didn't lie,' Owen managed to say. 'I just didn't tell you about it.' His father's grip on his arm increased, his thumb digging in hard. Willing himself not to show how much it hurt, Owen tried not to wince.

'Mr Fletcher,' Gretchen said, her voice crisp and clear, 'if anyone is responsible, it's me. I should have approached you and asked for your permission to teach Owen. I apologize for any offence that oversight on my part may have caused you.'

Ron Fletcher stared at her. 'That's the trouble with people like you: you poke your nose in where it's not wanted and think you can talk your way out of anything with a fancily worded apology. But I'll thank you to mind your own business. This is a matter between me and my boy and he's going to be punished for his lies. What's more, as of now, there'll be no more lessons, and if I ever hear that

511

he's been here again, I'll make damned sure you regret it. That goes for your sister as well.'

'Are you threatening me, Mr Fletcher?'

He let out a nasty laugh and took a step towards her. Towering over her, he said, 'I'm just asking you to keep away from my son. As his father, I decide who he mixes with and I don't want him mixing with the likes of you.'

Later, back at home, as soon as the door was closed, his father threw Owen against the wall, caught him by the throat and lifted him off the ground so that his feet were dangling and he was struggling to breathe. 'If you *ever* defy me and go there again, I swear I'll burn that house down with those two ugly bitches inside it. And after I've done that, I'll decide what I'll do to you and your mother. Now get out of my sight.'

It took Owen three days to summon the courage to confront his father. He waited for his mother to go to the shop and approached him in the lounge where he was stoking up the fire, the weather having turned unexpectedly cold. Owen stood behind him, close enough to show that he wasn't scared. 'If you do anything bad again to Mum and me,' he said, 'or to Gretchen and Lillian, I'll tell people about you.'

His father stopped what he was doing, but he didn't turn round. 'And who will you tell?'

'My teacher at school. Then . . . then I'll go to the police as well.'

'Will you now? And what will you tell them?'

'I'll tell them everything. How you hit Mum and me. I'll tell them about the bruises and how Mum cries.'

'It's called discipline, Owen. It's what a father has to do. Especially with boys who lie. And you're a liar, which means I have to beat it out of you.' He went back to pushing lumps of coal into place on the fire with the poker. 'It's for your own good. You'll thank me one day.'

'What about Mum?' Owen forced himself to ask. 'Why do you hit her?'

'For the same reason. She lies to me. You both lie to me. You're as bad as each other.'

'We're not bad,' Owen said defiantly. 'It's you who's bad.'

Suddenly his father lurched to his feet, grabbed hold of him and pushed him to the floor, grinding his face into the hearthrug. It was when Owen smelt burning that the pain started and he began to scream and scream, kicking his legs, doing everything he could to get away. But his father was too strong for him and pinned him down until he was finished.

'Tell anyone and this is what I'll do to your mother,' his father hissed in his ear when the worst of the pain began to subside and he'd stopped screaming.

A week later Gretchen and Lillian helped Owen and his mother to escape. They gave them money and arranged for a taxi to take them to the station. From there they went to London before they finally ended up in Basildon. It had always been a great sadness to Owen that he and his mother lost contact with the two women who had done so much for them. Initially they did stay in touch by letter, but because they moved so regularly, Gretchen and Lillian's letters often didn't reach them. Many years later, when Owen passed his Grade Eight piano exam, he decided to write and thank them for the encouragement they had given him when he'd been a boy. All he could remember of their address was: The Hidden Cottage, Little Pelham, Northamptonshire. He never heard back from them and was left to conclude that they had either moved, or died.

As a child Owen had never questioned why his mother didn't just leave her husband, because as a child those questions don't really enter your head. But as an adult, he had asked himself the question and knew that there wasn't a simple answer. But mostly it was fear that made a person stay with a violent and abusive partner and Owen's mother had been terrified of her husband, not just for what he might do to her, but what he might do to Owen. By staying with her husband she had thought she was protecting her son, but when Ron Fletcher had taken that poker from the fire and pressed it against Owen's shoulder and scarred him for life, she had known he was capable of anything and they had to get away.

Ron Fletcher had come looking for them on several occasions. One time he almost caught up with them, but thank God they had always managed to stay one step ahead. When he died they were finally able to breathe a long sigh of relief.

A lifetime on, Owen could still feel the searing pain and smell the awful stench of burning flesh. Another legacy from those days was that he detested violence of any sort; he couldn't watch a boxing match or a fight scene in a film without feeling sick in the pit of his stomach.

A breeze blew in at the window, bringing with it the sound of a blackbird chirruping shrilly down in the garden. Dragging himself back from the past, Owen turned away from the window and repositioned the stepladder by the chimney breast so he could get to work with the scraper on an area of wallpaper that had so far resisted removal.

As he climbed the steps, he wondered as he had before about the way Jeff had spoken to him last Saturday. He hadn't seen that level of pent-up anger in another man since his father. He would never go so far as to describe Jeff as a vicious bully like Ron Fletcher, and certainly Mia had never once hinted that he'd ever ruled the roost with his fists, but bullies had many disguises and often just needed the right tipping point to reveal their true colours.

And that was what worried Owen as he remembered the frozen look of guilt on Mia's face when she realized they had been spotted by Wendy. 'We're doing nothing wrong, Mia,' he'd said. 'Act normally and smile at the woman.' Which was exactly what he did. To do anything else would have made them look guiltier still. Wendy had smiled back at him through the glass. He'd been damned sure the cheery smile on her face had been as false as his. Owen had expected Mia to be angry with him for putting her in the position he had, but she had said nothing, had looked sadly at him and said she ought to go now.

Jabbing too hard with the scraper, a powdery chunk of plaster came away from the wall and fell to the floor. It coincided with an almighty crash, followed by a volley of banging that made Owen start and drop the scraper. Steadying himself on the stepladder, he worked out that the deafening racket was coming from the front door. Just as his startling powers of intuition brought him to this conclusion, the banging stopped. He climbed down the ladder and in the silence that followed, he found himself irrationally rooted to the spot.

He was about to do the sensible thing – go and see who it was trying to batter his door down – when the noise started up again, this time at the back of the house, just as loudly, just as violently. He went over to the open window, and leant out. But he couldn't see who it was because the door was hidden beneath the sloping roof of the veranda.

When he heard his name being called, he knew exactly who it was. It was as if his thoughts only minutes ago had been a presentiment of what was about to happen. With real dread in his step, he went downstairs.

There was no one on the veranda when he opened the door. But when he took a wary step forward, Jeff appeared from the side of the house, where the log store was. In his hand, he had the axe that Owen had left there earlier that morning after chopping logs. His first reaction was to laugh at the absurdity of what he was seeing, but there was nothing remotely funny about the expression on Jeff's face.

'You bastard!' Jeff yelled, his face red, his eyes wild. He was seriously pumped up. 'You lying, cheating, bastard!'

'Jeff, put the axe down, OK?'

'Don't you take that patronizing tone of voice with me. I knew you were too good to be true. All that nicey-nicey stuff you've fooled everyone else with – I wasn't taken in for a minute. The second I set eyes on you, I knew you were trouble.'

'Look, whatever it is you want to discuss with me, let's do it calmly and reasonably.' Owen moved slowly across the veranda and stood at the top of the steps that led down to the garden.

'You think I can be calm when I know you've been screwing my wife behind my back? Not a chance!'

Owen took a step down from the veranda. Then another. He was playing for time. Trying to figure out the best way to handle this. Denial seemed the most sensible option – it was probably what Mia would want him to do, and besides, just what could Wendy have said, other than supposition based on very little when you got down to it? But what if Mia had already confessed to what they'd done? If that was the case, a denial from him would be futile and enrage Jeff yet more. And he looked plenty agitated as it was. Still playing for time, he said, 'If you don't like me, Jeff, that's fair enough, but I have no intention of patronizing you. Now how about you—'

'Shut up! Just shut the hell up, will you? Do you think I've come here to chat man to man and then leave, saying, "That's all right, old sport, I quite understand you couldn't keep your hands off my wife"? Is that what you expect?'

With a shiver of genuine fear, Owen honestly didn't know what to expect. *Expect the unexpected*, echoed inside his head. 'Jeff,' he said, deciding to be straight with him, 'tell me what you know.'

Something flashed in Jeff's eyes. 'I told you, I *know* about you and my wife. And you're going to pay for trying to break up our marriage! Let's see how you feel at losing something you value.' He spat the words out and suddenly turning his back on Owen, he marched away.

What now?

Following after him, Owen then realized what Jeff had in mind to do.

The first swing of the axe smashed the headlight on the driver's side of the E-Type, the second took out the headlight on the passenger's side. Next Jeff went for the bonnet, crashing the axe down with a crunch.

Owen yelled at him to stop. Then: 'Stop, or I'll call the police!'

At that Jeff let out a cry of frustration – the blade of the axe was firmly embedded in the metal of the wrecked bonnet and he couldn't budge it. Owen quickly made his move. It was time to stop the madness. Up close he could see a sheen of sweat on Jeff's face; he could also smell the disgustingly sour aroma of vomit.

'I bloody well hope you feel better for doing that,' he said. It was a cheap taunt and one he regretted in a second.

Having assumed Jeff's anger was spent, he wasn't prepared for the fist that caught him on the side of the head. Stars sparked behind his eyes and he rocked on his feet, then with a guttural roar Jeff came at him again, grabbed him and slammed a fist into his jaw. Owen reeled backwards, lost his balance and fell to the ground with a thud. But still Jeff wasn't finished and once more he came at Owen, this time with his foot, kicking him in the ribs. Instinctively Owen brought his knees up to his chest to protect himself as yet another kick landed – this time it was his head, and pain exploded like a firework inside his skull.

'I'm going to break every bone in your body,' Jeff yelled at him as he unleashed yet another ferocious kick followed by another and another.

For a terrifying moment, as he tried to clear his vision that was spangled with stars, Owen thought that nothing would stop Jeff, that caught up in this frenzy of violence he was no longer in control of himself and would go on kicking until he was exhausted.

Knowing he had to defend himself, that he had to fight the paralysis that had gripped him, Owen tried to get to his feet, but as he reached out to push himself up, Jeff grunted and raised his foot and brought it down hard on his hand. Owen let out a cry of pain and tried again to get to his feet, but another kick to the side of his head felled him and Jeff let rip with a blood-curdling cry. The sound filled Owen with real terror and he knew that Jeff really had lost it. Nothing would stop him now.

But suddenly the kicking did stop. The awful blood-curdling noise continued though, and when Owen dared to look at Jeff, what he saw had him convinced he was hallucinating, for he was staring at something straight out of Hitchcock's film, *The Birds*.

CHAPTER 56

He wasn't hallucinating; Putin really was attacking Jeff!

The noise was terrible. Screeching and squawking, the bird was going crazy, flapping its wings, throwing itself at Jeff and pecking viciously at whatever bit of him he could get at. His arms flailing, Jeff was yelling and thrashing around in a blind panic, trying to get away from the bird. But keeping up the onslaught, Putin was forcing Jeff across the lawn and towards the lake; it was as if the bird was planning to push him in.

Dizzy and wincing with pain, Owen got to his feet. He should intervene. He staggered across the lawn and added his voice to the melee, shouting at the bird to stop. With his back to Owen, the bird didn't react. Why would it? It wasn't as if the bird could speak or understand English!

'Stand still, Jeff!' he then tried. 'Don't move!'

But Jeff wasn't hearing him.

Circling round, Owen placed himself so that he was directly in Putin's line of vision. At once, miraculously, the bird fell silent and stopped what it was doing. It stared at Owen, lowered its wings, tilted its head and seemingly let out a breath, its feathers rising and then settling. Throwing a sideways glance at Jeff, the bird shook itself and sauntered off.

In the deathly hush, Owen looked at Jeff. The man's face was white and he was visibly trembling. Jeff opened his mouth to speak but no words came out. He began to shake harder, then very slowly his body crumpled and his legs gave way and he dropped to the ground.

At first Owen didn't grasp what Jeff was doing, but then he realized that he was crying. It started quietly, a sort of stifled moan, and then gathered force until it was a full-blown howl coming deep from his guts and he was calling out Daisy's name over and over, begging her to forgive him as he lay prostrate on the grass. But then like a man possessed, he began to babble incomprehensibly.

Owen looked on. He didn't know what else to do. Then gradually, some of what Jeff was saying started to make sense. Sense of a kind. And with shock Owen realized that Jeff wasn't asking for forgiveness for the row he'd had with his daughter which Mia had told him about, but for something he had done the night of Daisy's death. It was something Owen was certain Mia knew nothing about.

Despite the immense pain he was in, Owen half carried, half dragged Jeff up to the house.

He took him inside, sat him at the kitchen table

and using the hand that Jeff hadn't stamped on, he shakily poured two glasses of brandy. He passed one of the glasses across the table.

'Drink it,' he said. He raised his own to his mouth and knocked it back in one go, the liquid burning his throat. How much would he have to drink to block out the pain? he thought.

He put his empty glass down on the draining board and looked at his left hand. Already it was bruised and hideously swollen and he could barely move his throbbing fingers. He noticed then that the face of his watch was cracked and for a split second he felt more annoyed about that than any broken bones he might have.

He took the watch off, laid it next to his empty glass and then gingerly with his right hand touched the side of his head that hurt the most. He felt wetness and when he looked at his fingertips, he saw they were red. An old and familiar feeling of shame consumed him as he thought of himself on the receiving end of Jeff's fury, when he had literally frozen, haunted by the memories of witnessing his father's anger and terrifying loss of control.

As an adult he had firmly believed that his aversion to anything of a violent nature didn't make him less of a man, and he wanted to believe that now. But he couldn't deny that a part of him unequivocally wished he hadn't been paralysed by fear, that he had beaten Jeff to a pulp. He knew, though, that had he done it, he would never have been able to live with himself, not when it would have meant that he had become no better than his father.

A long, shuddering groan from behind him made him turn and he observed Jeff with pity. Pity, and not hatred, because the snivelling, tear-stained man sitting in his kitchen, his head in his hands, looked every inch a broken man.

As if feeling Owen's gaze on him, Jeff slowly raised his head. 'You look like shit,' he said, his voice croaky.

'I feel it,' Owen said. 'And while we're exchanging compliments, you don't look much cop either.'

Shrugging off his coat and dropping it to the floor, Jeff said, 'What the hell was that bird doing out there?'

'I don't think he approved of what you were doing,' Owen replied.

'Any more of that brandy going?'

Owen filled his glass.

'I shouldn't have done what I did to you,' Jeff said, after he'd taken a swallow and seemed to pull himself together.

'No you shouldn't.'

'I was angry. I still am.'

'I get that. But you lost control. You could have killed me.'

'I wanted to. I really did. Every bit of me wanted to keep on kicking until you didn't exist any more.'

'And would that have made your marriage right?'

Jeff took a long inhalation of breath and let it out slowly. 'You know nothing about my marriage.

You've known Mia for no more than a few months; you don't know the first thing about us as a couple.'

'I know Mia isn't happy.'

Jeff jerked his head up. 'Of course she isn't happy; she's just lost a child, for God's sake!'

Not caring if his words hurt Jeff, not after what he'd just done to him, he said, 'She wasn't happy before Daisy's death. You need to face that.'

Jeff flinched. 'When did it start? And don't lie to me.'

'Her unhappiness?'

'*No!* The affair. Or was it just a fling, another name to add to the long list of your conquests? What was the plan, to screw your way round the village?'

Owen regarded him with contempt. 'I'm not that kind of a man.'

'So it was an affair?'

'I fell in love with Mia. I didn't mean to. But it happened.'

'Love? You haven't known her long enough to love her. What you're talking about is sex.'

Owen closed his eyes and pinched the bridge of his nose. When he opened his eyes, he said, 'It's not about sex, Jeff.'

'Of course it is! It's always about sex. For a man it's never about anything else.'

And if you truly believe that, no wonder Mia strayed, Owen thought. Feeling lightheaded, he pulled out a chair and sat opposite Jeff.

'Does she think she's in love with you?' Jeff asked.

'I can't speak for Mia. What I do know is that she was going to leave you, but when Daisy died, she changed her mind. From then on, she refused to see me again. She told me that you needed her, that you had no one else to turn to in your grief.'

Jeff looked shocked. 'She said that?'

Owen nodded.

'So it's out of pity she's stayed with me?' He drained his glass. 'Pity,' he repeated flatly. 'I don't want her pity. I want her love. Her loyalty. I want what we used to have.'

Thinking of the confession he'd overheard in the garden, Owen said, 'And for that, what do you give her? Do you give her love and *loyalty* in return?'

'I've given her everything!'

'You really believe that?'

'I suppose in your arrogance you think you can give her more, don't you?'

'I can't give her anything,' Owen said flatly. 'I told you, Mia broke it off between us after Daisy's death.'

At the mention of Daisy's name, Jeff's eyes sparked and his composure faltered. '*Stop it!* Stop talking about Daisy in the same breath as your sordid affair with her mother!' Abruptly his blood-shot eyes welled with tears and he covered his face with his hands and wept anew.

Owen went to find a box of tissues, and it was when he was out of the room that he realized something important – something that had he not been feeling so rough he would have realized sooner – every question Jeff had asked clearly indicated that he hadn't spoken to Mia about the affair, which further suggested he hadn't heard of it from her either. And that left Owen with the only possible conclusion he could reach: Wendy Parr had done her worst and word had gone round. Which meant that very likely Mia had no idea that Jeff had come here to confront him.

When he returned to the kitchen, Jeff was still crying loudly and without restraint. Mia had told him in Olney that she hadn't once seen her husband cry over Daisy, not even the day of the funeral, and Owen wondered, given the extreme nature of this expression of grief from Jeff, if it was his first genuine outpouring. Was it possible that the shock of learning about the affair between Mia and Owen had released something inside him and brought him to this cataclysmic point?

Owen put the box of tissues on the table. Jeff snatched a tissue from the box and pressed it to his eyes. 'I should go,' he mumbled.

Owen had every reason to agree, but he said, 'You don't have to.'

'Why? Do you want to see me suffer some more? Are you getting a kick out of it?'

'An unfortunate choice of words, but no, I'm not getting a kick out of seeing you this way. I don't like seeing anyone suffer. Least of all a man who's grieving for his daughter.'

'Don't waste your sympathy on me.'

Owen shook his head. After what Jeff had done to him, he had every right to throw the man out and call the police, as he'd earlier threatened, and have him arrested for assault. But the truth was – and his motives were wholly selfish – he didn't want Jeff to leave until his hypocrisy had been exposed.

He pushed the bottle of brandy across the table. 'Help yourself to another,' he said.

Jeff did and for some five minutes he sat in silence just steadily drinking. Twice he blew his nose and wiped his eyes. Finally he said, 'I hate men like you. The type women always fall for.'

'I wouldn't know about that.'

'Come off it! You've worked a perfect scam on Muriel and her cohorts, had them completely wrapped around your little finger since the day you arrived.'

'I'd hardly call being neighbourly or offering help as working a perfect scam. Can I ask you something? Why are you still sitting here? What do you want from me?'

'I'm trying to understand you. Everyone in the village speaks so highly of you, and I just don't get it. There again, your stock is going to crash and burn dramatically when this all comes out.'

'The full details needn't come out.'

'What? You think I'm going to pretend you and Mia haven't been having an affair behind my back?'

'It rather depends on what it is you want, I'd have thought. If you want to keep Mia and make your marriage work, it would be better to carry on as if nothing's happened.'

'Not possible. Not now. How do you think I got to know about it? It's already the talk of the village.'

It was just as Owen had feared. 'You could brazen it out by ignoring the gossip,' he said.

'Oh yes, that would suit you perfectly, wouldn't it? That way you still get to smell of roses.'

Owen leant forward. 'No, what would suit me is if you faced up to the truth and realized that if Mia had been happy she wouldn't have had an affair with me.' He shook his head wearily. 'None of this was meant to happen. I came to Little Pelham for a quiet life. I just wanted to get on with starting over again.'

'Well, it has happened, and you need to face up to the consequences of your actions.'

'What about *you*, Jeff? What about you facing up to the consequences of *your* actions?'

'My actions? What the hell do you mean?'

'What about the row you had the last time you saw Daisy? How does that weigh on your conscience? Is that what your grief for her is really about? Your guilt at how much you hurt Daisy and were never able to tell her how sorry you were?'

Jeff's face reddened and he gripped the glass in his hand. 'How do you know about that?'

'Mia told me how desperately upset Daisy was.' Owen could see a muscle twitching at Jeff's jaw;

it was a warning for him to stop, to back off, but after what he'd gone through at the hands of this man, he'd be damned if he'd keep quiet.

'You see, Jeff,' he continued, 'it wasn't just about sex between us; Mia and I talked. When was the last time you talked openly and honestly with Mia and listened to her? When was it ever not about *you*?'

Scraping his chair back, Jeff jumped to his feet. 'You have no right to speak to me this way.'

Very calmly, very stiffly, Owen stood up too. 'After what you did to me, I'll say what I want. And you know what, I'd love for you to admit the real reason why you lost control earlier. I haven't witnessed violence on that level since I was a child and my father beat the hell out of those he should have cared most about. So what is it with you, Jeff? What made you lose control? The realization that you've messed up? That you drove your daughter away with your suffocating love for her, and now you're facing the knowledge that your wife wanted to leave you as well? None of that puts you in the running for husband or father of the year, does it?'

His face puce, Jeff stared at him, his bloodshot eyes once again filling.

'So what did make you lose control?' Owen went on. 'Because that's what happened out there, wasn't it? You said yourself earlier that you wanted to kick me until I no longer existed. That's about as savage as it gets.'

'You're not going to get the police involved, are you?' Jeff asked anxiously, his glaze flicking over Owen and the damage he'd inflicted.

'No. But only because I love Mia and don't want to add to her problems. Plus, I think you have enough to deal with right now. What are you going to say to Mia?'

'Is that any of your business?'

'Since I'm the cause of what's happened, I think it is. And I warn you, if you so much as breathe over her, I *will* go to the police.'

'For God's sake!' Jeff exclaimed. 'I'd never do anything like that.'

Staring him straight in the eye, Owen said, 'Right now I'm having trouble believing that.' He raised his painfully throbbing hand. 'I'm guessing you've broken at least three fingers.'

'I said earlier I shouldn't have done that to you.'

'Who's to say you won't lose control again? Now why don't you tell me about Monte Carlo and the two women you paid to have sex with?'

Jeff looked startled and the colour drained from his face. 'How do you know about that?' he murmured.

'Before I brought you in from the garden you were – for want of a better expression – out of your mind and begging your daughter's forgiveness for the way you spent the night when she—'

'No! Don't say any more. Not that. Please not that.'

'Considering that you're condemning Mia for

being unfaithful, don't you think you should be honest about your own act of betrayal?'

Jeff shook his head. 'What I did was different.' He swallowed. 'But if I could turn back the clock, I would. You have no idea how guilty I feel about that night. That I was doing that while my poor Daisy . . .' His voice broke and his words ground to a halt.

'We all do things we regret,' Owen said. 'The lesson we should learn is not to judge others when they do something wrong. Better to show compassion than condemnation.'

'Is that what you expect me to do with Mia?'

'I expect you to do the right thing. You need to be honest with Mia and more importantly with yourself.'

'And if I don't, I suppose you'll be the first to tell Mia what I did in Monte Carlo?'

'She won't hear it from me. It's for you to tell her. And now I think you should go.'

Left alone, pain and tiredness hit Owen full on. His head ached, his ribs ached, as did his back, shoulders, arms and legs. There wasn't a bit of him that didn't feel stiff or sore. When his vision began to blur and he felt nauseous, he thought, *Oh hell, concussion*. Just what he needed.

CHAPTER 57

The moment Jeff walked into the kitchen and threw his coat onto a chair, Mia knew that he had found out about her affair with Owen. Haggard and ashen, his eyes sunken and rimmed red, his hair and clothes dishevelled, he looked awful.

She calmly listened to his anger. His disbelief. And his condemnation. She did it because everything he accused her of was true; she had nothing with which to defend herself. It was almost a relief to listen to his tirade – she could feel the black cloud of guilt that had been hanging over her since the summer begin to lift.

When he'd finished and asked her if she wasn't going to say something, she said, 'How did you find out?'

'I overheard Bev talking about it. We're the talk of the village.' His words were heavily weighted with sarcasm.

'Oh.'

'Is that all you have to say?' he asked incredulously.

She could see her calmness was infuriating him.

'I don't know what else to say. Other than I'm sorry. And I'm sorry that you had to hear it that way.'

'I bet you are! Well, I'll tell you this much: Owen-bloody-Fletcher had a lot more to say on the matter.'

'You've spoken to Owen?'

'Damned right I have. That's where I've been.'

It was then that the calmness she'd been feeling left Mia and she felt a shiver of anxiety. She gave Jeff a long, penetrating look and noted there was a strong smell of alcohol coming off him. 'Why did you go to Owen?' she asked. 'Why didn't you come to me first?'

His tone querulous, he said, 'Would you have preferred I had it out with you in front of your customers?'

'So you went to have it out with Owen?' she said, ignoring his question. 'And how exactly did you go about that? As if I couldn't guess,' she added, realizing now why he looked so dishevelled. She also now noticed the grass and mud stains on his trousers.

When he didn't reply but went to the cupboard to help himself to a glass of whisky, she said, 'That's your solution, is it? To resort to violence?'

'It's what any man in my position would do,' he fired back at her. 'You're my wife, for God's sake!'

Her hackles rose. 'And that gives you the right to hit someone? How pathetic of you.'

'What about what you did?' he rounded on her. 'How would you describe your behaviour?'

'It was wrong what I did; I fully acknowledge that. I should never have involved Owen in my unhappiness.'

'Not wrong to have cheated on me, then?' he responded, his mouth twisting into an ugly line, his eyes narrowed.

She looked at him, this man who was her husband, and tried to feel something for him. Some glimmer of affection. Or at least understanding. But she couldn't.

'We'll talk when I get back,' she said, picking up her keys from the worktop.

He stared at her as if he couldn't believe his ears. 'Where are you going?'

'I have to drive to the airport, to pick up Jensen and the others.'

Jeff listened to the sound of the back door slamming. Mia never slammed doors. She didn't go in for storming out of rooms either. She was always quietly composed. It was one of the things that he used to love about her, wondering what was going on beneath the surface.

In this instance, he knew exactly what she was thinking. She despised him. He'd seen it in her eyes, heard it in her voice.

It was her shameless indifference to what she'd done that got to him, and it was that that had stopped him from telling her the truth about Monte Carlo. All he'd needed from her was some real contrition for what she'd done and he would have been honest with her. But her manner, the way she'd gone on the attack and criticized him, had incensed and silenced him.

When he'd walked back from The Hidden Cottage in the fading light he had intended to share with her his own confession, if only because he was scared that Owen wouldn't be able to stop himself from blurting it out the first opportunity he got. Better that it came from him, he'd reasoned, than a gloating Owen Fletcher. He'd planned to use it to his advantage, to maintain that they were quits: they'd both done something wrong, and now they could put it behind them. Except he wasn't really sure that he could. What Mia had done was far worse. She'd had an affair. Nobody has an affair by accident; it's a calculated step. Whereas he'd drunk more than he should have and had made a simple error of judgement.

He looked at the glass in his hand and, deciding he'd had enough to drink, he put it down. He heard Owen's voice in his head describing him as having been out of his mind. He reckoned he must have been. Nothing else could explain what had happened. First the violence, then the total loss of control when he'd broken down and cried. He pictured himself lying on the grass and crying like he'd never cried before. Even as a child he'd never bawled like that. He hoped he never did again. Just thinking about the pain of it, and the humiliation of being seen in that state, made the blood pound in his head and his hands begin to shake.

He changed his mind about the whisky and picked up the glass in front of him and drank from it deeply.

Out of his mind.

Try as he might, he couldn't remember anything about begging Daisy's forgiveness for that regrettable night in Monte Carlo. It was a complete blank to him. He must have done it or how else would Owen have known about it?

Something he didn't entirely understand had happened to him this afternoon. After all these months of not crying for Daisy, a switch had been flicked inside him and finally it had all erupted from him in an agonizing, unstoppable force. Only last weekend he had wondered if he was in some sort of limbo of delayed shock; now he had his answer.

Darkness had fallen and as he stared at his reflection in the window, he wondered what would happen next. Right now, he didn't have the energy to figure it out. He was exhausted. All he wanted to do was crawl upstairs and sleep.

Mia had deliberately left early so that she had time to stop off at The Hidden Cottage; she needed to hear from Owen what had gone on. She also wanted to apologize. This should never have happened. She should have kept away from him the moment she recognized that there was a mutual attraction between them.

In the brightness from the security light that had

flashed on, she parked behind Owen's Jaguar. Out of her car she saw to her horror that an axe had been driven into the bonnet of the E-Type. Shards of glass lay on the ground where the headlights had been smashed. *What have you done, Jeff?*

Alarmed, she made her way round to the back of the house. She knocked on the door and waited for a response.

Nothing.

She tried the handle and, taking a deep breath, pushed the door open. She called to Owen.

Again, no response.

Straining her eyes in the dark, she went inside. 'Owen,' she called again, at the same time fumbling for a light switch, 'it's me, Mia.'

She found the switch. A quick look around downstairs established that Owen wasn't there. Still calling his name and with her unease growing, she went up the stairs. She was on the landing when she heard him.

'Mia, is that you?'

Relief flooded through her at the sound of his voice.

She found him in his bedroom, lying on the bed. 'Sorry about the mess,' he said, raising his head from the pillow. 'I was stripping wallpaper. Do you mind if I don't put the light on? I've got a hell of a headache.'

She carefully made her way round a stepladder and stood at the side of the bed. Even in the dim light, she could see that he was suffering from more than just a headache. Shocked, she said, 'What happened? Please don't say Jeff did this.'

'Erm . . . well, yes, we had a bit of a scuffle.'

'A scuffle,' she repeated under her breath. 'He told me he'd been here after he'd heard about us, but . . . but never did I think he'd do *this* to you.'

'It's OK. It probably looks worse than it really is.'

She sat on the edge of the bed. 'Owen, it's not OK; you need to see a doctor.'

'I'd rather not. Self-diagnosis says I have a bog-standard case of concussion – headache and nausea with a bit of dizziness and some flashing stars thrown in just to jazz things up.'

'How could he? I thought maybe a punch or two, but this,' she looked at the congealed blood on the side of Owen's head and his gruesomely swollen hand, 'this is awful.'

'He was angry. He'd just discovered I'd been having an affair with his wife.'

'That's no excuse. I swear I'll never forgive him. Oh, Owen, I'm so very sorry. It's all my fault. I should never have dragged you in to my problems.'

'You hardly dragged me.'

'I still think you should see a doctor. Why don't you let me take you to A and E?'

'I'll be fine. Really. If I see a doctor I'll be asked what happened and I haven't the energy to lie convincingly. I think it's best the fewer people who know the truth, the better. And I really can't face four hours of queuing in A and E.'

'All right,' she agreed reluctantly, 'but let me at least take a good look at you, just to put my mind at rest. Where do you hurt most?'

'Difficult to say; there isn't a bit of me that doesn't hurt. Your husband was very thorough when he kicked the shit out of me.'

'He *kicked* you?'

'Like a football. He was very angry.'

She reeled at his words and reining in her revulsion for Jeff, she insisted that Owen close his eyes so that she could put the bedside lamp on and examine him properly. 'I need to undress you,' she said.

He smiled weakly. 'You promise not to take advantage of me?'

She smiled back at him and after switching on the lamp, she asked him to sit up so she could remove his shirt. What she saw horrified her and she covered her mouth to stifle a small cry. His back, shoulders, chest and stomach were covered in red and purple livid bruises. How could Jeff have committed such an act of barbarism? She bit her lip and then inspected the side of Owen's head and found a ragged gash about two inches long.

'How's it looking?' he asked.

'I'm no expert, but I think you should have stitches.'

'Could you just clean it up for me? There's a first-aid kit in the bathroom cabinet you could use.'

When she returned to the bedroom, having been

downstairs to find a bowl to put hot water in, he was out of bed. He had taken his jeans off and was standing in front of the mirror looking at the bruises, which also covered his legs. 'Bit of a mess, aren't I?' he remarked with a grimace.

In a rush of sickened disbelief, she said, 'Only a monster could have beaten you like that.'

'Not a monster, just a very angry man who hadn't yet dealt with his grief. Or his guilt.'

She put the bowl on the bedside table, along with the first-aid kit. She opened it and took out some cotton wool balls. Dipping one into the water, she said, 'Sit down and let me clean that cut on your head.' She worked steadily and as gently as she could, not wanting to hurt him.

When she was happy the wound on his head was as clean as she could make it, she cut away some hair and applied a dressing. Next she turned her attention to the rest of him. 'What did Jeff do to your hand?' she asked, appalled at how swollen and bruised his fingers were.

'You don't want to know.'

'What if something's broken?'

'Almost certainly there is. If I straighten them, can you just try bandaging the fingers?'

She shook her head. 'Owen, I have to take you to hospital.'

'No,' he said firmly. 'I'll be fine.'

She did as he wanted and when she'd finished, she said, 'I can't be with a man who's capable of such violence.'

'Good call, I'd say.' He suddenly looked and sounded very sleepy, almost a little drunk and he swayed towards her.

She looked into his eyes and saw that they were glassy. She knew it wasn't a good sign.

She went across to the chest of drawers and found a clean T-shirt for him. Very carefully she pulled it over his head, then manoeuvred his arms into the sleeves. His eyes were closed as she gently nudged him back against the pillows. Pulling the duvet up and unable to resist it, she kissed him lightly on the forehead. He sighed. 'That was nice,' he said sleepily. She then stroked the side of his face until his breathing fell into a steady rhythm and he slept.

She laid a hand gently on his shoulder and considered what she should do next. She couldn't possibly leave Owen alone, but she had to get to Heathrow for Jensen.

There was only one person she could ask to help. Downstairs she found her mobile in her bag, and called Muriel. Without asking why, Muriel said she'd be there in ten minutes.

Back in Owen's bedroom, Mia tidied away the first-aid kit, tipped the water down the sink in the bathroom and then just as she was putting the bowl back by the side of the bed in case Owen was sick, he turned onto his side and his eyelids flickered open. 'It must have been a horrible shock for you hearing what Jeff did in Monte Carlo,' he said drowsily.

She knelt on the floor beside him. 'What's that?'

'The women he was with.'

'What women?'

Owen's eyelids closed; he was drifting back to sleep.

'Owen,' she pressed. 'Tell me. What women?'

He came to again. 'You know, about the two call girls Jeff was with the night Daisy died. He told you, didn't he? I told him he had to be honest with you.'

She wouldn't have believed that her opinion of Jeff could sink any lower, but it just had. 'No, he didn't tell me that,' she murmured. 'It must have slipped his mind.'

From downstairs she heard knocking. Thank God for Muriel, she thought grimly.

Owen woke with the distinct feeling that someone was in the room with him.

Remembering that Mia had been there with him earlier, he opened his eyes expectantly. Facing the wardrobe, he saw that no one was there. Turning over towards the window, in the light cast from the lamp, he saw a familiar figure sitting in a chair some three feet away.

'Ah, the patient awakes. Another five minutes and I was under orders to prod you.'

'Muriel. What the devil are you doing here?'

She put down the mug she was drinking from. 'Mia had to go to Heathrow to collect Jensen and co and I've been called in to be your very own

543

Florence Nightingale. How are you feeling? Any nausea? If the answer's yes and you're going to be sick, you must give me fair warning so I can exit stage left at speed.'

He sat up gingerly. 'You're quite safe, I don't feel at all sick.'

'And the head? Still got a thumping headache?'

'Less so than before.'

'Excellent.' She got up from the chair and came towards him. 'I've also been told to check on the state of your eyes.' She peered at him closely. 'Mmm . . . magnificent come-to-bed eyes and not the least bit glassy.'

'Back off, Muriel, you're scaring me.'

'And you, young man, have got yourself in a lot of trouble from what I hear. There's another cuppa in the pot. Shall I pour one for you and you can tell me all about it?'

He nodded and watched her go over to the chest of drawers where there was a tray of tea things. 'What time is it?' he asked.

She looked at her watch. 'Twenty past eight.' She removed the bowl on the bedside table and replaced it with a mug of strong tea. 'Mia was adamant that you mustn't sleep for too long, she wanted to be sure that you weren't going to conk out on us.'

'I wouldn't dare.'

'Good. Now let me get settled and you can tell me all. Mia gave me the barest details, but you can fill in the blanks for me.'

544

He reached for his mug and flinched as a sharp pain shot through his ribcage. 'Are you sure you can't fill them in for yourself?' he said. 'I can't imagine that you haven't got your finger fully on the pulse.'

'I hope you're not suggesting that I'm an idle gossiper.'

'Not at all. I just know that very little gets past you, Muriel. You knew about us, didn't you?'

'I guessed the night of my dinner party that you were both attracted to each other.'

'What gave us away?'

'There was a moment when you looked at each other and I swear sparks flew across the table. And there was me trying to fix you up with Georgina. You quite spoilt my plans for you both.'

'I'm sorry. Did Georgina guess that night as well?'

'Are you kidding? Georgina was too sloshed to know how many legs and arms she was in possession of, never mind pick up on any subtle nuances around the table.'

'Or not so subtle, as it proved to be. Why didn't you say something to me or Mia?'

'Not my place. My golden rule is never to get involved in other people's marriages or relationships. Much too risky. And before you ask, I haven't discussed it with anyone else either.'

Owen drank some of his tea. 'What's your opinion of Jeff?'

'Classic example of a man with a colossal ego who needs to be fully in control at all times. That's not to say I don't like him – he's always been fine in small doses and very helpful in the village when help has been required. I can't say I've ever really understood what the glue is in Mia's marriage to him, other than the children, but since I've never been married, I don't consider myself qualified to judge or truly comprehend.' She took a long sip of her tea. 'I think it would be fair to say I've tolerated him for Mia's sake. It's what friends do.'

He drank some more of his tea, pleased that Muriel was being so honest with him. 'It was good of you to come here,' he said.

'Again, I did it because Mia's a friend. As are you, Owen.'

'Thank you. So what's the current situation? How far has Wendy spread the gossip?'

'Pretty extensively, I'm afraid. If she's to be believed, the pair of you were rolling around on the floor of The Birdcage Cafe going at it hammer and tongs.'

He shook his head. 'It's ironic that she should see us when we weren't actually doing anything wrong. Presumably you knew, or had guessed, that Mia had stopped seeing me after Daisy's accident.'

'Yes. I put it down to guilt, to her wanting to wipe the slate clean in some way.'

'You're right, it was.'

'I think a lot of slates are in need of being cleaned right now.'

'Meaning?'

'Mia said that you told her Jeff had been with two call girls the night of Daisy's death, which does, at least, explain why he didn't answer his mobile when she was trying to get hold of him.'

'What do you mean, I told her? Surely Jeff did.'

'No, I distinctly recall her saying you told her. Apparently you were drifting in and out of sleep at the time. You weren't making it up, were you? Or having a hallucinogenic dream?'

Alarmed, Owen said, 'Muriel, are you sure about this?'

'Absolutely sure. It's not me who has concussion, you know.'

'But this is bad. Seriously bad. I never meant to tell her. I told Jeff I wouldn't. Oh my God, what have I done?' He put down his mug, pushed back the duvet and swung his legs out of bed.

'Hey, where do you think you're going?'

'I can't sit here knowing what you've just told me. How did she seem? Was she very upset?' He looked about him. 'Where the hell are my jeans?'

'Owen, calm down. Mia was angry rather than upset. And trust me, I lectured her at length to drive carefully. I suggested that I should go to the airport and she stay here with you, but she decided against that, didn't want to put me to any more trouble. She promised to text me when she arrived.'

'Has she?'

'Yes. Now get back into bed before I roll up my sleeves and I'm forced to give you a cold bed bath. And don't think I won't!'

CHAPTER 58

They had reached the point of no return. It was over between them.

An eye for an eye, a betrayal for a betrayal – that's how Jeff could have played it, but he hadn't. He'd stood there in their kitchen and thrown Mia's guilt at her while hiding his own, and that, on top of the savage beating he'd given Owen, was unforgivable.

Not until the following day, when she had challenged him with what Owen had inadvertently told her the night before, did he admit his own infidelity. It was the last conversation they'd had and a week had passed since then.

Jeff's first reaction had been to go on the attack. 'Owen said he wouldn't tell you! Not that I should have trusted him to keep his word. Why would he after what the two of you have been doing?'

When Mia had said that she felt he was missing the point, that it was irrelevant how she'd found out, he'd said, 'So I make one mistake and that's it? After everything I've done for you and this family?'

'You surely can't be serious?' she'd said. 'You've

done nothing but divide this family. It's been me who's held it together all these years. I'm sorry, Jeff, but I've spent the greater part of my life trying to save you from yourself, and now I'm going to save myself.'

He'd stared at her uncomprehendingly, but then that was exactly what she had anticipated. Right to the end he would somehow be able to kid himself that the dark realities of life had nothing to do with him, that anything that remotely resembled a truth was an exaggeration or a fabrication to suit someone else's misguided viewpoint. For Jeff, emotional issues were a distraction, something to be avoided at all costs for fear that they might hit home. It was that wall of determined avoidance, she could only assume, that had at last crumbled and led to him breaking down at The Hidden Cottage. Finally an emotion had hit its target and his grief for Daisy had been thoroughly exposed.

Still staring at her, he'd said, 'It was you who had the affair.'

'And it was you who paid for sex,' she replied, 'so that makes us equally culpable.'

'But what I did didn't mean anything,' he exclaimed fiercely. 'It was just sex, a one-off thing.'

'It still counts, Jeff. I'd feel more respect for you had it been a proper affair and you'd been in love with another woman.'

He'd given her a sour look. 'If you had come with me to Monte Carlo, it wouldn't have happened.

550

But you were too busy having your *proper affair* with Owen to be bothered with me, weren't you?' His tone was nasty and his eyes cold and steely.

'If it makes you feel better, I'll happily take the blame. And the consequences. You can paint yourself as the wronged husband if you want, but nothing will justify what you did to Owen. You're damned lucky he hasn't gone to the police. You could go to prison for a vicious attack like that.'

For the first time, he'd looked rattled. 'I told him I was sorry.'

'So he says. But do you really think that's enough?'

'I lost it, Mia. The red mist came down and I was out of my mind.'

'That's as maybe, but I can't be around a man who's capable of losing control to that extent.'

'It was grief that made me do it. Owen understood that.'

'Oh, I understand, Jeff, but I can't condone it. Nor will I condone or forget that you were prepared to let me think I was the only one to have done anything wrong. If Owen hadn't told me, would you have kept quiet?'

'I was going to tell you. I'd planned to. I really had. But you didn't give me a chance to get the words out.'

'My fault again,' she'd said bitterly. 'I might have known.' With nothing more to say, she'd added, 'I think it would be better if you didn't come home next weekend.'

Bristling, he'd replied defiantly, 'This is my home as much as it is yours. You can't throw me out.'

'I'm not throwing you out. I just can't bear to be anywhere near you for the time being. If it suits you better, you can stay and I'll go.'

'Straight to lover boy, I suppose?' he'd sneered.

'That's not what I plan to do. If necessary I'll stay with Muriel.'

In the days that followed, Mia had known there were plenty of rumours flying around the village as people continued vicariously to enjoy the thrill of the unfolding drama. Word had quickly spread – delivered first-class by Karl the postman – that Owen's car had been trashed and it didn't take too many guesses to work out who had done it.

But it wasn't until now, when they were all gathered in the village hall for the talent show, that people had got their first glimpse of Owen since last weekend and they could see for themselves that it wasn't only a car that had been harmed. Some were savouring the chance to gawp, while others looked shocked.

That night when she had collected Jensen and Tattie and Madison from the airport, Mia had kept her counsel until she was dropping them off. Taking Jensen aside, she had given him a hurried account of what had gone on. 'I'm sorry I lied to you about Owen,' she'd said. 'I hated doing that to you. But I just couldn't tell you the truth; I felt too ashamed. And it was over by then anyway.'

'And now?' he'd asked.

She'd shaken her head. 'Nothing's changed. But I'm going to stay the night at The Hidden Cottage. I don't want Owen on his own, not until I'm sure he's all right.'

'Can I give you some advice, Mum? Don't lose the opportunity to be happy. Grab the chance while you can. Do whatever it takes. You know you have my backing.'

Tears filling her eyes, she'd patted his arm and kissed him goodbye.

Returning to Owen's, she had thanked Muriel for helping and after making herself something to eat downstairs in the kitchen, she had slept in the chair next to his bed.

In the morning his hand looked even worse and he was clearly in pain. She had told him he had no choice; she was taking him to A & E. He had given in grudgingly and allowed her to help him dress. 'I didn't realize you were so bossy,' he'd said as she carefully eased him into his jacket.

'Lots of things you don't know about me,' she'd replied.

She had been right to insist that he be properly checked out; X-rays showed he had four broken fingers and two cracked ribs. He was suitably strapped up, his fingers splinted and bandaged, and asked several times how he'd come by the injuries and each time he said he'd fallen down the stairs.

She observed Owen now as he and the other two judges – the Reverend Jane Beaumont and her husband, Richard – gave their comments on Joe's hilarious Jessie J impression – it didn't bear thinking how Joe had squeezed himself into those electric-blue Lycra leggings. Mia was amazed at Owen's forbearance and his courage to face people here this evening.

Originally he was going to be one of the acts, playing the piano, but even Muriel had to accept that it would be a stretch for him to perform in his current state, so he'd been roped in as a judge instead, to replace Randall who, in company with several others, had succumbed to the cold doing the rounds. Muriel had been adamant that she wanted Owen involved, if only to secure his place within the village – that of a key and fully partici-pating member – and to show he wasn't afraid of a bit of gossip. A typical case of understatement from Muriel!

Knowing his presence would attract the wrong sort of attention, Owen had doubted the appro-priateness of his involvement tonight, but Muriel was having none of it. 'Don't you dare bail out on me,' she'd told him. 'I need every man, woman and child to make this work. At the rate we're going I'll be doing an act myself if anyone else lets me down.'

To one side of Mia was Jensen and on the other was Eliza with Simon, who, Mia was happy to know, had become a permanent fixture in her daughter's life. Madison was backstage with Luke and Edmund, and Georgina was there keeping them calm while they waited to take their turn to do their act. Up on the small purpose-built stage, dressed in a shimmering silver full-length dress with white faux fur draped around her shoulders, Tattie was compèring the show as Marilyn Monroe.

Next to Mia, Jensen started to fidget, drumming his fingers on his leg while bouncing his knee up and down at a furious rate. She was reminded of when he'd been a boy and was nervous. She nudged him. 'She'll be fine. Owen told you she can play her piece in her sleep.'

He smiled ruefully. 'Now I know what you must have felt like watching us as kids. Does it get any easier?'

'Not really.'

Up on the stage, Tattie introduced the next contestant. 'Ladies and gentlemen, girls and boys, put your hands together and give it up for Madison Morrow!'

Everyone applauded and Jensen let out an ear-piercing whistle. Like the pro she was, Madison ignored them and settled herself at the piano that had been positioned in the middle of the stage. She had chosen one of her exam pieces to play, which Owen had been teaching her – the tarantella. She flexed her fingers, straightened her back and began.

In the hushed hall she played beautifully and when she came to the end of her piece, she stood to take her bow. Everyone clapped and cheered and Jensen stuck his fingers in his mouth for another ear-splitting whistle.

When the applause died down, and with her arm around Madison's shoulders, just as she had with all the contestants, Tattie turned to the judges and asked them for their comments. 'And be very careful what you say,' she said. Turning pink with embarrassment, Madison poked her mother with an elbow.

The judges were unanimous; Madison definitely had talent. The vicar said that she wanted to sign her up straight away to play in church; Owen said he didn't care if he was accused of bias, but he couldn't find a single fault with her playing; and Richard said she was a star and a credit to the school.

Madison took another bow and, clutching her music, she left the stage, but not before sneaking a look over her shoulder at Jensen, who gave her a thumbs-up. She beamed back at him.

The piano was then moved to the side of the stage and Tattie announced the next act – Jedward. When Luke and Edmund bounced into view like a couple of hyperactive kangaroos, the hall erupted with laughter and applause. They started off well enough miming to the music that was belting out, throwing their arms in the air and shaking their heads, but then they seemed to forget everything they had practised with Georgina and after Luke tripped Edmund up, they started to chase one another round the stage. It was bedlam and the audience loved it. They were still chasing each other when the music stopped and it was only when Georgina came on stage and grabbed them both that they seemed to remember where they were.

'From the sublime to the ridiculous,' Eliza said with a laugh as everyone cheered madly.

In spite of everything that had happened, Mia had kept her word to help with refreshments and when the interval was over, she and Georgina were left to clear up. With the hatch to the kitchen closed, surveying the chaos of crockery and glasses, Mia said, 'Shall I wash and you dry?'

'Fine by me.'

With music and applause now coming from the other side of the hatch, they set to work. Mia had been so very concerned that her friendship with Georgina might have been damaged because of her affair with Owen, but Georgina had been reassuringly understanding. However, she had been surprised – surprised that she hadn't noticed anything, but more importantly that Mia hadn't confided in her. Not just about Owen, but how bad things were with Jeff. But then she'd made a confession about her own marriage and shared with Mia that things hadn't always been as rosy as friends and family had thought. 'At one point I actually thought of leaving him,' Georgina said, 'but then I found I was pregnant and everything changed. I never told a soul,' she went on. 'It was pride; I couldn't bear for anyone to know that we weren't the happy couple everybody believed us to be.'

The plates, cups and saucers all washed, Mia was refilling the sink with clean water to make a start on the glasses when Georgina said, 'Mia, after everything that's happened, you won't leave the village, will you?'

Mia paused, uncertain. 'To be honest, I'm not entirely sure what lies ahead for me. But I don't see myself continuing to live at Medlar House. I doubt whether Jeff will either.'

'Does that mean you're divorcing him?'

'I certainly can't stay married to him. Not after what he did to Owen.'

'Dare I ask, what about you and Owen?'

Mia shook her head. 'I know what you're getting at, but I can't do that.'

'Why not? You're not worrying what others will think, are you?'

'I'm beyond caring what anyone else thinks. But I need time to sort myself out. I've been all over the place with my emotions since—' She hesitated, her mood instantly sombre. It was still painfully difficult to talk about Daisy's death, especially in terms of simplistically referencing things that happened pre or post the night her daughter died. 'I just need time,' she repeated.

Georgina eyed her sceptically. 'Do you want my opinion?' she asked.

'I suspect I'm going to hear it whatever I think,' she said with a faint smile.

'In that case, listen very carefully to what I'm going to say. Don't be too hard on yourself.

558

Imagine it was Jensen or Eliza in your shoes, and think of the advice you would give them so they could live life to the full and be happy. Will you promise me you'll do that?'

Mia opened her mouth to respond, but her words evaporated. She stared at Georgina dumbly. Her mind whirled. And a part of her actually trembled. It was shock at suddenly seeing things from an entirely different perspective.

'Mia?'

She dried her hands and compelled to do something she hadn't been able to do since Daisy's death, she hugged Georgina. Really hugged her. It felt good. 'Thank you,' she said breathlessly, her eyes brimming. 'Thank you for everything.'

Looking confused, Georgina said, 'What for?'

'For being such a good friend, and for opening my eyes. And for being so understanding. Especially about Owen.'

'Forget it. All in the past. It's your future that's more important now.'

'You're right,' Mia said.

The next morning Owen slept in; it was almost nine o'clock when he woke.

Pushing the duvet away from him, he got stiffly out of bed and went over to the window. He drew back the curtains and saw Putin strutting across the lawn, head down, as if deep in thought. Every morning for the last week the bird had been here, not shrieking its head off as it usually did at the crack of dawn, just marching about as though keeping an eye on Owen. Mia said he was Owen's very own guardian angel.

He went downstairs to make some coffee. He filled the machine with water, added coffee, flicked the switch and then put two slices of bread into the toaster. With his left hand as good as useless, everything took him twice as long to do. Overall the pain throughout his body was less intense now, but coughing or sneezing was agony, as was bending. But then even sitting down or standing up was painful. The doctor said it would take four to six weeks for his ribs to heal and about the same for his fingers, maybe longer.

He was back upstairs slowly getting dressed when he heard his mobile ring; it was Bea.

'We've just got back from holiday and heard the news from Rich,' she said without preamble. 'What the hell's been going on there?'

'Oh, so Rich has been shooting his mouth off, has he?' Owen said. 'I knew I shouldn't have told him.'

'Never mind Rich, tell me how you are.'

'I've been better, it's fair to say.'

'Owen, don't waste your breath on your customary forte for making light of something. Give me the details.'

So he told Bea and when he'd finished, she said, 'Come and stay with us for a while; it sounds hell there.'

'It's not. Far from it. Besides, I can't drive; I'm here for the duration. More to the point, I don't want to be too far from Mia.'

'My God, Owen, she had better be worth all this she's putting you through.'

'She is. She really is.'

When he'd finished the call and was sitting on the edge of the bed, contemplating the immense task of bending down to put on his socks, he heard a knock at the back door, followed by the sound of Mia's voice – he'd given her a key so she could let herself in. 'Up here,' he called to her.

He heard her light footsteps hurrying on the stairs and he smiled when she came in. Every morning she came to boss him around. That was how he described her visits to help with anything he couldn't manage. She called it her care in the community work.

Always attuned to the slightest change in her, he said, 'Are you all right? You look tired.'

'I had trouble sleeping,' she said, coming over to the bed. 'Lots on my mind.'

Taking the socks from him, she knelt on the floor and put them on for him. She then found his shoes and put those on as well. There was nothing fundamentally intimate about someone putting your socks and shoes on for you, but for Owen it felt excruciatingly intimate, and while he was grateful for everything Mia did for him, he hated being treated as an invalid. He was also concerned, knowing how Mia's mind could work, that she felt guilty at what Jeff had done and coming here to help him was another sacrifice she was prepared to make.

'Thank you,' he said. 'And don't take this the wrong way, but there's no need for you to do this, I can manage.'

Still kneeling in front of him, she said, 'Are you sure? It's no bother for me. Or are you worried that I care what people might be saying because I come here every day?' Before he could reply, she said, 'I don't give a damn about gossip. All I care about is you being well again.'

Hearing the heated conviction in her voice, and with her lovely defiant face so close to his, he was dangerously tempted to tilt her chin up with his good hand and kiss her. But he daren't. Despite seeing her every day, there had been no physical contact between them, apart from the practical job of helping him into his clothes, and no matter how much he hoped it could be otherwise, he wasn't about to ruin things. For now she was relaxed in his company and was being a good friend to him; that had to be enough. Although he did have the vaguest feeling that the night she came here after Jeff had gone berserk she had kissed his forehead. Though the state he'd been in, he could have dreamt it.

'Well,' he said, wishing she'd get up from the floor and stop making this so difficult for him, 'I can see you're in a feisty mood this morning. I'd better be on my best behaviour. So what was on your mind that you couldn't sleep? Too much talent-show excitement? Was it the thought of Joe in those awful Lycra leggings?'

The defiance went from her face and was replaced with a more solemn expression. 'It was something Georgina said to me last night, about living life to the full and being happy.'

He cautioned himself to tread warily. She'd told him before that she could no longer stay married to Jeff, but as to what came next she hadn't said, and he hadn't asked. Any question from him would be too loaded. 'Happiness,' he said carefully, 'is often something we have to allow ourselves to feel.'

'I know. But once you're convinced of a thing, it's hard to shake off that belief.'

Once more choosing his words with care, he said, 'Do you think you can, Mia? Or will you always go on punishing yourself for something you didn't do? Daisy's death wasn't your fault. Being unfaithful to Jeff had nothing to do with it. I understand the sacrifice you feel you have to make, but it's wrong.'

'That's what I was thinking about last night. Again it was something Georgina said. She told me to imagine it was Jensen or Eliza in my situation and to think what advice I would give them.'

'And what advice would you give?'

'I'd say and do everything I could to stop them making the biggest mistake of their life.' Her eyes dark, she raised a hand and touched his cheek.

'So if you could be patient with me, I think I could perhaps follow that advice myself.'

He swallowed. 'Perhaps my wits are a little dull from the after-effects of concussion, but could you explain exactly what you mean by that?'

'I mean I don't want to rush things, but I want there to be an *us*. I want the chance to be happy with you.'

Now he couldn't resist her. He leant forward to kiss her and immediately let out a yelp of pain.

At once she got up from the floor and was on the bed beside him, her face full of concern. 'I can't even kiss you now,' he groaned. 'What a useless wreck I am.'

Her gaze burning into his, she said, 'But I can kiss you.' And she did. It was a beautiful kiss, long and lingering, and made his heart beat double time.

When she pulled away, he said, 'Do you think if I took enough painkillers we could risk making love?'

She shook her head and smiled. 'Don't even think about it. No sex until you can manage to put your own socks and shoes on.'

CHAPTER 59

Sunday afternoon in Brussels and after a difficult week at work when the slightest thing had pushed him perilously close to the edge of his patience and sanity, Jeff lay sprawled on the sofa in his pyjamas and dressing gown. He hadn't bothered to wash, shave or dress since Friday. To do anything other than lie here took too much energy. The television was on with twenty-four-hour rolling news, but it was merely background noise. Occasionally he turned up the volume to drown out the racket coming from the apartment above.

Somebody new had moved in and had spent the weekend shunting furniture around and playing music at full blast. Earlier this morning he'd had enough of the din and, charged with a rush of adrenaline, he'd been on the verge of storming up there to let rip. He'd got as far as the hall when he'd caught sight of himself in the mirror in his dressing gown and had at once shambled back to the sofa. Where he lay in a state of bewildered shock, made worse by increasing shame and regret.

How had it happened? How had any of it

happened? He'd lost everything: first Daisy and now Mia, along with his life in Little Pelham.

None of which he could have foreseen. One of the questions amongst the many that he kept asking himself was: had he known what was in store for him, would he, or could he, have done anything different to prevent it happening? And what more had Mia wanted from him? What more could he have given? He doubted that Mia knew the answer herself as otherwise she would have told him. That's what wives did; they didn't hold back with their criticism or thoughts on how men should improve themselves.

But no, he wouldn't pursue that line of thought any further. He didn't want to risk thinking of anything that made him angry for fear of succumbing again to the awful rage of last weekend. Every night, just as he was falling asleep, he'd be jerked wide awake by the sickening memory of his aggression. Every day his shame grew, just as it had over that night in Monte Carlo.

If only he hadn't gone to The Hidden Cottage straight after he'd overheard Bev relishing the grubby gossip she'd got from her cousin about Mia and Owen. Had he not made that mistake, he would undoubtedly have garnered some sympathy in the village as the wronged husband and Owen would have been held in contempt. Even if he had thrown a punch or two, people would have sided with him, saying it was what any man would do in the circumstances. But losing control in the way he had was another matter altogether. So it was Jeff who would be condemned and reviled; he would never escape the stain of what he'd done, and as a consequence, he knew he didn't have the guts to show his face in the village again.

Mia hadn't said the words yet, but divorce was inevitable. As was the sale of Medlar House. In due course he would ask Mia to pack up Daisy's things and send them here. He trusted her to do that much for him.

He had come close to ringing Mia to ask her to have a rethink, to consider putting everything behind them and move away from Little Pelham and start over somewhere new. The idea had momentarily given him hope, had also made him recognize the value of what he'd had with Mia. Good and bad times, they had a shared history – a history that included Daisy – and he didn't want to lose it. All he had to do was convince her he was truly sorry and she would come round. She always had. But when he'd really thought about it he'd been forced to acknowledge that his heart wasn't in it. He no longer had the hunger in him he'd once had – the hunger and drive that used to make him fight tooth and nail for something he wanted was gone.

It was a depressing realization and, alone in his misery, he was left feeling there was nothing in the world that he remotely cared about any more.

CHAPTER 60

It was a year to the day since Owen had moved here and as he looked out at the lake in the languid stillness of the silvery moonlight, he believed that The Hidden Cottage really was, as Mia liked to say, an answer to a mad, mad world.

Standing at the end of the wooden jetty, which Mia had lined with tea-lights, he waited for her to finish talking on the phone with Eliza, and wondered what she was up to. All he knew was that she had a surprise for him, a way to celebrate his first anniversary of moving to the village.

Earlier in the evening, after he'd finished cutting the grass, he'd been shooed away from the house and ordered to go for a drink at the Fox and Goose with Jensen and told not to return until it was dark. The only clue he had was that he might like to wear something warm. It was a cool May night, not cold, but with a clear star-pricked sky above him, the temperature was likely to drop and so he was well prepared with a scarf and one of his old ObeSkiWear fleeces.

In the distance he could hear music drifting across the fields. There was a concert on at Castle

568

Ashby tonight with an assortment of eighties bands and singers performing – the appetite for nostalgia showed no sign of abating.

He turned to look back up the garden to the house. With the light on in the sitting room, he could see Mia standing at the French windows, a phone pressed to her ear. She waved to him and gestured she would be a few minutes more. He responded with a gesture of his own, relaying that there was no hurry.

No hurry at all, he thought as he returned his gaze to the shimmering metallic surface of the lake. That was how it had been since November last year. Nothing had been rushed or forced. He had held himself in check, determined to give Mia the space she needed to come to terms with all that she had lost.

At the end of January she had transferred Mia's Hats from the barn at Medlar House to a lease-hold shop in Olney and moved into the flat above. With an excellent footfall of passing trade, the business had gone from strength to strength and Mia was busier than ever. Owen had offered her a cushion of money to ease things until her divorce settlement had been decided, but she had refused a penny from him; he'd known full well she wouldn't accept any financial help, just as she'd known he wouldn't be able to stop himself from making the offer. Instead she had allowed him to help, as much as he could with a hand that hadn't quite healed, with the refurbishment of the property. Jensen had helped as well, along with Tattie, and even Eliza and Simon had mucked in one weekend.

The fun of getting the place ready for its grand opening day, and seeing how excited Mia was, had reminded Owen of when he and Bea had set up in business together. It didn't make him hanker for those days, though; he was more than happy with teaching children – and a few adults – to learn to play the piano. It was the most rewarding thing he had ever undertaken and the number of students he taught continued to grow. He had applied to do a teaching diploma and was waiting to hear if he had been accepted. He had hoped to apply last December, but four broken fingers had put paid to that.

He bore Jeff no malice, could see no point in doing so, and was relieved that as far as the divorce and the financial settlement went, Jeff was playing it fair with Mia. Medlar House had sold quickly, faster than Mia had anticipated, and had been bought by a family who lived in nearby Yardley Hastings; they were expected to move in next month.

Jeff was now living in Dubai. He'd left Rieke Hirzel in December last year and had gone to work for a Dutch engineering firm, one that offered him a fresh start in the UAE. According to Jensen and Eliza, who had dinner with him only a few weeks ago when he was in London on business, he was in a better state of mind now. 'Life in the sun suits him,' Jensen had reported back to Mia. 'It seems to have mellowed him.'

All things considered, a complete change of scene was probably the best thing Jeff could have opted for. And that wasn't self-interest on Owen's part, but a genuinely objective opinion. After all, having made a fresh start for himself here in Little Pelham, he knew what he was talking about.

Even Rich, who had been hugely dubious about the abrupt change in lifestyle, had grudgingly acknowledged that Owen was looking better than he'd seen him in a long while, though naturally he tempered his admission with the threat that nobody was fond of a smug git and Owen had better not let his sickening contentment as a member of the idle rich go to his head. His comment had caused Catherine to laugh and accuse Rich of needing to take a leaf out of Owen's book. 'A little balance in your life wouldn't go amiss,' she'd said. She and Rich had been staying the weekend with Owen over New Year before heading off to Austria for a skiing holiday. They had invited Owen and Mia to join them, but Owen had wimped out, reluctant to put his ribs to the test so soon.

It had been a great New Year, however, with he and Mia hosting a free-for-all open house party on New Year's Eve culminating in fireworks provided by Rich. Plenty of people from the village came, including Muriel and Georgina and the twins, Beth and her parents, Joe, and Bob Parr

571

(ironically Wendy had become the subject of much tongue-wagging, having left Bob before Christmas to go and run a bar in Cyprus with an ex-boyfriend she'd hooked up with on Facebook), and, of course, Mia's family were there as well.

At the pub this evening, Jensen had spoken at length about the difficult relationship he'd had with his father while growing up and how he was attempting to build bridges. He'd admitted that it was proving tough, trying to undo years of bad habits – a need to put each other down – but he was set on doing it for Tattie and Madison's sake. Which was why he had gone with Eliza to meet Jeff in London. Apparently, and with Mia's approval, it had been Eliza's idea to extend the olive branch, to show Jeff that no matter what, he was still their father and that he counted. 'You should have seen his face when I invited him to the wedding,' Jensen said. 'His expression was priceless. Then once he'd recovered from the shock he asked how much it was going to cost him. In a way it was almost reassuring to see a flash of the old cynicism in him, to know he hadn't changed too much.'

'Will he come?' Owen had asked.

'He said he'd have to check his diary. Which I think we can take as a no. I expect he's still embarrassed to face people here. And he probably wouldn't be that comfortable seeing you and Mum together; too soon for that for him.'

Owen had said he'd bow out if it made things

easier, but Jensen had shaken his head and said he didn't think that was necessary. 'Actually,' he went on, 'I reckon the real reason he won't come is Daisy – too many reminders here for him. Whereas for Mum, it's the opposite; she likes being surrounded by the memories. You know the kind of thing – this is where Daisy walked, this is where she sat on the green – it's a comfort for her, as if she's still here. I feel it myself at times.'

Owen had a lot of time for Jensen. He liked his frankness and the fact that he had accepted Owen into his mother's life so readily. He and Tattie were getting married in St George's next month and the reception was to be held here at The Hidden Cottage. Tattie's parents were flying over and every time Owen saw Madison for a piano lesson, she brought him up to date on the wedding plans, including her bridesmaid's dress. Since she had passed her Grade One piano exam with merit in December, Madison was a changed girl; her confidence and self-belief had grown enormously.

Owen often wondered what Gretchen and Lillian would make of their ten-year-old protégé, all grown up and encouraging others just as they had. He liked to think they would view it as a legacy and be proud and happy to take the credit for what they had inspired him to do.

Having done some research amongst the more elderly residents of the village, Owen had eventually tracked down a woman who had moved into a care home in Northampton some years ago and who could actually recall Gretchen and Lillian. She had apologized for her memory not being what it once was, but she was pretty sure that in the early eighties one of the two women had gone into hospital with pneumonia and had never recovered. Following her death, the remaining sister moved away; she didn't know where.

It saddened Owen to think of the sisters being separated, and he hoped that it wasn't Lillian who had been left alone. His memory of her was she had seemed the more fragile of the two and he didn't like to think of her struggling on her own.

Mia ended the call with Eliza, happy to hear that she and Simon would be coming up next Saturday for the village fete. Like Tattie and Madison, Simon had become a part of the family and Mia always looked forward to seeing him. He'd been a good influence on Eliza and had achieved what no one else had ever managed, he'd taught her to laugh at herself more and to realize that she didn't have to try so hard, that she had absolutely nothing to prove. But most of all, he had taught Eliza that she was loved because of who she was and not what she could do. As a mother, Mia regretted that she hadn't been the one to convince her daughter of this, but then as Jensen had told her, there are some life lessons a parent can't teach a child.

Leaving just the outside light on, Mia locked the back door and, breathing in the night air that was milky-sweet with the smell of freshly mown grass, she made her way down the garden. Facing away from her and illuminated by the flickering tea-lights on the jetty, Owen was deep in thought – she could tell from the stillness of his body. She called his name softly, not wanting to make him jump – not when he was standing so close to the water!

'You were looking very serious,' she said when he turned.

'I was thinking of Gretchen and Lillian,' he said. 'And now,' he added, pulling her into his arms, 'I'm thinking of you and what you have in store for me.'

She smiled. 'Wait and see.'

Droplets of water sparkled in the moonlight as she pulled on the oars and rowed towards the island. Holding a lantern aloft to help guide them, Owen sat in the prow of the boat.

Having never rowed in her life until Owen showed her how, Mia loved it – she found it to be wonderfully relaxing. It was what she did when she needed to think things through. The lake was also where she came to be alone and think about Daisy. She still cried when she thought of her youngest child's life cut so brutally short, but she had accepted that the mourning process would continue for a long time yet, maybe for ever.

She felt the same about her marriage to Jeff; it could never be eradicated from her thoughts. How could it be? And why should it? It was a fundamental part of her, had shaped and defined her for the greater part of her life. She hoped Jeff would find happiness in his new life in Dubai; she had the feeling that he would. As Muriel liked to say, you couldn't keep a man like Jeff Channing down for long.

It was when Mia had shown the new owners round Medlar House that she had realized something that had never crossed her mind before. The couple had asked her what the word 'medlar' meant and she had explained that it was a tree and that the fruit, which resembled a crab apple, was only edible when it had begun to decay. Afterwards she had thought of the poignant symbolism of this in relation to her own situation: that only when she had been forced to accept the truly rotten state of her marriage and had thrown aside her reasons to stand by Jeff had she allowed herself the chance to enjoy the sweetness of a new and better life.

When they reached the island and the prow of the boat nudged against the bank, Owen hopped out and while he secured the boat, she drew in the oars and then took his hand. In the softly glowing light from the lantern, he smiled when he saw what she'd laid on inside the summerhouse. 'Are you planning to seduce me here?' he asked.

'I might be,' she said, guiding him to a chair.

She took a box of matches from the table that was covered with a white linen cloth, onto which she'd placed plates, champagne flutes, napkins and a candelabra. She lit the candles first, then moved to the lanterns she had put in front of the summerhouse. Next she fetched the bottle of champagne from the bucket of ice and, wiping it dry, dispensed with the wire and foil and eased the cork out with a satisfying pop. She filled the flutes, put them to one side, then uncovered a chocolate fudge cake, which she knew was a favourite of Owen's, having made one for his birthday in March.

He leant forward keenly. 'Mmm . . . this gets better and better,' he said.

'And I've even laid on music for you,' she said as a burst of Tony Hadley singing 'Gold' drifted across the fields.

The cake cut, she passed him his glass of champagne and sat in the chair beside him. 'A toast to you and The Hidden Cottage,' she said. 'The two of you were destined to be together. May you always be truly happy here. And,' she added, 'to Gretchen and Lillian, because if it wasn't for them you would never have returned and we wouldn't have met.'

His eyes shining in the candlelight, his expression thoughtful, he chinked his glass against hers and raised it to his lips. 'To Gretchen and Lillian,' he echoed so quietly his words were almost inaudible.

They drank some more of their champagne and then moved on to the cake.

When he'd finished eating, she asked if he'd like his present now.

'You have a present for me?'

She nodded excitedly. It was a surprise she had been working on for some time, although she couldn't take the credit for it, not really. 'Close your eyes,' she said. He did and bending down, she reached under the tablecloth for the box she had hidden there. *'Ta-daar!'* she said after she'd placed it on his lap.

He opened his eyes and looked with amusement at the hatbox. 'A hat? Oh, you shouldn't have.'

She smiled. 'Go on, take the lid off.'

After he'd pushed aside the scrunched layers of tissue paper, he didn't speak, just stared into the box and then at her, and then back to what lay inside. He slowly shook his head. 'I don't believe it. How? How did you know? And where? Mia, this is amazing. Where did you find it?'

'It's a long story, but basically I roped in Jensen and Simon, who are far better at this sort of thing than me. They scoured the internet and in the end it was Simon who discovered this copy in Germany.'

He shook his head again. 'I . . . I don't know what to say.' As if the present was the most precious artefact in the world, he held it carefully in his hands and moved closer to the candlelight to see better.

'Look inside the box again,' she said. 'There's something else there for you.'

She watched him delve beneath another layer of tissue paper and once more his silence and awed expression betrayed just what this meant to him.

'An original vinyl copy,' she explained, 'and a CD Simon made especially for you. It turns out that Simon is a hardcore audio purist and has a state-of-the-art turntable and collects vinyl LPs. Eliza calls it his dark side. As luck would have it, he's so into it he has some sort of nifty software that removes all the scratches and hisses when he converts vinyl to disc, so with a bit of luck that CD should give you near-perfect sound quality.'

'Mia, this isn't *near* perfect, this *is* perfect. I can't believe you've gone to this much trouble, and all without letting on. I didn't have a clue what you were up to.'

She smiled. 'It was hard keeping it from you. When Simon told me he'd tracked the record down to a dealer in Frankfurt who sells classical rarities on vinyl, I was so excited the first thing I wanted to do was tell you.'

He leant over and kissed her. 'The fact that you've done this says you know what it means to me. Thank you. But I can't even remember telling you that Gretchen and Lillian had made a record. Did I tell you?'

'You mentioned it just once, when you first told me about them and why this house is so special to you and it stuck in my mind. I had hoped to find the record for your birthday, but better late than never.'

He leant over and kissed her again. 'You did a far better job than me. I tried years ago to get hold of something they'd recorded and got nowhere; I kept hitting a dead end and eventually gave up.'

'That's the magic of the internet – it's so huge these days it's easier to search for things now. But it's not me you need to thank, it's Simon; he was the one who kept on digging. Once he started, he simply wouldn't let it go.'

Studying the photograph on the front of the LP cover, which showed two strikingly regal women sitting bolt upright in front of a piano, with the title – *Brahms and Schubert Piano Duets by Gretchen and Lillian Lampton* – Owen said, 'It's weird seeing them as young women when I only knew them as old. Though to be fair, they probably weren't that elderly; I guess they seemed old because they were so badly disfigured from the fire they'd survived.'

'Not forgetting that to a young boy, anyone over twenty seems ancient,' Mia said as he turned the LP over to read the track listing on the back.

He smiled. 'They were probably about the same age as Muriel is now, and who would dare call her old?'

He put the LP and CD back in the hatbox and placed it safely out of harm's way on the floor in front of the table. He then shifted his chair nearer to Mia and took her hand, lacing his fingers through hers. For a few moments he stared out at the water, its silvery surface glistening like mercury in the moonlight. It was very quiet; the music over at Castle Ashby had finished and the only sound came from the moths attracted to the light from the lanterns, their wings flapping like capes.

'I have something to ask you,' she said.

He turned. 'Actually, I have something to ask you as well.'

'OK, you go first then.'

'It's about our arrangement. You living in Olney and staying with me as and when. And . . . well, I was wondering if you wanted to review matters.'

'Funnily enough, that's exactly what I wanted to ask you.'

'Really?'

'Tattie and I have been talking—'

'About our sleeping arrangements?'

'No,' she said with a smile. 'Her eco party bag business is growing fast and she needs somewhere bigger than their loft to work out of and I've suggested she takes over the flat at the shop.' She paused a beat. 'So I was going to ask you if I—'

'Yes,' he said.

'Yes what?'

'Yes *please*?'

She tipped her head back and laughed. 'No, I meant, what are you saying yes to?'

'Yes to you moving in with me. Come on, Mia, you know I've wanted you to do it right from the start.'

'I know, but I needed some time on my own to find my feet.'

'And you've found them?'

'I think so.'

'That's good. Now we can get on with the serious business of living together and shocking Little Pelham all over again.'

He touched the side of her face with great gentleness and kissed her. It was a kiss of intense feeling, tender yet passionate and filled her with the deepest love for him.

For a while neither of them spoke, each absorbed in their own thoughts. In the stillness, Owen bent forward and passed her glass of champagne to her and picked up his own.

'You made an excellent toast earlier,' he said. 'Now I'd like to amend it slightly. Here's to *us* and The Hidden Cottage – may it always bring us happiness.'

Gazing at his face in the candlelight – that face she had come to love so much – she smiled. 'It will,' she said with great certainty. 'It will.'